Charleston Hearts

THE FULL SERIES COLLECTION

MELISSA STORM

Editor: Megan Harris
Cover & Graphics Designer: Mallory Rock
Proofreader: Falcon Storm & Jasmine Jordan

This is a work of fiction. Names, characters, organizations, places, events, and incidents are either products of the author's imagination or are used fictitiously. Any resemblance to actual persons, living or dead, or actual events is purely coincidental.

Partridge & Pear Press

A New Life

CHARLESTON HEARTS #1

To Sky Princess and Mila:
My own personal Chihuahua miracles

About this Book

Some say that whenever it snows in Charleston, God is giving a miracle to his most favorite of places. So, I reckon, the blizzard that bleached the entire sky that December must have been a blessing of epic proportions. It was certainly a miracle that I'd forgotten my cell phone after giving my Christmas Eve sermon and had to race back to the sanctuary in order to retrieve it.

Otherwise, how would anyone have ever known that right there in our famous nativity scene, a trembling, little Chihuahua had given birth to a litter of puppies? Yes, right there in the manger. O Holy Night for sure!

This is a story about how those special pups came to change our church—and all the people in it—for the better. Most especially my poor daughter, Abigail. Being the preacher's kid is never easy. I know, because I grew up as one, too. But losing your spouse right while expecting to become a parent for the first time?

Well, that's enough to make even the strongest of believers question God's plans. I know I did. But then those blessed little dogs found us... And, well, I'll let you read the story to find out what happened next!

A NEW LIFE is a touching and poignant story from a New York Times bestselling author that will warm your heart, bless your soul, and leave you smiling.

Prologue

PASTOR ADAM

Some say that whenever it snows in Charleston, God is giving a miracle to His most favorite of places. I tried to remember that as the cold reaching fingers of the wind poked and prodded my cheeks, nose, and everything else not already covered up by my scratchy winter getup.

But the more I tried to be optimistic about the shocking turn in the weather forecast, the harder that miraculous snow swirled. Soon it had bleached out the entire sky so that it was hard to tell where earth ended and the heavens began. We had a veritable snow storm on our hands just in time for the celebration of His birth.

I mumbled a quick prayer that those traveling tonight would remain safe and hugged my threadbare coat tighter around my shoulders. Head down, I fought against the wind, marching ever closer toward my destination.

Leave it to me to get so caught up in my Christmas Eve sermon that I'd forget my cell phone right there on the pulpit! Lucky thing I did, though, because as I finally reached the front doors of the sanctuary, I discovered a most disturbing sight.

Our locally famous nativity scene had been on the fritz all week, but

now the angels' glowing halos had plum run out of power, casting the entire display into darkness. And on Christmas Eve, no less.

Ignoring the cold, which had found its way straight up underneath my clothes, I stepped closer to investigate the source of our power outage. Last summer old Mrs. Clementine had taken it upon herself to plant a little garden right outside the church. How could I say no to her request when she said all the food from our newly christened vegetable patch would be donated to feed the hungry?

And so with more than a little trepidation, I said *yes*, and unfortunately so did every little critter within a twenty mile radius. Even with the crops resting for the winter, I had no doubt that one of Mrs. Clementine's rabbit friends had tried to make a home of Christ's manger—and a snack of His power cords.

Upon closer inspection, I found that—yes, just as I'd suspected—a tiny ball of brown fluff had nestled into the nativity right there between Mary, Joseph, and the kindly shepherds who'd come to pay their respects.

Darn varmits!

Well, that's what I wanted to think, but then I stopped myself. These poor creatures hadn't expected the sudden snowfall either. They just wanted to get warm, and maybe God had sent me back to offer assistance on His behalf.

My toes began to go numb, but I tried to ignore that tingly sharpness as I stepped in for a closer look at the trembling animal.

Imagine my surprise when I found not just one creature, but five!

Right there next to the little Lord Jesus lay a mother dog and her four newborn pups. How they'd managed to survive this long was truly by the grace of God.

I didn't want to leave them, but I couldn't carry them all at once either. At least not on my own. After retrieving the box that our latest batch of hymnals had arrived packed inside, I stripped off my scarf and made a little nest. Then one by one, I lifted the mama and her puppies into the cardboard carrier and brought them into our church to get warm.

My lungs could scarcely take in a single breath of air until I made sure

that each pup was alive and well. Only by the glory of God each of these tiny newborns moved just enough to show me they were okay. You must understand these dogs were hardly bigger than my own thumb. They could have easily been mistaken for rat pups if not for that brave mama dog.

A quick search on my newly retrieved phone confirmed that these were not just any dogs. They were the most diminutive of all dog breeds.

I didn't even stop to question why the Almighty had sent me five Chihuahuas in need as an early gift for His birthday. I didn't have to, because right then I knew beyond the shadow of any doubt these dogs were meant to find us. Surviving that cold Christmas Eve outdoors was only the first of many miracles that mama dog and her pup would bring to our congregation...

Chapter 1

ABIGAIL

Abigail Sutton sat in the dark living room waiting for her father to return from his Christmas Eve sermon. Much to his chagrin, she'd refused to attend church with him that evening. She also wouldn't go tomorrow morning, next Sunday, or any other day for the rest of her life as long as she could avoid it.

Avoiding church when your father was the pastor took quite some effort, but Abigail had committed herself to just that. The last time she'd stepped foot into the Eternal Grace sanctuary had been for her husband's funeral, which had forever tainted the place as far as she was concerned.

It had destroyed her relationship with God, too.

She'd happily praised His name all her life, and for what? The first time she'd truly needed God, He'd failed to show up. What good is having an all-powerful Heavenly Father if he couldn't even take the one second that was needed to shield her husband from the bomb blast that had claimed him far too soon?

Then there was the guilt.

Abigail herself had been the one to convince Owen to take a second tour of duty before they'd settle down to start their family. If she'd just asked him to stay home, they'd be together singing holiday hymns at church with her father and planning the start of their family side by side, hand in hand.

Instead, Abigail sat alone. She'd moved back in with her father about two months ago. Back to her childhood home in Charleston.

It was an odd thing returning to your hometown when you thought you'd already left it behind. It was almost as if her life with Owen hadn't even happened, like the world wasn't just burying his body but also his memory. But it couldn't get rid of her husband that easily, for Abigail still had two very good reminders.

One was the glistening gold band on her finger. They said people wore rings on their second smallest finger because it had a vein linked straight to the heart. She'd always liked that.

Her other reminder of Owen was also near to her heart, as in literally growing just beneath it. Their child. The last piece of Owen anyone would ever have in this world.

She didn't know how to feel about becoming a mother and a widow at almost the exact same time. She'd only found out about her pregnancy a few weeks before the solider with downcast eyes and a blank expression had delivered the folded flag to her doorstep. She'd called to tell Owen the news even though it was still early, and conventional wisdom said not to tell anyone until the first "dangerous" twelve weeks had passed.

But the news of their child was supposed to keep him safe, give him something that much more special to which he'd returned. Instead, she would always have to wonder if it had been the distraction that knocked him off his game and ultimately ended his life way out there in that horrible desert so far from home.

She hated picturing it, but she couldn't stop either. Every time Abigail closed her eyes, she saw her Owen smiling and wiping away tears of joy at their wedding. But in an instant, his handsome face would be replaced by a bloodied, torn visage mangled by pain. It was this last haunting version of Owen that remained with her, and it didn't even look like him.

But what about their baby? If it turned out to be a boy, would it look like Owen? The *real* Owen?

She didn't know whether that would make things easier or not. Would having a little boy the spitting image of his father break her heart every time she looked at him—or would it soothe her?

Abigail wished she didn't have to consider these things. She wished she could be a normal mother expecting her first child and expecting her husband home healthy, happy, and in time for dinner.

A part of her also wished that she had never met Owen at all. Each time Abigail thought this, though, a tremendous wave of guilt overtook her.

When would the tears stop coming? When would the guilt stop eating her from the inside out? When would she actually be happy about this baby?

Never couldn't possibly be the answer, but it was the one she expected. She'd given God her everything, only for Him to take it all away at the first chance He got.

She glanced at the clock on her cell phone. Her father should have been home at least half an hour ago. She groaned and curled her legs up beneath her on the chair. It wasn't that she needed his company, but she liked to have benchmarks by which she could measure the passage of time.

Her biggest comfort these days was simply that time pressed ever onward. After all, it was supposed to heal all wounds. And Abigail had few other options left when it came to finding some way—any way—to begin to feel normal again.

Another five minutes passed before she heard the sound of her father fiddling with the doorknob outside. "Abigail, can you help?" he called through the thick wooden door. "I have a surprise!"

Slowly, she lifted herself from the chair, bracing herself for whatever came next. She'd asked him not to make a big fuss of Christmas this year, but that didn't mean he'd chosen to listen. Her sweet father was always coming up with grand schemes, and they all too often involved her. Even before Abigail had moved back home, he'd often call her out of the blue and stop by the base to invite her on an impromptu day trip.

Normally she loved his zeal for life, but lately it was just too much. She needed him to be calm, reserved, forgettable. Then maybe she could put these painful days of grieving behind her, too.

Somehow she doubted that would happen. She took a deep breath, then placed a shaking hand on the door knob and twisted it open. The surprise that greeted her on the doorstep was quite possibly the last thing she'd ever have expected...

Chapter 2

ABIGAIL

Abigail took a step back as her father rushed past her into the house. In his arms he carried an old cardboard box. He'd taken off his coat and flung it over the top so that she couldn't see what was inside.

She heard it, though—a mix of whimpers and squeaks that surely meant they were in for a calamitous holiday.

"Oh no." Abigail gave her father a stern look. "Did a squirrel have babies in the attic again? You know you don't have the time to look after them. You were too upset last time when—"

"Yes, I know what happened last time." Her father turned to her with a huge grin on his wind-chapped face. "But this time will be different."

She gave him a fatigued sigh. She hated to dampen his spirits, but she just didn't have the energy for yet another ill-fated rescue attempts. "Different how?"

"Well, they aren't squirrels, and I'm not raising them." His eyes glowed like the beginning sparks of a fire. There was no stopping him now. "You are," he concluded with an enormous Cheshire grin.

Abigail wanted to argue that she didn't have a maternal bone in her body, but the baby growing inside her seemed to imply otherwise.

"Take a look," he said, setting the box on the carpeted floor and finally raising his coat to offer her a peek inside.

"Puppies!" she shouted, eyeing the wriggling balls of pink, black, and brown with hesitation. "Where did you get a box of puppies? And *how* when you were supposed to be giving the Christmas Eve sermon?"

He waved his hand dismissively. "This happened after."

Abigail slowly approached and let the mother dog sniff her hand. She was half fawn colored and half white with giant ears flanking either side of her head. She looked from her nursing pups to Abigail and squinted before letting out a tremor that shook her whole body.

"Oh my gosh!" Abigail cried. "Is she okay?"

"That's Mama Mary, and she'll be just fine. She got her babies to safety. I found them cuddled in the manger right next to the little Lord Jesus himself."

"I suppose that's why you named her Mama Mary," Abigail said with a smirk. Even her cold, dead heart warmed a bit to the sweet puppies and their heroic mother. "And there are four puppies. Did you name them after the four gospels?"

He laughed as they both stood transfixed by the squirming pups before them. "They don't have names yet, although that isn't a bad idea. I figured we'd let the Sunday school kids bestow the honor."

"Wait, does that mean you're planning to keep them?" She glanced to her father in shock. While he'd always loved all of God's creatures, he'd never exactly been a pet person. What had happened with the squirrels several years ago had been quite the anomaly—and she thought they'd all learned their lesson from it.

When a sheepish grin lit her father's face, she knew there was no way she'd be able to convince him to take the dogs to a shelter.

"I thought they could be a Christmas gift. The fact they found us in that storm has got to be a sign. This isn't just one miracle—it's a whole litter."

"And Mama Mary makes five. Five dogs!" She wanted to be supportive, but someone needed to be realistic here. "How on earth are we going to give a proper home to five dogs?" she demanded.

Her father was completely nonplussed by Abigail's attempts to protest. He simply smiled and pointed above. "The Lord will provide a way," he said.

"You always say that."

"It's always true."

Abigail hid the smile that tried to creep across her normally placid face. If nothing else, her father was consistent, and that was something she'd always found comforting. In that way, it was nice to be home. She should be grateful that she at least had a loving home to return to. It was hard to imagine things could be worse, but of course they always could.

These nearly frozen over pupsicles were proof enough of that.

"You know we at least have to look for the owners," she pointed out softly.

"I know that, but I also know nothing will come of it. I prayed a lot on the drive over. God wanted us to have these dogs. That's why He sent them." He rubbed his hands and blew air into them, then let them hover over the pups, using this makeshift heater to warm them further.

So God saw to it that these five dogs were saved, but my husband wasn't important enough to warrant his attention? Abigail thought bitterly, hating herself as she did. She should be happy that the little animals hadn't caught their deaths outside, not jealous.

Not angry.

She'd never been like that before, and she didn't want to be like that now. "Maybe you're right, but we still owe it to..." She hesitated. "To, uh, Mama Mary and her children to at least try."

"I agree," he answered simply. "This won't be like the time with the squirrels," he added as an afterthought.

Oh, those darned squirrels... Truth be told, she liked the puppies better already, but she would keep that to herself.

Chapter 3

ABIGAIL

After moving the box from the table to the floor, Abigail sat with the dogs while her father zipped around the house procuring arrangements for them. An old pillow with an even older throw blanket draped on top became their bed, a pair of ceramic cereal bowls converted into food and water dishes, and a space heater set atop an overturned milk crate helped to warm the area.

"Now I'm going to make Mama Mary a dinner like she's never had before," he said, kneeling down to scratch the dog between its ears before popping back up and heading toward the kitchen.

"Don't tell me you're planning to feed her the Christmas ham," Abigail called after him, half-believing he would.

His laughter floated over from the stove. "No, that would take too long. But I figure our good girl has earned herself a nice New York strip."

The mother Chihuahua grunted in affirmation, and Abigail could swear she heard the dog's belly rumble. She couldn't stop the chuckle that bubbled to the surface. It felt both amazing and like the worst kind of betrayal to Owen's memory. This was far too soon for her to be happy over something so trivial.

She grew silent as she watched the little puppies nurse at their mama's side. While they squirmed and whined freely, the mother dog stayed mostly still and quiet—like Abigail herself. The last thing she needed was to get attached to a sick dog, only to have it die before the morning sun.

"I think we need to take them in to see a vet," she called to her father.

He answered back after a series of three loud plops and sizzles that told her he was making steaks for more than just the one of them. "I called around, but no one's open tonight or tomorrow."

She tried to think, at last remembering who it was they knew for this kind of thing. "What about Mr. Manganiello? Doesn't he work with animals?"

"He's celebrating Christmas with his family same as everyone else. Besides, we've got this. You and me, just like the old days."

Ah, the old days... back when Abigail's biggest problem had been whether or not she could convince her father to let her attend the freshman dance with dreamy Gavin Holbrook as her date. After much pleading he'd said yes, but only on the condition that he could chaperone. Abigail had never been so mortified in her entire life, but that hadn't stopped Gavin from sneaking a kiss on the front doorstep before they'd said goodnight.

How long ago that seemed. She'd lived and died many times in the decade and a half between ninth grade and the new, sadder life she struggled through now. Each day was a gift, that's what she'd believed before. These days, she knew better.

And yet...

Her heart would break all over again if this poor mother dog didn't live to see her puppies grow into strong, full-grown ankle biters. Abigail didn't know much about dogs, but she knew enough to know that Chihuahuas were fierce, yappy little things.

Why couldn't her father have found a litter of Golden Retriever puppies instead?

Guilt hardened in her stomach once more as Abigail watched Mama Mary breathe heavily and close her eyes.

"Hey, hey," she said gently, nudging the dog until it opened its eyes again. "We're going to get through this. Don't give up."

She continued to stroke the dog's patchy fur and murmur to it while her father prepared their dinners. Judging from the poor thing's condition, she'd either never had an owner or had been missing for a very long time. What if her owner had been searching for her all this time? What if the dog had finally found help for her puppies but it turned out to be too late for her? She tried not to think about that. After all, there was nothing she could do to prevent either outcome. She could simply ease the pain that came before.

"Did you and Mama get some good bonding in?" her father asked, watching her from the door frame.

"It's hard not to root for her," Abigail admitted. "But I still don't think we should keep them long term."

"Banish the thought." He clucked his tongue and wagged a finger at her. "When God sends you a gift, you don't just send it back. These pups were meant to find our church, and that's where they belong."

"So now they're the church's pets?" she said flatly. It seemed her father's plans for these dogs were growing by the minute. Before the end of the night he'd have them signed up to compete for blue ribbons at the Westminster Kennel Club.

He chuckled as if privy to her private speculations. "Not pets. I was thinking more like working dogs."

Abigail forced down a giggle of her own. It would have cost her too much to let laughter in twice that day. "Working dogs? But they're so small! What are they going to do? Pull a sled the next time it snows?"

Her father's eyes glimmered, but he said nothing as he returned to the kitchen.

Abigail eased herself up from the floor and followed him. "What kind of work are they going to do for the church?"

"Whatever the Lord decides is good enough for me," he answered, plopping another steak into the frying pan.

"Wait. You're serious, aren't you?"

"As a heart attack" came the response.

"I always knew you were crazy, but this seems beyond your normal. You know all of Charleston will be talking about this before no time at all."

"Good, let them talk. Maybe then they'll come to church to see for themselves."

"More like they'll come to see the infamous Church Dogs of Charleston."

"Now, that does have a nice ring to it," he answered with yet another chuckle before turning and pushing a tea plate stacked with sliced steak into her hands. "Go see if you can get some food in that poor dog. After that, we'll work on you."

Chapter 4

ABIGAIL

Abigail could scarcely sleep that night. After her third time waking up in the wee hours, she officially gave up and went to hold vigil over the Chihuahuas.

Once in the living room, she found a plate of sugar cookies and gingerbread men waiting beside a glass of milk. Had her father put these out for tradition's sake, or did he have a feeling she'd rouse early and need a snack?

Why they were there didn't much matter, because food was one of the few joys Abigail still luxuriated in from time to time. She chose a gingerbread figure with chocolate icing hair and a red licorice smile, and bit into it with delight.

This one had to be her.

Growing up, she and her father had decorated dozens upon dozens of cookies each year, fashioning each to look like someone they knew from the church. She'd taken that tradition with her when she married Owen and moved into base housing. In fact, last year they'd had quite the laugh over her interpretation of his commanding officer.

This year, she'd skipped out on baking with her father. She'd skipped out on many things, not quite ready to attempt normality just yet. The baby inside her, she knew, presented a ticking clock. She'd need to be strong, healthy, and happy when he or she arrived. It wouldn't be fair to push her grief onto the child. After all, the poor thing would already be starting life one parent short.

Abigail took another bite of the warm cookie and glanced over to the basket of sleeping puppies nearby.

Mama Mary caught her eye, her little nose sniffing high in the air as if she needed two senses to confirm she had a visitor. And then, the tiny dog gently worked her way out of the basket and waddled over to Abigail.

"What is it, girl?" Abigail asked.

The dog cocked her head to one side, then slowly pulled herself into an upright position. Her two front paws clawed at the air in the most adorable bout of begging Abigail had ever witnessed in her whole life.

She smiled at the mother dog, glad to see she was already feeling so much better. "I'm not sure this is good for you, sweetie," she explained, frowning at the frosting smeared across her fingers even after the cookie had disappeared into her mouth. "Actually, they're not very good for me, either. Let's see if we can find something better in the kitchen."

Together, the mom and mom-to-be trotted into the kitchen and peeked into the fridge. It was flowing with abundance even more than usual. It seemed that this time of year every little old lady in her father's congregation wanted to help feed the poor single pastor—especially this year since he now came with a tragic widowed daughter and a yet-to-be-born grandchild.

Abigail selected a chicken and rice casserole from amongst the bounty and pulled it from the fridge. "We really need to pick you up some proper dog food as soon as the stores open again," she said, dishing out a serving for each of them. She stuck her plate in the microwave and put Mama Mary's on the tiled floor.

The dog sniffed it and sat without taking even the tiniest of bites. She glared at Abigail as if trying to tell her something. Just what that was, Abigail hadn't the faintest idea.

"Sorry, I don't speak dog," she said, grabbing her plate from the microwave before it could beep and disturb the still sleeping members of their household—especially the puppies. Their mother deserved whatever little bit of break she could get, especially if it meant getting more meat on her fragile bones.

Abigail carried her plate over to her favorite chair, surprised when Mama Mary chose to follow her out to the living room and continue her begging there.

"I just gave you some," Abigail reminded her, gesturing toward the kitchen where the other helping of fine Southern comfort food sat untouched.

For some reason unbeknownst to Abigail, these words encouraged the dog who attempted to jump up on the chair with her. However, she couldn't quite make the whole leap and fell back down to the floor.

"What?" Abigail laughed despite herself. "Do you want mine?"

The little dog glanced from Abigail's face to her plate and back again, causing her to laugh even harder. This time she didn't even scold herself for the happy gesture. Well, at least not much.

"Okay, have it your way," she said, offering the plate to the hungry Chihuahua who immediately dug in and made fast work of cleaning the plate.

Abigail was just about to return to the kitchen to warm a second plate for herself when her father appeared at the end of the hallway, rubbing sleep from his eyes. "Morning already?" he asked with a giant overhead stretch.

"Not exactly," Abigail admitted, feeling a bit more reserved now that another human was around. Somehow it was easier to let her cruel inner dialogue rest in Mary's presence. Maybe because, inexplicably, it felt as if the dog understood in a way even Abigail's father couldn't—in a way she had yet to figure out for herself, too.

"Us girls were just having a late night snack," she added, continuing to the kitchen and thrusting open the fridge. "Want some?"

"Oh, what are we having? Actually, you know what? It doesn't matter. I'll have two, please."

That was her father, though. If it was worth doing, then it was worth overdoing, which was exactly why they now had five new dogs to take care of. It was also why his pants had become increasingly snug around the middle after she'd left to make a new home with her husband.

Well, she was back now, and if she couldn't straighten out her own life, maybe she could at least do some good in her father's.

She smiled coyly to herself as she served him a single portion.

It was for his own good, after all.

Chapter 5

PASTOR ADAM

I knew my daughter and that mama dog would be thick as thieves in no time at all. Only "no time at all" happened faster than even I'd dared to hope. By the time I woke up the next morning, I found Abigail smiling and laughing just like she used to in a time not so long ago.

What I'd give to have that time and that happy, hopeful version of Abigail back for good.

Of course, I still remember clear as a bell when I first heard the news of my poor son-in-law's departure. Abigail had been crying so hard I could scarcely understand the words as she spoke them. Somehow I knew before she even had to confirm the tragic passing. I knew my daughter inside out, but nothing I could have done would have prepared her for this untimely loss.

Regardless of all that, I still question myself to this day. If I'd worked harder to keep Abigail's mama around, would she have an easier time dealing with the loss of her husband?

These questions remained impossible to answer, but that didn't mean I'd ever stop asking them. Just that night, for example, I had lain awake in bed, thinking, praying, wishing, wondering if my baby girl would ever come back to me. The Lord works in mysterious ways, but sometimes it's quite difficult to see His plan when you're standing right in the middle of it.

Abigail herself seemed to have decided that there was no plan, or if there was, then it meant His only aim was to torment her in this life and quite possibly also the next. Even though I understood her need to question, it still broke my heart to watch her shut God out—and, in turn, to shut me out, too.

You have to understand, it wasn't so long ago that my wife, Rachael, abandoned the both of us—only, unlike Owen, she chose to do it. I know Abigail's husband would have given anything to stay with her and guide their child through life.

Even still, I sometimes wonder what Rachael is doing with her life these days, but I also know not to pick at that particular wound. It's why I haven't succumbed to the allure of Facebook even though so many of my congregants do sorely wish I'd start an account there. The best way to avoid temptation is to *avoid temptation*, if you know what I mean.

Whether I should have talked with Abigail more about her mother, I still don't know. But what could it help now? In my heart and by the eyes of God, I'm still married to Rachael, even though she chose to walk away from our life together and has never once looked back.

Had I been a bad husband to her?

Was I a bad father to Abigail?

Whatever the answers might be, the only thing I want now is for my daughter to smile again. Well, that, and to find her way back into the Lord's waiting arms. I pray for her many times each day. It's like breathing —a sacred routine I need in order to keep on keeping on.

That's why when He sent those dogs I knew for a fact that my prayers were well on their way to being answered, and then... this morning, I saw the beginnings of that answer take shape. God is good!

Chapter 6

ABIGAIL

Abigail fell asleep in her favorite wingback chair sometime between three and four a.m. When she finally awoke to start the day, the room was brightly lit by the morning sun and her father had returned to the kitchen to make his famous Sunday morning fry-up.

Never mind that today was Friday.

And Christmas.

She padded over to the kitchen and gave her father a kiss on the cheek.

"Merry Christmas," he said, wrapping his arm around her in a tight, warm hug.

She returned his holiday wishes and asked, "What do you have planned for today? I'm sure the church is keeping you on a very busy schedule as always."

He grinned and shook his head. "Not this time. Today I have the full day free to celebrate with you and our five new family members."

Abigail scrunched up her nose in confusion until she realized… the dogs, he meant the dogs. "Well, don't back out of any plans on my account. I'll be fine on my own."

He clucked his tongue and dismissed her hesitation with that same self-assured smile he always offered when she had no choice in a matter.

"That's what you say every day," he pointed out. "But *today* is Christmas. And I'm not taking no for an answer."

Abigail brushed a loose strand of hair behind her ear. She probably looked a fright. "Okay, but what's the question?" she teased.

"No question. Just you, me, and the dogs celebrating His birth and eating lots of good food. Now while I finish up in here, why don't you go check the stockings?"

Abigail smiled at the memory of so many years before. She and her father had a veritable treasure trove of holiday traditions, and unpacking her stocking was one of her most favorite.

"There's one for the little squirt, too!" her father called after her as she traced her way to the fireplace.

Reflexively, she brought a hand to her belly. Next year she'd have an actual, real live baby with her—a small piece of Owen who would need her to show him the world and all its wonders.

That meant she had less than a year left to rediscover them for herself. No pressure. Nope. None at all.

She gently unhooked both stockings from the mantle place and sat cross-legged on the floor to inspect their contents.

Mama Mary sidled up to her, tail wagging furiously as her four puppies whimpered and searched the bed for their missing mother.

"I bet it's exhausting," Abigail confided in her. "Having four! I can barely picture having one. I don't think I'm ready."

The little brown and white dog came closer and pushed her head under Abigail's palm.

Abigail smiled and petted the dog as requested. This tiny little thing had braved incredible obstacles to keep her babies safe. Would Abigail know to do the same once her child was in this world? Would she simply snap out of it and do what was needed?

She wished she could know for sure. Maybe then she wouldn't worry quite so much. For now, though, she had a stocking to unpack.

"C'mere," she called to the Chihuahua, patting her lap and waiting for the eager dog to climb up into it. "We'll open them together."

She started with her own, a handsome green velvet stocking with her name written across the top in red glitter. She'd had the same one since grade school. Truly, some things never did change, while others...

"Okay," she told the dog, then sucked in a deep breath to steady herself and reach her hand inside. The first thing she found was a stick of peppermint lip balm. After that, a white chocolate bar—her favorite.

She continued to extract item after item from the stocking. Most were pretty run-of–the-mill Christmas things: ornaments, costume jewelry, treats. But at the very bottom she found something quite different. A little book was wedged into the giant stocking's toe.

Even before she'd pulled it out, she knew what it was. The gold-gilded pages and tiny engraved letters on the cover confirmed it.

Her father had returned her very first Bible to her.

"Why did you give this to me?" Abigail demanded of her father when he came to join her in the living room, handing her a plate overflowing with all her favorite breakfast foods.

"It's tradition."

"Not the stocking. *This*." She held the little Bible up for him to see—as if he could forget.

Mary skittered off her lap and returned to her puppies.

"What? *The Bible?* It's not a dirty word, you know. You can say it."

"Fine. Why did you give me the *Bible*? You know how I feel about this stuff now."

"This stuff, huh?" He shook his head and took a seat beside her on the floor. "I know you're in a sad place right now, which is why I thought you might want to be reminded of happier times so that you could see that maybe life isn't all bad."

"Happier times like when my mother abandoned me?" she asked, tucking the little book back into her stocking—out of sight, out of mind —before taking a deep, shuddering breath. Most days she tried not to spare a single thought for her selfish runaway mom, especially on the holidays. She hadn't earned the right to be a part of their world. Not anymore.

"We had a good life together, you and me," her father said with a sigh of his own. "We still do."

Abigail brought her knees up to her chest and hugged them tight. She didn't have the strength for this—not now, not ever. "I'm sorry, Dad. I don't mean to take this out on you. It's kind of why I wanted to be alone today."

"And it's exactly why I wouldn't leave you to your own devices." He lowered himself to the floor beside her, sitting close but not reaching out to touch her. "Wallowing solves nothing, baby girl. Owen wouldn't want you to live this way."

"It's only been a few months," Abigail sputtered, unable to look at him. "At least give me time to deal with my grief."

"Take all the time you need. I just want to make sure you know you're not alone. You've got me, and you've got God."

When Abigail continued to stare stonily at her feet, he added, "The dogs, too. They're here for you, and I'm willing to bet you need them just as much as they need you."

Chapter 7

ABIGAIL

They spent the rest of Christmas day watching their favorite holiday movies and keeping a close eye on Mama Mary and her puppies. By the end of it, Abigail was glad her father hadn't left her alone, but she also felt exhausted from the lack of sleep the night before coupled with all the time spent being social today—even if it was just with her dad.

"I'm going to hit the hay," she announced, hugging him goodnight. "Thank you for today."

As she padded to her room, she heard the scratch of little toenails following close behind. Sure enough, she turned to see the mother Chihuahua standing right at her heels.

"Good night, Mama Mary," she cooed. "See you in the morning."

But when she began walking again, the dog continued on after her.

"Hey, what are you doing? Go back to your puppies," Abigail urged her.

But Mama Mary just plopped her butt down and beat her twitching tail against the wood floor.

"Well, will you look at that! Looks like she needs you just as much as those puppies need her," her father said, rising from his chair with a chuckle. "Let's get them settled in your room."

"Why do you like me so much?" Abigail asked the Chihuahua, who merely tilted her head and widened her dark eyes in response.

Her father continued to laugh as he squeezed past with the makeshift bed of puppies. "Well, why wouldn't she? I mean, what's not to love?"

Oh, everything, Abigail wanted to respond, but bit her tongue. She'd once liked the person she was, but lately she didn't even recognize what she'd become. Could a few months really change a person so completely? And, even more worryingly, would she ever find her way back?

At least taking care of Mary and her litter of wee ones would provide a bit of a distraction to the unending monotony that filled her days lately. But she worried about allowing herself to become too attached. What if the dogs were also ripped away like a bloody bandage? What if she lost them the way she had lost Owen?

It hurt to open herself back up, even if it was just to a scraggly little dog. And yet, how could she say no when the brave mother Chihuahua clearly craved her friendship?

"You can stay with me tonight," she told the dog at last. "But tomorrow we're going to find your owners. They must be worried sick."

Her father sent her a knowing glance. "Since you're planning to go out, would you also get dog food, a new bed, a crate, collars, leashes... basically the works?"

Abigail sighed and paused in the doorway to her bedroom. "What? No, I'm not going out. I thought I could start an Internet search. I'd be happy to order whatever supplies you need from Amazon, but don't you think you're jumping the gun just a bit here?"

"What I think," he said, studying his daughter with a tender expression now, "is that you haven't left the house for weeks. This will be good for you. Besides, it's high time."

"But you said to take as long as I need to," she reminded him. Of course, she wanted to get better, but that was much easier said than done.

Being around other people—people who recognized her as the good pastor's daughter, no less—would only make things harder.

"Getting on with life doesn't mean you're letting go of Owen," he said, eyeing her cautiously.

He knows he's pushing me. He's doing it on purpose! she realized, though she was completely unsurprised by this revelation. After all, it was her father's way. If there was some poor soul in need of fixing, he was always first in line to volunteer for the job.

Her father shrugged as if that were enough to downplay his meddling. "All you need to do is go to the pet store, get what we need, then come right back. I'm way behind on prepping my sermon for Sunday. You'd be doing me a big favor. Mama Mary, too."

Abigail knew she would eventually have to stop hiding, but it still felt too soon to face the pitiful glances and repetitive platitudes of the various people about town. Grief wasn't a team sport, and she had no extra energy to help others deal with Owen's death. She hardly had enough to keep herself going.

Even if it was just a quick little trip to the pet store, she knew it would take a lot out of her. She also knew if she didn't go, her father would continue to pick at her until she finally caved. When it came right down to it, she might as well get it out of the way now.

"Okay," she conceded at last, bringing forth a big grin from her father. Even Mama Mary seemed to smile as she returned to nursing her puppies and watched the conversation unfold from her new spot in Abigail's room.

"But," she added, "if I do this, you can't force me to leave the house again for at least another week." She wasn't going to give in unless she could get a little out of this agreement, too.

"If that's what it takes," her father said, continuing down the hall without another word. Something told her he was already plotting how to break the deal they'd only just made.

He sure was lucky she loved him so much!

Chapter 8

ABIGAIL

The next morning, Abigail slid into her favorite pair of sweatpants, threw her hair in a messy bun, and headed to the pet store as soon as it opened. She normally didn't like big chain establishments, but the idea of being one of many anonymous shoppers in pet supply super stores around the country appealed to her that day.

Her waistband cut into her stomach as she sunk down into the driver's seat of her poor neglected vehicle. Soon she'd be able to feel the baby kick, and shortly after that, others would notice the growing bump at her midsection. She zipped up her loose hoodie, hoping it would be enough to hide her tummy from gossiping onlookers, then put the car in drive.

Having been born and bred in Charleston, she hadn't had much opportunity to drive through snow. Luckily, last night's blizzard had mostly melted into slush. Add to that the fact few cars were out on the road so early on the day after Christmas and she could handle it just fine. With any luck, she could get in and out of the store without running into anyone she knew, then within half an hour she'd be able to put this whole miserable errand behind her.

Abigail thanked her lucky stars when she noticed only one other vehicle in the enormous parking lot. She could do this. She could buy dog food without incident or embarrassment. Because if she couldn't, there would truly be no hope left for her.

First the dog food, then the world.

It felt silly putting so much importance on a simple errand, but it was the first normal thing she'd done since receiving news of Owen's death all those weeks ago. She grabbed a buggy from the carousel out front and pushed it into the overly bright store with the wind blowing at her back, urging her forward.

Right, dog food.

She'd never had a dog before so wasn't sure what the best brand was and didn't feel like pulling out her phone and researching in the middle of the aisle. With no other options left, she grabbed a bag that sported a dog who looked like Mama Mary on the front. She also grabbed a few cans of wet food that apparently tasted like filet mignon—*well, la-dee-dah*—before continuing to the next aisle.

Less than ten minutes later, her buggy was bursting with an assortment of toys, treats, and comfort items, all for Mama Mary and her puppies.

Which reminded her she'd forgotten to print out the flyer she'd designed to help locate the mother dog's owner. She'd wanted to give it to the cashier and request that she share it with anyone who stopped by, but it was too late for that now—and she definitely wasn't leaving the house again if she could avoid it.

So back to Plan A, then.

She'd start a social media campaign with the goal of reuniting Mary with her real owners. Back before she became a hometown hermit, she'd boasted a thriving freelance graphic design business. Perhaps those skills could help attract the right eyes in this scenario, too, and could help find Mary's owner quicker. After all, a picture said a thousand words—and a pretty picture got the point across that much better.

She smiled to herself. It was decided then, and she was almost home free. With a sharp turn of her shopping buggy, she headed toward the checkout lane, hoping she had everything her father had requested and that she had a large enough wad of bills in her pocket to cover the expense.

"Excuse me, Miss?" a husky voice called from behind her.

Abigail froze. She knew that voice, or at least a younger version of it. But she wasn't supposed to see anyone she knew here. She was supposed to be an anonymous shopper. She—

"Um, you dropped this." He wheeled his buggy next to hers and handed her a stuffed dinosaur toy.

Why, of all the rotten luck... It took all Abigail's Southern gentility to avoid cursing a string of not-so-nice words at the top of her lungs right there in the middle of the mega mart.

"Wait, Abigail Elliott? Is that you?" His chocolate eyes widened and his voice grew light, happy. "Well, fancy running into you here."

She hesitated before offering an uncomfortable smile and saying, "Hi, Gavin."

Yes, that same Gavin who'd escorted her to the freshman dance, the same Gavin who had once made her heart beat with wild abandon...

He was the same Gavin, but she wasn't the same Abigail.

Chapter 9

ABIGAIL

A bigail's heart pounded like an unwelcome visitor inside her chest. She'd worried about running into one of the little old ladies from her father's church, but never would she have guessed she'd be standing in the middle of an empty store the day after Christmas making small talk with her eighth grade crush turned ninth grade boyfriend.

Just the mere mention of Gavin Holbrook had once sent a swoony sigh rumbling right through her. Now, it set off a sigh of a different kind all together.

Oblivious to her torment, Gavin's smile widened to show off a row of perfectly straight teeth. Apparently all those years of braces had done him right. "I haven't seen you in forever," he whispered as if she were a thing to be worshipped rather than avoided.

Before Abigail could hesitate, he'd wrapped both arms around her in a tight hug. Of course, this sent her heart galloping even quicker. She glanced past his shoulder and into his buggy where an enormous tub of cat litter sat beside a bag of cat kibble and a baggie of cat nip.

"It's okay. I'm fine," she said, trying to remember if Gavin had owned a pet feline growing up or if he'd only recently become a cat person.

"Well, of course you're fine," he answered, pulling back to study her at hardly an arm's length. How she wished he would move on, or at least move back. "The years have been more than fine to you. You look great!"

She shook her head and slipped out of his hug with as much grace as she could muster given the situation. It was strange that he hadn't apologized for her loss yet. Most people did that the moment they laid eyes on her. Still, any minute now, he'd remember the news about Abigail's husband and pull into full-on pity mode.

"You must be back for the holidays, right? How much longer are you here? Can I take you out to dinner?" He paused to flash another megawatt smile her way before concluding with, "You know, for old time's sake?"

She watched in slow motion as Gavin's gaze fell toward her hand and the small but sparkling diamond she still wore every day to honor her vow to Owen.

"Oh," he said. "I didn't realize... I mean, let's go out as just friends. Because we are, right? Friends?"

She frowned, feeling mortified for Gavin. How could he not know? "Didn't you hear about...?" Abigail let her voice trail off.

"That you got married? I guess I hadn't. A belated congratulations." He smiled again, a lesser smile this time.

"No." She twisted her hands together. While she'd dreaded everyone knowing, it was somehow worse that Gavin hadn't heard—that she'd need to be the one to tell him.

"I mean I was married, but..." She paused and risked a glance up at him, who watched her with wide eyes. He really didn't know. "Um, he died."

Gavin cursed under his breath. "I had no idea. I'm so sorry, Abigail."

"And I'm pregnant," she added without hesitation, hoping that this reveal would curtail any lingering attraction he may harbor for her.

"With your...? I don't know how to say this right." Gavin turned red as he struggled to find the appropriate words. "With your husband's baby?"

She nodded. This was the end now. He'd make an excuse and run off. They always did. Nobody knew how to handle Abigail these days. Only her father even still tried.

Gavin's expression grew tender as if he could reach right in and feel the pain in her heart. "So it's a really recent loss then?"

Abigail nodded and choked back a sob. She wasn't sure how she'd expected him to respond, but it certainly wasn't with the tender hug that followed. That made two hugs in the space of five minutes, she noted.

Gavin held her as she cried right there in the middle of the pet emporium. Luckily, no one else was there to see save a few stray workers who gave them a wide berth.

"Well, now I'm definitely not taking no for an answer," he said with a smile as the two of them pulled apart. "When are we having dinner?"

"Dinner? No, I can't. I'm not ready to date. I'm not sure I'll ever be."

He shook his head. "No, not a date. As friends, like I said before. It seems like you could use a friend now more than ever."

"But..." She couldn't think of an argument to offer, but she also had no reason to say yes. It was so much easier to hide out alone in her father's house, especially now that she had the company of the Chihuahuas and a personal mission to find Mama Mary's owner.

"I promise no funny business," Gavin said, which is the same thing he'd told her father when arriving to pick her up for freshman year homecoming.

The déjà vu made Abigail titter softly, just like she would have back in high school when chatting with a cute boy, a boy like Gavin.

Gavin grabbed hold of this opportunity and refused to let go. "So you do remember what fun we used to have? Remember how we used to stay up and talk on the phone past midnight?"

She nodded and twisted her hands on the bar of her buggy, eager to make her escape.

"We could do that again," he pressed. "I'll catch you up on my life, and you catch me up on yours. Or don't. Look, I don't know the protocol for this. I don't want to pressure you, but it really does seem like you could use someone in your corner."

She sniffed and tried to smile. When that didn't work, she said, "You mean because I'm crying in the middle of the pet store on the day after Christmas?"

He shrugged before offering her another whole-hearted grin. "Well, that, and I've gotta believe we ran into each other like this for a reason. We're the only two people in all of Charleston up and about right now, almost like it's fate."

"I don't believe in fate," Abigail answered quickly.

"But you could use a friend," he pointed out.

Oh, he was persistent.

She liked that in a way, but did Abigail really want a friend? She found it tiring enough to hang out with her father, and she loved him more than anyone else left in this world. Then again, what could one dinner hurt? Now that he knew her situation, there was no way he'd put the moves on her, and he always had been a good listener...

Okay, then. It was decided.

"Do you like puppies?" she asked with a guarded smile.

Chapter 10

PASTOR ADAM

Well, imagine my surprise when Abigail returned home with company. I recognized that school boy Gavin right away, and from the awkward expression plastered clear across his face, it seemed he remembered me, too.

Had it really been fifteen years since I'd reminded him to treat my daughter as the lady she is, else he'd be meeting the business end of my shotgun?

True, I didn't have a shotgun then—still don't—but he didn't know that. And it seemed my words had stuck with him over the years, too. He hauled in all the heaviest bags and supplies while Abigail moseyed in with a mostly empty shopping bag that held soft toys for when the puppies were old enough to begin using their choppers.

They still hadn't opened their eyes, and from the talking to I'd had with Mr. Manganiello just a short bit ago, it seemed they wouldn't for at least another week. I smiled just thinking where the pups would be in seven days' time—and, more importantly, where my daughter might be with them. Especially if it only took one small trip out of the house for her to make—or in this case, remake—a friend all on her own.

"Mr. Elliott," the all grown-up version of little Gavin said with a curt nod in my direction.

"I prefer Pastor Adam," I told him, trying to recall when exactly was the last time I'd seen him in church on any given Sunday.

"Oh, right," he said with a laugh. "I forgot since... Well, my folks moved us to the Chapel Assembly when I started dating Abigail. Said my mind needed to be on God—and not girls."

"Good of them," I answered with a chuckle. Seems his parents had their priorities straight, and I hoped he did, too. Especially if he planned to spend any significant amount of time with my Abigail. Come to think of it, I couldn't even remember why he and my daughter had called their young love quits all those years ago. Hopefully that meant it wasn't too gruesome.

"I got the things you asked for," Abigail said, shooting me a warning look. But warning me of what? I honestly hadn't the faintest.

"Gavin wanted to see the puppies," she explained, leading the friend turned stranger turned back into friend again to her bedroom.

I cleared my throat, ready to protest, but my daughter turned back toward me with such vim and vigor in her eyes that I swallowed my words back down. Instead, I followed along more of a force of habit than a lack of trust in my girl. Besides, I had too many questions about this new development in our day that I'd rather not leave her answering them to chance. I needed to find out why Gavin was here and what he wanted with Abigail whatever way I could.

"They're so tiny," he said, using the tip of his index finger to stroke each of our church dogs in turn. "They can't be more than a couple of days old."

"Probably not," she agreed.

"Do you know anything about dogs?" I asked from where I stood, leaning against the door frame with my arms crossed over my chest.

"Afraid not," he said with a grimace. "I'm more of a cat person."

If I'd been born a Catholic, I would have crossed myself in response to that one. Of course I loved all of God's creatures, but I'd always loved dogs just a little bit extra. We hadn't had them while Abigail was growing up because her mother Rachael had been allergic—and, well, a part of me always hoped she'd walk back into our lives and pick up where she left off.

"Be nice, Dad," Abigail warned again, a look of exasperation etched across her normally sorrowful face. At least exasperation was an improvement.

"I'm always nice," I answered, an idea popping into my mind as I watched the two young people coddle Mama Mary and her puppies. "It sure is nice to see you again, Dr. Holbrook."

"It's good to see you both, too," he answered with a brief, questioning glance my way. "Although I'm sorry about the circumstances."

This raised more questions than it answered. I'd called the man a doctor, hoping he would correct me and reveal his true profession—but he'd stayed blessedly silent.

"So, how is the medical business treating you these days?" I pressed further.

Abigail sighed, but Gavin answered me all the same. "I hear it's good, but I'm not in that business myself, so couldn't say for sure."

"Daddy, could we please have some privacy?" Abigail asked, her exasperation had turned to outright frustration.

"Oh, yes. I'll just be on my way. Good to see you again," I said, knowing when I'd been defeated at my own game.

Still, Gavin and I exchanged nods, then I carried myself away, hoping I'd still be able to overhear any conversation from the living room.

Chapter 11

ABIGAIL

Abigail brought her hands to her cheeks to hide the sudden rush of heat. Her pale skin meant that she would often turn red at even the slightest provocation. If Gavin noticed her sudden shyness, he at least didn't say anything to further embarrass her. Her father had done enough of that already.

"Sorry about him," she whispered when she was certain the meddling pastor had moved out of earshot.

Gavin laughed, and his eyes crinkled at the corners just as they always had. She liked that some things didn't change, no matter how much life threw at you.

"I think it's sweet how concerned he is over you," he said after a pause. "And that he thought he was being so stealthy with all that Dr. Holbrook business."

He rolled his eyes, then turned his attention back to the puppies. "I think this one's my favorite," he said, gently petting a mostly black puppy with a little white line running down the top of her head all the way to her impossibly tiny nose.

"How can you have a favorite?" she asked, grabbing tight to the topic change and running with it. "They all act the same."

"Nah, you can already see their personalities coming through. See how this one pushes its way in over the other puppies and makes sure it gets the best spot? He's a spunky little guy and will be a lot of fun when he's old enough to play."

"*She*," Abigail corrected. "That one's a girl."

Gavin drew his hand away from the puppy and turned to face Abigail. "Oops. I guess my lack of dog knowledge is showing. What's her name?"

"She doesn't have one yet. None of them do except for Mama Mary," she admitted, even though she'd definitely been tempted to preempt her father's waiting period and just name the puppies herself. "Dad says he's going to let the Sunday School kids pick names."

"Oh, boy. That probably means they'll all be named after princesses and superheroes then." Gavin leaned in toward the puppies again and gave the mother dog a scratch between her ears.

"Well, there are worse ways to name a dog, I suppose." Abigail thought of the little one growing inside her belly. She didn't have any names picked out for him or her yet, either. Nothing felt right in a world where her child would be born half an orphan. She guessed if it were a boy she could name him for Owen, but what if she had a girl? She had no idea which she preferred or whether she would love her child on sight as all good mothers were supposed to do. None of it felt real yet even though the clock continued to tick away without missing a single second.

"What's wrong?" Gavin asked, his brow crumpled with concern.

"Nothing," she answered reflexively and swiped at dry, itchy eyes. "Well, actually everything, but that's not your fault."

Gavin cleared his throat, then waited for her to look up at him before he spoke. "I hate seeing you like this. You were always this bright beam of sunshine growing up." His smile faltered before returning full blast. "Actually, I think I had a crush on you ever since the first day I met you on the swings in Kindergarten. Remember that?"

"No," Abigail answered with a shake of her head. "I'm sorry. I really don't."

He placed his hand on hers and gave it a quick squeeze before letting go. "When we were finally placed in the same class in second grade, I insisted the teacher sit me right behind you."

Now this she couldn't believe. Gavin hadn't said a single kind word to her until middle school at the absolute earliest. "But you were awful to me in second grade!" she argued. "I went home crying more than once."

"Yeah, little boys aren't the best at romance." He chuckled, drawing a soft giggle from her as well. "But I finally got it right in eighth grade when I asked you to the end-of-year dance and even braved your father to come pick you up."

"That was a good night," Abigail said with a wistful sigh. She could still remember almost every minute of that special day. "I remember thinking the gymnasium looked absolutely magical."

"Yeah, a great night followed by a great year. But then stupid teenager stuff got in the way and we broke up. I never stopped caring about you, though, you know. Junior year I tried to rack up the courage to ask you to prom, but then Pippa Jackson asked me first and I figured I might as well go with her rather than risk you saying *no*."

"I would've said *yes*," Abigail realized with a start. "I ended up staying home because all of my friends had dates except for me."

"Unbelievable," Gavin teased with a roll of his eyes. "Seems we had a few different near misses in our day, but still, here we are again. Together."

She sighed and wondered what more she could say to convince Gavin she wasn't ready for a relationship—not now and possibly not ever again.

"As friends," he added before she had to correct him. "I know you're hurting and I want to help. I care about you, Abigail, and besides, I'm not looking for a relationship either."

She raised an eyebrow in his direction. "Oh? Is that so?"

"Work keeps me busy. Your father was half right, by the way. I actually am a doctor, but for teeth." He flashed his pearly whites at her as if they alone offered the proof she needed.

She scrunched up her face at that reveal. "You grew up to be a dentist?" She'd never pictured Gavin as a dentist. Truth be told, she couldn't really picture him as anything rather than the boy she knew in high school.

"Nah, an endodontist. We're way better than your run-of-the-mill dentists."

She knew that word, and it wasn't a good one. Owen had been severe pain before finally visiting the base-recommended endodontist for an emergency root canal. And now Gavin was saying this was what he had voluntarily chosen to do for a living? Too bizarre.

"Aren't you the guys who give people root canals?" she asked, trying her best to keep a straight face. This felt just like the old days when they'd tease each other about who got the higher score on a test or who could skip a rock further across the beach. "Hate to break it to you, but nobody likes a root canal."

But Gavin was clearly a man who loved what he did and was ready to defend it. "See, that's where you're wrong," he argued. "Everyone talks about how bad they are, but it's really the pain leading up to them that's bad. Actually, root canals end that pain, and that makes me a professional pain ender."

Abigail studied him for a moment, noting how his blond hair hung shaggy over his forehead and how he'd grown into the long arms and legs he'd sported as a teen. He seemed sincere and without a hidden agenda. It didn't make any sense, but then again, they'd both grown up so much in the years since high school. Gavin had become a doctor, for goodness' sake. She needed to give him a chance. At the very least his company offered less pressure than her father's. Maybe it wouldn't be the worst thing in the world to have a friend she could confide in.

"So you want to end my pain?" she asked after taking a dry gulp.

"Yes, ma'am." Always the good Southern boy. Always sincere, a gentle-man. He hadn't changed one bit other than this crazy new job of his.

She watched as his eyes lit with mischief.

"I'm not too sure a root canal would help here," Gavin said with a shrug. "But we can always try it just in case."

Abigail laughed softly and bumped her shoulder into his as the puppies continued to scramble for the best nursing spot.

Yes, it felt nice to have a friend.

Chapter 12

ABIGAIL

Abigail watched as her father did up his tie in front of the old antique mirror that hung in their foyer.

"Are you sure you won't come this morning?" he asked, making eye contact with her reflection and offering a wheedling smile.

She pretended to think it over, already knowing full well what her answer would be. *"Hmm.* Didn't you promise not to ask me to leave the house again for at least a week after the whole thing yesterday?"

He shrugged and patted his tie flat after finishing the knot. "I thought maybe things had changed since you invited that Gavin fella over. And besides, the kids will be naming the puppies today. Don't you want to be a part of that?"

"No, I haven't changed my mind, and, no, I don't need to be there. The puppies are too little to go anyway. Take the pictures I gave you to help inspire the kids, and I'll stay here to watch after the dogs in person."

Her father turned abruptly and placed a hand on her shoulder, regarding her with a frown that told her exactly what was coming. They had the same conversation every Sunday since she'd moved back home.

"One of these days you're going to have to make peace with God," he said softly.

"Maybe, but today's not that day."

He looked like he wanted to say more but swallowed back whatever it was and cleared his throat, then gave her a kiss on the cheek instead.

Abigail watched him go, then waited until she heard her father's car start up in the drive before finally letting out a long, shaky breath. Today was the day she planned to find Mama Mary's owners. Even though only a few days had passed since her father brought the Chihuahuas home from his Christmas Eve sermon, she already felt herself getting attached—and that was a huge problem.

It would be just her luck for the cuddly creatures to get ripped away by their rightful owners just as Abigail had finally allowed herself to fall in love with them. She needed to find them sooner than later, even if her dad and all the Sunday school kids would be sorely disappointed at the loss of their "church dogs." After all, the longer they waited, the harder it would be on everyone.

She'd already taken photos of the mother dog from multiple angles and designed a handful of sharable social media graphics and printed flyers that she hoped her father might be willing to distribute around town to save her the trouble. Now she just needed to figure out where to post her notices online, and if all went according to plan, the dogs would be returned to their original owners by nightfall.

What kind of person loses a heavily pregnant dog in the middle of a snow storm? she wondered. And what if that bout of negligence wasn't just a one-time thing? What if Mama Mary often escaped or got lost on the streets? Would it really be best for the dogs—especially the tiny puppies— to go back to an owner like that?

She shook her head, hoping to dislodge the guilt that had set up shop inside her head. But the gesture didn't help. Nothing did. The guilt would probably stick with her no matter what she decided. After all, not trying to find the owners wasn't an option either. Why did this have to be so hard?

She fired up her laptop which—other than designing the graphics to aid in her search—had been badly neglected as of late. Once it had finished running a slew of updates, she logged into Facebook to begin posting her found dog campaign far and wide. A little red notification drew her eyes to the friend requests section where a smiling picture of Gavin greeted her.

She clicked accept and almost immediately received a private message: *Pffhew! For a while there I wasn't sure you were going to be my friend.*

Gavin's name blinked at her until she clicked the window to type out her response: *I'm not on much. Just logged in to see if I can find the dogs' owner.*

Need any help?

I'll let you know. Thanks.

She hated to be abrupt, but if she didn't focus now, she'd never find who Mama Mary belonged to. When it seemed like Gavin had nothing more to say, she minimized their chat and did a search for rescue groups in the area. She was able to join two straightaway, but the others all had a membership approval process, meaning she'd already reached a dead end for the time being.

Frustrating.

Before logging off and waiting for the dogs to awake from their morning nap, she decided to check her newsfeed. Most of the updates were either from members of her father's church or her friends from back on base. It felt odd seeing them continue with their lives as if nothing had changed when everything in Abigail's world was different.

She quickly scrolled past anything that made her heart ache for Owen, finally stopping on a beautiful image of a fair-haired woman sitting in the snow with a gorgeous pair of huskies. *A FREE BOOK FOR THE ADVENTURER IN YOU* was written in huge block letters beside them.

Abigail clicked on the ad and was taken to a simple website with a place to enter her email and receive a free copy of the author's bestselling book based on her adventures with sled dog racing. Abigail doubted there was an "adventurer in her," as the ad claimed, but at the very least, this free book could help to pass time.

She entered her email and downloaded a copy to her computer.

Returning to Facebook, she spotted an ad for the local gynecological office asking her if she'd scheduled her yearly pap smear. It was creepy how much the social media site knew about her, and these very specific ads proved it. No, she hadn't scheduled a pap smear lately, which she suspected Facebook already knew, but she did need to find a new doctor for her prenatal care. Other than taking her vitamins and trying to eat somewhat healthy, she'd done very little to take care of her baby.

Part of her was terrified she'd burst into tears and not be able to stop crying when she came face to face with the baby on the big ultrasound screen—without Owen there to hold her hand and experience the moment with her. But she'd already waited too long as it was. She needed to be a good mother to her child, no matter how hard it was on her heart.

Abigail held one hand over her pulsing chest and used the other to click into the doctor's website. It was time to stop hiding from what needed to be done.

Chapter 13
ABIGAIL

Later that day, Abigail's father came home to tell her the children had named the puppies Brownie, Cookie, Cupcake, and Muffin —apparently, they had all been craving some rich desserts that morning. The names they'd picked were kind of cute, though, and surprisingly they did match the puppies quite well.

The white one with brown spots resembled a chocolate chip cookie. The mostly black puppy with a white stripe on its forehead could be a burnt brownie, she supposed, while the fawn colored dog reminded her of a banana nut muffin, leaving the one that most resembled its mother to be their Cupcake.

Ugh. It would be harder to give them up now that they had names. Of course, they might not have to ever say goodbye at the rate her search was going. She'd been approved to join a couple more groups and a few dozen people had reposted her pictures, but so far there were absolutely no leads.

She'd need to get the dogs into a vet soon. Maybe the staff there would have some ideas of where to search next. Heck, they might even recognize Mama Mary and know how to get in touch with her owner.

Abigail decided to make an appointment for the dogs once business hours started up again the next morning. Everything was slower because of the holidays, and that would continue for at least another week. She shuddered at the thought of ringing in a new year and thus ushering in her first full year as a widow. It would also be the year she welcomed her first—and probably only—child into the world.

There would be many more firsts on her own now that all her lasts with Owen were through. What a horrible epiphany!

The only lucky thing that happened all day was that the OBGYN's website allowed her to book her appointment directly online. Miraculously, they even had an opening for the following morning, which she nabbed right up. If her calculations were right, she'd be able to discover the baby's sex during her ultrasound tomorrow. This realization made her incredibly nervous. It would make everything that much more real, that much more imminent.

She chose not to mention the appointment to her father over dinner that night, knowing he'd insist on coming with her. Truth be told, she would rather face the doctor alone. After all, she'd need to get used to handling her parenting tasks solo—might as well start now.

She hardly caught a wink of sleep before waking up far too early the following morning. Mama Mary and her puppies continued to snuggle on the new fleece-lined dog bed she had purchased for them the day she'd run into Gavin who, by the way, hadn't messaged her again since she'd brushed him off the day before.

It was for the best. Thank goodness.

She'd already foolishly allowed herself to wonder what her life would be like now, if the two of them hadn't broken up back then, if she'd never fallen for Owen at all because she was still smitten with her high school sweetheart. This, of course, begged the question about whether it was better to have loved and lost...

Lately, she didn't think it was.

If she'd never met Owen, then she wouldn't be aching for him now. She wouldn't be facing a life alone as a single mother living with her pastor father in the same house she'd grown up in.

Of course, she felt terrible for thinking like that. It was almost like throwing away her memories of him altogether. If it had been the other way around, if she'd died instead of him, what would *his* life be like now? Well, *he* wouldn't be expecting a baby, for one. But would he mourn her or would he cry a little and move on?

Owen had always been the better person of the two of them, so no doubt he would choose the right response... whatever that was.

Abigail's phone buzzed on her dresser with an appointment reminder. Once again, she'd let giant snatches of time pass without doing anything more than wallowing in her own misery. She really needed to cut that out... if only she could figure out how.

Struggling up from the bed, she pulled on her favorite pair of jeans. When the button dug into her growing belly, she unsnapped them and used the same ponytail holder trick she'd used in college when that wretched freshman fifteen had settled over her hips. A quick loop around the button and a bit of a tug transformed her too-tight jeans into makeshift maternity wear.

This was the beginning.

She wouldn't be able to put off buying actual maternity clothes for too much longer, but maybe she could purchase them online and avoid having to go out to handle the dreaded task.

This made two outings in three days now, and she knew she'd need to help her father take the dogs into the vet that evening as well.

Just breathe. You've got this, she reminded herself.

After a quick splash of water on her face and a second ponytail holder to tie back her hair, Abigail took a series of deep breaths and headed out of the house.

Soon she would see her baby live on the big ultrasound screen. She'd even find out whether it would be a girl or a boy. That was a big deal, right? A huge deal!

So why wasn't she excited?

Chapter 14

ABIGAIL

Abigail held her breath as the ultrasound tech squeezed a line of cold gel onto her belly.

The tech hummed merrily as she slid the wand across Abigail's distended abdomen. "Do you want to know what you're having, or are we leaving it a secret until the big day?" she asked with the kind of smile that implied she absolutely loved her job.

"Sure," Abigail answered, trying to match the other woman's enthusiasm. This was her baby, after all. It was okay to get excited. It's what she was *supposed to* be feeling.

The tech continued to make occasional small talk as she took and retook various measurements. Luckily, she didn't ask about the father, a small miracle for which Abigail was extremely grateful. Instead, she said, "Your baby is measuring on the small side. Not small enough to be worried, but it explains why you're not showing much yet. Have you felt the baby kick?"

"Not yet," Abigail answered with a frown. Yes, a kick would definitely make her baby feel more real. So far she'd had a physically easy pregnancy and, for the most part, had kept her mind on Owen's loss rather than bonding with the child. "Should I have?"

"Many women do by now, but it's not uncommon for women undergoing their first pregnancy to feel the baby moving closer to twenty-six weeks. You're at about twenty. Maybe nineteen."

"What will it feel like? When the baby moves?" she asked, moving her eyes from the grainy image of her sleeping baby on the screen over to the other woman.

The tech gave a wistful smile as she continued to stare at the baby's heart thumping on the black and white monitor. "Every mother describes it a little differently. None of my girls were very rough and tumble on the inside or the out, so to me it felt something like bubbles popping or butterfly wings flapping."

"Girls," Abigail said, trying to feel something—maybe hope, maybe dread, just *something*—at the thought of having a daughter of her own. "Am I having a girl, too?"

The tech's eyes widened and she dropped her voice conspiratorially. "Are you ready to find out?"

"Yes." Abigail held her breath as she waited for the tech to reposition her wand. Suddenly she desperately needed to know what she was up against. Maybe decorating a nursery and shopping for an infant wardrobe would help her finally move on past her grief and begin to feel excited that she wouldn't be the lone member of the Elliott-Sutton family any longer.

The tech snapped a picture of the screen and traced her cursor across the image to outline the baby's private bits. "Congrats, Mama. You're having a boy."

Abigail closed her eyes to keep in the tears that had begun to form. She still didn't know whether she felt happy about this news or saddened by it. The only thing she knew for sure is that she wished Owen were here to experience it with her. If she still believed in God, she could tell herself that her late husband was smiling down at her...

But she just couldn't.

"Do you know what you're going to name him?" the tech asked, moving the wand in slippery circles as she searched for the next spot to measure.

"Yes," Abigail answered, surprising herself. This was one decision she didn't need to deliberate over at all. She knew exactly what her little boy was meant to be called.

"Owen," she whispered to the tech before saying it again louder, clearer. *Owen.*

Perhaps now the name would bring her joy. Perhaps now she could finally look forward instead of back.

"That's a nice name," the other woman said, not pressing for more. Somehow she just seemed to understand what Abigail needed from this exchange—and, even more importantly, what she didn't.

When Abigail and Owen had first started dating, she'd looked up the meaning of his name on a parenting website. Now they had come full circle, it seemed. Owen was a Welsh name, she remembered, meaning "desire born." But Abigail had never desired raising a child without his father. She had never desired becoming a widow in her twenties. Would new desires in life finally find her once this second Owen was born?

Owen, Jr. she thought, immediately deciding never to call her child that or the resulting nickname—OJ. She would teach her son how to be a strong man, a good and honest one. And if she had a hard time doing that on her own, she knew her own father would always be there to support him, to support them.

And she couldn't think of a better man to serve as a role model for her son. After all, he had given up his whole world to make sure that hers had been magical growing up. Safe.

It wasn't his fault that life had thrown her such an unfair curve ball. But was it really God's, either? Her father had spent his entire life in pursuit of living a good life, of leading others to Jesus. He was the best man she knew. Could his beliefs really be fundamentally flawed?

...Or was it Abigail herself who was wrong? Damaged? Deeply flawed?

She looked again toward the monitor and watched as her son twisted into a new position, bringing his hands up to his mouth and eliciting a yelp of joy from the tech.

"Oh, look! Someone finally decided to join us. Hi, little guy," she said with a smile that matched the one that had stretched across Abigail's face, too.

"Hi, little Owen," she whispered, wiping away the beginnings of fresh tears. "I'm your mama."

Chapter 15

PATOR ADAM

I returned home from a morning meeting with the church elders to discover my only daughter had snuck off in my absence. Of course, almost immediately, I found myself wondering if she'd gone out with that Gavin fellow. And if that were the case, should I be grateful to him or suspicious of his motives?

Hmm, a tough question indeed.

A quick check on the puppies found all four content with full bellies. Mama Mary seemed to be well fed, too, so I left the five of them to whatever mid-day routine they'd established amongst themselves and continued my search of the rest of the house for my missing Abigail.

As I opened doors and flung back covers, I attempted a little bit of math in my head. Mind you, math had never been my strong suit, but desperate times, desperate measures and such.

Okay, I told myself. *I found the puppies Thursday night. Abigail found Gavin Saturday morning. And now it was early Monday afternoon.* By last count, I was still up five dogs, up one questionable ex-boyfriend, and down one daughter.

Hmmm, indeed.

Maybe a few more calculations would help me sort this out.

Numbers, numbers... Owen's funeral had been about *three* months ago, which meant Abigail's baby was about *five* months along. Meanwhile my wife had been missing approximately *eighteen* years and seven months, give or take a week.

I had no idea where this left me now. I hadn't moved on relationally in close to two decades, but I had kept my head up and kept going on as if life were normal for my daughter's sake. Was she ready to do the same for her child?

Also, my wife was still—presumably—out there somewhere very much alive. We knew Owen's body rested peacefully six feet under while his soul enjoyed eternal paradise with His maker.

That made things different between Abigail and me.

But just how different, I found it difficult to quantify. If you divided my length of mourning by her length of mourning so far, carried the two, and multiplied by a factor of...

Nope, I surely had no idea how to solve for X when it came to this one. Or even what X represented, for that matter.

That was when my phone rang, zapping me straight out of my mathematical conundrum. The caller ID told me it was none other than my missing Abigail.

"Hello," I answered with a smile that almost made it hurt to talk. I'm not sure whether I was happier to have found Abigail's whereabouts or to be free of trying to calculate... whatever it was I had begun to calculate.

Her voice came out soft, so soft it was hard to hear over the thumping of my own heart.

"Speak up, dear," I shouted into the phone, trying to lead by example. "Are you okay?"

"I'm perfect," she said with that omnipresent sniffle of hers. *Perfect* was a word I hadn't heard her utter since the days before Owen's passing, which really made me wonder where she could be and why she was calling now. Luckily, I didn't have to ask.

She rushed straight into sharing her news, informing me, "I'm having a boy."

A boy. A boy!

I swear to you, more wonderful words have never been spoken, not before and not since. My baby girl was having a baby boy.

What really sent my heart spinning with happiness, though, was the pride in her voice as she made this announcement, the gratitude and love.

Soon Abigail would have a son, and I'd have my daughter back.

Plus, one very special grandchild to spoil rotten as only pappies, pawpaws, and gramps are welcome to do. I couldn't wait for my turn to come.

Chapter 16

ABIGAIL

A sudden burst of sadness overtook Abigail as the glass door to the doctor's office swung shut behind her. It was there in that tiny office she had felt the first flickers of excitement about becoming a mother, *there* she had truly committed herself to doing whatever it took to give little Owen the best life possible.

And that started with healing his mother.

Despite her newfound determination, she had no idea where to begin with such a lofty task. There was so much she needed to fix, so many parts of herself she needed to find again. The challenge seemed practically insurmountable.

But she simply had to find a way, no matter how long it took.

Head down, she hurried down the corridor that led back to the parking lot.

Maybe she could start with setting up the nursery. She'd been out of work for a while now, but she also had a modest sum remaining from big Owen's life insurance policy. If she was mostly frugal, with a few special splurge items here and there, she could craft something quite special for little Owen.

She just had to—

Oof!

"I'm so sorry," she sputtered into the stranger's chest. That's what she got for not watching where she was going. "I didn't mean to—"

Her voice fell away the moment she glanced up and spotted Dr. Gavin Holbrook smiling down at her with a bemused expression. "Fancy running into you here," he said with a smirk.

"You said that last time," she pointed out.

"And it's even truer this time. Where are you headed in such a hurry?"

"The baby store," she admitted. "I just found out I'm having a boy."

"Well, congratulations!" he said with not the slightest indication that he felt anything other than immense happiness for her. "I'd say this calls for a celebration. I was just about to take my lunch break. Can you delay your shopping for—oh—I'd say an hour?"

She hesitated for a moment before remembering her resolution to be better for her baby. Friends were good and healthy. She needed this.

"Sure," she said with a smile as she reached into her purse for her keys. It got easier each time she forced a smile. Maybe soon she wouldn't have to fake it anymore. "But do you mind if I drive?"

Gavin sucked in a deep breath and leaned forward as if to reveal a secret. "*Uh oh.* Seems like someone still remembers what happened during driver's ed sophomore year."

She rolled her eyes at him. Some secret! "I'm pretty sure everyone in the tri-county area remembers. Who could forget some random guy driving straight into the school flagpole his first time out behind the wheel?"

"Hey! That wasn't some random guy. That was me!" He grabbed the lapels of his white lab coat and stood taller.

Abigail couldn't help but smirk at his ill-founded pride. "I'm not sure owning it makes the whole thing any better."

"Well, I assure you I'm a much better driver now." He rooted in his pocket and pulled out a giant cluster of keys adorned with a pink fuzzy puff of a keychain.

She studied him for a moment before bursting out into her first whole laugh in what felt like ages. "As much confidence as all this inspires, I'd still rather not take any chances," she said when at last she had sobered enough to manage words.

"Have it your way." Gavin sighed and shoved his keys back into his pocket. "But if you're driving, I'm treating."

"If you insist," Abigail said as they wove through the parking lot and toward her old, beat-up sedan. She'd need to find something much safer before her baby arrived.

"Unbelievable," Gavin said, staring at her as if she'd sprouted a second head. "Is this the same car you had in high school?"

"Well, yes and no," she admitted, turning the key in the door because she hadn't bothered to replace the batteries in the automatic opener yet.

"It either is or it isn't. How can it be both?"

"Nice to know you live in a world without gray areas," she said, shooting a playful wink his way before sinking down into the driver's seat. It really did feel like old times with Gavin at her side, as if all the years since high school had melted away—all the problems, pain, and hurt.

"My car in high school was a '96 Saturn SL2," she explained after Gavin had joined her inside. "This is a '00."

"So you basically bought the same ancient car a second time?"

"Well, not exactly the same, but I couldn't find any '96s," she explained.

"But why?" he demanded. "This car is like twenty years old now. That's practically as old as we are!"

She shrugged, feeling scrutinized by his direct gaze. "Cars aren't super important to me. My first one always served me well, so when it was time to replace it I figured, why not get another just like it?"

Gavin stared slack-jawed at her, saying nothing.

"I guess maybe I'm a little bit sentimental," she admitted.

His eyes widened and his head jutted forward. "A little bit?"

"Okay, a lot. But so what? There are more important things in life than cars." She jabbed her key in the ignition and brought the engine to life, if for no other reason than to show Gavin that—yes—this dusty old car was reliable and—yes—it got her around just fine.

"You haven't changed at all," he said, appraising her with mirth in his eyes. "It's one of the things I always liked about you."

She turned away from him, wondering if it was too late to get out of this lunch. "What? How could you possibly say that? You only just found out about the car."

"Yeah, but not that you hang on to things that are important to you. Remember your room in high school? It had pink walls and unicorn decals. You still had all this white furniture with crystal knobs. It was the same set you—"

"Had in grade school," she finished for him. "I know." She risked a glance his way, unable to hide the embarrassed smile that burned its way onto her face. "It's still the same even now, you know."

"I figured it might be. The room you're sleeping in now with the puppies, though. It's not the same one you had back then."

"No," she said, looking over her shoulder before backing out of the parking spot at last.

"Why not? If you're so nostalgic, why keep your old room the same but not use it when you came back home?"

"My new room has my bedroom set from back at the base. With my husband." She set her mouth in a firm line, hoping he wouldn't ask any more questions for a while.

Gavin sank back in his chair and rubbed his hands on his pant legs. "You're a complex woman, Abigail Elliott."

"Abigail Elliott-Sutton," she corrected.

"It's like your two bedrooms, huh? You're hanging on to both."

She frowned. Why should she have to explain herself? So what if she cherished things a little more than was normal? Not everyone lost their husbands in their mid-twenties or their mothers in early grade school. She had to hang onto what mattered, because in some cases it was all she had left. But how could you explain that to someone who had never known loss?

"Relax," Gavin said, startling her as he placed a hand on her arm. The car swerved toward the curb in response. "I don't mean to give you a hard time. I like that things matter to you. It makes me think that maybe I mattered, too. Maybe I still matter." He paused before adding, "As a friend."

It was only then that Abigail realized he was absolutely right. Reviving her friendship with Gavin was the perfect way to rediscover who she'd been and bring back that happier, kinder person for her son.

She owed it to her baby, and she owed it to herself. Besides, it seemed Gavin was a little sentimental, too. He brought up the past even more than she did. "You do matter," she told him. "And I'm glad we're friends again."

Chapter 17

ABIGAIL

Abigail followed Gavin's directions as he navigated them through Charleston's Historic District straight to a locally famous restaurant called Poogan's Porch. If you were to ask her father, he'd claim that Poogan's was not quite as locally famous as their church's yearly nativity scene, but then again, he'd say the same thing about the Carolina Panthers as well.

"This doesn't seem like a quick lunch to me," she scolded her impromptu lunch date while eyeing the quaint yellow restaurant and its not so quaint double-decker box porch.

"I was in the mood for some Lowcountry cooking," he said, holding the door open for her so she could pass inside. "Besides, they get folks in and out quickly at lunch time. We'll be just fine."

Gavin pulled out a chair for Abigail, then pulled his keys from his pocket before taking a seat of his own. "We'll have two sweet teas and two orders of shrimp and grits," he told the hostess with a smile.

"Ordering for me, are you?" Abigail teased. Lucky for him, she liked just about everything. She also hadn't had shrimp and grits for a very long time, and everyone knew Poogan's Porch served them up best.

"Why order anything else when this one dish is perfection?" he asked with a sly smile. "I'm sure the others are perfectly delicious in their own right, but it doesn't seem I'll ever find out. As soon as I walk in that door, I know exactly what I want."

"And that's the shrimp and grits, huh?" She could think of far worse food addictions—far worse addictions, period. These days it felt almost as if she'd grown addicted to grief and solitude. Shrimp and grits would have been a much better choice.

"Precisely," he said, bringing her ribbing session to a close.

"Okay, so I have to ask. What's with the giant pink thing on your keys?" Abigail said, gesturing toward the giant heap of metal and fluff that sat beside his water glass.

"What, this old thing?" he asked with a laugh, picking up the bunch and handing it over to her. "A very special little lady gave me this pink poof and I haven't had the heart to take it off my keys, no matter how emasculating it might be."

Half a dozen questions raced through Abigail's mind. What child was so important to Gavin that he kept that silly thing proudly on display? Was he a father? A proud uncle? What wasn't he telling her, and would it be too nosy if she asked outright?

"You haven't told me much about you," she hedged. "Other than that you're a professional pain remover."

"Not much to tell," he responded with a shrug, casually dropping the keys into his lap and out of view, which didn't go unnoticed by Abigail.

"But you had a lot to say about your job."

"My job is my life these days. That and my Puss."

Abigail choked on her water. "Excuse me?"

He laughed at her expression of horror. "Puss in Boots, my cat. He's why I was at the pet store the other day. Why we found each other again."

She rapped her fingers on the table, resisting the urge to take another sip of water in case Gavin said something equally shocking once more. "You must know that's not a great name for a cat."

"Why not?" he chortled as his blue eyes danced with mischief. He clearly enjoyed making her squirm. "It was good enough for Antonio Banderas, it's good enough for me."

"Um." Abigail leaned back as the waitress poured their drinks from a sweating pitcher of tea.

"Oh, c'mon. You know *Shrek!* The movie with the big green guy? Besides, it was fun to get a shock out of you," he teased. "Normally, I just call my cat 'Boots.' He's mostly brown tabby, but he's got these little white socks on his feet that are quite distinctive."

"So why not name him Socks?" she asked flatly, praying her cheeks hadn't turned as red as the lobster being served up two tables over.

He shook his head. "Nah, everyone names cats like him Socks. I had to be at least a little different."

"Gavin Holbrook," Abigail drawled, "I'd say you're *a lot* different."

"And I'd say that's quite the compliment." He raised his freshly filled sweet tea glass and clinked it to the edge of Abigail's. She decided not to mention that it hadn't been meant as a compliment. Weird or not, Gavin was all himself and she admired that—wished she could be more like it herself.

"So you like root canals and cats. What else?" she prompted, looking back toward the spot where his keys and that giant pink pom-pom had rested only minutes before.

"Well, you already know I like you. That makes three things," Gavin answered between sips of his tea.

Abigail frowned. She'd already told him everything worth knowing about her these days, and he still kept the better part of himself hidden. It didn't seem like a very good basis for rekindling their friendship. "Three things isn't a lot to go by when getting to know a person," she offered peaceably.

"But you already know me."

"Maybe, but that doesn't change the fact you're hiding something."

His smile faltered. "I'm not hiding. I just like to focus on the positive. Especially when you already have so much to be sad about without me heaping on."

"Gavin," she whispered. "What is it? You can tell me."

He ran both hands through his sandy blond hair before taking a deep breath and nodding. "I'll tell you, but I don't want to focus on it. I want this lunch to be about old friends reconnecting. Believe me, I spend enough time wallowing when I'm on my own."

She gulped, hating that she had brought his pain to the surface like this. She wouldn't have even guessed a single thing was wrong if not for his sudden change of demeanor. "You don't have to if—"

Gavin cleared his throat and set his glass back on the table, failing to make eye contact as he spoke. "No, I should. I need to get used to talking about it, and you've been so forthcoming with me. It's just..."

He snapped his line of vision back up to meet hers, and Abigail saw an intensity in his eyes she'd never seen before—not in all the times she'd spent mooning over those eyes in school and not in their time spent together as adults, either.

He regarded her silently before finally revealing, "As it turns out, you aren't the only one who's lost someone important to you."

Chapter 18

ABIGAIL

Abigail folded her hands in her lap and waited for Gavin to say more.

He closed his eyes and smiled as if picturing the most beautiful scene he could imagine behind his eyelids. "Her name was Millie—the little girl who gave me that keychain—and she was three years old at the time. She wasn't my daughter, but it sure felt like it. First I fell in love with her mother and then with Millie herself the moment we were introduced. Her mother, Susie, and I were set to be married that spring with little Millie serving as both the maid of honor and the flower girl. I couldn't have been happier if I tried."

He opened his eyes again and frowned at Abigail so deeply it made her heart ache for him, for the man he'd once been. "But then around about this time two years ago, Millie's father came back into the picture. And what could I say to save myself? He hadn't been the best to either of them, but he said he was a changed man, that he wanted the three of them to be a family."

"Oh gosh, Gavin, I'm so, so sorry." She hated when people apologized for things that weren't their fault, but what else could she say? Just like her, Gavin had loved and lost. Big time.

He smiled weakly before continuing. "Susie spent days weighing over the decision. Maybe even weeks. But in the end she decided that Millie needed her father and it would be best for all of us if I were to break off contact completely."

Abigail shook her head, unable to believe Gavin had gone from almost married with a family to depressingly single within the blink of an eye. "So that was it?" she asked gently. "You never saw them again?"

"They moved to a new state, wouldn't even tell me where, and I moved back to Charleston, opened my practice, and threw myself into work like there was nothing else that mattered. Because, really, there wasn't."

"I can't say I blame you." Abigail wished she had the determination to keep working hard in the wake of her loss, but unlike Gavin, she'd lost the will to fight for herself.

"One day they were my whole world, and the next they were strangers. It was quite the shock to the system. It still hurts fresh as yesterday if I let it." He offered her a wistful smile. Even though no tears fell, Abigail couldn't help but wonder if they were ready and waiting. Or had Gavin simply reached the point where no more tears would come?

"That's why you reached out to me," she stated.

He nodded softly. "I needed a friend, too."

Abigail leaned across the table and clasped his hand. Was it worse that Susie chose to leave Gavin? That she intentionally cut him from her life, leading to not only loss but betrayal as well? Their situations weren't the same, but they certainly felt familiar to one another. Gavin had lost two people that meant everything to him, the poor guy.

"I'm happy to be your friend, but I don't know what to say to make it better," she admitted, finally understanding why people resorted to the same old platitudes over and over again. It felt better to say something cliché than to say nothing at all.

He sighed and gave her hand a squeeze before letting go. "That's the thing: words can't make it better. Only moving on does."

"Have you?" Abigail wanted to know. "Moved on?"

Gavin wrapped both hands around his half empty glass of tea. "I honestly don't know."

"Are you ready to?" She was pushing him now. She knew that, but somehow it felt as if curing Gavin would cure her as well, that it would prove recovery was at least possible. The problem was she had no idea what moving on past grief would even look like. Maybe there wasn't truly any way to ever really move on. Maybe you just buried your sadness underneath heaps of happier memories and prayed like heck that your pile wouldn't topple over.

Gavin shook his head—whether to say no or that he wasn't sure, Abigail couldn't figure out. Perhaps it didn't matter in the grand scheme of things.

"It sounds like you need a root canal," she said with a sly smile as she watched the waitress approach their table.

He laughed, the light returning to his eyes. "You're probably right about that. Root canals *do* make everything better. For now, though, I'll start with these." Gavin picked up his spoon and dipped it into his fresh bowl of shrimp and grits the moment the waitress set it in front of him.

"Thank you," Abigail said as she accepted her lunch as well.

They each savored their food in silence for a few moments before Gavin set his spoon down, wiped his mouth, and said, "It does help, you know. Throwing yourself into a project. My work keeps me sane, if not fully happy."

"I've been out of work for a while," she admitted. "It's hard to be creative without having that fire. I'm a graphic designer, by the way. In case I hadn't mentioned." She chose not to reveal her worry that her creative passion had been permanently doused, that it had left this world right alongside Owen.

"Doesn't need to be work," he answered between bites. "That's just what I chose. What about the puppies?"

The puppies. She'd only been away from them for a couple hours, but it seemed so much had happened since she left the house that morning. "I'm trying to find their owner but haven't had much luck yet. I also need to take them to the vet with my father this evening."

"I think they're your project," Gavin said with a genuine smile as he regarded her. "Haven't you felt better since your dad brought them home for you to look after?"

"A little," she said, pushing a particularly juicy shrimp around her bowl. "I like the dogs, but I don't want to get attached to them. You know how it is."

"I do. But I also know if you never let anyone in, then you can find yourself two years down the road every bit as broken as you are now."

He was right about that, and he clearly spoke from experience, too. It was easier to help the puppies who were here and needing her now. Little Owen still felt lightyears away. The puppies would be practically full grown by the time he was even born. Could they not only give her a head start on her parenting skills, but also help her heal on a deeper level? If Gavin was right, then yes. They absolutely could.

"Hey," Abigail protested halfheartedly. "I resemble that remark."

"Me too," Gavin answered with a wink before shoving another big bite in his mouth.

Chapter 19

ABIGAIL

After lunch, Abigail dropped Gavin back at his office and gave him a quick hug goodbye. "Thanks for everything," she whispered into his ear before they pulled apart. They exchanged numbers and promises to meet up for lunch sometime again soon, and then she made a quick stop off at the baby store before heading back home.

Hearing Gavin's tale of pain touched her in a way she hadn't expected. On the one hand, it was nice to know she had someone who could understand, someone other than her father who so desperately wanted to swoop in and fix everything for her.

On the other, it hurt her to see her friend hurting. He'd seemed so carefree one moment and so tortured the next. Would she never truly escape her grief? Would it be like a shackle that remained forever bound to her ankle, sabotaging her as she tried to stumble her way through life?

There were no easy answers. That much hadn't changed.

She tried to push their lunch from her mind and focus on the aisle that stretched before her brimming with seemingly every infant knick-knack in existence. She pushed through to the clothing display and selected a dapper little outfit for Owen. It had soft overalls sewn into the onesie and even sported a little bowtie. He would look so handsome dressed to the nines while still comfy cozy in the soft cotton get-up.

Just five more months until he'd be here with her. She tried to picture it but couldn't quite form an image. Would he have a full shock of red hair like his papa? Or would his hair be dark and silky like Abigail's? He could be born bald as a cue ball for all she knew. One thing she knew for sure, though, was that he'd be hers.

All hers.

There was still so much to prep for his arrival, but at least now she knew she could do it. Gavin was proof that one could live with pain and still thrive in other ways. He'd seemed so normal and happy before he revealed his big secret to her. It obviously still hurt him, but it didn't stop him from reaching out to her, either.

But why her? Why Abigail of all people?

It was clear he wasn't looking for a relationship now that he'd told her the sad truth hidden behind that goofy grin. So what was he looking to accomplish, and why did he think she would be the one to get him there?

Maybe he was just well and truly lonely.

Or maybe, a small, niggling voice whispered in the back of her brain, *it wasn't an accident at all. Maybe God put you in each other's paths for a reason.*

She shook off the thought, not having the energy or desire to unpack it at the moment, and headed to the cash register to purchase little Owen's first outfit.

❧

Back at home, Mama Mary whimpered and shook her teeny tail so furiously that her entire body followed right along with it.

"Did you miss me?" Abigail asked the dog with a laugh, noticing Mary had knocked one of her puppies off the bed in her eagerness to greet her.

"Let's put you back, little Cookie," she told the pup, kissing the top of its head before nestling it in beside its brothers and sister. She headed to the kitchen to refill the mother Chihuahua's water dish, then fired up her laptop.

Mama Mary groaned and waited for Abigail to pick her up and place her on the bed beside her. The little dog gave Abigail a quick lick then dove under the covers, probably eager to have a nap completely undisturbed by her babies. Soon Abigail would understand how that went for herself—just five months to go.

She watched as Mama Mary got comfortable and fell asleep with a series of happy whimpers, then opened up Facebook and found that two messages were waiting for her.

The first was from Gavin: *Thank you for today. It meant a lot.*

Why me? she asked herself again. She'd asked herself that same question when Gavin had started paying attention to her in high school. He'd always been more popular than her, more handsome and well-liked by their peers. So what did he want with boring old Abigail? She had even less to offer now, but that didn't stop him from wanting to spend time together.

She'd need a while to think about how she wanted to respond, so she clicked on the other message. It read: *Hi, my name is Marcus Barnes, and I think you found my dog.*

Chapter 20

PASTOR ADAM

From the very second Abigail told me about this Marcus Barnes and his apparent claim to the dogs, my spidey sense started going haywire.

"Why won't he let us meet him at his house?" I asked her after she'd informed me that we had to go to meet Marcus instead of to the vet as planned.

She shrugged away my concern as if it were nothing. "I don't know, but I'm sure he has a good reason for it."

"Well, did he present evidence of a photographic or any other nature?"

She just rolled her eyes at me, same as she'd been doing since she was a little thing herself. "Dad, listen to you. You sound like Nancy Drew or something. Why would he say the dogs are his if they're not?"

That's what I wanted to know, too. Of course, I wouldn't keep our church dogs away from their rightful owner, but this smelled more than a little fishy if you asked me. And if Abigail wasn't going to worry about it, I'd have to worry about it enough for both of us. Luckily, I'd already started in on that particular task.

"Ready to go?" my daughter asked, carrying Mama Mary tucked tight into her chest and leaving the box of puppies for me to manage.

"As I'll ever be," I said with a grunt as I followed her out to the driveway and allowed her to drive us to the nearby Micky D's.

❧

"You must be Marcus," Abigail said, striding right on up to a scraggly fella leaning up against an old GMC and smoking a cigarette.

Had she no sense of self-preservation?

Boy howdy, was it a good thing I'd talked her into letting me come along.

The man smiled in a way that told me he was thinking unconscionable things about my daughter. He was lucky I was the turn the other cheek type and not the shoot now, ask questions later type. "Did you bring the dog?"

"Yes, we have her and the puppies in the car." Abigail wrung her hands, and I could tell this pained her, too.

"We need proof before we hand them over," I shot in. I loved that it was in my daughter's nature to trust people, but God had already told me that these dogs belonged to the church. And I trusted my God Almighty over a million such Marcus Barneses.

The man sniffed. "Proof? My word not enough for you?"

"Oh, no," Abigail said in a hurry. "We didn't mean to—"

"No, good sir, it is not," I said, taking a step forward and motioning for Abigail to get behind me just in case this turned ugly. "How do we know that the dog is yours? How do we know she'll be better off with you than with us? She was half dead when we found her, and that doesn't exactly inspire confidence in your pet-keeping skills."

"She's mine because I say she is." He puffed up his chest, then just as quickly deflated. "Look, her name is Sausage, and I was worried sick about her, all right? Can I just have my dog back?"

"You got any pictures of Sausage on your phone? Something you can show us?" I demanded.

"If you're looking to shake me down for a reward, it's not going to work. Just give me my dog."

"Well, this is quite the pickle, because I'm not giving you a single dog without proof, and you refuse to provide it."

"I'm not looking for a fight. I just want my dog back," the man said.

"And we just want to make sure we're doing right by these dogs, and right now sending them home with you doesn't seem like the right decision at all."

"So, what then? You're just going to refuse to give them to me?"

"Tell you what," I said with a smile. "We can divide them in half, that way we each get some. The mother dog stays with us, though."

"So you're telling me it's some dogs or none at all? You're crazy, man."

"So you choose none at all? Fine by us. C'mon, Abigail, let's go home."

"Wait!" Marcus said, trailing after us like he was the little lost puppy in this scenario. "Fine, I'll take half, if that's the way it's gotta be."

"Get in the car, Abigail," I said with a patient smile before turning back to Marcus and explaining with triumph, "We will not be giving you any puppies today."

"What?" the man exploded. He'd clearly had more than his fill of me, and I definitely felt the same way about him. "You just said you'd give me half."

"I did say that, and I'll also say this: you need to read your *Bible* more, son. You just let me get away with a classic King Solomon," I said, referencing the story about the two mothers fighting for the same baby. That time, the King had said they'd cut the child in half. I was just talking about dividing puppies, but still, if he loved that mama dog at all, he would not have settled for our split decision. And he would have had at least one photo to back up his ownership claims.

Marcus Barnes watched dumbfounded as I slipped into the car and motioned for Abigail to drive us back home, dogs in tow.

"I don't know what he was playing at," I told my daughter, "but I think I'll give Officer Jackson a call just to see if he can't find out for us."

Chapter 21

ABIGAIL

The vet was very understanding about rescheduling their appointment after Abigail's abrupt cancellation. A good thing, too, because it seemed her father had been right all along. Mama Mary and her puppies were meant to find them.

After returning home from their distressing meeting with Marcus Barnes, her father had put in a call to his friend in the city police department. The man hadn't been smart enough to use a fake name when reaching out to Abigail, so the police were able to track him down that same evening and bust his puppy mill operation wide open.

How one pregnant mother Chihuahua had managed to escape her cage and run all the way to their church was anyone's guess, but by doing so she'd saved her puppies and countless others, too.

"Would you mind keeping hold of the dogs a little longer?" Officer Jackson asked when he called to share the news. "The local animal shelter doesn't have enough room for all the dogs we took from this guy, and we need all the help we can get."

"Say no more," her father answered promptly. "Eternal Grace is on the case."

Abigail watched in amazement as her father started up the church phone tree, amassing more than a dozen volunteers in less than an hour. She hugged Mama Mary close to her chest, finally willing to admit how much the dog had come to mean to her in such a short span of time.

"Do you believe God sent us these dogs now?" her father asked, picking up each little pup in turn and giving it a gentle kiss on the head.

Abigail nodded, still clutching the mother dog tight. "I guess you were right about them being miracle workers. Mama Mary saved so many other dogs because of her bravery."

"And you helped her do it because of that strong sense of right and wrong you've had ever since you were a little girl." He came over to pet Mama Mary and make cooing noises at her. "You weren't going to rest until we found that owner."

"Thanks, Dad." She gave her father a hug and a kiss on the cheek, basking in her and Mary's shared victory. She had done something important, something miraculous, and it felt wonderful.

The next morning, the vet confirmed that they had rescued the dogs just in time. "They're all strong and healthy," she said, shaking her head in disbelief. "Even brief exposure to the cold at their age should have done them in. I just don't understand. It's like it's a—"

"Miracle?" her father finished with a knowing smile. "That's what I said."

The vet laughed before pressing her stethoscope to Mama Mary's chest. "Yes, I guess you could call it a miracle. Someone was clearly looking out for these dogs."

"How's Mary doing? Is she healthy, too?" Abigail asked from her seat in the corner. Even though she still wasn't sure how she felt about God these days, she'd prayed for that little dog hard and long. Mary had overcome too much to not get her happily ever after now.

The vet frowned briefly before putting on a placating smile. "Yes, she appears healthy. But she's had litters before. It's hard to say how many, though I'd guess she was being bred nonstop since reaching sexual maturity."

"How old is she now?" Abigail chewed her lip nervously.

The vet shifted her stethoscope to Mary's back and listened in a couple different spots before turning her attention back to Abigail. "My best guess is three."

"Only three!" her father sputtered, his brows lifted in surprise. "She sure has seen a lot for her short time on earth."

The poor dog had suffered three years of captivity and forced breeding, three years of non-stop torment, Abigail realized. *So why does she trust me? She shouldn't trust anyone.*

"She's remarkably well-adjusted for what she's been through," the vet continued, confirming just what Abigail had been thinking.

"She's a hero," Abigail said, picking Mama Mary off the exam table and giving her a kiss between the ears. This amazing creature had chosen her. Perhaps she'd seen something in Abigail that Abigail had yet to discover in herself.

"So what next?" she asked the vet, eager to make their adoption of the church dogs official. She was never letting a single one of them out of her sight again—not if she could help it.

"We'll take up a collection at church to help pay for the veterinary care of the others who were rescued from the mill," her father said.

"And I'll perform those exams at cost," the vet added. "A rescue this size is a huge undertaking, but I can see the dogs are in great hands." She reached out to shake both of their hands before picking up her stack of folders and leaving them alone in the exam room.

"Praise the Lord," her father said. "We couldn't have asked for better news today."

"Are you really taking up a collection?" Abigail mumbled, not sure why she was surprised by this news.

"Of course." He smiled and puffed out his chest, always so proud of his church and the people who made up its family. "The congregation will want to help."

"*I* want to help," she said before she could change her mind. She still had a rough relationship with God, but she wanted to do her part to make the world better, to help in whatever way she could.

He gave her the side eye. "Does that mean you'll come to church this Sunday?"

"I could design flyers, or—"

"Or you could finally come back to church." He turned his full gaze on her, a warm smile took over his entire face. "Come tell everyone about the dogs and why they need help. Introduce them to Mama Mary and her pups. Maybe say hello to God while you're visiting His house."

"Okay," she said before taking a deep, shaky breath. "I'm in."

Chapter 22

ABIGAIL

Abigail texted Gavin to update him on the puppy mill bust, their vet visit, and her upcoming return to church. Almost immediately after she pressed send, her phone buzzed with an incoming call.

"Wow," Gavin said, not even bothering with hello. "All that in the space of twenty-four hours? You definitely don't do anything halfway."

"I guess not," she answered with a laugh.

Mama Mary cocked her head to the side as if trying to listen in to the conversation, which only caused Abigail to laugh harder.

"So you get to keep the dogs?" Gavin asked. Hope filled his voice, and the sound of a whirring drill accompanied it as well.

"Are you...? Are you doing a root canal while talking to me?"

"Maybe a little bit. I have you on speaker," he confessed without sounding the least bit apologetic.

"Gavin!" she shouted, plopping down onto her bed with a soft whoosh as the down repositioned itself in her comforter. "That's awful. You need to be one-hundred percent present for that. Your poor patient is probably terrified."

A muffled moan came from the other end of the call, and she couldn't tell whether it was the patient's way of expressing pain, terror, or laugher.

"Oh, *sure*," Gavin joked, drawing out that last word an unnatural length.

She could just picture him rolling his eyes, and it made her feel light and easy despite all the awful things that had happened in her life the past few months. They said that time healed all wounds, but sometimes it felt like going back in time was the only way to move forward. Perhaps that was why she was so sentimental, as Gavin had deftly pointed out.

"It's not like I've done a million of these before, but okay. Have it your way," he said with a dramatic and clearly faked sigh. "By the way, I'll be there with you and the dogs on Sunday, too. Okay, bye!"

He hung up before she could protest, presumably returning his full attention to his latest root canal victim.

Okay, well, I guess that's that.

She'd be seeing Gavin again on Sunday. Perhaps his presence would make the visit a little easier on her. Now she just needed to find a way to fill her time between now and then. It was only Tuesday, after all, and Sunday seemed a mighty long way off.

She leaned back against her headboard and let out a long, beleaguered sigh.

Mama Mary popped up from her bed and trotted over. Her petite paws hugged the edge of the mattress as she whined and begged for Abigail to pick her up.

"You can save fifty-seven dogs from a puppy mill, but you can't even jump onto the bed," Abigail said with a chuckle as she lifted the Chihuahua into her arms. Mary's triumphs and challenges spoke to Abigail in a way little else had. Even though the small things were hard, that didn't stop her from achieving big—some might say impossible—feats. Could that be a lesson for Abigail's own life? And for Gavin's, too?

"You know what?" Abigail told her canine friend. "I think I'll draw you. Stay there," she said, petting the little dog who was still trying to get comfortable on the bed. "I'll be right back."

The very moment Abigail got up, however, Mama Mary thumped down onto the floor after her and waddled down the hall right at her heels.

Most of Abigail's work had been digital over the past decade, but right now, returning to the basics appealed to her more than she could say. Her drawing charcoals had been tucked away in her old bedroom years ago, which meant she'd need to visit the abandoned shrine to her youth in order to claim them.

Everything sat just as she remembered it—white wood furniture, pink walls, and princess murals. Her mother had designed this room for her, which is why she'd never wanted to change it even as she grew up and her tastes changed. It was the beginning of the sentimentality that Gavin so admired in her. But really, she was afraid to let go of anything, not knowing if there would be a way to ever get it back.

This room would need to be converted into little Owen's nursery, she realized. It was the only spare room they had in the whole house. And it had sat unoccupied long enough.

Maybe her old bedroom set could make some other little girl happy, could turn her bedroom into a fairy wonderland as it had done for Abigail. It wasn't right to keep things to herself if they could help others. She'd always known that. Her father had instilled a sharp sense of morality in her, even if he was partially to blame for her inability to move on past the... well, *past*.

After all, he'd never dated, never remarried, and to her knowledge had never tried to find her mother after she'd left them both behind. Did she know she was about to become a grandmother? Was she even still alive?

Abigail hadn't the slightest clue, but she needed to stop focusing on the things she couldn't change, the things she couldn't have. Right now, she would grab tight to that tiny flicker of creativity Mama Mary had inspired and see if she could coax it into something bigger.

First she'd draw the best picture of her dog she could manage, and then she'd see about conquering other mountains.

Chapter 23

ABIGAIL

Sunday morning arrived even faster than Abigail had dared to hope. True to his word, Gavin stood waiting outside the front doors wearing a light gray suit and an expectant smile. It reminded her of that ninth grade dance all over again. Only this time she was wearing a pair of stretchy pants and a stretchy tunic style shirt. Her thick hair was pulled into a messy bun and hiding a huge tangle she'd been unable to comb out that morning.

Yes, unfortunately, pregnancy had made her always thick hair nightmarish and almost impossible to care for these days. At least her skin had remained smooth and blemish free, with only a few extra hairs poking through on her chin as a result of all those blasted hormones.

"You look beautiful," Gavin said, holding the door open for her and Mama Mary who walked at her side on a leash.

Abigail couldn't help but laugh at that one. "Thanks," she said with a goofy grin that mirrored the one Gavin so often bestowed upon her.

"What?" he asked, following in after her. "What did I do wrong?"

"Nothing," she assured him. "It's good to see you. I just feel a mite underdressed."

Gavin waved her off. "Nah, you're the pastor's daughter. You set the standard for fashion around here, if I remember correctly."

She laughed again, already thankful that he'd insisted on accompanying them to service today. "I'm not sure you do, but I'll take it."

"Hey, where are the puppies?" Gavin asked, searching around as if their carrier would materialize out of thin air.

"Back in my father's office. That way they can be with their mom between services, and nobody gets too hungry."

They stepped through the double doors into the sanctuary, and it felt as if all eyes had turned on them. Everyone was probably looking at Mama Mary, but Abigail couldn't help but feel scrutinized—judged—by the eager glances so many sent straight in their direction.

"Honey, up here!" her father called, jumping and waving his arms from near the pulpit.

Oh brother, she thought while hurrying over to her father as fast as her swollen feet would carry her.

"Morning, Gavin," her father said with a curt nod before wrapping Abigail in his arms and squeezing her tight.

"What are you doing?" Abigail hissed in her father's ear. "You literally just saw me five minutes ago in the car."

His smile didn't dampen one bit. He even winked at her to further punctuate his point. "I'm just happy to have you here. Back in church where you belong."

"Don't get used to it," she warned.

"What, me?" he asked, pretending to be taken aback. *"Never."*

The band chose that moment to start the music up, and her father motioned for them to sit right in the front row. If Mama Mary was startled by the loud instruments, she sure didn't show it. She sat proudly by Abigail's feet, thumping her little tail to the beat.

Abigail sang the words she knew so well as she glanced around the sanctuary she'd all but grown up inside. Last time she was here, white flowers had lined every surface and Owen's closed casket had been draped with a neat, unblemished United States flag. She'd hardly been able to stand as the officers had folded it up into a neat triangle and offered it to her, thanking her for her husband's service and for her own sacrifice.

Today the only flowers were leftover poinsettias from Christmas. Everything was bright, upbeat, and happy, but that didn't change the fact that people received their last rites here, that this church saw marriages that were doomed to fail, new lives that would end all too early... so much suffering.

Looking around on that cool Sunday morning, you would never guess that these four walls had seen so much pain, witnessed so many tragedies. It was just like Gavin and that goofy grin of his—pretty on the outside, but broken on the inside.

Was that all she could aspire to now? The veneer of happiness? Of fullness?

The band switched to a new song and—just like that—Abigail felt like she was going to be sick. She ran out of the sanctuary, Mary waddling along quickly at her heels. It wasn't morning sickness, but something else —the sudden violence of a horrible memory overtaking her system. In that moment it felt as if she were reliving the funeral all over again.

Why had she come today? She wasn't ready to be here yet. Maybe she never would be, and maybe that would be okay. Her father could teach little Owen about God and Jesus and just leave her out of it.

Mary stood on her hind legs and pawed Abigail's knees, a knowing look in her little charcoal eyes.

"I'll be okay," she told the dog. "It's just silly human stuff. You wouldn't understand."

She bent down to pet the sweet Chihuahua when an odd sensation stopped her mid-motion. She remained perfectly still, waiting to see if it would happen again.

That was when Gavin burst through the doors and rushed over to her side. "Are you okay?" he whisper-yelled. "You had me worried there."

She held up a hand and—

There it was again!

"Gavin," she cried, forgetting the need to remain silent. "Come quick!"

In an instant, he was at her side. Tears flowed freely as she reached for his hand and pressed it up against her abdomen.

And then it happened again.

And again.

"Oh my gosh, is that?" Gavin asked, his eyes shining as he stared at her belly in wonder.

"Little Owen says hello," she sobbed. "That was the first time I felt him kick."

"He must like it here," Gavin said with a cajoling smile. And even though he was teasing, Abigail knew he was absolutely, one-hundred percent right.

Chapter 24

ABIGAIL

When the music stopped playing, Abigail dragged both Gavin and Mama Mary back into the sanctuary. "I'm supposed to go on at the end of the announcements, and they come right after praise and worship. Let's go!"

Her father caught her eye from his place behind the pulpit and motioned for her to join him upfront. "Ladies and gentleman of the Eternal Grace congregation," he drawled. His Southern always came out in extra measure when he was before an audience. "I'd like to welcome my daughter, Abigail, to the pulpit along with a special guest she'll introduce to y'all shortly."

The crowd of church goers gasped and cooed as Mama Mary proudly pranced down the center aisle at Abigail's side. Gavin walked with them until he reached his seat in the front row and plopped right down into it.

That meant the rest of this was up to Abigail now.

Her father gave her a quick hug and kiss, then went to take a seat of his own to the side of the pulpit.

"Hi, everyone," she said into the little microphone that was hooked onto the wooden stand. The resulting feedback told her she'd leaned in too close.

The crowd that stretched out before her continued to smile expectantly. Most still had their eyes fixed on Mama Mary.

I can do this, Abigail told herself. *It's important.*

"Hi, everyone," she started again. "I'm Abigail Sutton-Elliott. Pastor Adam's my dad. Um, I know you guys haven't seen me in a while, and for that I'm sorry. I'm back today, though, with important news. Good news. And a plea for your help."

Murmurs rose from the sea of congregants before her.

She looked to her father who nodded encouragingly and motioned for her to continue. With a deep breath, she bent down to pick up her doggie companion and held her as high above the pulpit as she could manage.

"This is Mama Mary, and she's my hero," she told everyone. "If you have children in the Sunday school class—or if you're part of the Eternal Grace phone tree—you may already know part of her story. Here's the full thing." Abigail paused to take a deep, measured breath.

Gavin gave her the thumbs up, and she felt grateful again that he had come to support her today. Public speaking had never been a strength of hers—not like it was for her father. But maybe her passion for these pups would get her through it. After all, they were counting on her.

"Mama Mary escaped from a puppy mill during that huge snow storm on Christmas Eve," she continued, pausing to make eye contact with several members of the audience. "She was very pregnant at the time and actually came to our nativity scene to have her puppies that night."

She paused again while a gasp swept through the crowd.

"She had four little pups, who are all doing fine by the way, and my dad—Pastor Adam—found them before they could suffer too badly from the cold. They've been with us ever since, and earlier this week, we found out about the puppy mill Mama Mary escaped from. The police did a bust up and found a total of fifty-seven dogs being kept in just horrible conditions."

Her voice cracked, and she grew angry just thinking about what all those poor dogs had been through. How anyone could treat animals so cruelly... well, it proved that there was evil in this world just as much as there was good. She glanced to her father again, who was also wiping away a small, glistening tear.

"That's why I'm here to talk with you today. These dogs need our help. Some of you have already volunteered space in your homes. Mama Mary and I are here to ask that you reach deep into your hearts and give whatever amount you can to contribute to the veterinary care and to finding forever homes for each of these fifty-seven dogs."

The ushers rose and distributed the collection plates to the rows in front and back, and the band began to play soft music behind her.

Emboldened, Abigail stepped out from behind the pulpit so that everyone could see Mama Mary clearly. She raised her voice loud enough to reach the folks all the way in the back and then promised, "I also want you to know that Mama Mary and her puppies aren't going anywhere. Ever since my father found them, he knew God had sent them for our church. At first I didn't believe him, but then I got to know Mary and her puppies. And I remembered just what my father is capable of achieving when he puts his faith in the Almighty."

Laughter rose up from the congregation. They all knew her father every bit as well as she did. They loved him like she did, too.

"So I don't know everything yet," she continued with a smile of gratitude, "but I do know Mary and her four pups—Cookie, Brownie, Cupcake, and Muffin—will be around for years to come, to help our church in whatever way we need. Thank you."

Abigail gave another quick smile before she crept back to her seat beside Gavin who put his arm around her.

"Good job," he whispered.

And she believed him, too.

Chapter 25

PASTOR ADAM

L et me tell you just how proud I was of my baby girl that Sunday. I knew she had a hard time facing the Maker, and she'd always struggled with speaking in front of crowds, too—but that didn't stop her from coming through for those pups.

Everyone clapped as she took her seat. Me loudest of all.

Now it was my turn to speak out about something that was important to me. Despite all my hoping and praying, I knew I might not get another chance to deliver a sermon to my daughter, at least not anytime soon. So this one would have to count extra.

With a quick adjustment of my tie, I rose to take my spot behind the pulpit. Most of my sermons as of late had been about the Fruits of the Spirit, and my flock was no doubt expecting more of the same, but today I decided to depart from my carefully planned lecture series and speak to a topic I knew Abigail would be able to relate to beyond any shadow of a doubt—and that was our church dogs.

"Isn't my daughter beautiful, folks?" I asked, assuming my position at the front of the church, and was met with a ripple of approval through the sanctuary.

My darling daughter slid further down in her chair as if that would be enough to hide her. Well, she had to get used to people looking at her, admiring her, because much more of that would be coming soon.

"I'm so grateful to her that she introduced y'all to Mama Mary and told you her story, because Abigail is absolutely right. These pups are going to be with our church for a long time to come. Jesus said let the little children come to me, and that's just what this litter of pups did. They found Him in His church. *They found us.*" I paused here as I was apt to do whenever I needed a point to sink in deep.

"God has always been willing to use anyone and anything He can to get our attention, and this time He chose a litter of little dogs—of mini miracles—to deliver His message.

"Hmm, okay. So what might that message be?" I cocked my head to the side just like Mama Mary did whenever she was paying extra close attention to Abigail. "Well, let me ask you this: what message do you need to hear?"

Most people laughed. A few looked uncomfortable. Those were the ones I decided to focus on. Sometimes I prepared my sermons word for word to make sure I got them just right. Others, I played it by ear. Today was an *other* kind of day.

"We're all searching for something in this life—all praying, wishing, desperately hoping for that one thing that can change us and our lives for the better. What's *your* one thing? Take a moment to think about that, because we'll be coming back to it later."

I glanced toward Abigail who was nodding along without even realizing it. I knew her one thing because it was the same as mine—to put the grief aside, to stitch up our broken hearts, and learn to survive without our other halves. I wanted that for Abigail even more than I wanted it for myself. After all, I'd been living with my mess of a heart for years, and if I could spare my daughter that same fate, I'd consider myself a blessed man.

God could do it. He could do it for both of us.

"Got your one thing?" I asked the congregation.

They nodded, shouted yes, just generally expressed their readiness to hear what came next.

"Good," I said, letting that one word echo through the sanctuary a couple times before continuing on. "Now I bet it feels too big, too far, too heavy, but you know what? *If you have faith as small as a mustard seed, nothing—nothing!—will be impossible for you.* Wow... Do you know how small a mustard seed is?" I held my fingers in a circle so tiny hardly a speck of light filtered through. "Even smaller than that. Wow."

"Now look at this tiny dog," I said, walking over to Abigail and grabbing Mama Mary's leash so that I could trot her across the front of the sanctuary. "She's a Chihuahua. That's the smallest kind of dog in the whole wide world. She was pregnant—just about to give birth, as a matter of fact. She'd been kept in a cage her whole life. She'd been tormented, neglected, forgotten... but not by God."

I stooped down to pick that brave mama dog up and into my arms. "God gave her a strength she couldn't have had on her own. He guided her paws out of that prison and straight to His house where she and her pups would be safe. Now if God can make that time to save a little dog, what might He be willing to do for his own children? For you, brothers and sisters?"

A pause here gave everyone a bit more time to think before I asked with a humble smile, "How big—how impossible—does your one thing seem now?"

Various murmurs rose up over the congregation, but I wasn't done yet.

"I can do all things through Christ who strengthens me," I quoted from the scripture. "Not some things. All things! Not a few things..." I paused to allow my church to supply the answer.

"All things!" they cried in unison.

I smiled and nodded. "All things. Imagine that. *All things* in Christ."

When I glanced back over to my daughter, she was still nodding along, but now she was crying big, fat tears, and I didn't know whether they were joyful—or if I'd somehow pushed her even deeper into the depths of despair.

All things, I reminded myself. *Including helping my daughter to heal. Amen.*

Chapter 26
ABIGAIL

Abigail raced out of the sanctuary for the second time during that same service. With a quick hand gesture, she motioned for Gavin to stay behind as she tore a path to her father's office with Mama Mary following closely behind. As soon as she shut the door securely behind her, she placed the excited mother dog into the box with her puppies.

She didn't mean to run off, but she needed a few minutes on her own, and she needed a break from her father's hard-hitting words. He'd spoken right to the heart of her every fear. He'd said that God took time out to help Mama Mary and her litter, which was great... except that didn't change the fact He'd chosen to deny Owen that same protective care.

What made one life more important than the other?

Her father claimed she could do anything with a little bit of faith, and she'd memorized the verses he cited long ago as a Sunday school student—but today she considered them in a new light. Was she willfully remaining broken by slamming her heart's door to God?

She wished she knew. Oh, how she wished she knew.

Little Owen woke up and kicked her from the inside. What did he feel? What was he trying to communicate to her now? And why did it feel that everyone—even her unborn child and a handful of miraculous Chihuahuas—knew God better than she did?

"Owen," she whispered, not sure whether she was speaking to her husband or her child. Maybe she was saying something they both needed to hear. "I feel so lost. Like I'm standing just outside of where I need to be, but there's this big giant wall blocking me from going in. How do I tear down that wall when I don't have any strength left to fight?" she sobbed.

The door creaked open behind her and her father's voice floated in sure and strong. "Don't you remember the story of Jericho?"

She kept her back to him so he wouldn't see her patchy face. "Dad..."

"If you're already there, all you need to do is march. And maybe blow a trumpet if you have one." He crossed the room and took a seat on top of his desk, forcing her to look at him.

"This is serious," Abigail argued. What was he doing here with her? Shouldn't he still be preaching? Or had she really let so much time pass her by without noticing?

"I know, baby girl." He sighed and leaned forward with his hands on either knee. "I'm proud of you for coming today. Just know this: you don't have to figure it all out at once. To be honest, even I haven't got it all figured out yet."

This was not what Abigail needed to hear. It already felt impossible, carrying on, being happy again. For her father to tell her that the answers would come little by little—if at all—dimmed her hope even further.

"Then how can you tell others what to believe?" she needed to know. "How can you stand up there week after week telling others how to live a good life when you admit that you haven't figured it out yet?"

"It's not *me*. It's God speaking through me. And if you'll listen, He'll speak to you. If you let him, He'll speak through you. Just like He's doing with those dogs."

Abigail crossed her arms over her chest. He was always so predictable. Yes, he loved her, but his answers never wavered. He always, always brought it back to God.

"Why are you so sure these dogs were meant for us? They're just dogs," she said, feeling guilty even before the words had fully left her mouth.

"Faith like a mustard seed," he said with a nod and the start of a smile. "But here's a secret: if you don't have a whole mustard seed, that's okay, too. Take that half seed, that quarter seed, that one billionth of a seed, and water it. See what God can do then."

Did she have one billionth of a seed? Perhaps somewhere deep down in a part of her that she'd boarded up to protect from pain. But could it really be enough? Could something new grow from such a tiny fragment?

She shook her head and turned her face away so her father wouldn't see her frown. "You claim it's a miracle they found us, but what if it's just a coincidence? A freak accident even?"

"If it is, then it is," her father answered, surprising her for once as he placed a hand over his heart. "But I choose to believe in miracles. The world looks more beautiful that way. You don't have to be right to be happy. Think about that."

She cracked a small smile. This line of reasoning she could relate to. It didn't require her to sort through her feelings about God first. At last it gave her a place to start. "Are you saying ignorance is bliss?" she asked.

He cleared his throat and loosened his tie. It always ended up a mess by the end of his second service. He hated wearing that thing, but still he donned it some time or another every single Sunday.

"No, what I'm saying is I know you're struggling with God's decision to call Owen home," he offered gently. "You want to understand why, but maybe you *can't* understand. Maybe none of us can. So where does that leave you? Well, you can torture yourself trying to figure it out, or you can trust that God is good, that He loves you, and that He's got a plan."

"That somehow involves Chihuahuas?" Abigail asked with a smile. Although it sometimes annoyed her, his unwavering faith also provided a constant in a world that felt like a dizzying blur even at the best of times.

"Why, yes, I believe it does." He rose from the desk and straightened to full height, looking down the bridge of his nose at Abigail who was still folded in on herself. "And what do you believe?"

"I don't know," she admitted. And then after a pause, added, "And maybe this time, that's okay. Thank you, Dad. I love you."

"I love you, too, baby girl." His entire face lit up just as it always had whenever she told him she loved him. He'd tucked her in every night of her childhood, exchanged butterfly kisses and "I love you's" every single time, but still—still—hearing that affirmation from her meant the world to him. It meant the world to her, too. *Thank God for loving fathers.*

"And you know what else?" he asked.

"What?" Abigail asked, allowing him to pull her to his chest in a gentle hug.

"I don't think the Chihuahuas are the only miracle that found us this Christmas season." He smiled down at her, waiting to see if she'd been able to interpret his latest cryptic burst of gratitude.

She had not. "What do you mean?"

"I'll leave you to figure that out on your own," he said as he departed toward the door. "I've got a second sermon to deliver."

Chapter 27

ABIGAIL

Abigail stayed with Mama Mary and her pups until it was time to deliver her plea to the second service crowd. She was surprised to find that Gavin had waited for her despite her sudden departure.

"You okay?" he whispered as she took a seat beside him at the end of praise and worship.

She smiled and nodded. Shortly after, her father called her to the stage and she spoke with every bit as much passion as she had the first time, maybe even a little bit more... and then she was ready to go home. She'd faced more than enough for one day—especially after the emotionally draining talk with her father in his office.

"Need me to drive you home?" Gavin asked, leaning in to her when she returned to his side.

"Please," she whispered, grabbing his hand and leading both him and Mary back to the office to retrieve the puppies.

"You were gone for a while," he said, concern knitting his brow. "I would have come to find you if I knew where to look."

"No, it's okay." Abigail brushed a strand of loose hair behind her ear and picked up the box of squirmy Chihuahua babies. "I needed a little bit of time after..." She let her words trail off and made a rolling hand gesture instead.

"Yeah, that was something, all right." Gavin sucked in a deep breath, filling his chest and lifting his shoulders, then let it out again slowly. "It's been so long since my family changed churches, I guess I'd forgotten how great your father is at what he does."

That, she couldn't deny. People loved her father for a reason. She loved him for many reasons of her own, too. One of them was that he was always willing to say what needed to be said, even and especially when it was hard.

"Yeah," she said with a smile. "And that particular bout of preaching was meant for me, so it was a lot to take in."

"You're really lucky, you know," he said, taking the box from her but remaining close as he spoke softly. His sandy hair fell over his brows as he leaned in. "You're surrounded by love on all sides. Even the inside."

Gavin's goofy grin darted across his face before he turned serious again. "You're a special woman, Abigail, and sometimes it seems you're the only one who doesn't know that."

She forced a laugh, but Gavin held her eyes with his, refusing to treat his words as a joke. "How can you say that when we haven't known each other that long?" she asked.

Gavin cocked his head to the side, but kept his focus intently on her. "Haven't we?"

Abigail's cheeks grew warm. All of her grew warm. "I meant as adults."

"The core of who we are doesn't change, Abigail Elliott-Sutton, and you've always been beautiful in absolutely every sense of the word." He drew closer still, bending briefly to set the box aside before taking her in his arms.

"Gavin," she murmured into his shoulder. "I can't."

"I'm not asking for anything," he said. "I just want you to know that I'm here. I'm close. I'm ready to go to bat for you in whatever way you need. Right now, I know that's just as a friend, but maybe someday there will be a way for us to mean more to each other. I know you'll need a long time to heal, to find yourself again, but I'm not going anywhere. Do you understand?"

She nodded, unable to say anything in that moment. "I do," she choked out at last. This she understood. It was faith that had become a mystery to her, but love made perfect sense. Had Gavin really carried a torch for her all these years, or did the broken part of him fit together with the broken part of her?

She wanted to believe she could love him one day, but right now she honestly didn't know how her heart could ever make space for any man other than Owen.

Gavin's chest beat beneath her cheek and for a moment she let herself believe it was Owen's. The two men's hearts beat out the same tempo until Owen's had suddenly stopped.

What if she allowed herself to fall for Gavin, only to lose him, too?

Loving Gavin was terrifying, but so was not loving him. She felt as if she'd gotten stuck in an impossible place. Maybe she had.

Gavin pulled away, placing a hand on each of her shoulders and holding her at arm's length. "I'm not trying to scare you, and I'm not trying to saddle you with anything more than you can handle. I need time to heal, too, but ever since you came back into my life, I finally feel like I have a reason to try, to open myself back up again. I just want you to know that. Even if you don't feel the same way now, even if you never feel the same way, I just need you to know what's in my heart."

"Thank you, Gavin," she said, unable to add anything more. What was right in this situation? She'd loved Gavin before, but that was years ago— practically a whole lifetime. He said the core of who you are doesn't change, but what if he was wrong?

The only thing she knew for sure is that she needed some time by herself to figure things out.

God. Gavin. Everything.

Chapter 28

ABIGAIL

Abigail spent the rest of that day on her own. Neither her father nor Gavin pushed her for anything more. Instead, both thankfully left her to rest and recover from the tough conversations that had taken place in her father's tiny church office.

So, to pass the time, she finished reading the romantic adventure book she'd downloaded for free and immediately bought the next in the series. She also drew another picture of Mama Mary and just generally gave herself permission to relax for a change.

One afternoon stretched into two, which quickly became three. The monotony was at last broken when the puppies finally opened their beautiful eyes and looked into Abigail's for the very first time. She'd admit she cried, but then again, she always cried these days.

Now that the pups had open ears and eyes, they became feistier than ever. Mama Mary was no longer able to wander away and hide to take a nap on her own. Tending to the puppies became a full-time job now that they were moving toward independence and able to uncover heaps of trouble if not watched constantly.

To celebrate, Abigail decided to take the pups to a park for their first big outdoor adventure since that fateful Christmas Eve rescue. It didn't take her long, though, to realize her mistake. There was no way she could handle all four puppies and their mom at once.

She needed help.

But when she called her father to ask for him to meet her at the park—so that the trip wouldn't be a total bust—he said he'd been called in for a last-minute meeting at the church and suggested she call Gavin instead.

Abigail thought about that one for a few minutes before deciding to act. She'd been putting off Gavin's texts since his confession of love for her, and while she missed him, she just didn't know how to act casual in his company either. After a bit of hurried deliberation, she decided to head home on her own rather than requesting that Gavin join her at the park.

When she arrived back at her father's house, however, Gavin's over-sized truck stood waiting in the driveway. Unfortunately, Southern manners dictated she welcome him warmly rather than driving around the block a few times until he gave up and went away.

She cursed under her breath, put on her best smile, and ambled over to meet him with all five Chihuahuas nipping at her heels.

"Hi Gavin," she called, offering a small wave. "What a nice surprise."

He raised an eyebrow. "Is it?" he asked. "Because someone's been avoiding my texts all week."

"Well... I've been busy with the puppies, is all."

"Uh huh." He looked as if he wanted to hug her but thankfully held himself back.

Despite the awkwardness of this unplanned meeting, she had missed talking with him these past few days—missed seeing him, too. But how could she admit that without leading him on? Everything would be that much harder now that she knew he had feelings for her. She couldn't just get over her husband's death in a matter of months. It wouldn't be fair to Owen, but expecting Gavin to ignore his emotions and then relegating him to the role of a simple friendship wouldn't be fair to him.

So what was fair to Abigail, and—?

"I know what you're thinking," Gavin said with that goofy grin she found so much comfort in.

"Sorry," she muttered, all the while wondering: *Does he actually know? Am I that obvious?*

"You're not the one who needs to apologize," he said with a frown. "I put a lot of pressure on you the other day when that was the last thing I wanted to do."

"Gavin, stop, you don't have to—"

"Yes," he said pointedly. *"I do.* I owe you an apology, and I've also brought a peace offering. A deal, too, if you're willing to make it."

Okay, he definitely had her attention now. She waited to see what he would say or do next.

"Do you want the gift or the deal first?" he asked as a mischievous smile stretched from one cheek to the other.

"Umm..." She thought about it but had no idea what either could be, which made it impossible to choose. She'd always been bad about making choices, no matter how frivolous. And somehow she doubted this one was.

"Too slow!" Gavin cried, slapping the back of his truck. "You're getting the gift. Think you can grab the door for me?"

She ran back to the porch and opened first the screen door and then the heavy wooden front door. The small herd of Chihuahuas trotted merrily into the house. When she glanced back to the driveway again, she found Gavin struggling with a long piece of honey-colored wood.

"Gavin Holbrook," she scolded, placing her free hand on her hip "What did you do?"

"I told you that already. I got you a gift," he said after triumphantly extracting the furniture piece from his truck bed.

"That doesn't look like a small token of apology."

"Well, *small* is what you make of it. Right, Mama Mary?" he said to the dog who had come back outside to supervise the undertaking and now stood beside Gavin as if she, too, was in on the surprise.

"Does that work both ways?" Abigail asked, hardly able to suppress a laugh. "Because I don't think it does."

Gavin winked at her as he carried the first piece past her and through the open doors. "A friend of mine makes custom furniture, and he's been having a rough go of things lately," he explained with his back to her. "I figured this could be a great gift for you as well as a way to help him. Besides, you need one."

"What?" she asked as he brushed past her to return to his truck for a second trip.

"It's a crib," he said before, stretching over to grab more pieces. "Tommy offered to deliver it in one piece, but I don't know. I kind of wanted us to build it together. I hope that's okay." He popped back up and gave her a cautious smile.

"That's more than okay, Gavin. Thank you so much. This is a wonderful gift." Her heart warmed as she pictured the two of them fitting together the pieces to build something wonderful for little Owen.

He let out a big sigh of relief, then jumped right back into teasing her. "If you like this, just wait until you find out about the deal."

Chapter 29

ABIGAIL

Abigail watched from her perch by the door as Gavin brought in the last of the crib pieces. She liked having him here, liked being taken care of again—but was that enough to risk her heart a second time and so soon after her first love ended in utter heartbreak?

"Well, where should we build it?" Gavin asked, wiping a bead of sweat from his forehead as he surveyed the already filled living room with a befuddled expression.

She latched the door shut and stepped back into the house. Puppies ran around like crazy. Clearly the short period without supervision had already yielded significant damage. Little Muffin even tried to fit his mouth around a piece of the crib before Gavin shooed him off.

"I want to give the baby my pink room, but it's still filled with all my old things," she answered. "And I haven't had the chance to paint it yet, either. I doubt my little boy will appreciate all the pink princess decor that's in there."

"Well, c'mon then, we've got a lot of work to do." Gavin charged toward her old room, still remembering where it was after all these years—or maybe just getting lucky with his choice of doors.

"Gavin, wait!" Abigail hobbled after him. "We can't just set up the nursery right now."

He blinked twice. "Why not?"

She stared back at him blankly, completely unable to come up with an appropriate excuse.

Gavin smiled and tilted his head back. "Yup, that's what I thought," he said with a laugh. "Do you know what you want to do with all the old furniture?"

"I was thinking of donating it," she mumbled, standing in the doorway as he appraised each piece of furniture.

"Perfect. I have my truck, and it should all fit, so let's take it straight out." He pulled the mattress off the bed and set it against the wall. "Actually, wait. You shouldn't be lifting anything in your condition. Or smelling paint fumes, for that matter," he pointed out. "I guess I'll handle things in here. You rest."

"All I ever do is rest," Abigail admitted. "I want to help."

He glanced over his shoulder with a sinful smile. "Well, I wouldn't say no to a tall glass of iced tea, if you happen to have any just lying around."

She gasped and lifted a hand to her chest, playing her part of this charade perfectly. "Shut your mouth. You know Dad and I have always made it fresh."

"Then hop to, darling, while I take care of business in here." He winked and made a clicking noise before turning his attention back to the furniture.

Of course, maybe Abigail should have protested at least a little, but then again, she liked this playful, teasing side of Gavin. It made things easier between them, which is what they both sorely needed right now.

After fixing a glass of tea for Gavin and some lemonade for herself, she took off her shoes and padded back into her old bedroom. Gavin had already managed to clear the dresser and nightstand out, leaving the room emptier than she'd ever seen it in her entire life. It was truly amazing how quickly the remnants of a life could be removed, replaced.

Gavin drained half of his beverage in a single gulp, then made a contented smacking noise. "That hit the spot. Thank you."

She blushed despite herself. "You're welcome."

"So, do you already have the paint picked out, or do we still need to get some?" he asked before taking another long chug of sweet tea.

Abigail held her glass with both hands. The coolness felt nice even though the outdoors were still more than chilly enough. "I was thinking blue," she said, trying to picture the room after its forthcoming makeover. "It may be cliché, but it's also tried and true when it comes to baby boys. I haven't picked any up from the store yet, though."

"No worries," he told her without hesitation. "I can swing by after this."

"Why are you doing all this for me?" She took a measured sip to hide —and cool—the heat rising to her cheeks.

"I already said because you shouldn't be handling it in your condition, and because I care about you. It's what friends do. They show up and put up." He flashed her a debonair smile, but it didn't distract Abigail from the fact that her platonic male friend was the one who needed to help prepare for little Owen's arrival, and that was because her husband was sadly no longer in the picture.

At least Gavin had better endurance and a stronger back than her father. She'd give him that.

"If you're sure," she said before hiding her face behind her glass again.

"I'm sure." His hair fell onto his forehead from the force of his nod, and she realized she liked it that way—a little messy from an honest afternoon's work.

Abigail watched Gavin disassemble the bed frame with a screwdriver he just happened to have in his pocket. *Men.*

"So what's the deal?" she asked, suddenly remembering that he had come baring multiple gifts and promises.

"Not yet. We have to finish in here first."

"Finish as in build the crib, or finish as in polish off the entire nursery?"

"The second one," Gavin said with a grunt as he dislodged a metal beam from the side of the bed. "That'll give you something to look forward to."

Abigail could have argued, but she rather liked the idea of knowing something pleasant was coming in her near future. Despite all the years that had passed since their initial friendship, she trusted him to take care of her, not disappoint her.

And even though he had shown up at her house to take care of all manner of husbandly tasks, that awkward tension hadn't lasted long. It was easy to fall in step beside him, regardless of what his feelings might or might not mean for them in the future.

"Hey, Gavin," she said after a spell. "Remember that time some butthead kid drove straight into the school?"

He popped his head up and groaned. "Please don't tell me that's the only memory you have of us together."

Abigail raised a finger to her chin and pretended to think about that rather than provide the answer she knew he wanted to hear too quickly. "I remember lots of things about us," she said at last to put him out of his misery.

"Oh, yeah? Then prove it." He set his screwdriver down, shifted himself away from the bed, and placed his chin on his hands in a dramatic display of anticipation. "Tell me five memories. Your five favorite."

"No pressure, right?" She laughed. What a production this was getting to be.

"There's never any pressure," he assured her, "but I do like revisiting the bygone days."

She thought about sitting down beside them, but these days getting up easily wasn't always a guarantee, and she'd rather not struggle like that in front of Gavin. "Well, one of my absolute favorites is when we had lunch together at Poogan's Porch and you opened up to me." She leaned back against the wall and turned her face to him.

"That one just happened. Can it really qualify as a memory?"

"Well, *I* remember it fondly," she countered with a giggle.

"Okay. What else?" He ran a hand through his sandy hair, messing it up even more than before.

"Definitely the time you drove into the school." When she saw that Gavin was about to protest, Abigail hurried along with a second, less embarrassing memory. "Then there was the time you surprised me at my locker and asked me to the homecoming dance. The dance itself was amazing."

"Yeah, those are all—for the most part—good, but you have one more."

"Right now," she admitted. "Right here in this exact moment. I already know it's going to be one of my favorites."

Chapter 30

PASTOR ADAM

O kay, so here's the truth. I did not have a meeting that afternoon. But because I couldn't bear to lie to my daughter, I set one up on the fly. Luckily, this sweet young couple I'd been counseling was all too happy to stop by my office for a chat about their upcoming nuptials.

I figured the Lord would forgive me this teeny fib since I'd done my best to make right on it. Also, I assure you, I'd misled my daughter with only the purest of intentions.

Even if Abigail didn't see how much she opened herself back up to the world from the very moment Gavin Holbrook stepped back into our lives, it certainly didn't escape my notice. One moment she would barely talk to me, and the next she was smiling again. Laughing even.

Oh, the church dogs definitely played their part, but something about that young man reached my baby girl's heart in a way that I just couldn't. I'd seen it back when they were kids, too. That's why I'd threatened to shoot him. It's a father's duty to protect his girl from getting her heart broken—especially when it looks like her heart is already halfway out the door to its new home.

Even now, even still, the life came back into her whenever Dr.

Holbrook came around. So was it really all that wrong for me to try to help nudge them together?

Mind you, I prayed about it for a long time before my loving meddling began, and, yes, my plan is one-hundred percent God approved.

Now it was up to Abigail.

Of course, I was beside myself with joy when I returned home to find his truck parked outside, even though that meant I had to park at the curb myself. Inside, I found a storm of fluff roaring through the living room as the wide-eyed puppies chased each other's tails and competed for top spot in their little family pack. If you ask me, I think Brownie was ahead of the others by at least a few hard-earned points.

"Dad," Abigail said, appearing in the hall. "How was your meeting?"

"Good, good." I bobbed my head heartily in case she needed extra convincing. Then as casual as I could muster, I asked, "Was that Gavin's truck I saw out front?"

Her cheeks turned pink at the mention of that boy's name, and it didn't stop there. I swear to you, her forehead also blushed!

"Oh, yeah. He just stopped by to help with the nursery," she explained.

"That's nice of him," I said.

"Yeah." She smiled, and her pink skin darkened into a rich mulberry.

"Is he around? I'd like to say hello."

Abigail stepped aside and pointed back toward her old bedroom, then we both walked in to find Gavin wearing only jeans and a few odd splatters of paint as he dragged the roller back and forth across the walls, transforming the long-since faded pink into a vivid blue.

I cleared my throat.

"Hello, Pastor Elliott," the young man said before using the back of his arm to wipe the sweat from his brow. He'd clearly been working hard, but...

"Don't you think you might want to keep your shirt on in mixed company?" I pressed. His button up lay discarded in the corner of the room, and I rushed to retrieve it for him.

Abigail kept her eyes on me—too embarrassed, I suppose, to make eyes at the fella in my presence. "I haven't been in here, Dad. Gavin said the fumes are bad for me and the baby, so I've been shut in my room reading while he works in here."

Good man, I thought. *Thank you for respecting and protecting my daughter and grandson.*

"Yeah, and you shouldn't really be here now." Gavin set his roller back in the tray and shrugged into the shirt I'd just handed him. "Why don't we all go to the living room where there aren't any harmful chemicals floating in the air?"

"Hey, baby girl," I coaxed. "You should really listen to him. He is a doctor, after all."

"I'm going!" Abigail shouted, raising both arms above her head in surrender as she turned back to the hall.

When she'd gone, I closed the door up tight. "Got a second brush?" I asked and waited for Gavin to provide it.

We painted together in silence for a few moments until I finally decided to come right out with it. "What are your intentions with my daughter?" I demanded.

He startled, and a few drops of blue fell onto the tarp below. "I believe you asked me that before, sir, and my answer hasn't changed."

"Which is?" I pressed, not because I didn't remember but because I wanted to see if he had.

"To make her happy," he said matter-of-factly.

"Any funny business this time?"

"Not unless she'll first accept my grandmama's ring," he answered, surprising us both with the intensity of his confession.

"Good answer. Good man." I tossed my paintbrush aside and wrapped him in a hug.

There it was, my proof that our plans were aligned. God was on our side, too. Now all we needed was a measure of time and a bit of bravery from our dear Abigail.

Chapter 31

ABIGAIL

When Abigail arrived at the Eternal Grace Church for her father's service the following Sunday, she was surprised to find Gavin waiting for her just as he had the week before.

"How'd you know I would be here?" she pressed, giving him a hug hello even though the two of them had worked together on the nursery the previous evening.

Gavin shrugged before bursting into his signature goofball grin. "Lucky guess, but I figured you'd come since your little one enjoys it so much," he pointed out, bringing back that perfect memory of her baby's first kick.

"That he does," she answered, giving him a playful jab as they walked side by side into the sanctuary. "And now that he's started kicking me, he just won't stop. It's like he constantly wants to remind me that he's in there and that he'd like a bit more space, please and thank you."

"Smart guy. If I were him, I'd be doing whatever it takes to get your attention, too." He waited for Abigail to select their seats before plopping down beside her.

"Speaking of which," he continued as if there'd been no pause in the conversation at all. "I have a proposition for you both. Would the two of you like to accompany me on a picnic lunch after the service?"

"I don't know," Abigail teased, reaching both hands down to rest on her growing belly. "What do you think, little guy?"

"He says yes," Gavin quickly supplied.

She laughed, eliciting questioning glances from the family in the row behind them. "Do you two have a telepathic connection that I don't know about?"

"Nothing like that." He leaned in close and whispered to her, making their conversation private once again. "But I do know he likes it when you're happy, and trust me, this will make you both very happy."

"Do I finally get to hear your deal? Because the fact that you haven't told me yet is making me nuts!"

"Maybe," he said with a disarming smile that contradicted his noncommittal response.

Before Abigail could ask any more questions, the band started up. This marked the beginning of praise and worship and the end of their conversation...

For now.

&

After the service, Gavin begged and pleaded until Abigail at last agreed to let him drive to their secret picnic destination. Thankfully, he did not crash his truck into their old high school—or anything else, for that matter.

But he did drive a little faster than Abigail was normally comfortable with. "What's the hurry?" she wanted to know.

"Just excited to take you to one of my favorite places," he admitted, rolling down both windows and letting a cool breeze sweep through the truck's cab.

The crisp winter air blew Abigail's hair across her face, and it landed in her mouth whenever she tried to talk, but she didn't care.

"Are we going to the Angel Oak?" she asked, recognizing the path they were taking despite not having been out this way for longer than she cared to admit.

Gavin gasped, but still seemed please. "How'd you know?"

"Lucky guess," she teased, mimicking their conversation from earlier that morning. "I'm glad I'm right, though. I haven't been to the park over there since high school."

"That's way too long. I go at least once a season. Sometimes more."

"I've never seen it without its leaves," she admitted. "Do people still go year round?"

"I do. It's different each time," he said, pulling to a stop at the traffic light and turning to Abigail with utter joy written across his face. "Oh, but I wish you could've seen it on Christmas Eve when it was covered with snow. That's gotta be a once in a lifetime spectacle. But you know what? Sometimes lightning strikes twice, and that doesn't make the second time any less special."

Abigail stayed silent. It didn't seem like he was just talking about the tree, and she wasn't comfortable discussing a relationship yet.

"So, are you on team five hundred or fifteen hundred?"

She blinked over at him, completely lost. "What?"

"The Angel Oak," Gavin explained patiently. "How old do you think it is?"

Abigail thought back to what she'd learned about the tree. Not only was it the oldest living thing in Charleston, but some said it was the oldest thing in the United States period. She'd never thought much about it, always just considering the tree "really, really old." Both five hundred and fifteen hundred seemed impossibly large, and neither figure changed the majesty of that sprawling tree that sat alone, an island calling people from all over the world to come visit it.

"Five hundred, I guess," she said after considering it for a moment. "I'm practical like that. How about you?"

He laughed as he pressed down on the accelerator and jolted the truck back to life. "Definitely fifteen hundred."

"Why?"

He turned to her momentarily as he unleashed that favorite grin of hers. "Because I like believing in magic." His eyes were back on the busy Sunday traffic once more.

"Substitute miracles for magic, and you sound just like my father," she teased. Still, she wished she could believe like she used to. Would the old Abigail have chosen the magical response to Gavin's question instead of the practical one?

"He's not the worst person to sound like, I suppose." He pulled into the parking lot that serviced the Angel Oak park and began to search for a spot closest to the entrance. When at last he found one and cut the ignition, he turned toward Abigail and said, "He loves you like crazy, you know."

She nodded. "I know."

And so do you, she thought. Because the fact that Gavin wanted her was definitely insane. Couldn't he see that she wasn't going to be ready for a long time—if ever? Why not move on to somebody else?

Chapter 32

ABIGAIL

The Angel Oak was a true Lowcountry treasure. People came from all over the world to see it, but as is often the case when a treasure lies buried in your own backyard, Abigail hadn't paid it a second thought until Gavin brought her today.

The massive tree stretched clear up to the sky and in every direction besides. Some said it looked creepy with all those heavy, tangled branches reaching every which way, but Abigail liked to stick with the angel metaphor. Though if memory served, the name "Angel" came from the original owners of this land and not the heavenly host of beings.

"It's like this one tree is trying to hug the whole world," she murmured in awe as they walked a slow circle around its trunk. "Or at least all of Charleston."

Gavin nodded and put an arm around her shoulder. "I feel connected here. To the past, present, and people who are too far out of my reach."

"Like to Susie and Millie?" Abigail asked, remembering the sorrow that had reflected in his eyes when she told him his story of love—of a family—lost.

"Yes," he said, his face remaining neutral for once as they continued their walk. "The last several times I've come out, it's been for them."

He stopped and turned toward Abigail, then grabbed both of her hands and swung them loosely between their bodies. "This time I'm here for you, though. Actually, both of us. We're here for us."

"What do you mean?" she asked. Fear filled her chest. Surely he meant to discuss their romantic feelings and possibilities again when she still wasn't anywhere near ready.

He looked up toward the top of the tree, which they couldn't see from where they were standing. It appeared as if the Angel Oak ascended forever into the heavens.

"For the sake of argument, let's say this tree is actually fifteen hundred years old," Gavin said before lowering his gaze to look at Abigail once more. "If you round our ages up to thirty, this tree has still lived fifty times longer than either of us. It makes us seem so short-lived by comparison. Doesn't it?"

"You sound like my father again," she teased in an effort to lighten the air of seriousness that now hung between them. "I'm sure he's used this argument in one of his sermons about Methuselah."

"I sound like me," he said without the slightest bit of humor. "This is all of me talking to all of you in front of all of this." He motioned widely at the tree.

"I'm sorry. I didn't mean to interrupt," Abigail whispered. "The tree does make me feel small. In size, too."

"Small, but not unimportant," he corrected. "More like there are things that are bigger than us out there. There are things that are bigger than us right here."

She nodded, unsure of where he was going with this.

"Now assuming we're still thirty, think about what one day of your life so far represents. You've lived over ten thousand days and still have many more to go. What I'm asking for is three hundred and fifty of them."

Nearly a year. What could he possibly want with that? She didn't follow. "I don't understand..."

"Abigail, I love you," he said bluntly but made no effort to kiss or embrace her. "I don't think I ever stopped."

She hung her head. Why had he trapped her here for this? She didn't want to hurt him, but she had nothing she could give, either.

Not yet.

Gavin continued, "But we both need time to heal, to rebuild our friendship. That's why I'd like to offer you a deal. We ran into each other again, after all those years, on the day after Christmas. I think—if you're willing—we should take any talk of a relationship off the table for one whole year. Until next year on that same day. Let's focus on being there for each other as friends, on helping each other heal. Then on the day after Christmas, we can meet here at the Angel Oak again and decide once and for all what we mean to each other. It's just one year—a little less—but I think it will go a long way to healing us both."

He hesitated before grabbing her wrist and directing her eyes toward his. "What do you think?"

A million questions shone in his eyes, but only one that mattered. *If you don't love me today, do you think you might tomorrow? Do you think you can love me within a year?*

The idea of delaying that conversation for a full year both terrified her —because that would mean that it was still coming—and relieved her. Now she just had to decide which reaction was stronger, and whether she'd be willing to give his plan a try.

Chapter 33

ABIGAIL

As silly as it seemed at first, taking the prospect of a relationship off the table for one full year was just what Abigail needed to get past her hang-ups about spending time with Gavin. Over the weeks that followed, their friendship grew.

And so did the puppies.

Now their ears stood straight up like true Chihuahuas, and those huge ears combined with those tiny bodies made them that much cuter. Abigail still favored Mama Mary most of all, but as it turned out, she had room in her heart—and during her days—for each and every one of those pups.

Most nights, Gavin joined Abigail and her father for dinner at the kitchen table. They shared about their days, laughed, talked, and sometimes even caught a movie at the local cineplex.

Each morning, Gavin would text Abigail a status update about her baby. Every day brought a new fact about little Owen's development and about pregnancy and childbirth practices around the world. At twenty five weeks, her son was apparently the size of a rutabaga—though he was starting to look like an actual infant and even growing hair. She marveled at the changes happening inside her body. An entire life was growing inside of her. It wouldn't be long until little Owen was his own person, and that revelation shocked and amazed her each and every day.

On Valentine's Day, Gavin showed up with tacos—Abigail's number one pregnancy craving as of late—and a gift for her father, of all people. "First, we eat, then we have to take a little trip," he told them with a smile so big it spread around the entire room. Abigail guessed her baby might also be smiling in her womb, such was the infectiousness of Gavin with a surprise.

"What are we doing here?" her father remarked when Gavin drove them straight to the Eternal Grace Church and parked next to the two other cars in the lot that evening. "Not that I'd ever complain about the chance to spend time in God's house, mind you."

"You'll see," Gavin said, leading them toward the sanctuary.

Neither of the three ever missed a Sunday service now, but spending Valentine's Day with her father and with God... Well, that was a new one, all right.

The church secretary met them outside the double doors dressed in a becoming crushed velvet dress that graced her knees elegantly. Her hair was twisted into a neat and tidy updo, and her jewelry sparkled dazzlingly from her neck and earlobes.

"Mrs. Clementine, shouldn't you be out celebrating the holiday with your husband?" Abigail exclaimed upon seeing her there.

The old woman smiled but continued to block their entry. "That's where I'm heading next, but first, I wanted to be here for the look on your pa's face when—"

"Don't you dare, Mrs. Clementine," Gavin hissed. "We haven't managed to keep it a surprise for this long, only to spoil it at the last second!"

She slapped a manicured hand on her forehead. "Of course, you're right. You're right. C'mon inside, y'all. You're going to want to see this with your own eyes."

Abigail noticed the new addition to their sanctuary even before her father did. She gasped as she took in two large projector screens on either side of the church. Glancing toward the ceiling she, sure enough, saw a pair of projectors shooting colored beams at both.

Behind them, Gavin flipped off the light switches and the image on the screen became clear as day.

For all you do for others. Happy Valentine's Day, Pastor Adam! it said in white letters on a red background. Beneath that there was a very recent picture of Mama Mary and her pups posed in front of their locally famous nativity scene which had been put into storage weeks ago.

"How did you manage to do all this without either of us catching on?" Abigail asked with a stern look to Gavin while her father marched straight up to each projector and reached a trembling hand out toward the light.

"I have my ways," was the only answer Gavin would give. "Happy Valentine's Day, Abigail."

Her father returned and grabbed Gavin in a huge hug. He pulled Abigail in, too. "This is amazing. Thank you for giving the church such a wonderful gift. It will be much easier for everyone to read the words to our hymns now."

Mrs. Clementine spoke up for the first time since they'd entered the sanctuary. "It's not just for little old ladies with bad eyesight like me," she pointed out. "We can make slides to go along with your sermons and put them on the new church website for people to reference later—or to read for the first time in cases where they're too sick to attend in person."

"Can our church website do that?" her father asked in shock. "As far as I knew all it had was a few pictures, service times, and our address."

"It may need an update," Mrs. Clementine confessed, still wearing a broad smile. "But it will be very much appreciated by the congregation."

"You know," Gavin said, "with all the slides that will need to be put together each week plus the need for a new website, Eternal Grace may want to look to bringing a graphic designer on staff part-time. Now, where can we find one of those?"

Abigail's jaw dropped open. Of course. It was the perfect opportunity for her to stay busy and keep her skills up to date without putting too much pressure on her schedule as a soon-to-be mom. Gavin had done this for her father and for the church, but really, he had done it for her.

"I think that sounds like a mighty fine idea," her father said, placing an arm over her shoulder. "Mighty fine, indeed."

And that's the exact story of how Abigail finally returned to work in the wake of her loss. It was a good story, and one she knew she would revisit often. It was amazing what good friends, good family, and a good God could accomplish.

Chapter 34

ABIGAIL

The new job at church helped Abigail to fill her days more efficiently. It also energized her like she hadn't been in months. Rather than sleeping her days away, she spent her free time reading up on some of the best nationally recognized therapy dog programs and all the other great working roles dogs could fill in society.

It was one thing for her father to claim their church dogs were miraculous, and quite another to intentionally set them up to help change people's lives. True, most working dogs belonged to much larger breeds, but while it wasn't common for Chihuahuas to have jobs, it absolutely could be done.

There were so many different types of therapy dogs, it made her head spin. Ultimately, Abigail decided it would be best to teach their church dogs how to help people going through difficult life transitions and battling with depression. After all, Mama Mary had helped her with just that thing. And while she wasn't fully recovered, she was making progress every day. Sometimes just having a nonjudgmental ear and a friendly lick could work wonders.

When Abigail shared her intention to get Mary and her pups certified as therapy dogs, her father ate the idea right up. "Ahh, perfect. That's just what our church needs. I told you God had a plan."

She laughed, all the while appreciating what her father's faith coupled with her research could accomplish.

&

By the time she reached twenty-eight weeks pregnant, the puppies had all turned eight weeks old, which meant they were ready to be enrolled in obedience school. During the first class, three of four puppies piddled on the floor of the gymnasium, and the fourth attacked and shredded a pamphlet about the importance of training dogs young. Still, Abigail was not discouraged.

"Well, we can only go up from here," she confided in the pups while loading them back into the car to head home. "Maybe one of you will earn the title of 'most improved pup.' At least we can hope."

A sleek black SUV she didn't recognize was waiting for her in the driveway when she and the puppies returned. Abigail peeked inside, but the car sat empty. Hesitantly, she pushed the front door open and was greeted by her mother-in-law, who she hadn't seen since the day of Owen's funeral.

"Hello," Abigail said with a shaky voice, picking up Mama Mary who had run to greet her at the door and hugging the dog close. "It's nice to see you... Mom."

She'd always felt strange calling Owen's mother "Mom," but it had made him happy, which is why she did it anyway.

The older woman was tall and thin, with bright red hair and age spots where freckles had once been. Abigail had always liked her well enough, but it was hard for the two of them to spend time together after Owen had died.

They shared too many sad memories.

Mrs. Sutton approached her with tears in her eyes. "May I?" she asked, motioning toward Abigail's protruding belly.

Abigail nodded, and her mother-in-law placed a hand on each side of her belly. "Oh!" she cried. "He kicked me."

"He does that a lot," Abigail said. "I'm going to name him Owen, by the way."

Tears fell in earnest now, and Mrs. Sutton's face turned the same shade of burgundy as her hair. "That's a wonderful name. He would be so proud."

"I like to think he *is* proud," Abigail said gently. "That he's in Heaven experiencing every moment with us." Her faith had grown tremendously since her visit with Gavin to the Angel Oak. The faith she'd once resisted had brought her the beginnings of peace that she'd so desperately craved since her husband's passing.

"That's a nice thought, dear." Owen's mother smiled sadly.

"I didn't mean to cut you out of things," Abigail explained. "It's been hard, and I—"

"No need to apologize. I wasn't ready to see you yet, either," the mother confessed as she tightened a hand around the strap of her purse. "The only thing harder than losing your spouse, they say, is losing a child."

Abigail's heart ached for them both. "When the baby's born, I want you to be a part of his life. Same as you would be if Owen were still here. Family is too important to keep little Owen away from any of the people who love him."

"Thank you," Mrs. Sutton said. "I want to be there for him, and for you. It's just..." Her words trailed away as if they were still too painful to speak.

"*Hard,* I know," Abigail finished for her. "Believe me, I know."

"Actually, I don't think they've made a word strong enough for it yet." Mom let out a sad chuckle. "I finally got the courage to sort through all of Owen's old things. There were boxes upon boxes in the attic, in his old bedroom. There was so much, yet it didn't feel like enough to represent a whole life. Not even close."

Abigail nodded and listened, waiting for Mrs. Sutton to say more.

"I couldn't part with anything. Not yet," Owen's mother continued.

"It felt wrong to simply give it all away to people who didn't know him and wouldn't value any of the things that had once been so important

"And so..." She sniffed and wiped away tears before continuing. "I'm starting small by bringing some of these memories to you, so you can share them with Owen's son. I know you will both treasure them like I would, and that makes it a little bit easier. I packed a box for you. It's in my trunk."

"Thank you, Mom. I'd love to have it." Abigail wasn't sure what to do next. Should she hug Mrs. Sutton? Offer to retrieve the box from her car? Instead, she asked the easiest of the many questions on her mind. "Where's my dad?"

Mrs. Sutton gave her a sad smile. "He let me in, then went for a drive. Said we'd need time alone together before he was there to get in the way."

Yes, that sounded just like her dad, although it may have been easier if he was here to mediate for them.

The two women stood in awkward silence for a moment.

"Oh, let me go get the box for you," Owen's mother said after reaching in her purse for a crumpled tissue.

Abigail waited inside, both terrified and eager for what she might find.

If only she knew...

Chapter 35

PASTOR ADAM

Things in our little corner of the world had been going peachy keen for more than a month now. Thanks to Gavin's generous donation to the church, our little congregation welcomed in many new families who appreciated Eternal Grace's blend of modern technology mixed with classic praise and worship.

I swear to you, that boy was a genius. I'm really quite glad I didn't shoot him back in the day.

Best of all, Abigail stayed busy and happy with her new role at the church along with starting things up for the Chihuahuas and their career ambitions as therapy dogs. Yes, Abigail was happy as a clam...

Until one day she wasn't.

Oh, I knew trouble was coming when Mrs. Sutton showed up at our house. Not that she would do anything to hurt my Abigail. She was a decent enough woman, but pain seemed to be contagious around here lately.

And wouldn't you know it? I returned home from my drive about to find Mrs. Sutton's car gone and my daughter lying in tears on the living room floor. The puppies, whose bed had been moved out of Abigail's room and into the living room, all eagerly lapped at her tears while Mama

Mary remained nestled into her side, trying to offer comfort via warmth. A sizable cardboard box sat atop the table, its scattered contents covering the surface.

"Baby girl, *honey*," I whispered, coming as close as the puppies would allow. "What happened?"

She looked up at me with scratchy red eyes and a face to match. I'd only been gone for about an hour, but apparently the damage had been more than done.

"I can't talk about it right now," she told me. "I thought I was getting better, but this... this is too much." Her eyes guided me to the box that sat open on the table, inviting me to take a look and see for myself.

As hard as it was to turn away and leave Abigail to her sorrow, I needed to know what had upset her so greatly. Inside that box and all around it were mementos, tokens from Owen's life—an old high school letter jacket, a worn teddy bear, dozens of photo albums including several pictures that appeared to have been printed directly off of Facebook or some such site, and even an old baby book.

"It was nice of her to bring these by," I said with caution.

"Was it?" Abigail asked me with a cracked voice.

"Memories are worth cherishing," I answered, knowing full well that one day she'd be glad to have these things to look back on with her son.

"Memories hurt," she said, stroking Mama Mary's soft fur. "This hurts."

I placed the items back into the box and carried it to my bedroom, the one spot in the house where my daughter was least likely to come across it by accident.

"When you're ready for it," I told her upon returning, "all you have to do is ask."

"That's the thing," she said, her voice still shaky. "What if I'm never ready?"

"Then that's just fine, baby girl," I said, lowering myself to the floor even though it meant pushing several puppies out of my way in the process. "That's just fine."

Chapter 36

ABIGAIL

Abigail's father left her to her tears but remained nearby as she struggled through the flood of emotions that had hit her that day. She'd finally begun to look toward the future, toward her son and the life they would lead together, to the possibility of one day allowing herself to fall in love again.

But that box from Owen's mother was perfect proof that when you fell, you got hurt. She'd loved her husband with everything she had. They had built a life to live together, until suddenly it collapsed and Abigail found herself back home with her father.

So much optimism they'd had when decorating their home, arguing over whose family traditions they'd honor for each holiday, planning the perfect wedding and then seeing it through. They'd never expected for it to come crashing down all around them—that one of them wouldn't make it out of the mess alive.

Or that it would practically kill her, too.

Thanks to her father, the dogs, and—yes—Gavin, she'd been able to start rebuilding, but as it turned out, she was the little piggy who'd built her house from straw. One blow and everything came tumbling down around her.

She'd always been the sentimental type, or at least since her mother had disappeared and left her behind. Her way of moving on had apparently been not to think about Owen. One medium-sized box ended up being a giant trigger. Everything rushed back, the pain fresh and new and not patched up as she had started to believe.

Abigail knew she needed to be stronger. In fact, she didn't have a choice. Her son would arrive in about three months, and he'd depend on her for everything. If she couldn't even take care of herself, how could she care for a newborn baby?

It terrified her, the thought of failing her son—of failing Owen's son, his one living legacy. That she could be triggered by anything and at any moment meant that nothing was fully safe, no day guaranteed.

The most frightening thing of all, though, was that she had almost allowed it to happen again. Her friendship with Gavin had become vital to her these past few months. The more time that passed, the more she thought that—yes—she could really love him. She could really build a new life and future.

He'd once told her that sometimes lightning struck twice and that each time was equally special. The truth of the matter was that lightning strikes were terrible, painful disasters. She'd somehow managed to survive her first but wouldn't be strong enough if the lightning found her again.

One can recover from pain if the pain stops, but what if a fresh blaze destroyed everything that's left? She'd loved and lost Owen. Could she handle loving Gavin when there was always—always—the possibility she could lose him as well? She never thought her husband dying would happen, but it had.

Gavin could fall out of love with her, find someone else, change... he could die, too.

What was she thinking? It was already scary enough to have a baby on the way. It would take everything she had to keep him safe and raise him well. She didn't have anything to risk, couldn't possibly stand losing anything more. Because if she did, she wouldn't be able to nurture and provide for her son like he needed and deserved.

Sometimes you had to make sacrifices for the greater good. As horrible as it was to think about, that's exactly what Owen had done. He'd given his life for his country. Now Abigail would give her last chance at love for her son.

Things with Gavin needed to end. Even though he'd taken a relationship off the table until the day after Christmas, both of their feelings continued to stretch and grow. If she waited, he'd hurt that much more in the end.

Oh, she prayed he would know it wasn't his fault, that she didn't want to hurt him the way Susie had. But truth be told, she already had a family, too. And she owed it to them to protect her heart.

She was thinking about all this, determination growing within her, when Gavin arrived with an armful of knit baby blankets.

"My mother couldn't help herself," he said with a laugh before spying Abigail on the ground and her father at the table. "Oh no, what happened? Is the baby okay?"

"The baby's fine," she assured him, struggling to sit.

Gavin kneeled at her side to help her up.

How could she possibly begin the conversation they needed to have? She started weeping all over again. When would the tears stop? She'd shed so many tears this past year, she was practically a fountain of sorrow.

"What's wrong?" he coaxed gently.

Her father walked out of the room, and a moment later she heard his bedroom door latch shut behind him.

Gavin turned to her with a knitted brow and searching eyes, and Abigail said the only two words that pushed through into her brain.

"I can't."

Gavin forced a smile. It held none of the usual mirth or mischief. He already knew.

She didn't have to say more, but she owed it to him to try. "You've been such a good friend to me, but I don't think I can see you anymore."

His pain became visible on his face, in his posture. "Did I do something wrong?" he asked.

"No, you've been perfect," she said, crying and both wishing and not wishing that he would take her in his arms. "That's the problem."

"I pushed you too hard. It was too much, too fast." Gavin turned red as he searched for the reason why. But Abigail already knew he would never find it. He couldn't understand not having experienced it for himself, and for that she was very grateful.

Abigail placed a gentle kiss on his cheek—a kiss goodbye. "You've been perfect, but I'll never even be close to that. I'm too broken already."

He grabbed both of her hands. "You're perfect to me. Abigail, I love you."

"I wish I could let myself love you, Gavin, but I need to give everything I have left to my son. You understand that, don't you?"

Gavin turned away from her so she couldn't see the pain that mangled his face. But she heard it all the same. "You know where to find me if that ever changes," he said. "Goodbye, Abigail."

Chapter 37

ABIGAIL

Abigail was relieved that Gavin didn't try to fight for her. She'd made up her mind, and he respected that now. She sorely missed all the time they had spent together—he'd been a great friend—but threw herself into work at the church and with the dogs as well as preparing for little Owen's arrival.

As the days became weeks which then became months, Abigail found this second sting of loss transformed into a dull, quiet ache. This time, it had been on her own terms and with her child's best interests at heart. Gavin was a good man, and she didn't doubt he would find somebody wonderful to share his life with, someone far better than the wreck Abigail had become.

Then one day, Abigail woke up with a cramping pain that just wouldn't quit. When it still hadn't abated by dinner, her father forced her into his car so that he could drive her to the hospital. She was still two weeks out from her due date and understood that most first babies arrived late. Little Owen, however, did not seem to understand this, because less than twenty-four hours later, her beautiful baby boy joined her in that hospital room.

Her father didn't leave her side for a single moment. When they called

Owen's mother, she, too, tended to Abigail during the labor, creating a room full of love just as she'd hoped would be the case when welcoming her child into the world.

A flurry of folks from the church paraded in and out of the maternity ward, bringing their well wishes along with flowers for Abigail, gifts for the baby, and of course casseroles for her father. She wondered if Gavin had heard the news and if he would try to stop by and offer his congratulations. It felt odd not having him here when he had been so involved in preparing the nursery and had even gifted them the blanket that little Owen was swaddled in that day.

Looking into her son's perfect face now, though, she knew she would do anything to protect him for as long as she lived. Her life was no longer her own, and that was perfectly fine by Abigail.

When she awoke from a brief nap the next morning, she found a most unusual gift sitting on the window pane. While others brought more traditional flowers like daisies, daffodils, and tulips, this plant was all green. Upon closer inspection, she saw that it was a bonsai tree whose limbs had been twisted and shaped to resemble the far-reaching arms of the Angel Oak on John's Island. There was only one person that gift could be from, although the little tree arrived with no note attached.

She was glad to see that Gavin was still thinking of her fondly and hoped the absence of a note meant he had moved past the hurt she had burdened him with.

When little Owen stirred, she got up from the hospital bed. Her stitches still stung, but she felt freer than she had in months as she padded over to cuddle her child.

"Look at this, little man," she said, rocking him gently in her arms as they both approached the window. She knew he couldn't see far yet, but he loved listening to her voice, which meant she talked to him as much as she could think to say.

"This little tree represents a much bigger, older tree. In fact, we have our own special bit of magic right here in Charleston. One day when you're older, I'll take you to see it," she promised.

"Oh, good you're up!" her father said, pacing into the room as he clutched at his belly. "If I eat one more helping of casserole, I think the good Lord might call me home."

Abigail laughed. "Your grandpa is such a silly old man," she told her son, who had reached one hand out of his blanket and was stretching it toward her. "We're going to have to tell all the church ladies to stop feeding him so well."

"I'll hold you to that," her father said. "As it turns out, I just can't say no to a good plate of home cooking, but that's not why I'm happy to see you up."

"Oh?" Abigail lifted her son higher in her arms and kissed his fuzzy little head.

"I used my Godly connections to accomplish a little favor from the hospital staff, and well... bring her in, Mrs. Clementine."

And sure as day, Mama Mary trotted into the room like she owned the place. She even wore a tiny hospital gown and plastic booties on her feet. The moment she saw Abigail, she broke into a run, pulling her leash clean out of Mrs. Clementine's hand.

"Oh, Mary! Look, we're both mamas now!" Abigail cried, happy to see her best canine friend.

Mary barked happily, but Abigail shushed her. "Not now. You only just got here, and I don't want them to take you away before you have a chance to meet my little one. Would you help us out, Dad?"

Abigail settled back onto the bed with Owen in her arms, and her father came to sit beside her holding on to the sweet mother Chihuahua so she could say hello.

Mrs. Clementine snapped a picture and gushed, "How nice! The whole family's here!"

"Well, not the whole family," her father said.

Abigail opened her mouth to correct him. Gavin wasn't part of the family, not anymore, and it wasn't very nice of him to remind her of that on what should be a happy day.

Before she could say anything, though, her father continued, "We'll have to wait until we're at home to introduce Muffin, Cupcake, Cookie, and Brownie. They're probably still a mite too hyper to be around little Owen."

Abigail laughed and nodded, posed for another picture, then looked toward the bonsai replica of the Angel Oak. She had everything now, so why did she still miss Gavin?

Little Owen's face scrunched up, and he let out a goat-like cry.

"Oops, didn't know we were intruding on breakfast time," her father said, leading Mrs. Clementine and Mama Mary from the room. "We'll just wait outside until you're through."

Abigail listened for the click of the door behind them before fitting her son to her breast. As she watched him nurse, she remembered the reasons behind her decision to end her friendship with Gavin.

She needed to be strong for her child, and she needed to stay that way, too.

No matter what else happened.

Chapter 38

ABIGAIL

Abigail had always known that early motherhood would be a lot of hard work, but she was not prepared for the exhaustion that came with it. Whoever made the rule to sleep when the baby sleeps must have had a great little sleeper on her hands.

And although Owen wasn't terrible by any means, he would wake a few times each night to cry out for Abigail. This made it hard to track days. In a way, it had all been one very long day since he was born in May.

Her fatigue reached amazing new levels in early December when Owen began to crawl. He and the puppies, who were almost full grown now but just as feisty and playful as ever, could cause mischief together. And, oh, did they ever!

The worst of it happened a few days before Christmas when the cyclone of fur knocked their evergreen tree clear over. Luckily, little Owen wasn't involved in that particular fiasco, but he did pull a platter of cookies off of the end table when Abigail was distracted in cleaning up the mess of scattered ornaments and tinsel that the Chihuahuas had left in their wake.

"Your Christmas present is extra obedience classes," she told them while wagging her finger.

They all sat in a line and looked up at her with tails wagging merrily as if to show they were already the perfect little angels.

Mama Mary groaned and went to hide under Abigail's favorite chair, but not before first swiping a fallen cookie.

"That's not good for you!" Abigail cried, but now Owen had a cookie, too, which meant she had to choose which battle she preferred to fight that day.

"Ah-ha, gotcha!" she swiped the broken gingerbread man from Owen, who then began to cry. "Where are you, Dad?" Abigail moaned.

Of course, by the time he returned half an hour later, both puppies and human child had begun their afternoon naps, leaving the house serene and peaceful and nothing like it had been less than an hour ago.

"Looks like y'all had a nice day," her father said with a proud grin.

She simply laughed and swiped the tray of recovered cookies away from him before he could steal one for himself. "I wouldn't eat those if I were you."

"Do I want to know?" he asked with raised brows.

Abigail just shook her head and walked away. It was a chaotic life, but a blessed one.

T he following day was Christmas Eve. This time Abigail not only attended the service, but helped to lead it. Even Mama Mary and her pups made an appearance. Thankfully, Mrs. Clementine was all too happy to look after little Owen while his mother was busy with church duties. Abigail even made her an honorary grandmother, which meant she doted on Owen extra.

After church, they captured pictures of the Chihuahua family in that same locally famous nativity scene where they'd been born and first discovered.

"Happy Birthday, babies!" Abigail cried.

Owen clapped his pudgy hands with glee.

To think, just one year ago, Abigail had been all by herself. Her father had been there for her, but she'd shut him out. Everything had changed last Christmas with the discovery of those puppies, and now she and her father had Owen in their worlds, too.

Despite the added mischief, his childish antics were exactly what Abigail had needed to fill her days and her heart once more. It was hard to believe she'd ever doubted the love she would have for him. She enjoyed being a mother more than anything.

"It was a good day," her father said when they were back at home sitting before a roaring fire and noshing on a fresh batch of Christmas cookies. This time they had chocolate chip.

"It was," she agreed. "A long day."

"Merry Christmas, baby girl."

"Merry Christmas, Dad." Abigail closed her eyes and leaned back into the chair, enjoying the quiet comfort of the evening. She was surprised when her father spoke again.

"I know it somewhat breaks with tradition, but I was wondering if you might like to open your stocking tonight."

"That's okay, Dad," she answered with a satisfied sigh. "I don't mind waiting."

"Let me rephrase that. You should open your stocking tonight."

She opened her eyes and glanced at her father suspiciously. "Why?"

He winked at her in a move that was very St. Nick, especially given his ever growing bowl full of jelly. "Let's just say it has time sensitive material."

Abigail shrugged and went to retrieve her stocking from the mantel place. Immediately, she found that it was much lighter than it had been in years past. Reaching in, she found a single small item, which she wrapped her fingers around and pulled out.

It was a silver locket shaped like a heart. On the front were the initials RE.

"Was this Mom's?" she asked, feeling the weight of it in her palm.

His gaze softened. "Yes, I gave it to her the first Christmas after you were born. I figured this would be the perfect time to give it to you now that you're a mother yourself."

"Thank you, Dad," she said, practically short of breath from the sudden burst of excitement. "I love it."

"Open it," he prompted.

It took some doing since the necklace hadn't been worn in decades, but eventually Abigail was able to pry open the little heart. On one side she found a close up of her and Owen's faces on their wedding day, both very much in love and with no idea what the future would hold for them. The other side showed a candid shot of her and Gavin, heads leaned in close to each other as they both laughed over something she could no longer remember.

"What's this all about?" she asked, feeling hurt that her father would ruin this perfect gift by reminding her of both the men she had lost.

He took a deep breath before explaining. "Baby girl, as your father, it was my job to teach you faith, and I'm so proud of the strong Christian woman you've become. The next great man in your life, Owen, taught you love, and I will forever be thankful to him for that. But Gavin... Gavin taught you laughter when you needed it the most. Don't throw that away."

"You never moved on past Mom," she said, fully angry with him now. "How could you expect me to move on past Owen? That isn't fair."

"No," he said simply. "None of what's happened has been fair. The worst of it all is that you shut out someone who loves you just because you were scared."

"Of course I'm scared!" she shouted, praying the baby wouldn't wake from her carelessness. "I lost everything."

"And how blessed you are to have found it again," her father said before pushing himself up from his seat and leaving her alone in the darkening living room.

Chapter 39

ABIGAIL

On Christmas day, Abigail, her father, and little Owen joined her in-laws to celebrate. They lived about two hours away, but Abigail vowed to make the journey upstate to visit at least once per month so that the new grandparents wouldn't miss out on getting to know their grandson.

By the time they returned to Charleston that evening, Abigail was utterly exhausted from their long day of festivities coupled with the four hours of driving. The following day was Sunday, which meant her father would be in for another long day. She didn't know if she could handle it herself, though—or if Owen could, for that matter.

She turned off her alarm and decided to leave it to chance. By the time she awoke the following morning, her father had already left for first service. She was surprised that little Owen hadn't stirred and gently padded to his nursery, only to find her baby had been replaced by a single sheet of lined paper.

Abigail, it read in her father's jagged scrawl. *I took Owen with me to church. Mrs. Clementine would have my neck if I denied her Sunday cuddles with him. I didn't want to wake you, but I did want to tell you to* look in the top drawer of Owen's dresser. I know you'll make the right decision.

Love,

Dad

She clutched the note to her chest as she crossed the room to the honey oak dresser and pulled open the first drawer. In it lay her first Bible, the same one her father had regifted her last year. When she picked the tiny book up, her mother's locket fell onto the folded onesies below.

Why was he giving these to her now, and why had he brought them to Owen's room? She thought back to when she'd pulled the Bible from her stocking last year. He'd wanted to remind her of happier times and said that Owen wouldn't want her to wallow. This year, she'd found the locket tucked into the bottom of that same stocking, and he'd told her not to throw away her chance with Gavin.

But why was he harping on this? She'd found God again. She had a great job, a son whom she adored. She was happy again. The love she felt for her father, her son, her dogs, and her God had given her the strength she'd once lost. And now...

Oh, no.

Love wasn't weakness like she had allowed herself to believe. It wasn't something to be feared and sacrificing it wouldn't be doing her son any favors. Love was what had made her whole again. Love was what gave her strength, life.

And she'd thrown Gavin's love straight out the window, when it had been a big part of helping her to find a life worth living again. He'd given her all of himself, but she'd been stingy. Afraid. Unable.

What a terrible mistake she'd made.

She opened up the Bible and found a torn page from her father's page-a-day calendar. It talked about new hope, new chances, and on the center of the tiny sheet of paper, a giant 26 was written in big, bold strokes.

It was the day after Christmas, the same day she'd run into Gavin at the pet store last year, the same day they'd promised to meet under the

Angel Oak and decide whether their relationship should go further. He'd asked her for one year, and she hadn't even given him that.

She didn't deserve for him to be waiting for her under that magical old tree, but she had to at least try. She had to go and see if he remembered, if he still wanted her despite all the hurt she had caused them both.

"C'mon, Mama Mary," she called, not caring that she was still dressed in her pajamas. She needed to get to John's Island and fast, and she needed the moral support that only her special little dog could provide.

"Please, God. Please don't let it be too late," she prayed during the entire drive over. Her mother's locket lay against her collarbone, and she lifted a hand to stroke it. Her mother had walked away from a good man, but Abigail would not repeat her mistakes, not if she could help it.

She parked and jumped out of the car, racing around to grab Mama Mary from the passenger's side. She caught a glimpse of herself in the side mirror and gasped. She looked a fright, but she didn't care. She'd let silly things, incorrect notions, rob her of her joy before, and she was done making the same mistakes over and over again.

She clipped Mama Mary into her leash and walked toward the giant oak looming in the distance. Just as before, its branches reached out to hug all of Charleston. She squinted as she drew near, searching each face in the park.

And then she saw him.

"Gavin!" she cried, breaking into a full sprint with Mama Mary trailing behind. She let go of the leash so she could run faster, knowing her dog would follow along obediently.

He turned toward her, and that goofy grin she had missed so much lit his entire face. "You came!" he called to her, standing in place as she continued to run as fast as her legs would carry her.

"Gavin!" she cried again, reaching him at last and tackling him with a hug. And wouldn't you know it? There she was, crying again.

"You came," he repeated, brushing her messy hair away from her face.

"I finally realized a few things I should have known a long time ago," she said between pants for air.

"Such as?" he asked. It was then she noticed he was holding his breath. He still didn't know. He'd never known because she hadn't told him.

"That I love you. I want only you. Little Owen and I both need you in our lives."

"You love me?" he asked, his grin growing even wider than she'd once thought possible.

"So much," she whispered. "So much it hurts. I'm so sorry I sent you away. I was scared."

"I know." When he nodded his understanding, a fresh tear fell from his cheek and landed on Abigail's pajama shirt.

"I don't want to be scared anymore," she continued. "I want to be brave for you. For us. I love you so much, Gavin Holbrook."

"Are you done apologizing?" Gavin asked, raising his palm to stroke her cheek. "Because you have nothing to be sorry for. You're here now and that's more than I could have ever hoped for. I don't care about your past, Abigail Sutton-Elliott. I only want your future, and I hope that maybe one day you'd be willing to become Abigail Sutton-Elliot-Holbrook."

Before Abigail could ask whether Gavin was officially trying to propose to her, he brought his lips to hers in a delicate, inspiring, life-affirming kiss.

Sometimes love hurt.

Other times it healed, but always—always—it was a miracle.

Chapter 40

It may have taken a whole year, but finally my daughter found the gift waiting right in front of her. When I returned home from church that Sunday to find her and Gavin cuddled up together on my living room couch, I whooped so loud it made the puppies run in a barky blur searching the house for an intruder or some other such oddity that would explain my sudden outburst.

Gavin rose to meet me, extending his hand for a shake and taking a hug right along with it. "Thank you," he whispered into my ear. "Thank you for helping her see."

"I didn't do it for you," I said with a smile despite the harshness of my words. "I did it for my baby girl. I'd do anything for her."

Gavin laughed. "I remember the shotgun."

"There never was a shotgun," I admitted. "I just had to make sure you were good enough for my daughter."

"And what's the verdict?"

I hesitated to make him sweat a little before wrapping him in another hug, clapping him on the back, and saying, "Welcome to the family, son."

Of course, he's not an official part of the family yet, but Gavin's been one of us ever since he returned to our lives that fateful day after Christmas. It won't be long until things are official, though. The kids are planning their wedding for May at that very same oak tree that's become so important to them. I'll be officiating, and little Owen will serve as the best man and the ring bearer all in one.

Don't worry, the church dogs will be there with us, too. They wouldn't miss it for the world.

Are you ready to find out who the Church Dogs help next? When Harmony left Charleston, she vowed never to return. Now she's back and needs a miracle...

CLICK HERE to get your copy of *A Fresh Start*, so that you can keep reading this series today!

🐾

And make sure you're on Melissa's list so that you hear about all her new releases, special giveaways, and other sweet bonuses.

You can do that here: MelStorm.com/gift

Acknowledgments

I have wanted to write this book for such a long time. Once I fell in love with my own special Chihuahua girl, Sky Princess (and later her Mama Mila), I knew I needed to write a book series to celebrate them.

And, finally, here we are!

I always have so many people to thank, but I wanted to make this batch of acknowledgments special—so here we go, all the people who helped me make this book a reality, in chronological order of their contribution.

Thanks go to my family for encouraging my creativity and rarely saying no when I wanted yet another book to add to my massive home library.

To my husband, Falcon, for showing me what love was and that I was worthy of it. For taking care of things around the house so I can focus on writing, and for never failing to believe in me and encourage me to keep on going after my dreams. Just because you catch a dream doesn't mean you should ever stop chasing it, right?

To my daughter, Phoenix, for turning me into a certifiably crazy Chihuahua lady.

To my friend, Mina Jandou, for entrusting me first with Sky Princess and then Mama Mila. Thank you for bringing the magic of Chihuahuas into my life, thank you for loving them every bit as much as I do, and thank you for being your beautiful, wonderful self!

To my two Chihuahua girls for inspiring the series and lending such life-like qualities to Mama Mary and her puppies. To my non-Chi dogs as well, because I also love and am inspired by them.

To my cover designer, Mallory Rock, for bringing my vision to life with her art—and for suggesting that we use Sky Princess as one of the cover models!

To my fabulous assistant and friend, Angi Hegner. Thank you for getting excited about my books and forcing me to write them in a timely fashion, even though I definitely know I'm not easy to manage. And to Becky Muth and Shanae Johnson for also getting excited as my word count increased.

To Mallory Crowe for doing write-ins with me and just generally being awesome. You are thanked, my dear.

To my amazingly talented editor—and another of my many cheer-leaders—Megan Harris. She's the real deal, folks, and my work is the better for it.

To my proofreader, Jasmine Bryner, who always gives such great feed-back and insights while she's reading and lives the story right alongside me.

To my readers. To you. For letting my books into your heart and giving me a voice, for writing me such kind notes of encouragement, and for getting excited about the characters who are so near and dear to my heart.

And to anyone who's ever loved a Chihuahua, who's ever helped a dog in need, who's ever believed in miracles—no matter how small.

Thank you all. You are appreciated more than you know and loved more than you might expect!

A Fresh Start

CHARLESTON HEARTS #2

To Sky Princess and Mila:
My own personal Chihuahua loves

About this Book

Some folks are born with a silver spoon jutting right out of their mouths. Others are a bit more like Miss Harmony King. That poor thing bounced in and out of so many foster homes growing up, that even my head spun circles trying to keep track of them all.

Once Harmony hit eighteen, though, she disappeared from Charleston altogether. Fast forward nearly a decade, and now she's back, bent over a pew, and praying like her life depends on it. I'd reckon that just maybe it does.

Of course, I don't know why this young woman left our town, and I don't know why she's come back now—but one thing I do know beyond the shadow of a doubt is that God meant for us to find each other again.

So I told Harmony the story of the special Chihuahuas born in our church's nativity scene last Christmas Eve, and that our Muffin, in particular, wanted to help her if she'd let him. Yes, our church dogs have worked miracles before, and by the grace of the Almighty, I think they might just be about to perform another...

A FRESH START is a touching and poignant story from a New York Times bestselling author that will warm your heart, bless your soul, and leave you smiling.

Prologue

PASTOR ADAM

Some say that whenever it snows in Charleston, God is giving a miracle to His most favorite of places. I tried to remember that as the cold reaching fingers of the wind poked and prodded my cheeks, nose, and everything else not already covered up by my scratchy winter getup.

But the more I tried to be optimistic about the shocking turn in the weather forecast, the harder that miraculous snow swirled. Soon it had bleached out the entire sky so that it was hard to tell where earth ended and the heavens began. We had a veritable snow storm on our hands just in time for the celebration of His birth.

I mumbled a quick prayer that those traveling tonight would remain safe and hugged my threadbare coat tighter around my shoulders. Head down, I fought against the wind, marching ever closer toward my destination.

Leave it to me to get so caught up in my Christmas Eve sermon that I'd forget my cell phone right there on the pulpit! Lucky thing I did, though, because as I finally reached the front doors of the sanctuary, I discovered a most disturbing sight.

Our locally famous nativity scene had been on the fritz all week, but

now the angels' glowing halos had plum run out of power, casting the entire display into darkness. And on Christmas Eve, no less.

Ignoring the cold, which had found its way straight up underneath my clothes, I stepped closer to investigate the source of our power outage. Last summer old Mrs. Clementine had taken it upon herself to plant a little garden right outside the church. How could I say no to her request when she said all the food from our newly christened vegetable patch would be donated to feed the hungry?

And so with more than a little trepidation, I said *yes*, and unfortunately so did every little critter within a twenty mile radius. Even with the crops resting for the winter, I had no doubt that one of Mrs. Clementine's rabbit friends had tried to make a home of Christ's manger—and a snack of His power cords.

Upon closer inspection, I found that—yes, just as I'd suspected—a tiny ball of brown fluff had nestled into the nativity right there between Mary, Joseph, and the kindly shepherds who'd come to pay their respects.

Darn varmints!

Well, that's what I wanted to think, but then I stopped myself. These poor creatures hadn't expected the sudden snowfall either. They just wanted to get warm, and maybe God had sent me back to offer assistance on His behalf.

My toes began to go numb, but I tried to ignore that tingly sharpness as I stepped in for a closer look at the trembling animal.

Imagine my surprise when I found not just one creature, but five!

Right there next to the little Lord Jesus lay a mother dog and her four newborn pups. How they'd managed to survive this long was truly by the grace of God.

I didn't want to leave them, but I couldn't carry them all at once either. At least not on my own. After retrieving the box that our latest batch of hymnals had arrived packed inside, I stripped off my scarf and made a little nest. Then one by one, I lifted the mama and her puppies into the cardboard carrier and brought them into our church to get warm.

My lungs could scarcely take in a single breath of air until I made sure

that each pup was alive and well. Only by the glory of God each of these tiny newborns moved just enough to show me they were okay. You must understand these dogs were hardly bigger than my own thumb. They could have easily been mistaken for rat pups if not for that brave mama dog.

A quick search on my newly retrieved phone confirmed that these were not just any dogs. They were the most diminutive of all dog breeds.

I didn't even stop to question why the Almighty had sent me five Chihuahuas in need as an early gift for His birthday. I didn't have to, because right then I knew beyond the shadow of any doubt these dogs were meant to find us. Surviving that cold Christmas Eve outdoors was only the first of many miracles that mama dog and her pups would bring to our congregation...

Chapter 1

HARMONY

Thirteen months later

Harmony King had been running for a long time. At first, she was always running toward something—more specifically, toward freedom. Growing up in the foster care system would not be how she'd chosen to start life, and she definitely wouldn't have elected to remain a slave to that system until her eighteenth birthday finally set her loose.

But that's exactly what had happened, anyway.

All those years as a little girl with no home to call her own, she longed to live life her own way, to be the master of her own fate. Somehow, though, she'd only managed to continue her lifestyle of drifting from one place to the next without feeling any real connection.

It made her wonder: was she *born* broken, or had that just happened along the way?

Because, no question about it, something was majorly wrong with her.

That was part of why she'd returned to Charleston. As much as she'd fought to escape the Holy City as a teen, truth be told, it was the only place she'd even come close to belonging.

Her homes had shuffled about faster than a magician preparing his cards, but a kindly agent at Child Protection Services had fought to keep her in the same schools growing up. It was the only constant she'd had up until that point.

When she could, she would sneak away to the Eternal Grace Church and listen to the pastor regale his congregation with tales of fortitude, forgiveness, charity. Jesus had been a poor wanderer, too—and Harmony liked that. It made him relatable, although when she'd mentioned this to her foster mother at the time she'd earned a cold, hard slap on the cheek and her fastest reassignment to date.

This experience strained her relationship with the church, but she still managed to attend services at least once per month by scraping together any spare change she could find to purchase a bus ticket that would deliver her to the service and hopefully, one day, salvation.

Sometimes she'd even pretend the pastor was her long-lost father and that one day they'd realize their relation and hug each other, sobbing big, ol' tears for all the time they'd already lost. But Harmony knew this was just a dream. She knew nothing of her birth father other than that he could have been any number of men. Her mother, who had been the very worst kind of junkie, died when Harmony was just four. But sometimes, if she clenched her eyes shut real tight, she could call up the memory of her mother's face.

And some other times she'd wish her mother had died much earlier. Because if she had, baby Harmony would surely have been adopted. Angry, dramatic four-year-old Harmony had tempted no one into taking such an action.

Of course, she often wished that she'd never been born, but then immediately prayed for forgiveness to the Almighty. As far as she was concerned, God had put her on this earth for a reason, and it was her failing—not His—that she hadn't figured it out yet.

Most recently she'd been living in Alabama, but when she'd lost her job and gotten evicted by her landlord, she knew her time was up in that particular locale.

It was always her tongue that got her into trouble. Harmony could put the fear of God into just about anybody, which had been a necessary skill to fight off the unwanted advances of foster brothers and fathers, along with a fair-sized collection of schoolyard bullies, too. But it was also a skill she couldn't control even now. If someone made her angry, they were going to hear about it—and with colorful language to boot.

She was sure God didn't mind. The two of them had an understanding when it came to these things, but Harmony still wished she could learn a bit of discretion. It certainly would make her life easier. At least a little bit, anyway.

There was little she could depend on in this world, but God always came through in some way or another.

That was another reason she'd returned to Charleston now—to the church where she'd first discovered her faith, to the pastor she'd liked to imagine was her father, to the only place she'd really stayed long enough to form some good memories along with the bad.

And, oh, did she need those good memories now. She needed answers, too. Some kind of direction she'd yet to find in her nearly twenty-eight years.

Harmony dipped her head in reverence as she stepped into the sanctuary of Eternal Grace. After a quick glance around to confirm that she was alone, she did the only thing left to do. She dropped to her knees and prayed like her life depended on it. *Dear God. I need you. I'm so afraid...*

Chapter 2

HARMONY

Harmony prayed so long and so fervently that she all but lost track of time. When at last she lifted her bowed head, opened her eyes, and swiped at the tears that had flown freely down her face, she saw that she was no longer alone in the sanctuary.

"God's got ya," the same pastor she remembered from her youth said with a kindly smile and a quick nod. "Whatever it is, He knows, and He'll take care of you, too."

"Th-th-thank you," she stuttered. The embarrassment of being caught mid-prayer sent a sudden flash of warmth straight to her cheeks.

The pastor sank down a few seats away from Harmony and folded his hands in his lap. "Miss Harmony, it has been quite some time."

"You remember me?" She eyed him cautiously. Just how much *did* he remember, and why did he actually seem happy to see her now? Of all God's eternal mysteries, Harmony always found it most suspect when someone from her past welcomed her back into their presence with open arms. It had only happened a handful of times, but the most recent had been such a spectacular disaster that this situation now with the pastor gave her pause.

Pastor Adam carried on without even the slightest hesitation. He'd always had the gift of gab. Only he practiced it in far better ways than Harmony used her own version of the same... gift. "Of course I remember you. I've thought about you many times over the years, wondered how you were doing, sent up prayers. It's good to see you now."

"I didn't know where else to go," she confessed with a shrug. If she acted like this wasn't a big deal, then perhaps it wouldn't be. Then again, that ship had likely already sailed when she decided to flee her last home in the early hours of that morning and drive straight up to Charleston, with only the odd break here and there to use the bathroom and stretch her legs.

Pastor Adam smiled consolingly in that same way he always had whenever speaking of the disadvantaged, and Harmony King was definitely one of the disadvantaged—now more than ever.

"You did right by coming here. You're always welcome at Eternal Grace." He waited for her to say more, but when she didn't, he added, "I'm still an exceptionally good listener if you'd like to talk about what's troubling you."

Harmony thought about this. She liked Pastor Adam—trusted him, too—and yet her burdens felt too big to offload onto somebody else. In truth, she already knew that only God could save her now.

"I never found talking about my problems to be an effective method for solving them," she said with a sigh. "Instead, they just seem to shine a spotlight, make 'em that much uglier."

He chuckled softly. "True enough, Harmony. True enough."

They sat in companionable silence for a few moments, leaving Harmony to wonder if she might just excuse herself and head home for the evening—provided she could find a spare room to rent somewhere near to here.

Then the pastor spoke again. "Of course, you shouldn't tell me anything you aren't comfortable sharing, but it's been a long while since I saw you last and I'm mighty curious... What have you been up to all these years?" He watched her expectantly, hopefully, but she already knew that anything she chose to reveal about her life would surely come as a tremendous disappointment.

"I left the very first second I could," she told him without even a single shred of regret.

He nodded, keeping his eyes fixed on his hands folded neatly in his lap. "I remember that. It's why I've always wondered how you got on. Worried, too. Eighteen is awfully young to forge out and make a life for one's own."

"Yes, it was. After Charleston, I went up north. First to Tennessee, then Ohio. I worked as a waitress mostly, because I couldn't afford schooling." Harmony had gotten good at skimping on the details when presenting herself to others. She needed to say just enough to get the job, to snag the rental, but never too much. That would only make them suspicious, make them turn her away. For all of Harmony's misfortunes, she was still a decent person, but folks who hadn't been in her shoes often missed that small, important point.

"So you were in Ohio until now?" Pastor Adam continued, pushing her along slowly as was his way.

"Gosh, no. I've been all over the place. Every time I lost my job for running my mouth, I'd pack up and move again. But I never found a place that felt more like home than Charleston." She marveled at how her old accent had come back out in full force. In all her travels, she'd never lost her Southern accent but had often adapted it to fit her current region rather than her roots.

"What brings you back now?" The pastor's questions kept coming, and they were beginning to wear Harmony out.

"This time I wasn't just running away. I was running from something, too. Or rather someone." She shouldn't have said that. It was too much for anyone besides her to know.

The pastor didn't gasp or suggest she call the police. He merely nodded and said, "But running all the same. Are you here for good now?"

"I can't say for sure. It's hard to put down roots when the very nature of your childhood is hopping from one house to the next. It doesn't take long for my feet to start itching, wanting to journey somewhere new, see what else is out there." Yes, it was easier to pretend she wanted this life, because that made it easier to accept.

"I hope you find a reason to stay," the pastor confided. "And if you need any help, I'm happy to provide it. A home, a job, you tell me what you need, and I'll find a way to deliver. With His help, of course." He pointed to the ceiling and smiled.

"Thank you," she mumbled. "That means a lot."

She almost asked if he knew of a room she might rent, but if the last two years had taught her anything, it was that she should depend on herself—and only herself—to get things done.

She'd prayed that Alan would never find her, that he wouldn't hurt anyone else either, that she could find a way to belong and, like the pastor had said, a reason to stay and make her home in Charleston. She'd asked God to deliver her from the repercussions of her own mistakes, to once again set her free.

But she already felt the walls closing in, moving fast toward the Holy City, trapping her in the only kind of life she'd ever known and erasing any last vestige of hope.

Chapter 3

HARMONY

Harmony twiddled her thumbs, spinning them in circles around each other. She was ready to leave the church, but the pastor stayed sitting quietly in her company. She was just about to excuse herself when at last he spoke again.

"Actually, if memory serves, you never were good at accepting help from others," he said, scooting closer to her with a knowing smile as if she'd suddenly been found out. "And I reckon that hasn't much changed."

"No, sir." She grinned, though it was strange speaking to someone who knew her well enough to call out her habits. It had been years since anyone had figured her out. Well, anyone besides Alan.

They shared a good laugh, although Harmony was beginning to feel rather discomforted by the exchange. The longer she stayed, the sooner the pastor would see through her, the sooner the final pieces to which she so desperately clung would shatter, thus leaving the puzzle of her life wholly unsolvable.

"Well, in that case," Pastor Adam said, rising to his feet and motioning for Harmony to follow him. "I'm not going to wait for you to ask for help. I'm just going to up and offer it right now."

She followed obediently as he led the way to his tiny church office, but she still argued against his offer all the same. "That's very kind of you, but I'll do just fine on my own. I really should be going. It's getting—"

"Just you wait one second now." He retrieved his phone from on top of his old, wooden desk and motioned for her to shush. His thumbs worked the digital keyboard quickly and deftly for a man of his generation. After a couple minutes of silence, he slid the phone back into his pocket and smiled over at Harmony.

"There. Now that's taken care of, let's have a chat."

Harmony blinked hard. If she wasn't careful, she'd be trapped talking to the goodly pastor for all of eternity. *Another* one?

A deep chuckle rose from his belly and shook his growing midsection. Age hadn't been the kindest companion to Pastor Adam, but Harmony saw right away that the same honorable man she'd always known resided within the puffier, wrinklier exterior. "Yes, another one. Or, rather, a more specific one. Come."

He led her out to the church foyer where they now waited within spitting distance of the front doors. "I just spoke with my daughter, Abigail. Do you remember her?"

Harmony nodded. "Yes, we had some classes together. She was always nice to me."

"Good to hear it." He pulled out his phone again and shook it demonstratively. "That was her I texted just now, and well, she's on her way here."

"She's coming *now*?" She'd only wanted a place to pray, clear her head a bit, and regroup. She hadn't meant for this quick church trip to turn into a whole big thing. But such seemed to be the Charleston way and Pastor Adam's in particular. She figured his own personal motto should be *if it's worth doing, it's worth overdoing.* This afternoon was clearly proof of that.

"Right now." He tossed his phone from hand to hand, catching it each time but worrying Harmony he'd drop it and crack the screen all the same. She cringed at the memory of all the good phones she'd lost being careless.

The pastor must have caught her discomfort, because he suddenly stopped and dropped his phone back into his pocket. "And she's bringing Muffin," he said with what looked like it may have been a wink.

"That's nice of you both, but I'm really not hungry. I need to—"

He laughed again. "Not muffins, Muffin. Your new dog."

"Dog?" Well, that couldn't be right. Why on God's green earth would Pastor Adam think she needed or wanted a dog?

He eyed her so contentedly after delivering his announcement that she had to put an end to this crazy notion immediately.

"No, no, no. I think there's been some kind of mistake."

"Well, he's really more of a loaner dog, but—boy howdy—do you two need each other." He was dead serious about this, and she was dead set against it.

"I'm not really in the position to..." She let her words trail off. If she explained that she didn't yet have a job or a place to stay, then the pastor would no doubt spring to further action, call in more favors, keep her hostage until he was absolutely certain that she was fully provided for.

"Please," he said firmly and with a sad smile. "You need comforting, Harmony. You need someone who understands and won't ask too many questions. I'm only human, but Muffin, he's a certified therapy dog and one of God's most special miracles."

This assertion shocked her into silence. Didn't therapy dogs stay with their trainers? Why would the pastor—who hadn't seen her in nearly ten years, by the way—thrust a dog on her mere minutes after becoming reacquainted? It just didn't make any sense.

"This dog... Muffin... is a miracle?" she asked slowly to make sure she understood him right. Ten years was a long time. Perhaps Pastor Adam had gone crazy since she'd last seen him. Anything was possible, after all.

"Sure as I'm standing here. Have you heard the story of our church dogs before? It's been about a year since they found us now, a very good year."

"Um, no," Harmony said. *Don't appear ungrateful,* she reminded herself, *but don't get suckered into taking a dog, either!*

Pastor Adam stood straighter and spoke animatedly with his hands.

He'd clearly told this story many times before. "It was two Christmases back—like I said, just over a year. I forgot my phone at the pulpit after delivering the Christmas Eve sermon. When I went back—"

"Are you only telling Muffin's origin story just now? I'd have figured that would be the first thing out of your mouth." The pastor's daughter, Abigail, swept into the foyer with a baby on her hip and two tiny dogs walking beside her on leashes.

Harmony hadn't even heard her come in, such was the volume and the vigor of Pastor Adam's storytelling.

"Dad says you and Muffin are *destined* for each other," Abigail said with a big roll of her eyes. "Told me I had to be over lickety-split before you could second-guess things." She pressed a leash into Harmony's palm and closed her fingers around it tightly before stepping back and regarding Harmony with a grin. "So, here you go, this is Muffin."

The little dog barked, perhaps to say hello, perhaps because he was equally confused about their sudden arrangement. One thing was for sure: Pastor Adam really, really wanted her to have this dog... and how could she say no to the man who had given her so much over the years?

Well, crud. It looked like Harmony had herself a dog.

Chapter 4

HARMONY

Harmony stooped down to let the fawn and white Chihuahua sniff her hand. She'd been around enough dogs growing up to know that this little gesture of peace went a long way when it came to convincing a dog not to bite you.

Not that the pastor would foist a vicious dog upon her, but still... up until a few minutes ago, she hadn't expected him to foist any dog upon her at all.

Muffin licked her hand enthusiastically and didn't stop lapping at it until Harmony pulled back.

"She sure is friendly, but I'm afraid I don't know much about dogs." There it was, her final attempt to say no. Too bad she already knew it would fall upon deaf ears.

"Muffin's a *he*," Abigail corrected. "I know it sounds a little silly, but the Sunday school kids named all the puppies, and—well—they went with a bakery theme. Someday I'll have to introduce you to his siblings Cookie, Brownie, and Cupcake."

"And who's this?" Harmony looked toward the other dog who sat at attention beside Abigail. It was plumper than Muffin, but otherwise looked very much the same.

"This is Muffin's mother." She stared at both dogs lovingly, as if they, too, were her children. "We call her Mama Mary. You know, since she gave birth in a manger?"

Harmony couldn't contain her laughter. Truly she was in the presence of the holy family—or at least the canine version of it.

"You arrived just as I was getting to the good part," Pastor Adam said to his daughter, then jumped straight back into his animated tale of how the Church Dogs of Charleston had come to be.

By the time he reached the end, Harmony suspected her jaw might be hanging wide open. Even though it was terribly rude, she just couldn't help herself. This litter of pups had been through a lot, almost as much as Harmony herself, but she still didn't understand one very important thing...

"I can see they're an incredible group of dogs, but why do you want to give one to me? Shouldn't they stay with the church?"

"Not giving, *loaning*," the pastor corrected with a wag of his finger. "And Muffin is staying with the church. He's staying with you. We both know that the church is made up of people, not bricks and mortar. Keep coming back each Sunday, and maybe Tuesdays, too, for a bit of counseling. What say you, Miss King?"

She glanced down at her feet hidden within a pair of old, dirty Converse she'd had for ages. Harmony felt torn between considering the dog a kind gift and a terrible imposition. Perhaps Muffin would prove to be both.

"It's okay if you don't know dogs," Abigail said when no one else spoke. "I can teach you. In fact, if you're up for it, little Owen, Mama Mary, and I were just about to head to the dog park for a bit of exercise. I'm sure Muffin would love to accompany us, too. What do you say, Muffy?"

The little dog barked and wagged his tail so hard that his entire body shook. Maybe a doggie companion wouldn't be the worst thing in the world, but so far Harmony had been given far more questions than she'd received answers.

"I'd love to come, but what do I feed him? And won't he miss his family? And how often does he need exercise? And... well, I'm sure there are a million more questions I don't even know to ask yet." It all made her head spin. Did they really think she could take care of another life when she could barely manage her own? Why were they willing to take such a risk on her when she'd only just gotten back into town? Something didn't add up.

Abigail and Pastor Adam both chuckled.

The pastor placed a warm hand on Harmony's shoulder. "I wouldn't have asked you to take Muffin if I didn't think it would be the best decision for both of you. These pups have worked miracles before. It's what they were born to do. Let Muffin do his job. Let him help you. He's a good dog, and you deserve him. After all, the Lord works in mysterious ways, and lately, in the case of Eternal Grace, that's through these little shivering balls of fluff."

"And for a more direct answer to your question," Abigail said as she fished through her oversized shoulder bag and pulled out a stapled bundle of papers. "Here's your guide to caring for one of our church dogs. The answers to all your questions are right in here along with my number. Call me any time. It's my job to take care of these pups and to run the program. I'll be visiting you throughout the week to check in and make sure you are both getting along. I also have a care package waiting for you in my car. It has Muffin's favorite foods, toys, blankets, pretty much everything you need and then some."

"Welcome back to Charleston, Harmony," Pastor Adam said, holding his arms open to request a hug.

Harmony eagerly stepped into them and felt the warmth of his non-judging, omnipresent love.

"Welcome home."

As Harmony looked to Abigail, her adorable son, and each of the dogs, she saw that roots had risen up from the earth to anchor her to this city.

At least for a little while longer, at least for now, it looked like she'd be calling Charleston her home—and Muffin her roommate.

Chapter 5

PASTOR ADAM

As I live and breathe, I never expected to see Harmony King set foot in Charleston again. She was always a kind child, but so, so broken. It wasn't just the lack of a family that got her started off all wrong. The kids made sure she never forgot what she was missing.

I often encouraged my daughter, Abigail, to reach out to her, but she insisted that it would be social suicide to have the girl no one liked come to our house for a bit of food and kindness—no matter how much the poor thing needed both. Abigail herself never made matters worse for Harmony, but I often wonder how much it would have meant to that poor girl to have a stable friendship to lean on for support.

Of course, I still remember the first time she was shifted about the system. I was certain that she was lost to Eternal Grace forever, but she had an angel on her side working at the Child Protective Services. That angel kept her nearby enough so that she could attend church and stay in Abigail's class at school.

No, she didn't make it every Sunday after that, even though I suspected she might like to. I offered to pick her up before first service and drop her home after second, but she never agreed to accept my help. I suspect she didn't want to depend on anyone if she could help it, and I can see she's still very much the same.

That's why I entrusted Muffin to her.

Oh, I saw her hesitation, the fear that she was now responsible for another life when she'd barely figured out how to manage her own, but God doesn't give us more than we can handle—I know that for a fact. And from the very moment I set eyes on Harmony praying like her life depended on it, there in the middle of my mostly empty sanctuary, God leaned in real close to my heart and whispered, "This girl needs a miracle. Let's give one to her."

And around here, "miracle" is just a fancy word for "Chihuahua." Yes, Harmony needed our church dogs in her life. Mostly because she needed someone she could count on, and I suspect she's never quite had that before. She needs to learn to forgive those involved in what happened to her—hard as it may be—and she needs to learn to look forward to better things, let others in to enjoy them with her.

But for now?

A dog will do just fine.

More than fine—*miraculously.*

A little love can go a long way. Now it was up to Muffin to answer God's call and finally give Harmony the chance to live a life to His glory as well as to her own satisfaction.

God speed, little Muffin.

And God bless.

Chapter 6

HARMONY

Harmony hopped in her old clunker and followed Abigail out of the church parking lot and toward a nearby dog park. At the pastor's insistence, Muffin rode along with Harmony, sitting proudly on the passenger side seat with his tongue lolling straight out of his mouth.

Less than five minutes later, they pulled into a small parking lot outside of a hilly fenced-in area. It was a good bit of space for being so near the heart of the city and appeared to be lovingly cared for, too.

Oh, the things people would do for their dogs.

Would Harmony soon be a doting dog mom herself? She had to laugh as she pictured dressing herself and Muffin in matching outfits and carrying him around town in a designer shoulder bag.

No, that vision belonged to somebody else's life. It would never be part of Harmony's.

"Told you it wasn't a far drive," Abigail called, standing outside her car and waiting for Harmony to extract Muffin from the inside of hers.

Unfortunately, before she could figure out how to grab him and pull him out of there, the little dog evaded her reach and leapt straight out onto the ground where he ran in tight, crazy circles around her ankles.

Harmony bent down to grab him from the parking lot, but the little dog was still too quick.

Abigail laughed. "That's okay. He knows the way in. C'mon."

Together the two women, baby, and the more mild-mannered mother Chihuahua headed into the dog park.

"Looks like he may be taking advantage of your inexperience," Abigail explained, but she didn't seem too worried about it. "Muffin knows better than to act without waiting for orders first. Lord knows he's had more than enough obedience training. It's okay, though. It just means that I may have to drop in three times a week to start until Muffin learns to respect you as his new pack leader."

Harmony nodded along passively, even though she secretly worried that this little dog was quickly becoming her full-time job. How would she pay for rent or food or anything else if every waking moment was devoted to helping Muffin so he could, presumably and supposedly, help her?

The questions kept piling up, and they were beginning to give her a headache.

Abigail must have caught her worried expression, because she placed a consoling hand on Harmony's arm and said, "I know it must seem overwhelming right now, but believe me, soon it will all be a routine. One you'll love more than anything. Trust me, I was exactly where you are hardly more than a year ago, and I thought my father was crazy for taking in these five dogs out of nowhere, but he was right to do it. He was right about everything."

"The dogs helped you... um, *what* exactly?" Harmony asked, hoping she wasn't coming across as rude. Abigail and the pastor were both trying to be kind and help her. The last thing either needed was her signature ill temper to make the situation that much more difficult.

Abigail smiled and swept her gaze across the horizon. Both Chihuahuas were running so fast their feet barely connected with the ground before lifting up again. A handful of other dogs roughhoused nearby, but all seemed happy and friendly despite the muffled growls that rose into the air above the park.

"Remember to live," Abigail said thoughtfully. "That's what they helped *me* with. It might be different for you, though. Oh, sure, I didn't believe it at first either, and I can tell from your expression you've got more than a couple doubts about the situation, but just... trust it, okay? Can you do that?"

Harmony shrugged, and when Abigail's face crumpled she quickly turned that shrug into a nod—a hesitant one, but agreement all the same. The two women hadn't been close growing up, and Harmony doubted they could be close now, but it did seem like the pastor's daughter wanted to help.

"How long have you been married?" she asked, groping for a change of topic in hopes Abigail wouldn't pry deeper into her life or the events had heralded her return to Charleston.

"What makes you ask that?" Abigail responded, keeping her eyes glued to the Chihuahuas as they jumped into the fray with the bigger dogs.

Harmony pointed toward the baby. "You said this is Owen, right?"

Abigail's face fell, but only for a moment before she righted it again. "Oh, right! Well, I'm not married at the moment, but I am engaged. Just recently, as a matter of fact. Do you remember Gavin Holbrook from school?"

She pictured the tall, handsome jock from her youth. Many of the girls had harbored not-so-secret crushes on Gavin, but not Harmony. She'd talked herself out of crushing on anyone back then, and she wished she'd have continued the habit into adulthood, too. There never was any use setting herself up for future disappointment.

Still, she was happy for Abigail that she'd managed to find a small bit of happiness in this crazy world. But she was also a fair bit confused.

"Didn't your father raise a fuss about you being unmarried and—?"

Abigail rushed to correct her. "Oh, no, no, no. That's a whole big story. I'll tell it to you sometime, but today is about you and Muffin, not about me and little Owen here."

"Ok-ay," Harmony said slowly, stretching the word apart into two long syllables. Even though she was curious, she knew it wouldn't be fair to press the other woman about her past when she herself wanted to keep everything in her life a secret.

"But first, can I ask you something?" It seemed she needed a fresh topic change again, and her visit to the church had taken up far more time than she'd planned. It was time for Harmony to ask for help—better Abigail than the pastor, she supposed.

Abigail turned to her with a warm smile that looked so much like her father's. "Sure. You can ask me anything."

Harmony tried not to flush with embarrassment. She hated asking for help, but occasionally it was necessary. "Do you know where I might be able to rent a room for the next couple months?"

There, she'd done the needful and casually committed to at least sixty days in Charleston, and with Muffin at her side. It probably wasn't the worst thing in the world. She just hoped she wasn't compounding one mistake with another.

Chapter 7

HARMONY

Harmony listened as Abigail told her all about an older church lady who was in need of some company and had a room to spare. It was decided that the two of them would pay her a visit straight after the dog park, with the dogs and baby in tow.

Frankly, it was rather amazing how she'd only been in town for a couple of hours and already had a dog, a place to stay, and maybe even a friend. But that was Charleston for you. Most of the time, the people were so friendly it almost seemed suspect. Harmony had learned to no longer question the kindness of strangers. Instead, it was the known folks from her past who gave her pause.

After some time the mother Chihuahua, Mary, came back to rest in the shade of the park bench beneath them. Muffin, who had far more energy left to burn, found a stick along the fence line and began running in wide looping circles around the park to show all the other dogs his prized find.

One dog in particular took a special interest in this charade and gave chase. Of course, it was the biggest, scariest looking dog in the entire park —a lanky, gray behemoth with wiry hair and coal eyes. He had to have at least fifty pounds on Harmony and would probably be taller than her, too, if he were to stand up straight on his hind legs.

Had they been on the street, she would have crossed to the other side for safety. Instead, this great beast was galloping after her brand-new borrowed dog, and the last thing Harmony needed was to see that poor little critter get mauled to death right before her innocent eyes.

"Hey, Muffin! C'mere, doggie!" she called in a high-pitched, childish voice, bending forward and patting her knees, praying the dog would listen for his own good.

And he did... but so did the other dog, who came lumbering after.

"Hi, Pancake!" Abigail cooed. She didn't even need to bend forward to stroke the massive dog between his ears.

"Pancake?" The name seemed ludicrous, not a good fit for the massive dog at all. Not really the best name for any dog, if she was honest. "Are all the animals around here named after foods or what?"

Abigail laughed as her baby blew spit bubbles and reached toward Pancake with chubby hands. "Just our church dogs and, of course, this big guy here." She used a baby voice that made all three dogs wag their tails wildly with excitement. Even Mama Mary woke back up to join in the fray.

Harmony took a step back as Pancake flopped onto the ground and rolled on his back. "He's massive," she said with a shiver.

"Yeah, Irish Wolfhounds get pretty big. Pancake is actually on the smaller side, believe it or not."

"I choose not," Harmony quipped. Why would anyone want a pet that could so easily overpower them? At least her loaner dog was small and easy to carry around if needed.

A tall, slender man spotted them from across the park and came jogging over. "Sorry about him!" he called. "He always loves it when he gets a chance to play with little dogs. He didn't slime you, did he?"

"Hi, Nolan. No, we're fine. It's good to see you and Pancake," Abigail answered for the both of them.

Harmony quietly studied the man standing before her. She vaguely remembered the pipsqueak two years behind her in school who was also called Nolan, but this fellow looked nothing like him at all. He was at least six foot five with long, lean limbs, sandy blond hair, and a smattering of freckles splashed across his thin nose. The thing that made him truly handsome, though, was his shining green eyes, which studied her with amusement.

"Have we met?" he asked, offering her an ingratiating smile. "I feel like I'd remember meeting someone as breathtaking as you."

Oh, brother. Harmony had been hit on plenty of times. Men liked her curvy figure and long, dark hair that fell halfway down her back in tight waves. Pickup lines that included *breathtaking,* however, usually came from men far older than Nolan. Honestly, this smooth-talker was nowhere near as impressive as his hulking beast of a dog.

"That depends," she answered cautiously. "Are you Nolan Murphy?"

His slow grin seemed oversized for his face. "None other. It seems my reputation proceeds me, then."

"Yeah, it's not that." She looked away to hide a smirk. It was a special pleasure of hers to keep male egos in check. "We went to school together."

"You remember Harmony King, don't you?" Abigail prompted.

Harmony saw the exact moment recognition flashed in Nolan's emerald eyes. "Oh, you were the girl—"

"Without a home, yeah. That's me. Hi." It always sounded worse coming from someone else's mouth, which is why Harmony chose to beat him to the punch instead. From pickup lines to punch lines, it turned out this would be a very memorable trip to the dog park, after all.

Nolan frowned and twisted his hand in his dog's shaggy fur. "That's not what I was going to say, but forget it. Who cares about the past when we all live in the present?" He winked at them, and Abigail fell apart in friendly laughter.

Harmony remained silent. The longer this conversation continued on, the more awkward she felt. Why wouldn't Nolan just take his dog and go back to his side of the park already?

"I haven't seen you in ages," Nolan told her, smiling once more. "Are you newly back in town?"

"Very newly," Abigail answered for her.

"Well, welcome back," he continued as if it were perfectly normal for someone else to be carrying on Harmony's side of the conversation when she was standing right there herself. "Maybe I can take you out some time, show you how things have changed?"

Harmony shook her head and looked away. "I don't think so, Nolan."

"Oh, okay. Have a nice day, then." Thankfully, he turned away without pressing for any further explanation as to her rejection.

Abigail frowned but didn't pester her, either. Nolan was the literal last man on earth Harmony wanted to date, other than maybe her ex, Alan. It might not have directly been Nolan's fault, but it was his sister—his very flesh and blood—who had made school especially hard for Harmony. Megan Murphy was the meanest of the mean girls, and she never let Harmony forget where she'd come from or where she belonged.

Which was to say nowhere.

She hoped it wasn't a bad omen that she had found a Murphy so soon after returning to town...

Chapter 8

HARMONY

Harmony stood beside Abigail as she rang the doorbell beside the large mahogany door fitted with stained glass panels.

"Just you wait. I'm coming!" an older voice called from inside. A moment later the door eased open to reveal a woman with white-blonde hair on her head and a string of plump pearls around her neck.

"I have a boarder for you, Mrs. Clementine," Abigail said, immediately handing her baby to the older woman who immediately broke out in an enormous grin.

"Well, isn't that nice? And you must be her." The woman turned to Harmony and stuck out her free hand in greeting. "Name's Virginia Clementine, and who might you be?"

"I'm Harmony. Thank you for agreeing to take me in," she mumbled. No matter how many times she rented a spare room from some widowed blue blood or middle-aged blue collar, it never got any less embarrassing as she was first getting settled. She felt like an imposter that day, just as she always had in the past when rotating between foster homes as a child.

"Honey, you're the one doing me a favor. It's been awfully lonely since Mr. Clementine took his promotion earlier this year. They have him on a new plane across the country just about every single week. How do you like that?"

Harmony nodded and smiled. She didn't know the first thing about working jobs that would actually pay for you to travel. From the looks of the grand hall before her, the Clementines earned a pretty penny for their troubles.

Some *trouble*, seeing the world!

"Muffin's coming with her, too. I hope that's all right." Abigail motioned to the little dog who'd already started sniffing around the cupboards in search of a spare crumb or some other such dog-approved treasure.

"That'll be just fine," Virginia said. "Any chance you'll be leaving little Owen, too?"

"Not a prayer," Abigail answered curtly, and both women laughed as if falling cue cards.

"I'll just go get Muffin's things," Harmony said, feeling like the odd one out in what was supposed to be her new home, however temporarily.

It took two trips to get all of the Chihuahua's things inside and only one to grab her own. Figured.

"Let me help you take these upstairs," Abigail offered.

"It's my old sewing room," Virginia instructed as she rocked the baby back and forth with wide, bouncing steps. "Just at the top of the stairs."

Harmony's new room turned out to be pretty nice, one of the nicest she'd stayed in in quite some time. The queen-sized bed was fitted with what appeared to be a homemade quilt, and she wondered if perhaps Virginia had made it herself to help stave off a loneliness she'd felt for longer than she'd initially let on. A large bay window looked out onto the backyard which was lined with palmetto trees—the official state tree of South Carolina, if memory served.

"I'll just give you some time to yourself," Abigail said, leaning up against the doorframe. "Unless you need anything?" The other woman seemed almost hopeful that Harmony would ask her to stay, but she needed nothing at this time and some solitude might do her good.

"Thanks for all your help today," Harmony answered with a small smile.

The other woman hesitated, then strode forward and gave Harmony an impromptu hug. "I know you've been through a lot and that you aren't telling us everything just yet, but I want you to know that I'm here for you. My father and Mrs. Clementine, too."

And with that, Abigail padded out of the room and latched the door shut behind her.

Everyone seemed so eager to help Harmony now that she'd returned to their lives. Was it because they wished they'd have done more when she was still living within the Holy City? Perhaps, but the course of Harmony's life was already set. Any form of lasting happiness surely wasn't within reach, but at the very least she could get by without any new and lasting pains, either.

A life of small mediocrities wasn't much to strive for, but it was the best Harmony could hope for now.

She sat down on her new bed, finding it pleasantly springy. It was then she remembered that in all her praying, she'd forgotten to thank God for the giant blessing he'd given her. "Thank you, Father, for helping me flee. Thank you for blessing my journey and delivering me to safety."

For there was no doubt in Harmony's mind now that she was safe here with these people who wanted to help and would protect her if any real dangers were to find her hiding here within this giant plantation-style house.

Trouble always did have a way of finding her out when she least expected it, but this time she would be ready.

Chapter 9

HARMONY

A scuffling sound came from the closed door, and Harmony rose to open it. Muffin trotted right in and stood on his hind legs, begging to be picked up. He looked like a very tiny, very unscary modern-day T-Rex, which instantly endeared him to her.

"C'mere, you," she said, reaching for the five pound package of fur.

Muffin let out a shrill bark and scurried under the bed, then ran out of the room with a piece of cloth clutched in his jaws. Harmony chased after him as he ran down the staircase and into the living room where Mrs. Clementine sat sipping a glass of sweet tea as the television played softly in the background.

"Abigail, Owen, and Mama Mary just left," the old woman explained. "And I'll be turning in for the night soon myself."

"Oh, okay," Harmony answered. It seemed mighty early for bed, but who was she to judge? Old people were just more tired, and while her new landlady didn't seem exceptionally old, she did appear to be worn down by life more than her fair share.

"Mind if I give you the grand tour first?" Virginia asked with a slight raise of one eyebrow.

"Yes, please do." Harmony waited as the other woman grabbed a thick coaster with a cartoon pig dancing on its front and set her tea down on top of it.

"All right," she said, rising to her feet and drifting in the direction of the kitchen. Muffin ran after her, still carrying the cloth in his mouth and shaking his tiny head every few steps as if he could kill what wasn't even living.

Harmony sped up and grabbed the dog, then took what turned out to be a lace doily from his clutches.

Virginia laughed. "Oh, let him have it. I have a million and one spares lying around this place. God never blessed me with children to call my own, and instead of getting mad or sad, I just picked up a needle and thread." My, she did reveal the source of her pain right up front. Harmony was never so bold when meeting new people. Did it mean Mrs. Clementine trusted her, or was this simply her way?

"The quilt on my bed is beautiful," Harmony said with an encouraging nod. "You do great work."

"It beats sitting around wondering why the Lord chose not to bless me with one of life's greatest gifts. I figured I might as well find some other way to make the world a nicer place, and so I added a bit of beauty."

Harmony didn't know whether to smile, apologize, or reach for a change of topic. Luckily, Virginia shifted into tour guide mode, freeing her from the burden of figuring out an appropriate response.

"Cups are in there." She pointed to the cabinet next to the fridge. "This drawer is for silverware." She pulled a drawer in and out demonstratively. "This arrangement is for room and board, so please eat and drink whatever you want. I always have way more than I need just for me."

"That's very kind of you, Mrs. Clementine," Harmony said. She felt like she was back in school. *Yes, Mrs. Thank you, Mrs.*

The older woman waved Harmony off. "Call me Virginia, or better yet, Ginny. Some folk even call me Gin. C'mon, now let me show you where all the bathrooms are."

Harmony followed Ginny around the house for the next half hour trying her best to commit everything to memory, but mostly just offering a listening ear and a bit of companionship. By the time the tour ended, Harmony was more than ready to call it a day. To think it had started before dawn with a six-hour-plus drive up to Charleston, then there was the church, the dog park, and now her new home. She'd left one man behind and refused another.

And still, she didn't know what was next for her. Well, at least she had a solid foundation for figuring it out tomorrow with the first light of a new sun.

Muffin followed her upstairs to her room. Somehow he seemed to know that he belonged with her. Maybe in some ways animals were smarter than people, after all. This little doggie kept close watch over his new mistress and immediately hopped up onto the bed beside her and cuddled in beside her hip.

Today had been a good day, she decided, and for that she was endlessly thankful. Tomorrow could be an even better day just as long as she remembered to keep her expectations low and her mind open.

A new life was waiting for her. She just had to keep being brave and mindful of her limitations. If God had wanted something else for her, surely He would have given it to her by now.

It was okay, though. It would all be okay.

Harmony closed her eyes and stroked the Chihuahua's smooth fur until at last she drifted off into a deep, comfortable sleep.

Chapter 10

PASTOR ADAM

I opened my eyes wide the second the sun peeked over the slight hill in our yard. As the years piled on, I'd begun waking up earlier and earlier. I often joked with Abigail that soon I wouldn't need to go to bed at all.

Yes, the wee hours of the morning suited me perfectly for my own personal prayers and reflections. There was something so special about being alone with God the Father before the rest of the world woke up and started making demands on the both of us.

After a quick hello to the Lord and a bit of reading in my Bible, I decided it would be a good time to call Mrs. Clementine to check on our weary traveler. As always, my old friend picked up after just one ring.

"It's like you know I'm calling before I do," I told her with the first smile of the day creeping across my face.

"I reckon perhaps maybe I do," she answered, a common exchange for us. Despite her oddities, I'd grown quite fond of my church secretary over the years. Truth be told, before Abigail returned to town and little Owen and the church dogs joined us, too, Virginia Clementine was the closest thing I had to actual family living in Charleston. She'd always seemed grateful for my company, too, and I was happy that the Lord had found a way to help her right along with Harmony.

"How is she?" I asked when Mrs. Clementine didn't immediately offer up the information I sought.

"She's still sleeping upstairs will little Muffin," she whispered. "Whatever happened to that poor child?"

I shook my head. "She only seems like a child because we're getting so old these days, but I do remember her when she was in school. That was before you'd joined our congregation. Almost ten years ago."

"She's very well mannered." She dropped her voice a couple of notches before continuing on. "But I'm afraid if I even raise my voice too loud in surprise she'll wind up cowering in the corner."

I couldn't stop the sigh that escaped me. "Harmony was never one to back away from a fight and I doubt that's changed now, but still, I don't like hearing how plainly she wears her pain."

"Actually, I think it's the pain that wears her." A soft tinkling of wind chimes sounded on Mrs. Clementine's end of the conversation, and I pictured her sitting on her back porch with a hot mug of tea in her hands. Morning was the only time she deigned to drink it warm. Tea, she always said, was meant to be served iced cold and with a good pound of sugar. I could scarcely argue with logic like that.

I fired up the coffeemaker for myself so I could join her with a beverage on my end of the line. "God brought her back into our lives for a reason, but I haven't figured out what that reason is just yet."

She laughed at my feeble attempts to understand the problems of a young woman like Harmony. "You mean God hasn't shown you yet. Honestly, Pastor Elliott, sometimes I wonder if it shouldn't be me up there giving the sermons each Sunday. You have a way of getting so deep in your meddling that you forget to wait for God to show His hand."

"And you, Mrs. Clementine, never hesitate to call me out."

She clucked and I could picture her sitting up straight with pride in her wicker chair. "Well, goodness, somebody's gotta do it. Might as well be me."

We chattered about church business for a few moments before saying goodbye. As hard as it was, Mrs. Clementine was absolutely right. The only thing we could do for Harmony now was to wait.

Wait and pray.

And add a little love, too, while we were at it.

Chapter 11

HARMONY

Harmony woke up much later than usual the next day, and in those precious first moments between sleep and consciousness, she lost all recollection of the events that had taken place the day before. Her heart picked up speed as she opened her eyes, then relaxed again when the memories came rushing back.

Muffin, of course, was there to lick the corners of her eyes and the insides of her ears, whining with joy as he did.

"Well, good morning to you, too," she said, patting the dog on the head and offering him a weary smile.

Muffin took this opportunity to lick inside of her mouth, too.

"Gross!" She brushed the Chihuahua aside with a sweep of her arm and used the other to wipe vigorously at her mouth and tongue.

Muffin jumped off the bed and went to scratch at the door impatiently. Oh, right. He probably needed to pee. Harmony did, too, but at least she could be trusted not to mess on the carpet. So she grabbed a cardigan from the top of her suitcase, draped it over her shoulders, and led the little dog downstairs.

Her new landlady was nowhere to be seen, but the clock above the stove informed Harmony that it was nearly ten o'clock. The rest of the world was probably already at work for the day—and that included Mrs. Virginia Clementine, too.

Her stomach grumbled as she eased open the sliding glass door and let the little dog run out into the palmetto-lined yard. He, of course, chose the very largest tree to do his business, lifting his leg proudly to splash the base of the thick trunk and then shuffling his hind feet like a cat trying to cover up a mess in its litter box.

Does he miss his brothers and sisters? Harmony idly wondered and for a moment felt jealous of her new companion. This little dog had more of a support network, more of a family than she'd ever had even for just one single day in her life.

Lucky little thing.

She sighed and leaned back against the house as she watched Muffin entertain himself by alternating bouts of sniffing with fast, flying leaps around the yard. When he'd seemed to tire himself out, she let him back inside and took him up to her room.

"You're going to be on your own for a little while," Harmony informed him as she pulled on her nicest pair of pants and a button-down shirt. "I need to go find a job so I can afford to pay for your kibble."

Muffin sat down on the edge of the rug and womped his tail on the ground.

"How do I look?" she asked him after dragging a tube of lip gloss across her lips and posing for her reflection in the mirror.

The Chihuahua tilted his head to the side and released a shiver so fierce that he practically fell over from the sudden motion.

"I don't think I speak your language just yet. Any chance of you learning English?" She should have felt ridiculous, carrying on a one-sided conversation with a dog, but Harmony actually found it quite comforting to have someone who would simply listen without forcing his opinions onto her.

Muffin tilted his head to the other side, ran in a tight circle, and then went back to scratch at the door.

"Sorry, Muffs. You've gotta stay here for now, but tell you what—if I do manage to find a job today, I'll bring you back a big bone to celebrate."

In response, Muffin dropped his tail between his legs, pressed his ears back against his head, and went to sulk under the bed. That was how Harmony felt about the situation, too, but she needed a job to keep her mind busy just as much as she needed it to pay the bills.

She and Virginia hadn't discussed the rental amount last night, meaning Harmony wasn't sure if she even had enough to cover the first week, let alone a few months or more of letting the room. The sooner she had a job, the sooner she'd have one less thing to worry about.

Please guide my steps today, she prayed silently as she passed halfway through the kitchen and paused near the fridge. After a quick debate on whether or not she should fix herself a bowl of cereal, she decided it was best not to impose upon Mrs. Clementine's kindness until she knew she'd have a way to cover the expense of her room and board.

With that decision made, Harmony's stomach grumbled again. It would have to make do with a handful of breath mints from the stash she kept buried somewhere in her purse.

"I'll find something. I will," she told her reflection in the rearview mirror. Desperation had a way of producing results, after all, and Charleston had hundreds of restaurants. Surely one of them would be in need of an experienced waitress.

Now all she had to do was keep her big mouth in line and remember to smile—*smile nonstop, never stop smiling.*

Harmony frowned at herself in the rearview mirror. Perhaps to get it out of her system, or perhaps because some part of her knew that trouble would find her no matter where she went, no matter how far away she got from Alan.

The best she could hope for was to delay the inevitable—and to find herself a job.

Here goes nothing...

Chapter 12

HARMONY

Harmony drove downtown and parked on the street in the first open spot she found. After using the last of her quarters to feed the meter, she began to search for an eatery that was hiring.

In the past, Harmony would have extended her hunt for a new job to the many retail shops that lined the city streets, but a few years back she'd faced such abuse from an unhappy customer that she'd vowed to only work at restaurants from that day forward. It didn't help that she'd told that rude customer exactly where she could place her non-returnable item —and it wasn't back in the box.

Oh, bless that bitter woman's heart!

She'd chosen downtown for her search not just for the variety of choices, but also because she preferred to avoid franchise restaurants if she could. Harmony had been through many jobs in the nine years since she'd set out on her own and had a fair number of rules when it came to selecting a good one: check the reviews on Yelp to make sure people like the food, order a meal to make sure they have good reason to like it, choose a place that's one of a kind even if it's a bit of a hole in the wall, and —most importantly—never date a coworker.

If there was one thing Harmony went through faster than jobs, it was dates. Maybe it was because she'd been waiting so long to have a family that she needed to make sure any man to whom she gave a permanent spot in her life fit said spot just right. Maybe it was because she was truly better off alone. Whatever the case, men had always disappointed Harmony, and she rarely gave them more than three dates to prove they weren't the one.

Alan had been the one exception. He'd hung on for nearly a year. Problem was, he didn't know when to let go. And even when Harmony suggested it was time to say goodbye, he dug his heels in and refused to let her leave.

Well, she sure showed him. She'd not only left their town, but she'd also put the entire state of Georgia between them for good measure.

Bless his heart, too!

Okay, she needed to stop mentally blessing everyone's hearts before she worked herself into total and irreversible agitation. Introducing herself to perspective employers when she'd already worked herself into a rage wouldn't suit her end goals one bit.

She popped another breath mint into her mouth and shoved the nearly empty container deep into her purse. Slow, centering breaths brought her back to a place where everyone's hearts had not been personally blessed and the birds once again sang merrily from their hidden perches within the trees and rooftops of the colorful buildings downtown.

Across the street a little window sign read "Now Hiring" in big, red letters. *Yes!*

Harmony looked both ways before jaywalking her way over to the other side. She never once took her eyes off that sign for fear it might up and disappear before she reached it. Now that she was standing right in front of the place, she did a quick Internet search.

"O'Brien's, Charleston," she murmured to herself as she typed the text into her browser. The Yelp reviews were good, an average of four-point-seven stars. The prices were mid-range and the hours were six to twelve. Every single item on the menu was related to breakfast—some offerings were classic and others she couldn't even begin to picture from the ridiculous-sounding names.

Whatever the case, it seemed like a good place to apply. If she worked here, she could get her hours in early and then spend the rest of the day however she pleased.

Perfect.

She pushed into the dining room and took in the bright interior with freshly upholstered booths and shining tile floors. The place appeared close to empty now that closing time was only an hour away. She hoped it was much busier during peak hours, but right now, beggars couldn't be choosers—and Harmony was definitely a beggar.

"Good morning, darlin'!" a blonde-haired, big-bosomed waitress called from behind a pot of coffee. "Go ahead and take a seat, and I'll be with you in two shakes of a lamb's tail."

Harmony strode across the dining room. Her shoes squeaked on the tiled floor but she tried not to feel embarrassed. "Actually, I'm here about the help wanted sign."

"Oh, that!" The woman, whose nametag read Jolene, returned the coffee pot to its warmer than brushed her hands on her apron as she grinned up at Harmony. "It's been there forever."

Harmony forced a smile until it hurt. "Are you not hiring anymore?" she asked as if the answer didn't have the power to determine her future happiness.

Luckily, Jolene talked fast and freely, putting Harmony's doubts aside almost as soon as they'd surfaced. "Oh, no. We are! We'd just kind of lost hope. That is, until you showed up. What's your name, sugar?"

Harmony introduced herself to Jolene, all the while wondering if this would be the easiest job she'd ever landed. It seemed the waitress was ready to hire her based on the fact that she'd simply shown up and asked.

"Well, Miss Harmony King, the boss isn't in today, but he trusts my opinion and he likes everybody besides. If you want the job, it's yours." Jolene caught her reflection in the stainless steel backsplash behind the coffee counter and fluffed her hair.

Was it really going to be this easy? Harmony shifted awkwardly from one foot to the other. "Um, don't you want my references or employment history?"

Jolene waved her off. "Nah, those don't matter so much. The best way to find out if you've got what it takes is to put you on the floor. Be here at five thirty tomorrow and we'll get you started."

They shook on it, and Harmony jotted down her number and address on the back of a placemat just in case Jolene needed to get in touch with her before then. That was all it took to put even more roots down in Charleston.

It hadn't been this easy in a long time, and Harmony knew her streak of good luck couldn't last. Yes, the coffee cup was definitely half-full, but at least she had something to drink.

Chapter 13

HARMONY

Harmony returned to the house and pushed her new key in the lock. A joyous fit of barking sounded from just on the other side of the door. Had Muffin managed to escape her room? She hoped he hadn't destroyed anything in the short time she'd been out, especially since she'd kept her promise and brought him a rawhide to celebrate her new job at O'Brien's. She'd also ordered a bit of takeout for herself so she could try out the restaurant's fare for herself before peddling it to customers.

When the door didn't open, she twisted the key the other way and gave it a good jiggle.

When finally she gained entry, she found Virginia waiting in the entryway. "Oh, I never lock it. I suppose I should, but I've always found it best to believe the best of others."

She chuckled, and Harmony bit her tongue. It was as if the old woman were rolling out the welcome mat for any robber within a hundred mile radius. Luckily, Harmony herself had nothing worth stealing, especially among all the many beautiful things the Clementines owned.

"I found a job," Harmony informed her, then told her the story of meeting Jolene at the diner.

Muffin stood on his hind legs with his head pointed straight up at Harmony's purse. A small whine escaped his throat and interrupted Ginny's story about that time when Jolene had botched her own baptism as a youngster.

"Sorry," Harmony said with a sigh. "I promised him a treat to celebrate the new job, and I guess he can smell it waiting for him." She pulled the rawhide from her purse and removed the shrink-wrap plastic. The thing was practically as big as Muffin himself, but he had no trouble picking it up and trotting off to enjoy it somewhere in peace.

Virginia shrugged into a pretty baby pink jacket. "I need to get back to the church. I just stopped in for a quick lunch break. By the way, you don't need to leave Muffin cooped up in your room all day. I know him and the other church dogs quite well and don't mind giving him free rein of the house. Same goes for you. Consider this whole place your home, not just that tiny room upstairs. Okay, I best be off. Bye!"

Harmony said goodbye, then headed to the kitchen to pour herself a glass of water and grab a fork for her omelet. She took everything back up to her room and sat cross-legged on her bed as she ate. While she appreciated Virginia welcoming her into her home, she also found the hospitality to be a bit overwhelming. Harmony had always found it far easier to belong in a small space—her room, her corner, her bed—than to have too much space in which to roam about. More space meant more chances for trouble, more chances for finding yourself in someone else's space, and that someone else becoming downright angry about it.

That's how she'd first met Alan. His first words to her had been, "That's where I sit." And those words were quickly followed by a sharp elbow to her ribs.

They'd both found themselves in one of those homes that collected foster kids like it collected head lice. What could one more hurt? And so they'd opened their home to Harmony and their wallets to the check from the state that came with her.

At the time there were four others, mostly older boys who could be put to work around the house and yard as needed. Alan was the youngest of them and it seemed he was grateful to finally have someone under him in the pecking order.

He'd been terrible to Harmony, but that had only lasted three weeks before he ticked off their foster mom and was sent packing. She never thought of him again until she randomly bumped into him in Mobile, Alabama a little over a year back. He'd apologized a blue streak, saying he'd been an angry kid but he was a different man now—a better one.

And Harmony believed him, partially because she understood the anger and partially because she had no reason not to. They began to seek each other out more and more until at last Alan had kissed her straight on the lips and declared himself in love.

For whatever reason, she believed that, too. Not only that, but she told him she loved him as well. And for a few glorious months she'd thought all the pieces of her life were finally popping into place. She and Alan spent every free moment with each other, and because she was happy, she kept her tongue in line and managed to keep her job for a record period.

Then he went and ruined it by asking her to move in with him.

The request surprised her as the notion didn't seem at all romantic. They'd both grown up tripping over several other kids in cramped rooms that should have only bunked two tops. Harmony liked having a space all to herself, and she wasn't ready to give that up yet.

Besides, moving in together would invariably lead to pressure to have sex, and she had long since promised God she would wait until marriage. It was a deal they had made when she was growing up. She'd asked God to keep her body safe from hands that would hurt her or take liberties not due to them, and in exchange, she would remain celibate until the day she decided to become somebody's wife—provided that day ever came at all.

Of course, Alan made the situation even worse by asking her to marry him later that week. She wasn't ready for that, either. Didn't he know she was still trying to learn to take care of herself properly? There was no way she was ready to double that burden by joining her life with someone else's on a permanent basis.

She'd politely declined, but in so doing had drawn a jagged red mark through the timeline of their relationship. The good times were all behind them, and what was to follow would only get worse by the day. This is what confirmed it for Harmony. People didn't change. Alan hadn't tossed aside his anger; he'd only buried it deep down.

And she'd foolishly come along with a shovel.

Chapter 14

HARMONY

The next morning, Harmony turned up at O'Brien's twenty minutes early for her shift. She always found it best to be extra punctual in the beginning so that her employers would forgive occasional necessary tardies later on.

Jolene was nowhere in sight, but the kitchen light appeared to be on. Harmony rapped gently at the glass.

A shockingly tall man emerged from the back and approached the door with squinted eyes. "Harmony?"

"Good morning, Nolan." She recognized him by his height more than his face. "Do you work here, too?"

"Own it, actually." He unlatched the door and let her slip inside. Thank goodness she'd discouraged his interest in her at the dog park a couple days back. Otherwise she'd have had to quit right there on the spot.

"Thank you for hiring me," she said, glancing around for something she could do both to prove herself useful and to escape Nolan's watchful gaze.

"I didn't hire you. Jolene did." He pointed toward the industrial-sized coffeemaker. "Want to get that started?"

"Oh, yeah. Yeah, sure." Coffee she could do. Working so close to someone she found so handsome, well...that had yet to be determined. The last thing she wanted after the whole ordeal with Alan was another relationship, especially with someone she already knew to be from bad stock. If Megan Murphy had tormented her all through school without ever feeling guilty about it, then her brother's moral compass couldn't be much better. It didn't matter that he was trying so hard to charm her now. His tune would swiftly change once her rejection sunk in.

"I'm glad she did, by the way," he called after her with an amused lilt in his voice.

At this point, her inner thought train had pulled so far out from the station, Harmony couldn't even remember what the two of them had been talking about. When she turned, he was still watching her from the same place by the door where he'd been standing before.

A small smile crept across his face and turned ridiculously large, like that of a little boy who hadn't quite grown into his features yet. "How's Muffin doing?" Nolan wanted to know.

Harmony shook her head. "What?"

"Your new dog?" There was that smirk again, the same smirk that seemed to imply he found her both tiresome and adorable. She did not like it one bit.

"Oh, right. Well, I'm only borrowing him for a spell, but he's doing just fine." She reached up to tuck a stray curl behind her ear.

Nolan's eyes lingered on her as she attempted to work.

"Am I doing something wrong?" she demanded, spinning around and placing a hand on each hip as she glowered at him. "Because you're kind of staring."

Oh, no, not yet! Rein in that temper. You can't afford to lose this job over something so silly as a man looking at you.

He laughed and shook his head. "Sorry about that. I'm just surprised you're here is all."

"Didn't Jolene tell you she'd hired me? I gave her all my information. Look, if this isn't going to work, I can go right now." She prayed he wouldn't call her on her bluff.

"Whoa there!" Nolan put both hands up in front of him as if he were dealing with a spooked horse. "Jolene had your information but accidentally misplaced it. She couldn't remember your name exactly, only what you looked like." He blew out an exaggerated puff of air. "But that's Jolene for you—great with people, terrible with names. When she described you, I had a sneaking suspicion, but I didn't know for sure until you turned up."

"Well, here I am, turned up and ready to work." She snapped the coffee basket back into place and pressed the brew button. "What do you need next? Should I check the condiment caddies? Refill the ketchup bottles?"

He stayed rooted to the spot and his eyes glued right on her face despite Harmony's constant moving about. "You sure know your way around a dining room, don't you?"

"I've done this rodeo before, but I kind of find it hard to work while I talk, especially while I'm still learning the ins and outs of someplace new." She crossed her arms over her chest and frowned.

He cocked his head, the same as Muffin liked to do. "So I need to stop distracting you. Is that what you're implying?"

"It's what I'm outright saying... sir." She added the sign marker of respect after an unnaturally long pause, but it seemed the best way to remind him of their positions. Surely he wouldn't want to date an employee, especially if O'Brien's actually needed the extra help as badly as Jolene had claimed.

He crossed his arms over his chest and studied her for a moment without speaking, then he licked his lips and said, "Why don't you take a few minutes to get acquainted with the menu? Jolene will be here soon, and then she can walk you through the rest."

She nodded and paced her way back toward the hostess stand to grab one of the oversized menus, then sank into the nearest booth and opened it up.

Nolan watched her every movement until he finally—*finally!*—

returned to the back of the house to work on getting the kitchen ready for breakfast.

Though she did her best to learn the ingredients in each dish, the words blurred before her eyes. The last time a man had paid such close attention to her, it had turned into the stormy relationship that had sent her running straight out of Alabama.

Chapter 15

PATOR ADAM

When I called Mrs. Clementine this morning to check in on our visitor, she informed me that our girl had found a job working at O'Brien's. Seeing as I hadn't treated myself to a meal out in quite some time, I decided to pay her a visit around about eleven o'clock when I knew most of the crowd would be cleared out and she'd have some time to talk.

"Morning, Pastor Adam!" Jolene Brown called with two giant heaps of pancakes stacked high on her tray. "Take a seat and I'll be with you in a moment."

I waved hello and then took a seat in a booth toward the back of the restaurant.

Harmony found me not two minutes later. "Virginia told you about my job," she said, tapping her fingers at the edge of my table before grabbing a little notepad from her apron and a pen from behind her ear. "What can I get you to eat?"

I declined the menu she offered. "Whatever you recommend," I told her with a smile I hoped she'd find reassuring.

She scrunched her mouth to one side, then said, "I don't know enough to recommend anything, although judging from the rush today, our French toast seems to be quite well received."

I laughed. French toast at an Irish restaurant—of all the things! Well, to each their own. "That sounds great," I told her. "How has your first day been?"

Harmony shrugged. "Good enough, I suppose."

I nodded. Harmony had never been the effusive type. She'd always had to be drawn out a bit before she would freely share what was on her mind. "And how are you and Muffin getting on?"

She couldn't hide the small smile that spread to her lips. "Better than I expected."

"And Mrs. Clementine?"

"A very gracious host."

I raised an eyebrow. *But?*

"What makes you say there's a but?"

"Well, there aren't a lot of other words you're saying, so I figured just maybe something was holding you back."

She sighed, glanced back at the kitchen over her shoulder, and then took a seat across from me in the booth. "But I have no idea what comes next," she confided.

"Folks worry too much about tomorrow. Just live today the best you can and tomorrow will take care of itself."

Harmony bit her lip. Was it to keep from saying something she thought I wouldn't appreciate? "You're right," she said after a moment. "Of course, you're right. Um, I should get back to work."

She didn't give me the chance to argue, and before I knew it, she had skittered off to the back of the house. Jolene brought me my French toast several minutes later, and I didn't see Harmony again the entire duration of my breakfast.

"The new girl a friend of yours?" Jolene asked later when she was refilling my half-full coffee mug.

I let the steam warm my face, inhaling the rich, earthy scent. Normally I didn't drink caffeine so late in the day, but partaking in a proper sit-down breakfast without a mug of coffee to go with it just might qualify as a sin. "Mmm, from a long time back," I told her.

"That's good," the waitress said before dropping her voice a couple notches and leaning closer to my table. "Because it seems she could really use one."

"Can't we all?" was my response.

Jolene laughed as she swept away from my table, her full hips swinging back and forth. A lot of men about town liked those hips very much, but none had ever managed to nail down their owner for a lifetime commitment.

I finished my meal and drained the last of my coffee knowing full well I'd be up later than I'd normally like that night, then left a tip for each of them and headed out.

I'd made it halfway down the block when the door to the restaurant burst back open and footsteps pounded toward me. When I turned, I saw Harmony standing with her arms crossed against the cold.

"Thank you for all your help," she said. "You really help me to feel like maybe I do belong here after all."

"Ain't no maybe about it." I turned to face her right there on the sidewalk. "Welcome home, Miss King."

If I'd been wearing a hat, I'd have tipped it in her direction. But since I wasn't, I just smiled and carried on my way.

Chapter 16

HARMONY

At Nolan's instruction, Harmony flipped the open sign to closed and pulled the blinds shut. Her shift had been busier than she'd expected, but she'd fallen into a nice rhythm with Jolene and ended up with a handsome wad of tips in her apron by the end of the breakfast rush.

"Oh, hold the door!" Jolene called, hurrying toward her just as she was about to flip the lock. "Thank you, sugar. See you tomorrow!" And she was out the door before Harmony had time to question it.

When she turned back toward the dining room, she found Nolan wiping down the warming shelf and staring daggers—or more accurately, hearts and flowers—her way. "I told her she could go on early. Carolina—that's her daughter—is home from college on winter break, and I know Jolene wants all the time she can get before she has to head back. Besides, it gives the two of us time to talk."

Harmony scratched at her elbow and glanced around the emptied out space. "You sure do like to talk," she mumbled just hardly above a whisper, but Nolan heard her anyway and let out a boisterous chuckle in response.

"As a matter of fact, talking *is* my favorite. You did a great job today.

MELISSA STORM

The customers loved you." His eyes fell to her mouth as if he wanted to say more but didn't know if it would be welcome.

Harmony scowled at him, but Nolan didn't seem to get the message.

"I thought about it all day, and I do remember you from our school days. You were the cool girl that didn't care what anybody else thought of her. I liked that about you even though I was probably too young to register on your social radar."

Harmony turned her back to him and let out a deep breath. He really had no idea. Of course she had cared what others thought of her. She was a teenaged girl, for crying out loud! And it was Nolan's own sister who had made her days in class almost as difficult as her nights in foster care.

Once Harmony had managed to catch the movie *Carrie* playing on a cable news channel in one of those very rare occurrences where she had a house to herself for the evening. After that, she had spent months praying to God that He'd gift her with the same psychic abilities with which she could defend herself.

Granted, Megan Murphy and her lackeys had never gone so far as to shower her in pig's blood, but she suspected that was because her wild, wicked tongue made them just a little bit afraid of her. However much they were or weren't afraid of Harmony then, it was enough to avoid any physical altercations and—quite thankfully—expulsion, too.

She turned back around and offered Nolan a gracious smile without saying anything. She didn't trust herself with words just yet.

Please stay quiet. Please stay quiet, she tried to whisper to him telepathically, but as it turned out, God still hadn't granted her Carrie's gift even all these years later.

"Would it be weird if the two of us had some breakfast together?" Nolan asked, coming out from behind the kitchen wall. "Because if you give me just five minutes, I could—"

"Yes!" Harmony said too loudly to be considered polite. "Yes, it would be weird. You're my boss. You shouldn't be hitting on me or forcing me to talk when I've made it very clear I'm not interested. It's highly inappropriate."

220

Nolan's face fell. "I'm sorry if I made you uncomfortable. I just thought you could use a friend."

"Well, I can't. Okay?" She glared at him, wondering if she should cut her losses and run right then and there.

Her new boss just kept talking, and he kept being nice, too, which irked her to no end. "I can still make you breakfast, if you're hungry. You look like you could use a hot meal in you."

Something unpleasant bubbled inside Harmony, and before she knew it, she'd boiled over. She cursed at Nolan, then added, "Will you just leave me alone already?" Too late she realized that this was not how you talked to your new employer if you wanted to keep your job and, despite everything, she did.

Well, shoot.

If Nolan was angry, he did an admirable job of hiding it. Instead, his eyes softened and he asked, "Who hurt you so bad, Harmony? Who made you afraid of the world?"

His kindness in the face of her temper shook her just enough to bring Harmony back to her center. "You really don't know, do you?"

"Know what?" he asked gently, risking a step closer, but only one.

"You may as well scramble up those eggs. This could take a while."

Chapter 17

HARMONY

Less than ten minutes later they were both sitting before steaming plates of that day's breakfast special: eggs, bacon, sausage, grits, and fried green tomatoes.

"Why is this place called O'Brien's if your last name is Murphy?" Harmony asked Nolan as she sprinkled a liberal dose of pepper into her eggs.

"So *now* you want to make small talk?" Nolan shook his head. "Because earlier when I tried to do the same, you kind of cussed me out."

Her face burned hot as he watched and waited for her response. "Sorry about that," she mumbled.

Nolan reached out and took her hand. After giving it a quick, friendly squeeze, he let go again. "It's okay. I understand, and it's one of the things I like about you."

Harmony let out a sarcastic laugh. "That I'm mean?"

"That you're *passionate.*" His eyes widened as he said that last word to add an extra pop of emphasis.

"You think you know me, but you're wrong. I'm not passionate about a single thing on God's green earth. I just have a wicked temper."

"Well, you're fighting hard for something. Maybe it's time you figured out what that is."

She laughed again and set her fork down on the edge of the plate. "Next you're going to tell me you moonlight as a shrink. Wait, do you?"

"No, but I have a passion for people." So he was an amateur counselor then, or just had a profoundly unusual interest in Harmony herself. She didn't much care for either option.

"And I have a passion for avoiding people," she shot back with a grin. At least her wit didn't fail her when it came to Nolan Murphy, even if her judgment seemed to be somewhat on the fritz.

He took a giant chug of orange juice, then wiped his mouth with the back of his hand. "The O'Briens are my cousins. None of them wanted to devote their life to the restaurant business, so it fell to me."

"What?" So much for having her wits about her.

"You asked about the restaurant, and now you know. So then, I believe you were going to tell me something important, which is why you deigned to have breakfast with me."

She smiled despite herself. Nolan was wearing her down, which could prove to be very dangerous if she wasn't careful. "It's good, by the way. The food."

He nodded and took a bite from the center part of his grits where all the butter had pooled, turning it into an extra delicious treat.

Harmony did the same. By the time she worked up the courage to tell him her story, they'd both already finished their full and very generous servings of grits.

"You asked who hurt me," she said. "The simple answer is everyone. The more complicated answer is your sister specifically."

Nolan dropped his fork and it clattered onto the table with a *clink, clink, clink.* "Megan?"

"She was horrible to me. Never let me forget I was foster trash and that I was in that position because my parents didn't want me enough to stay alive and nobody else wanted me enough to give me a forever home. She called it a forever home like I was some stray dog waiting to be adopted from the shelter. Well, I guess she was right about that part." But, no, even dogs got adopted eventually. Harmony had remained without a home her entire childhood. She often wondered why they hadn't just euthanized her if she was really such a burden to everyone who crossed her path.

Nolan stopped eating and stayed stock still, then started shaking his head as if in disbelief. "I just...I had no idea. Did she hit you, too? Hurt you in other ways?"

Why did it have to leave a bruise for people to consider the abuse she'd been through real? "No physical violence, no. Only damaged me to my emotional core which, in my very humble opinion, is far worse."

Nolan crossed his arms and leaned back against the seat, continuing to shake his head, though he appeared to believe her now. "No wonder you hate me."

"I don't hate you," she said reflexively, realizing then that in some ways she did. Fortunately, this talk was helping her to get beyond those feelings —not too far, but it was a start. "Okay, I *did* hate you, but I kind of hate most people. Don't take it personally."

His eyes fell to her mouth as he asked, "Do you hate me still?"

"You gave me a job." She shoved a forkful of eggs into her mouth as soon as she spoke those words, hoping to turn his attention elsewhere.

And his unblinking gaze moved to her eyes. "That's not what I asked."

Harmony finished chewing and swallowed hard. The eggs had gone cold on her tongue. "No, I don't hate you, Nolan, but I don't share your interest, either."

"Because of my sister? I'm sorry she made school hard for you. She did the same thing to me, too. We weren't close then, and we aren't close now, so please don't assume I'm anything like her."

She took another bite to avoid talking. What else was there to say?

Nolan seemed to have it figured out. His eyes flashed with something she couldn't quite identify, then he said, "Would it help if I told you she dropped out of college and works as a cashier at Publix and is generally a very unhappy person?"

"No, seeing as I never went to college, am newly hired as a waitress, and am as unhappy as they come." There she went acting ungrateful again. She was happy to have the job, but she needed Nolan to lose that light that shone in his eyes whenever he looked at her. The fastest and easiest way to do that was to quash the beginning sparks of his attraction before they had the chance to grow into something truly dangerous.

He leaned toward her again, apparently not even the slightest bit deterred. "I don't believe that."

She shrugged. "Believe it or don't. It's no skin off my nose."

"Why'd you come back to Charleston? Why now?"

"It felt the safest place for me," she answered honestly, even though she knew full well it would be the first place Alan searched for her when he realized she'd left Alabama. She'd just have to deal with that when they got to it.

Nolan leaned forward again; his eyes held a new intensity as he studied her. "Are you in danger?"

"Not any more than usual," she answered truthfully. "Anyway, I'm sorry I was rude to you. Please don't fire me. I'll be better, I swear."

"I'm not going to fire you, Harmony, and I'll stop pressuring you to go out with me, but I would really like to be your friend if you'll let me." He put his hand on hers so that her much smaller fingers disappeared beneath his palm. A warmth she couldn't deny spread from her hand all the way up her arm and into her heart.

"I guess I can live with that," she whispered, hoping that it would prove to be true.

Chapter 18

HARMONY

The week that followed turned out to be strangely sublime. Harmony worked each morning at O'Brien's, then spent the afternoons snuggling with Muffin and exchanging backstories with Virginia as the older woman taught her to work a pair of knitting needles.

She saw Pastor Adam and Abigail more days than not, and with all the folks who now regularly frequented her life, she was beginning to feel a strange sense of belonging. A warmth glowed inside of her at the thought, but fear still shook her to the core.

Alan could still come to find her.

Would still come to find her.

She would have to run again and leave all these good people behind.

Muffin would be all right. He could go back to the church, and maybe in her next town she could adopt a dog in need to be her permanent companion. Because, yes, despite her initial hesitation, the little yapper had grown on her.

She hated the thought of another human in bed with her and had not once let Alan sleep over when they were dating, even though he'd begged on many occasions and even tried to force himself on her once or twice, too. But having Muffin glued to her side throughout the night gave her a special feeling of comfort she'd never quite had before.

For all his craziness and all their years apart, Pastor Adam had known exactly what she needed when he paired her with the spirited Chihuahua. Maybe one day Harmony would take to carrying him with her in a fancy shoulder bag after all.

She felt safer when Muffin was near, too. For one thing, he had a way of barking at even the slightest unexpected sound from outdoors. That meant no one could sneak up and surprise her. And for another, she knew Muffin would always have her side and didn't even doubt he'd bite a few ankles if he sensed danger.

It was amazing what five pounds of love could do to transform one's state of mind, or more specifically, *her* state of mind.

Harmony tied off the final row of stitches on her newly finished handicraft and lifted it triumphantly for Mrs. Clementine to admire. "Ta da, my first scarf!" she cried, feeling really quite proud despite the crooked rows and loose knit of the garment.

"Oh, let me get a picture." The landlady grabbed her phone and Harmony posed happily with her creation. Yes, life seemed worryingly simple these past several days.

And every day another of her walls crumbled, the people who were near to her moving deeper and deeper into her heart. Was this what God wanted for her? Is that why He'd sent her migrating back to the Holy City? Or was she being foolish to believe that things could ever change for her, especially after so many years of hardship?

It was almost as if she'd stumbled onto a family of her own. If Pastor Adam was her stand-in father, then surely Mrs. Clementine would be her mother and Abigail a sister, even little Owen a nephew. Jolene had become a close friend. As to Nolan, well, she was still deciding where he belonged in her life. Big brother didn't seem like the right label given their mutual attraction, but she sure as sugar didn't think of him as a husband, potential or otherwise.

That would be the day!

After her experience with Alan, she doubted she'd ever be able to stomach the idea of marriage at all. He'd, of course, asked her many times to become his wife, and each time she'd declined. She'd known something was off between them, but she didn't know enough to figure out what, didn't know how a healthy relationship should actually look.

Matter of fact, she still didn't know. Maybe it wasn't all that important for her to figure out, though.

Maybe it was enough to keep living each day on its own like stitches in a row—loop enough together and you could make something truly beautiful.

"I have some patterns if you'd like to start a new project," Virginia said as she showed Harmony the burst of pictures she'd taken just then. "Or I could show you how to macramé, needlepoint, or quilt. You name it, and we'll do it."

"It's a little chilly outside these days," Harmony said after a moment's thought. "Could you teach me to knit a sweater for Muffin?"

Yes, she was only a few degrees away from crazy when it came to fondness for her new dog, and perhaps a few dozen loops or so away from having a strong base for her new life.

Just so long as her past didn't come calling, her future might turn out very bright indeed.

Chapter 19

HARMONY

Harmony was granted the following day off work. Well, more like Nolan had insisted she take at least one day's break each week and refused to argue the point. Luckily, the tips at O'Brien's were good and the people friendly. She'd already paid Virginia for an entire month's room and board and still had a bit of cash on hand for something fun to pass the time.

She started with a long, leisurely visit to the dog park, because Muffin deserved a treat on their day off together, too. After that, she swung by the craft store and picked out a new pair of knitting needles in her favorite color, a shiny metallic red, along with a few attractive skeins of yarn as a thank you to Virginia for all the lessons and for so generously sharing her stash.

In that same strip mall sat a salon called Beauty by Belle. Harmony had never been much for pampering or fussing over her appearance, but now that she thought of it, a change did seem long overdue. Alan had loved her long, dark wavy hair. It would be freeing to change it up, not to mention so much easier to get ready in the morning.

She pushed her way into the mostly empty salon where a tiny, jingling bell announced her arrival.

"Have a seat, shugs, and I'll be right with you!" someone called from the back.

Harmony plopped into the chair closest to the door and studied herself in the mirror. She'd worn her minimalist makeup the same way since high school and had never done anything trendy or daring with her hair. Yes, it was definitely time for a change—perhaps a radical one. At worst she wouldn't like it and would find herself stuck with an unpleasant change until her hair grew back with a vengeance. At best she'd be euphoric with the new look and less recognizable should Alan come searching for her.

Because even though a good bit of time had passed, she still didn't believe she was out of the woods yet. He'd turn up eventually and find a very different Harmony waiting for him. Maybe he'd stop being attracted to her, too.

If only she could be so lucky.

"What can I do for you today?" a red-headed woman who looked to be about Harmony's age asked as she came up behind her in the chair. She wore a brightly colored maxi dress in a light floral pattern and thick combat boots that had surely seen better days.

"Something totally different," Harmony announced with an excited bounce of her shoulders.

The stylist wrinkled her nose. "Are you sure? Cuz a lot of time women come up in here saying the same thing but then wind up complaining that it's *too* different. And I lose myself a customer. Name's Avery, by the way, Avery Hollis."

"I'm Harmony, and—yes—I am 100% sure. Can you make it the exact opposite of what it's like now? I can take it." She waited, praying the woman would not only agree but come up with something fabulous.

Avery walked a slow circle around Harmony, taking in all her angles. "So seeing as you're long, dark, and curly as a before, I'm guessing you might like short, straight, and blonde as an after? How much time have you got?"

"As much time as it takes," Harmony said, wiggling her butt in the chair with anticipation.

"Belle!" the stylist hollered toward the back of the house, startling Harmony by her sudden switch in volume. "Can you whip up a batch of bleach for me?"

"Sure thing!" came the cheery response.

"First I'll do a quick cut," Avery explained, snapping her scissors playfully. "Then we'll bleach ya, dye ya, and finally, we'll finish you up with an angled bob. Good?"

"Great." Harmony could hardly wait. Maybe all the time she now spent creating pretty things with Virginia was starting to rub off on her a bit more than she'd realized.

Avery spun her chair in a full circle. Her eyes widened as she said, "All right. Looks like we're going to have ourselves some fun this afternoon. Now, seeing as we'll be here for quite some time, you may as well start with your life story. Make it good. I do so love being entertained while I work."

Harmony swallowed, coughed, then licked her lips to stall for time.

"Oh, honey! Relax! You don't have to tell me anything you don't want to. It's just a lot of people use this chair as if'n they're in a shrink's office. You won't believe the things folks will confide in me when I'm wielding these here scissors."

"Actually," Harmony said, coming up with an idea she rather liked. "I'd much rather hear about you."

Avery crossed her arms and shifted her weight so that one hip jutted out to the side. "About me, huh? Well, whatcha want to know?"

Harmony shrugged. "Start at the beginning?"

The stylist put one hand on her hip and snipped the scissors animatedly in her other hand as she thought. It was only then Harmony noticed just how thin the other woman was. Her full collarbone jutted out from her chest like a cylinder had just been stuck on for good measure. She could also see the faint outlines of her uppermost ribs.

Avery caught Harmony staring and quickly turned toward the counter that held her supplies. "Is it a bit cold in here?" she asked as she extracted a lumpy cardigan from the bottom drawer and shoved her arms into it, clearly embarrassed by the exchange.

"Have you seen Josephine Hannah's newest movie yet?" Harmony asked with a smile, hoping the change of topic would set Avery back at ease.

"The one that takes place in Alaska, you mean?" The stylist took a deep breath and began to spritz her client's hair with a hot pink water bottle.

"That's the one. I haven't found the time just yet, but I heard it's her best to date. They say she actually fell in love while filming it, you know."

"With that hunky fireman?" Avery set the water bottle down and took the first of many snips with her scissors.

"Yes, he's a real cutie. Isn't he?" Harmony said amicably, even though Josephine Hannah's newest flame was not even close to her type. She preferred tall, blonde, and pushy, but no way was she ever going to admit that aloud.

"He sure is, but have you seen the new actor who's playing opposite Jo-Han in her next film?"

The two women laughed and carried on as new acquaintances with shared interests do. Harmony suspected she wasn't the only one who preferred to keep the conversation light and easy. She said a silent prayer that everything was all right in Avery's world and that everything would stay right with hers.

Oh, and that they wouldn't run out of handsome celebrities to discuss before Harmony's new hairstyle was finished.

Chapter 20

PASTOR ADAM

That day I brought Cupcake to my office with me for a bit of added company. The poor pup had been particularly disheartened since our Muffin moved out on assignment, so Abigail and I both tried to show her some extra love when we could.

I had a couple appointments scheduled for newlywed counseling, but mostly a quiet day to tend to my devotions and prepare my next sermon. Mrs. Clementine came in for a short while to discuss numbers and bills and whatnot, but I told her—as I always do—that I'd much rather she take charge of that so I'd know it was in capable hands instead of my own fumbling fingers.

By four o'clock, I was getting ready to head on home, but an unexpected visitor found me before I'd made any of the usual motions to leave. Cupcake stood ramrod straight and stared at the door, a low growl sounding from her throat.

"Oh, you, hush now," I told the Chihuahua as I nudged her gently with the side of my foot, then called to our guest, "C'mon in!"

A fashionable young woman strode in with sunny yellow locks cut short against her neck. It took me a good thirty seconds to realize I knew her. "Harmony?" I gasped and covered my mouth with my hand in an attempt to minimize the rudeness of my unplanned gesture.

"I changed my hair," she said with a small grin.

"I see that," was my reply. "It's quite becoming."

Truth was, I liked her hair better in its previous incarnation, but Harmony seemed lighter, happier with this change, which made me like it very well for the aforementioned reasons.

"Thank you," she mouthed without quite voicing the words aloud.

"How can I help you this afternoon?" I prompted. Folks like Harmony didn't just show up unannounced for no reason.

She glanced around my office, then, seeing Cupcake, stooped down to pick her up and shower her with kisses. Ha, I'd known there was a dog person hidden in there!

When that Chihuahua was acceptably covered in kisses, Harmony looked back up at me and said, "Seeing as my head feels tons lighter, I figured it might also be time to unburden my soul." She shrugged as if she hadn't just said something monumental, especially for her.

"If you're looking to confess, there's a nice Catholic church right down the street," I joked. "But if you're here to seek counsel, then I'm all ears."

"Actually, it's a bit of both." She sank onto the couch and Cupcake settled onto her lap, then flipped on her side to demand a belly rub.

"Go ahead when you're ready and I'll do my best to help in whatever way I can."

She smiled, frowned, smiled again. Clearly it wasn't easy for her to be here, and I appreciated that she had sought me out despite her reservations. "I want to tell you why I came back to Charleston," she began, and the words that followed sent a special blend of sadness and rage to my very core.

That poor, poor child...

Chapter 21

HARMONY

"I'm here to talk about Alan." Harmony kept her eyes glued to the dog in her lap as she spoke. That made it easier to tell the full details of what had happened to trigger her Charleston homecoming. "I just heard word for Jolene that he's back in town and looking for me. Figured that meant it was time someone knew the full story. In case..." Her voice cracked, and she paused, unable to finish voicing the horrible thought aloud.

"Go ahead," the pastor told her. "I'm a good listener."

She let out a slow, shaky breath. Might as well start from the beginning, or at least their reintroduction as adults.

"Well, at first being with him was really nice," she told the pastor. "Like I'd finally found someone who understood what I'd been through and didn't judge me for it. It was freeing in a way, knowing he just got it without me having to say a word, that it wouldn't be a problem later."

Pastor Adam nodded and steepled his fingers in front of his face as he listened. His expression remained neutral, although Harmony was certain hers flashed a full range of emotions.

"He was the perfect boyfriend as long as I never did anything to upset him. That's why it took me so long to notice something was wrong." She paused and shook her head. There were no tears left to cry, not for Alan and certainly not for herself. "I remember thinking that I was so lucky, that I'd finally found a family and that Alan and I were it, that we'd be together forever. He was attentive, showered me with compliments, was generous with his time and what little money he had, but it seemed there was a darkness in him."

She shivered as she recalled the first time she'd watched as something change in his eyes. The love he always wore transformed into the brightest burning hatred she'd ever seen in anyone. "One night I went out with some friends after work. I hadn't called to let Alan know since he had plans himself that evening, but when I got home, he was standing by my open door, waiting, glaring out into the darkness. He'd busted in, said he was worried when I hadn't answered my phone, thought something was wrong, that he loved me so much and couldn't stand the thought of anything happening to me. I'd told him my phone died, apologized a million times, and then we moved on. Things were good again for another few weeks after that."

The Pastor leaned back in his chair and crossed his arms over his chest, staying quiet because she still had words pouring out of her. Now that she'd started this difficult conversation, she just couldn't bring herself to stop until she reached the very end.

"He started checking in more often, making sure I called him once in the afternoon and once in the evening, asking about even the minutest details of my day. I started to consider myself lucky again, chalked it up to him just having had a bad day that one time. We all have bad days, right?"

Pastor Adam frowned, but nodded his head all the same.

Harmony let out a sad laugh and shivered again. The little dog in her lap had fallen asleep to the sound of her voice and was now having a dream that spurred her to twitch his legs and make tiny, whimpering sounds.

She took a deep breath and continued. "When he asked me to move in with him, I can honestly say I considered it, but in the end, I decided I'd rather keep my promise to God about staying pure. He took it hard, and even though he tried to hide his dissatisfaction, I felt something shift between us again. Not even a week later he asked me to marry him. He wanted to drive off to city hall that very moment—no more waiting, not even for a day.

"I knew he thought he was sweeping me up in this big, romantic moment, but honestly, I was scared. It was like the connection between us had severed and he no longer understood what I wanted or how I felt. When I said no, he asked if I was breaking up with him. I said no to that, too.

"And he started crying big, fat tears like I'd never seen a man cry before. He said if he lost me, he'd go crazy. He wouldn't know what to do. Maybe he would just kill himself now, he said, to save us both the trouble. I convinced him to stop crying, stop saying those horrible things. Told him I loved him, held him for a long time."

Pastor Adam sucked air in through his teeth, suggesting he knew exactly what was coming next.

And so she continued. "The next day he was obscenely happy, happier than I'd ever seen him. He'd brought over takeout from our favorite Chinese place, and we sat together on the couch to eat it and watch reruns on the cable TV. On a commercial break, he turned to me and said he'd given it a lot of thought... mind you, it had been less than twenty-four hours since our altercation the night before. He'd given it lots of thought, he said, and we didn't need a piece of paper in order to be married. We were already married in our hearts and we belonged to each other, and then he kissed me. He wouldn't stop. He pushed farther and farther, way past anything we'd ever done before, covered my body with his, and I could feel..."

Her voice cracked. "I could feel what he had planned, and it wasn't what I wanted. Not one bit. He kept coming at me even when I begged him to stop, and so I bit him. Hard. I bit him so hard, his lip was just spewing blood, and he called me awful names, then threw me off the couch so hard that the glass coffee table shattered from the force of me slamming into it. I ran and locked myself in the bathroom, begging him to go away.

"The next morning, my landlord stopped by, told me there had been too many complaints from the other tenants and I had until the end of the day to pack my things and move on. Alan didn't come round that day, I have no idea why. He called and seemed fine. We made plans to meet the next day because I figured that would keep him away long enough for me to get gone without him having to know where.

"He called at midnight to say he loved me. I didn't let him know that I had slept on a coworker's couch, that I had tossed most of my earthly possessions in a dumpster outside my old building. And the next day I woke up before the sun, grabbed my backpack, and left for Charleston."

She paused. Her shaky eyes locked onto his as she revealed, "The next person I spoke to was you."

Chapter 22

HARMONY

Harmony felt better now that someone else knew about what she'd been through with Alan, along with the disturbing fact that it likely wasn't over yet. Pastor Adam re-extended his offer for regular counseling and also suggested she go to the police, said he had a good friend in law enforcement who could keep an eye out for trouble.

She told him she'd consider both offers, thanked him for listening, and headed home to Virginia's. Along the way she wondered if she should try to purchase a gun to defend herself from the inevitable. She even went so far as to pull into the lot outside the tiny shack-like building that sold firearms and ammunition.

But no, she couldn't.

As much as she didn't want to die, she'd much rather Alan kill her than have to live with the knowledge that she'd willingly chosen to end someone else's life. Even if it was self-defense and she was thus never punished for taking action, her mind would still slowly deteriorate. Ultimately, she'd go mad with the guilt.

And that wasn't a price she was willing to pay.

Not even to guarantee her own safety.

She'd need to rely on her own wits, watchfulness, and a tiny

Chihuahua who would do anything to keep her safe. Thankfully, God was always with her, too.

At home, she found Nolan and Pancake sitting on the front porch waiting for her return.

"Jolene told me everything!" he said, rushing forth to give her a tight hug. "Why didn't you tell me you were in danger?"

She pushed back from his chest, trying to ignore how good it felt to be wrapped in his strong embrace, to have someone who cared. "What makes you think I'm in danger?"

"Well, for starters, you're shaking like a leaf. Also, Jolene has her way of getting a good read on people. She said that the man who came for you was on the search for no good." His normally cheerful face twisted with rage. It figured he'd heard the news as well. Jolene told everything to everybody, but at least she'd kept mum when it came to Alan's request for information.

"Did you get his name?" she asked, unable to deny her fear anymore.

Nolan shook his head and swore under his breath. "No, he wouldn't give it. Jolene said he was just under six foot tall with dark hair and eyes. He was wearing track pants and a concert shirt but she couldn't remember the band."

"Sounds like Alan to a T. No one else would be looking for me besides him."

"What does he want?" Nolan placed a hand on her arm. He was shaking, too.

"I don't know. Revenge on me for leaving him? Or, maybe just the opposite, that he wants to convince me to give him another try." Harmony sucked air through her teeth, but it wasn't enough to steady her or calm Nolan.

"You've got to be kidding me." He ran both hands through his hair and kicked at the pavement leading up to Mrs. Clementine's wrap-around porch.

"I wouldn't kid about something like this," she shot back. "I left and got as far as I could as quick as I could for a reason."

"Did he hurt you? Before you left? Was he...?" Nolan shook with rage so much so that she now felt the need to place a calming hand on his arm.

"Yes," Harmony told him. "Yes, he did hurt me, and I'm pretty sure he'd do it again if he got the chance. I'm not sure he meant to but—"

"But nothing!" Nolan exploded, causing Harmony to take a step back. "It's never okay. Never."

Pancake stood to his full height and let out a low growl. Inside the house, Muffin barked manically, begging to be let out to join whatever fight was unfolding.

"I have to get him before he goes nuts," she said to Nolan. "Try to calm down some. I don't want Muffin thinking he has to protect me from you."

The little dog squeezed through the doorway before Harmony could even open the door wider than a few inches. Once outside, he raced in a big loop, searching for the source of the agitation. When he deemed Nolan and Pancake to be of no danger, he trotted back to Harmony and stood on his hind legs, asking to be picked up.

"It's okay, Muffs." She scratched the little dog between his ears. He looked so proud of his guard-dogging efforts that she couldn't help but smile.

"I won't let him hurt you," Nolan said in a flat, eerie voice. "If I have to stakeout this place every night just to make sure you're safe, I will."

She blinked hard. "What are you going to do, Nolan? Park your car down the street and watch for suspicious characters?"

"If that's what it takes." He crossed his arms, and the gesture made him seem impossibly large, just like his oversized dog.

"Look, I appreciate the support, I do. But why don't you just come inside for a bit to calm down? Virginia usually has supper on the table by now, and I'm sure she'd be happy to have you join us."

He let out a frustrated sigh. "But Harmony—"

"But nothing. I've survived all these twenty-seven years. Surely I can survive the night. Unless you're saying I'm not strong enough to look after myself."

"It's not that."

"Then what is it?"

He took a deep breath, then let his shoulders fall. A moment later, he pulled out a small smile and said, "What do you suppose Mrs. Clementine has cooked tonight?"

"Let's go find out." Harmony opened the door and waited for him and Pancake to pass inside, then took one last look toward the street. When she saw that no strange or familiar cars idled nearby, she shut the door firmly behind her and, with it, her fears.

She could let Alan rule every second of her world the way he wanted to, or she could push her worry deep down and try to get on with her life.

For now, she chose the latter.

Chapter 23

HARMONY

Harmony leaned forward to whisper into Nolan's ear—actually, given their height difference, it was more like his shoulder. "Not a word of this to Virginia. I'd hate for her to worry."

"But—"

She jabbed her finger into his chest hard, which cut that argument off at the quick, then shook the same finger in front of his face and warned, "Not. A. Word."

"Have it your way," he said, kicking off his shoes in a defeated gesture, then lining them up neatly side-by-side in the coat closet. "But seeing as I already know and I'm already worried, I hope you can tell me more later."

"Fine," she agreed. "But later."

"Virginia," Harmony called as they headed toward the kitchen with both dogs trailing behind. "We have visitors!"

They found her standing in front of a fry pan tending to a simmering batch of greens that had been smothered to within an inch of their life with butter.

"Smells great," Nolan said, taking a long, appreciative sniff of the air that hung heavy in the kitchen. "Thanks for having me and Pancake. That is, if you'll have us. I didn't exactly hear Harmony ask."

Harmony's jaw fell open. Now he was lecturing her on proper decorum? Of all the teachers in the world, he hardly seemed the most qualified in this particular subject.

Mrs. Clementine, however, was in her element. "Of course!" the old woman crooned. "The more, the merrier. I always make too much and end up bringing the leftovers to Pastor Elliott the day after. I'm afraid it's starting to show on his waistline. You, however, look like you have plenty of room to expand on that tall frame of yours."

Harmony laughed as she pictured Nolan with a spare tire to match the pastor's, and it softened her feelings toward him once again. Still, she hoped the lack of leftovers wouldn't disappoint Pastor Adam too much, especially after the conversation they'd had earlier that evening.

"What are we having tonight?" she asked. "And how can I help?"

Virginia shook the pan then settled it back on the burner. "Just a chicken and rice casserole. I realized afterward that I forgot to include even an ounce of vegetables, so I busted out the turnip greens to right that situation. Harmony, would you please go ahead and pour the tea?"

Ten minutes later, they were settled around the table with the delicious spread before them.

"I must confess," Ginny said as she glanced from her plate to Nolan. "I'm a bit nervous for a professional like yourself to be tasting my food. If I'd known in advance that you'd be gracing us with your company I'd have whipped out *The Joy of Cooking*. Maybe tried one of those fancy French recipes."

"Oh, please. I scramble eggs and flip flapjacks. This—" He paused to load up his fork with a heaping bite that contained a little of everything. "—Is much more impressive." He even made a series of loud, appreciative sounds to prove his point.

Both dogs whined and shook their fluffy butts but stayed sitting where Harmony had instructed for them to wait.

"I'm glad it meets your approval." Virginia noticeably relaxed now that she had Nolan's good opinion. "Now, to what do we owe the pleasure?"

Harmony kicked him under the table to remind him of their deal.

"Oh, ouch, um…" Nolan, who was terrible at being subtle, swallowed his bite, took a sip of sweet tea, and then started over. "I came by to ask Harmony on a date, and she invited me in for your famous home cooking instead."

"Oh, Harmony," her landlady said with a sigh. "While I do appreciate the company, you'll have a much more enjoyable courtship without me tagging along as your third wheel."

"Point taken," Harmony said peaceably, wracking her brain for a change of topic.

But before she could come up with something satisfactory, Ginny spoke again. "You two do make such a nice couple. I could see the chemistry between you right away. Look, even your dogs are just smitten with each other."

Everyone glanced toward Muffin and Pancake. The two of whom had decided to lay down and cuddle up in each other's warmth as they watched for any stray bit of food that might be dropped from the table.

"They sure are," Nolan said, and then everyone laughed as both dogs tilted their heads in the same direction, almost like a synchronized dance—never mind that the little dog's entire body was still smaller than just the great Wolfhound's head.

"Love is funny like that," Virginia said. "If you'd told me all those years ago that I'd wind up married to Mr. Clementine, I'd have argued with you until I was blue in the face. Yet here we are, more than thirty years later, and still just as happy as the day we said 'I do.'"

Harmony smiled and nodded. In all the time she had been living with Virginia, she had not even met the man once, and he'd only called to talk to his wife a handful of times. While she loved Mrs. Clementine dearly, Harmony often asked herself whether her new friend was in denial or simply trying her best to hide her collapsing marriage from others. Harmony did what she could by praying for them each and every night.

If their relationship, however, showed what happily married looked like, then she was definitely better off alone.

Chapter 24

HARMONY

The next day started to feel normal again despite the scare Alan's appearance had been given to everyone. Jolene, of course, rushed to tell her version of the run-in with Harmony's ex, but Nolan mostly hung back in the kitchen and focused on his work. Once they'd finished their closing duties, he offered to escort Harmony back to Virginia's house.

"I kind of have my own car," she told him with a forced laugh.

"I'll follow you. C'mon." He checked and double-checked that the restaurant was locked up tight, then walked with her to the parking lot where they'd left both their cars that morning.

"I appreciate what you're trying to do for me, but really, it's not necessary."

"Who says I'm doing this for you? I'll worry about you the whole rest of the day if I don't see for myself that you get home safely."

Harmony fought back the fear that began to settle in her gut. It had been like this with Alan once, too. He'd wanted to be with her all the time, go everywhere she went, and called to check in frequently whenever they were apart. At first she'd thought it was because he loved her so much.

Sadly, by the time she realized that it was all about controlling her, she was already too deeply involved.

Nolan had been nothing but kind to her. But still...

Could history repeat itself, turning him into either his mean sister or her crazy ex? She hated that everything set her on edge, that she couldn't simply trust and enjoy her budding friendship with the nice man, but in the past, everyone had always let her down.

Why would Nolan be any different?

Even people who seemed nice in the start could still disappoint you. In fact, they were often the ones who wound up hurting you worst of anybody. It only made sense to keep the walls up around her heart and her life. If Nolan wanted to see her home, fine...but she wouldn't let him in. She wouldn't let him use her potentially dangerous ex as an excuse to get his hooks into her just as deep as Alan's had once been.

"You can see me home," she told him, stopping at her car door without getting in. "But you can't come in. Not today."

He nodded and broke into a smile as if she were the one doing him a favor in this situation. "That's perfect. I've got my basketball league this afternoon anyway. No extra time for visiting." Figured he played basketball. He was probably the best player on the team, too. Few men around these parts came within an inch of his great height.

She eyed him suspiciously. Was he merely telling her what he thought she wanted to hear, or did he truly only care about making sure she was safe?

"Look," he said, tossing his keys up in the air and then catching him in his opposite fist deftly. "I know you've been through some awful stuff. I also know enough to know that I don't know the half of it."

He laughed at his jumbled turn of phrase. "The point is, I promised to be your friend, and as part of that, I want you to know that you can trust me."

"I do trust you," she argued, knowing even as she spoke the words that they weren't true. It was nothing against Nolan—she simply preferred not

247

to trust *anyone*. It was the surest way to make sure she didn't get hurt again.

"You're getting there," he said. "But I can see that you need more time. You shouldn't just blindly trust people. You're right about that, but I'm also right when I say that I'm going to earn your trust fair and square."

She couldn't help but admire his determination. It was well matched to her stubbornness. "We'll see about that," she said with a poorly disguised grin.

"Oh, we will." He winked at her, and she wasn't sure why. "For starters, I want you to know that our talk the other day didn't fall on deaf ears. I had it out with my sister."

This surprised her. What could Nolan possibly have to gain by confronting Megan? How would it help anything?

"She remembers putting you through hell and says she's very sorry."

Harmony let out a sarcastic laugh. She just couldn't help it.

"I know. Likely story, right? Except she did seem genuinely apologetic, and she even asked if she could meet with you in person to say sorry."

Static pricked at the hairs on Harmony's arms. "Nolan! You didn't invite her to the restaurant, did you?"

"No, I wouldn't do that. She doesn't even know you're working here. I told her I'd ask you along to the Eternal Grace Church picnic later this month, and if you agreed she could apologize then and there. Gives you some time to think and prepare. Although I do hope you'll say yes."

"Yes," Harmony said without hesitation.

His eyes lit up and a smile began to creep from one cheek to the other.

"Yes, I'll think about it," she clarified. "Not yes I'll go. That has yet to be determined."

"Fair enough," he said, slapping his hand on the hood of her car and then bending forward to open her driver's side door. "Now let's get you home. If we stand here chit-chatting any longer, I'm afraid I'll be late for my practice."

Harmony reached up and gave him a quick hug. "Thank you for being my friend," she said. "I know it's not easy, but I'm glad you're up for the challenge."

Nolan cleared his throat and squeezed her tight. "I sure am," he agreed. "I sure am."

Chapter 25

PASTOR ADAM

Our spring potluck arrived just as the daffodils that lined the church flowerbeds had begun to unfurl their happy yellow petals to greet the season. Mrs. Clementine had planted them as one of her first acts when she took up the role as church secretary, and every season I was grateful to see them, seeing as they heralded warmer weather as well as the anniversary of our Lord and Savior's resurrection.

Last autumn she'd elected to remove the vegetable patch in favor of more flowers, and to say I was grateful would be an understatement of biblical proportions. I much preferred the pretty tulips that had taken the cucumbers' and tomatoes' places, and we had far fewer critters who showed up to wreak havoc on the brightly colored flowers.

Our church yard wasn't enormous, but we still insisted on having a picnic there at the change of each season and invited not just our whole congregation, but the entire town of Charleston.

Some folks came to eat and run, and that was just fine by me. Others lingered inside, while the more adventurous set up blankets outdoors where they could enjoy our newly awakened gardens.

This was to be my grandson's first spring potluck, seeing as he was born at the end of the season the year prior. He'd be walking any day now, too. Gavin and Abigail were all too proud to show him off to the folks that were ECP churchgoers—that's Easter, Christmas, Potluck—and they all gushed and gushed over his cuteness.

Rightfully so, I might add.

Yes, Gavin and Abigail made quite the beautiful couple. It wasn't just their faces that looked good together, but their hearts matched, too. Hallelujah, the Lord is good!

Mama Mary stayed glued to Abigail's side as she always did, but the younger church dogs roamed freely about the lot to greet our guests and beg for scraps. We placed several signs around the yard reminding folks not to feed the Chihuahuas but still, I suspect their tummies ended up full and well fed all the same.

One of the dogs bounded up to me and began to whine and scratch at my shins. It took me a moment to realize it was our working-on-location church dog, Muffin. Which meant...

"Harmony!" I cried the moment I saw her and stretched my arms wide to saddle her with a hug. I'd had a few weeks to get accustomed to her new hairstyle now, and it had grown on me. "I'm so happy you came."

"Well, you can thank this guy," she said with a half-smile, bumping her shoulder into Nolan Murphy's arm.

I turned to the tall chap and offered him a smile since his hands appeared to full to join me in a shake. "Nolan, it's good to see you, too."

"I brought some grits and sausage for the spread," he said, lifting up a crock pot that he'd carried over with him.

"Tables are over there under the tent," I instructed.

Nolan nodded and headed off decisively in the direction I had pointed while Harmony remained back standing beside me.

"I thought about your offer for counseling some more," she said, dropping her voice so quiet I could hardly hear her. "I'd like to do it, provided the offer still stands."

I took her hand in both of mine and gave it a good, firm shake. "See you Tuesday."

She agreed and then skipped off to join Nolan by the food.

Okay, so she didn't skip, but she didn't sulk, either. There was a certain peppiness to her step that hadn't been there before, and seeing as I'd been in love once before myself and had counseled countless others on the merits of 1 Corinthians 13, I knew exactly what had gotten into Miss Harmony King.

That Nolan was good for her.

And even if she hadn't realized it yet, I had no doubts. And so I made sure to mentally leave a section of my schedule open for their inevitable premarital counseling.

Chapter 26

HARMONY

Harmony let Nolan hold her hand as he guided her toward his sister.

Megan, who was setting up a store-bought veggie tray on the far end of the food tent, smiled as she spotted the two of them heading her way.

"Harmony," she cried. A look of anguish washed over her face, making her otherwise pretty features appear mangled. "I'm so glad you agreed to come!"

"Hello, Megan," she said, tucking her short, blonde hair behind her ears on both sides. Truth be told, she'd almost backed out of the whole affair. What good would seeing her former bully do for her now that she had a far more threatening figure stalking the outer edges of her life?

Alan hadn't shown himself again, at least not that she'd seen or heard. Still, Nolan insisted on escorting her home after each and every shift. He waited in the parking lot for her arrival in the mornings as well. True to his word, he never pushed Harmony for more of an explanation about her past or for more of a relationship than she could handle, putting her initial worries aside.

Now the biggest lingering concern was why Alan hadn't found her yet. Could he have really given up so quickly? It seemed unlikely, and yet as each day passed, Harmony began to feel more and more at ease in her new life.

Now's not the time for this. She willed her thoughts to be silent and focused her attention on Megan, who stood waiting before her with an expectant, awkward smile.

"Should we get some food before we catch up?" Nolan's sister asked. Like her brother, she had light blonde hair and freckles. Unlike him, however, Megan's good looks seemed to have peaked in high school. She was still attractive enough, especially when she smiled, but was nowhere near the knockout she'd once been.

Still, Harmony found herself envying the woman's tall, slender frame and ample chest. She'd been among the first of the girls at their school to bloom into a woman, while Harmony had been one of the last. Thinking about it now, Harmony felt that familiar old surge of jealousy swell.

"I'm not too hungry," she said waving a hand dismissively. The last thing she needed was to throw up church food on her former bully—no matter how funny it might be to revisit that moment later. "Could we talk first and grab food a bit later?"

"Sure, okay." Megan led them away from the food tent and toward a blanket she'd set up near the edge of the daffodils.

Harmony sat first, and Nolan sank down beside her, sitting close enough to lend his warmth without the two of them actually having to touch.

Megan swayed back and forth before finally lowering herself to her knees and then leaning back on her heels. That tormented look was back, and Harmony wondered if Megan had ever thought about her at all between high school graduation and Nolan's mention of her earlier that month.

Focusing her gaze on Harmony, she frowned and said, "I really, truly am so sorry for how I treated you during our school days. I'm just torn up about it."

Sure you are, Harmony thought bitterly. She'd long since stopped dwelling on the bad things Megan had done to her back then, but it didn't make facing the woman now any easier.

"I was going through some rough stuff back then. Not that it excuses how I behaved but..." She licked her lips and looked away.

Going through stuff for more than six years? That's a lot of stuff. Harmony thought the words on the inside but managed to plaster on a smile on the outside.

"It's okay," Harmony told her. "I understand and I'm not angry anymore."

Megan breathed a huge sigh of relief and then settled into a more comfortable position. "Really? Do you mean it?"

"I do," Harmony said with a nod.

Nolan reached over and squeezed her hand.

"I forgive you," she said.

"Oh, Harmony!" Suddenly Megan had hurled herself across the blanket and now had Harmony wrapped in a rather uncomfortable hug. "You have no idea what a relief that is to hear. I really am so, so sorry and hope we can start over. Can we?"

"Sure," came her answer.

Nolan moved to let go of her hand but she hung on tight. While it was nice that his sister had apologized and clearly she felt better about it, Harmony felt just the same as she always had.

Sorry didn't erase all the tears that had already been shed. Sometimes mistakes couldn't be reversed. The best anyone could do was to try to learn from them and then move on. It seemed that Megan at least had tried to do that, but it didn't make Harmony want to become best friends with her all of a sudden, either.

"Tell me about you," Megan said. Her eyes sparkled in the same way her brother's often did. "How long have you been back in Charleston? Where are you staying?"

"Little over a month now, and I'm renting a room from Virginia Clementine."

"Oh, she's such a nice lady," Megan said, clasping her hands together as if Harmony was a puppy who'd just performed a cute trick right on cue. "What else? What did you do after we graduated? What are you doing now?"

Harmony took a deep breath and began her story, or at least the PG version with no curse words, no scary parts, and—most importantly—no bad guys.

Chapter 27

HARMONY

Harmony sat chatting politely with Megan for about an hour, but by then, she'd reached the limit for how much chitchat she could handle in one day without losing her temper. Nolan saw it, too.

"Hey," he said softly when Megan had turned to talk to a woman whom Harmony didn't recognize but that Megan appeared to know well. "Want to get out of here?"

She nodded, not even teasing him about the fact he'd used yet another bad pick-up line on her.

Nolan wasted no time rising to his feet and stretching his arms high overhead. A giant, theatrical yawn drew his sister's attention to him. "Welp. That's enough sun and socializing for one day," he announced. "Harmony, do you mind if we head out of here early? I'm sorry, but my Irish skin just can't take anymore without bursting into a punishing amount of freckles."

"Sure, seeing as you're my ride. Thanks for that, by the way." She stood now, too.

Megan smirked at her brother. "The Irishman in the sun excuse doesn't really work when you're with family," she pointed out. "But you and Harmony make a really cute couple, so I'm cool with it."

They both accepted hugs from Nolan's sister. Neither corrected her about the status of their couplehood, which meant their escape was swift.

"Thanks again," she told him once they were safely settled in his car. "I don't think I could have lasted much longer."

"You betcha. Coming at all took some serious guts," he agreed with a nod while keeping his eyes focused on the road ahead. "Add it to the long list of things I really like about you."

She rolled her eyes. "Whatever you say."

"Where to now, Madame?" He adjusted both hands on the wheel and sat straighter in his seat, the very portrait of a proper chauffer. It was adorable, but still, Harmony was very tired.

"Home?" She looked down at Muffin, who sat proudly on her lap with his tongue lolling out the side of his mouth. He didn't seem ready to call it a day, even though the short outing had exhausted Harmony.

"Nope, I'm not letting you off the hook that easy. You promised we'd spend the potluck together, and that thing is nowhere close to over."

Muffin barked in agreement, then stood with his front legs against the door and scratched at the window until Harmony relented and rolled it down for him.

"So you're taking me hostage?" she asked with one eyebrow quirked.

"Only until..." He glanced at his car's dash to get the time. "Four o'clock?"

"I guess that's fair. What would you like to do?"

"I have the perfect plan, but first we need to swing by and pick up Pancake. It wouldn't be fair to let Muffin have all the fun when he's stuck at home."

At the mention of his name, the fawn-colored Chihuahua popped down from his perch at the window and scurried over to Nolan's lap.

Harmony had to grab the little dog quickly so as not to interfere with his driving. "We headed to the dog park?" she asked with a laugh. "That sounds fun and is clearly needed."

He smiled. "Nope, it's even better than that. And nope, I'm not going to tell before we get there."

Harmony crossed her arms over her chest in mock outrage. "Don't I even get a hint?"

"A hint? Hmmm." He thought for a moment, even going so far as to scratch his chin like an old-fashioned detective.

She couldn't help but laugh. Spending time with Nolan was becoming easier by the day. In fact, she could honestly say it had become her favorite part of most days. She was so glad that she'd agreed to be friends and that he hadn't pushed her for more that she could offer.

Nolan stopped for a traffic light, then turned toward Harmony in his seat. "Here's your hint: it was one of my favorite places as a kid. And a teen. And now, actually."

Harmony groaned. "But, Mr. Murphy, sir, I don't want to go into work on my day off!"

"Ha ha," he said pointedly, even going so far as to stick out his tongue at her. "This place is way cooler than O'Brien's, but don't tell anyone—and I mean *anyone*—I said that."

"Okay, what makes you like it so much, then? Expand the hint, please."

The light shifted back to green, and Nolan let out a dreamy sigh as he turned his attention back to the road. "It's funny, I loved it as a kid because of all the excitement. Now I love it because of the calm. Strange how the same place can represent two very different things even to the same person, isn't it?"

She nodded. That was exactly how she felt about the whole of Charleston. On the one hand, it was the site of her unhappy childhood, while on the other, she was building a life she rather liked here now.

"Add to that the fact dogs are clearly allowed if we're going to pick up Pancake, and I still don't have enough to go on," she said thoughtfully. "You're going to have to give me more."

He considered this for a moment before agreeing. "Okay. How about I share my favorite memory of that place, then?"

"I'd love to hear it, especially if it's going to give me clues. Have I told you how much I don't like surprises?" Surprises for a foster kid were almost never of the welcome variety, and Harmony had continued her disdain for them with her into adulthood.

A smile crept across his face as he adjusted his hands on the steering wheel once more. "I promise you'll like this one. In fact, I think it's just what you need after the day you've had. Have I mentioned how gutsy I think you are for meeting with Megan?"

She groaned again. "Okay, on with the story, please."

"It's one of my earliest memories actually. For years, we hosted the Murphy-O'Brien family reunions there. My cousins would fly in from all over the country, and it was usually the only time we saw each other for the entire year. Being little boys, we each tried to prove how tough we were. Mind you, none of us were as tough as you."

Harmony laughed at this particular assertion but enjoyed his story all the same.

"It was great fun. We made weapons out of sticks and chased each other around all day, then at night, just before the sun went down, our dads sent us to find driftwood along the shore. We, of course, had a competition to see who could collect the most. I was so proud when I realized I'd won, but what was even better was the massive bonfire that we built after. We sat on the sand watching the flames stretch to the sky, and then we roasted hotdogs and marshmallows and had ourselves a right feast. I fell asleep staring into that fire and begged to make another every year that followed."

Harmony closed her eyes and pictured the scene as Nolan had described it. Even though he'd tried to be secretive, words like driftwood and shore gave his location away all the same. "Did you?" she asked, imagining the tall pyre reaching for the sky.

He chuckled sadly and shook his head. "No, apparently, our parents had unknowingly broken the law and were slapped with a heavy fine. I'm still grateful for the one bonfire we managed, though. To me, it was priceless."

"That's a beautiful memory, but you know you sound like a MasterCard commercial, right?" Harmony reached over and put a hand on his shoulder.

And he brought up his hand to rest on top of hers, almost as if he were keeping it captive, as if he never wanted her to let go. "Fair enough. And if you were paying attention, then you already know where we're going."

Sure enough, they arrived about twenty minutes later with both dogs in tow. The beach had never looked quite so beautiful to Harmony as it did that day.

Chapter 28

HARMONY

Harmony and Nolan took off their shoes, rolled up their pants, and strolled through the chilly surf. Seeing as most folks were still at the church potluck or else waiting for a warmer day to visit the beach, they mostly had the place to themselves.

Well, them and the two wildly happy dogs who ran big, looping circles around them as they progressed along the shoreline.

"You're right about it being peaceful," Harmony said. Even the shock of the cold ocean water between her toes felt like an important part of the experience. All they needed now was a bit of moonlight for the perfect romantic moment. Only... she'd taken romance completely off the table, and despite occasional moments of longing like the one she was facing now, Harmony knew she'd been right to do so.

Nolan remained thoughtful as their heels pressed down into the wet sand, leaving uneven tracks behind them.

"Thank you for sharing your memory about the bonfire. It's almost like I was right there with you."

"It would have been a very different kind of memory had you been there," he answered with a nostalgic grin. "Probably even better."

Harmony chuckled and reached for his hand, then caught herself and pulled back again. "Would you believe I've never been to a bonfire?"

Nolan stopped walking and regarded her suspiciously. "Never?"

She shook her head and giggled. "Nope, no campfires, either."

"What?" he practically shouted. "Why the heck not?"

"One of the joys of being a foster kid. None of our temporary guardians were too concerned about making memories with us."

His face fell, and before she knew it, he'd pulled her to his chest in a hug.

She laughed nervously against him but didn't push away. "Nolan. Really, it's okay."

Nolan stroked her hair and made calming noises as if she were the one who was upset and needed to be calmed. He clucked his tongue and mumbled half to himself, "If you've never had a fire, I'm guessing you've also never had s'mores, and that will not do."

"I know what s'mores are," she countered, leaning back to glare into his eyes. "And I doubt I'm so deprived that it warrants all these theatrics."

He squeezed her close again. "You're wrong about that, and we're going to fix it. We're going to fix it tonight."

"Nolan, really, it's fine."

"It isn't yet, but it will be soon." He released her, then turned back and started walking in the direction from which they'd first come.

The dogs spotted the sudden shift and chased after him, barking merrily as they pushed through the gentle waves. Pancake stopped often to make sure his little buddy was still with him, making Harmony's heart swell with love for both creatures.

She followed after man and dogs, moving in double time to catch up with Nolan's long, determined stride. "I'm having a nice time at the beach. Can't s'mores wait?"

He kept moving at his impossibly quick pace without even looking back. "Spoken like someone who's never tried the little pieces of heaven," he called over the sound of gulls crying and waves lapping at the shore. "Yes, we'll definitely need to fix that."

Harmony laughed and shook her head, even though secretly she was quite flattered that Nolan wanted her to experience all of his favorite memories. It was almost as if she were making up for all the time lost during her childhood. Getting a second chance to do things right.

"Okay, so what now?" she asked when the car loomed back into view.

"I'm going to drop you off at home, head to the store to grab some supplies, and then come back to introduce you to the best dessert this world has to offer. Hey, do you know if Mrs. Clementine has a fire pit?" He grabbed his keys from his pocket and unlocked the car. Its lights flashed in greetings.

Harmony's legs had begun to ache from the sudden burst of exercise, but luckily it was nearing its natural end. "I don't know, but I can ask," she said. "And why can't I come with you to get supplies? It's not like the recipe is a secret."

He turned to her for a moment, mischief flashing in his green eyes. "No, but I have a surprise for you nonetheless."

"*Nonetheless?* Who says nonetheless? And what did I tell you about surprises?"

"Trust me, it will be worth it."

It was then Harmony realized that she *did* trust him. Not just a little, not just partially, but all the way. She wasn't sure when the shift had occurred or what it meant for the future of their friendship—or her job, for that matter—but she'd have to unpack that later.

Right now, they had urgent s'mores business to attend to.

Chapter 29

HARMONY

The sun had already begun to set by the time Nolan and Pancake returned to Mrs. Clementine's house. Sure enough, Virginia had an old fire pit buried in her garden shed that she allowed Harmony to dig out for use in their so-called s'mores emergency.

She fitted Muffin's newly knit sweater onto his tiny, shivering body, knowing the night air would be too cold for him without the added layer of fuzz. And, really, she was quite proud of her handiwork. She'd alternated two skeins of yarn to create adorable blue and yellow stripes. Virginia had even helped her out by making a tiny hat to go with it. Now Muffin looked too cute for words in this new ensemble, although he seemed to believe his hat made a better chew toy than fashion accessory.

"Sorry it took me so long!" Nolan cried, setting a few very full grocery bags on the countertop.

Pancake, whose massive head reached over the counter without any added stretching on his part, sniffed determinedly at the corner of one of the bags.

His owner pushed the dog aside with his hip. "First Harmony, then you!" he told the Irish Wolfhound.

"I thought dogs couldn't have chocolate," Harmony reminded him gently. In fact, she was sure of it. Abigail's church dog manual had been very clear on the point—no chocolate, raisins, onions, and about a dozen other things as well.

"They can't." Nolan drew what looked like a camouflaged fishing pole out from a bag and began to crank its handle. The little metal prongs on the end spun slowly in what had to be the most ridiculous roasting stick in the entire world.

"That's why they're having sausages while we have the good stuff. Wouldn't want to leave the puppers out of this important memory," Nolan continued, handing her the camo stick rod hybrid thing, then pulling a second matching one from the bag.

There were still two and a half full grocery bags on the counter.

"How much do you expect us to eat?" Harmony asked, tossing a glance at the unnecessarily exorbitant amount of supplies.

"At least three s'mores each," he answered with a smile. "Since this is your first time, you need to have the classic, the alternate, and the original. That makes three." He put up three fingers as if this somehow further confirmed his assertion.

"I had no idea it was so involved." She nodded then broke apart in giggles. Leave it to Nolan to turn everything into a production.

"Well, obviously, that's why I'm here to teach you!"

"Obviously," she said, unable to hide her excitement and unwilling to even try. Nolan's enthusiasm was infectious, and she was eating it right up.

After a bit more rummaging, he grabbed the bags and headed for the sliding glass door.

Harmony rushed forward to open it for him and, in short order, they had a modest fire flickering before them. Virginia had also lent them two folded camping chairs to use for this backyard adventure. It seemed that woman was prepared for any eventuality, and Harmony felt grateful for it and to her.

She sat now with her knees pressed together and the roast stick dangling loosely from one hand.

"Are you ready?" Nolan's eyes shone brighter than the fire. She wondered if this whole thing was providing him with the chance to relive one of his favorite firsts as well.

She nodded and pointed her stick toward the sky. "Marshmallow me up, baby."

And although Harmony was very careful with how she positioned her stick, her marshmallow broke into flames almost immediately after setting it near the fire.

"Whoa!" Nolan cried, blowing it out for her and unwrapping a package of graham crackers as quickly as his fingers would allow. "That's okay! The burnt bits add flavor," he told her as he pressed a graham cracker square on either side of the marshmallow and pulled it off her stick.

Harmony unwrapped the waiting Hershey bar, added a slab of chocolate, and then took a giant, appreciative bite. "How can something so simple be so wonderful?" she mumbled around her very large, very delicious mouthful.

"That's the beauty of the s'mores, and of life, too," he said with a goofy grin. "Okay, so you've had the classic. Now you need to have the alternate. The only difference is that you make it with a peanut butter cup instead of pure chocolate."

"Sign me up for one of those," she said eagerly, relieved she'd chosen not to eat much at the potluck since she now planned to dine on s'mores until her stomach couldn't take it anymore.

The alternate s'mores were just as delicious as the originals. Harmony was glad Nolan had decided that making desserts over the fire would be the perfect way to end their special day together. This was one first she regretted not having much, much earlier in life.

"Ready for the original? It's my own recipe that I just developed today, actually." He looked so excited she could hardly stand it. Had he always been this adorable, or did her newfound trust add an extra layer of attraction that hadn't been there before?

"Ooh," she gushed, enjoying herself immensely. "What's in it? If it's as good as the others, then I'm in."

"It's definitely just as good," Nolan promised. "It's also totally different."

She pointed at him as if he'd just said something brilliant. "I guess that's why you call it the original."

"Actually, I call it the Harmony. The Harmony S'more." He kept his eyes fixed on her, awaiting the inevitable reaction.

"You named it after me?" She suddenly felt incredibly touched by the gesture, by this whole day she'd had with Nolan.

"I had to, seeing as you inspired it."

"How'd I do that?"

"Allow me to explain." He paused to add a marshmallow to each of their roasting sticks. "We start with the marshmallow, which is sweet, fun to look at, and also required to make this a s'more."

Harmony giggled. "And also liable to catch fire at a moment's notice, right?"

Nolan laughed, too. "Nope. For that, we have the gingersnap." He pulled out a Tupperware of what appeared to be homemade cookies. "Hard exterior, filled with interesting, unexpected flavors and—let's be honest here—also thoroughly Southern."

"I like where you're headed so far. What's next?"

"I'm glad you asked, because this is the best part." He brought a glass jar out from the bag followed in short order by a plastic butter knife. "Strawberry jam. Not what you'd expect to round out your s'mores, yet somehow it's perfect just the same. It also represents your guts."

"That's a little bit gross, but I like it all the same. Definitely a good description of me."

They both laughed as their marshmallows finished roasting, and Nolan spread jam on a pair of gingersnaps in preparation. When the full dessert was built, Harmony studied it a moment before taking a bite. "The Harmony S'more, huh?"

"The Harmony S'more," he echoed. "The perfect blend of spicy and sweet. Just like you."

Their eyes locked and neither said anything until a bit of hot marshmallow goop oozed onto Harmony's finger, bringing her focus back to the morsel before her.

She took a big bite and silently prayed that she wasn't about to go doing something so foolish as falling in love with Nolan Murphy.

Chapter 30

PASTOR ADAM

The church potluck last weekend was a smashing success, and I couldn't be happier. Even though its primary purpose was to offer fellowship among our members and the community at large, Eternal Grace still managed to raise enough money to fund our Resurrection Sunday stage play, complete with costumes, beautifully painted backdrops, and all the bells and whistles. I know the kids are beside themselves with excitement, and so am I.

Tonight my daughter, grandson, the church dogs, and I decided to enjoy a quiet night at home. My future son-in-law Gavin dropped by, too. Even though it will be much lonelier for me when Abigail and little Owen move out, I'm looking forward to officially welcoming this kind-hearted young man into the family.

He's a good man, made even better by the fact that he cooked supper for us tonight—and better than better for the fact that it was really quite tasty. I'm not too proud to admit that I helped myself to seconds and thirds of his pot roast stew. If we hadn't cleared the pot, I'd likely still be at the table helping myself to fourths and fifths!

"How about *Finding Nemo?*" Abigail asked with her remote pointed at the TV undecidedly. "Little Owen loves the fish tank at his pediatrician's office.

Suddenly, I was quite grateful that Gavin hadn't served us fish fry that evening in light of Abigail's film choice. We set Owen up on the floor with far more toys than a child his age could ever need. He crawled back and forth after them, rising to stand on shaky little toes a few times before plopping back down on his diapered bottom. Only occasionally did he look to the little orange fish on the screen, but each time he did, he gave us a huge gummy grin which, to me, counts *Nemo* among our success.

The cartoon film had just introduced us to a gnarly pod of sea turtles when my phone began to ring.

"Oh, not tonight, Dad. It's family night!" Abigail protested.

Seeing as I was feeling mighty comfortable right where I was seated, I let the phone stay in my pocket and the call go to voicemail.

But then it rang again.

Abigail paused the movie and sighed. "Go ahead. It might be important."

Though I hadn't yet received a call from this number, it was one I'd saved all the same—and it belonged to none other than Harmony King.

I pressed to answer the call, but before I could even say hello, a stifled cry met my ears. "Harmony?" I asked, panic gripping my old, worried heart. "Is everything okay?"

She cried more than spoke, but still I managed to understand two very important words. "He's here."

I didn't have to ask who he was. Instantly I knew that it was that same fellow she'd run so far to escape. As far as I was concerned, *Danger* would have been a better name for him than *Alan*.

"Call Nolan," I told Abigail and Gavin. "And the police. Send them to Mrs. Clementine's."

They both sprung to action while I stayed on the line with Harmony. "Where are you? Where is he?"

Her voice was a little surer now, a little easier to understand. "He's at the front door. I ran upstairs to my room, locked the door, and am hiding under the bed."

Good, so they had at least two locked doors between them. Still, this man had broken in on her before, and I had no doubt that he'd do it again.

"Hurry," I mouthed to Abigail who was on the phone with the police.

"Where's Mrs. Clementine?" Fear tightened around me like a noose. I had to make sure my old friend wasn't also in harm's way. I didn't know Alan well enough to determine whether he'd stoop to hurting her, too, on his path to Harmony.

"Out," Harmony whispered. "I don't know where. Muffin's with me under the bed."

"Good, good. Stay put. The police and Nolan are on their way."

Gavin caught my eye and shook his head. "I couldn't get Nolan, so I left a voicemail."

"The police are on their way," I updated Harmony. Praying, praying, praying for their quick arrival on the scene.

"I'm so—" Harmony's words were cut off by a loud, shrill string of barks.

If Alan hadn't already discovered her, then surely Muffin had just given away that poor girl's location.

The line went dead.

Chapter 31

HARMONY

Muffin slipped free of Harmony's grip and began barking like a maniac. The door downstairs creaked open and, soon after, heavy footsteps hurried toward her room.

"Please, God. Please," she prayed through the tears, unsure exactly what she was asking. Perhaps it was that Alan would change his mind, give up, move on—then no one would have to get hurt in this.

Her Chihuahua companion whined and scratched frantically at the door, leading the intruder right to her.

She felt too terrified to call out to him, to look for a weapon with which she could defend herself, to do anything other than cry.

The doorknob rattled but didn't open.

A knock on the door came next.

Harmony covered her mouth with both hands to silence her sobs. If she could just stay hidden for a few more minutes, the police would come to save her.

Her phone buzzed beside her with an incoming call, and the buzzing against the carpet seemed to ring out like thunder.

She hadn't even realized she'd dropped the call with Pastor Adam, but now Nolan was calling her back and possibly sealing her fate.

Oh, God, save me.

"Harmony?" Nolan's voice was among the last she expected to hear on the other side of that door. Could it really be him? Where was Alan? She'd seen him with her own eyes right through the living room window before she'd run to hide in her locked room. Had he really gone?

"Nolan?" she chanced, her voice a nasal moan like as if she were trying to hold back a sneeze.

"Yeah, it's me," he responded with another useless turn of the door-knob. She'd never heard a sweeter sound. Nolan's voice meant she was safe, just as he'd promised. "Are you okay?" he asked with another rap on the door.

Harmony freed herself from under the bed almost as quickly as she'd initially dived beneath it. Stumbling to the door as quick as her shaking legs would take her, she sobbed freely. And then, a moment later, they were together at the threshold to her room.

Muffin let out a deep, throaty bark, and it almost sounded like he was reprimanding Nolan for not making it there fast enough.

Harmony laughed through the tears and pushed her face into Nolan's strong chest. "Pastor Adam said he couldn't reach you. How did you get inside? How did you know to come?" she mumbled into his shirt.

Nolan swayed gently with her and stroked her hair just as he had done upon learning she'd never eaten s'mores. Oh, how that memory now seemed a million miles away. "Mrs. Clementine once showed me where she keeps the spare key in that stone garden frog. I had to get to you, and you weren't answering the door."

"But how did you know I was in trouble?" Did it matter? All that mattered now was that he was here and Alan wasn't. And yet he'd be back again soon. She knew that beyond a shadow of a doubt. Now that she'd come face to face with her ex here in Charleston, she felt the fear even deeper in her bones.

"Megan." Nolan tensed upon speaking his sister's name, and without even looking at his face, Harmony could feel just how angry he'd become. "She called me up in a panic, saying she may have done something wrong."

Harmony pulled away from him and went to sit on the bed. Her legs felt too weak to hold her for another second. "She told Alan where I live?" she asked in disbelief.

"She didn't mean to." He crossed his arms as tension rolled off him in waves. "But she made a very stupid choice."

Harmony, too, felt her fear turning to anger. "How? What happened?" she demanded.

"Remember how I told you she works at Publix?"

Harmony nodded and hugged a still very distressed and shaking Muffin to her chest. *Calm down, calm down,* she willed herself. If Megan had put her in danger, then at least Nolan had come in an attempt to save her. It had been an honest mistake, though. And Nolan was right—a stupid one.

He shook his head and frowned. "A man came into the store asking around about you. He said he was an old friend and eager to reconnect with you."

"And she believed him?" Harmony spat. *It's not his fault. Control your temper.*

"Afraid so. She told him exactly where to find you. It didn't even occur to her that the man might've been lying until a coworker came to talk to her about the creepy guy trying to find Harmony King. That's when she called me."

"Oh my gosh," Harmony cried. "She can't just tell people where I live! That's gotta be illegal!" The cops were on their way. They'd know whether what Megan did was punishable.

"I'm so sorry, and Megan is, too. Tell me what I can do to make things better."

Harmony ran through the countless options in her mind. It made the most sense to pack her bags and leave, go somewhere Alan wouldn't know to look for her. But she was sick of running every time life got a little hard. Sure, Alan was more than just a small threat, but if she ran away from the good things that she'd begun to build here in Charleston, he'd still be controlling every aspect of her life—just like he wanted.

"He wasn't here when you arrived?" she asked. She needed to focus on the facts, on staying safe going forward, not getting revenge on Megan for her stupidity.

Nolan appeared almost apologetic. "No, I didn't see him."

"He'll be back, and probably soon now that he knows where I live now."

"Then I'll be here, too. This is partially my fault. If I hadn't made you meet with my sister at the potluck, none of this would be happening now."

Harmony felt disconnected from her emotions as she spoke, but at least she'd managed to tamp the anger down. "No, he would have found me eventually. I have no doubt about that."

Now it was Nolan who seemed afraid. "And what would you have done if he got to you this time? What are you going to do when he finds you next time?"

"I don't know," she admitted.

He sank down onto the bed beside her and ran his hands through his hair. "That's not good enough, Harmony."

"I'm sorry, but it's the truth. I've never been in this situation before."

"With a crazy ex stalking you?"

"Well, yeah, but also not wanting to leave. Earlier I would have just run away to somewhere new, but I don't want to go."

He regarded her for a moment, neither smiling nor frowning. His face gave nothing away. Finally, Nolan said, "I don't want you to go, either."

Chapter 32

HARMONY

Harmony and Muffin walked with Nolan downstairs to the living room. The fear she'd felt just minutes earlier clung to her bedroom like an odious perfume, and she didn't want to stay in there any longer than she had to.

True to his word, Nolan refused to leave, even after Harmony assured him she would be okay. A lie, but still she hated how her problems had taken on a life of their own, ensnaring all those around her who had dared to care. Unbelievably, she even felt kind of bad for Megan who had unwittingly put her in such danger. She'd be beside herself with guilt, no doubt.

Yes, normally Harmony would have wasted no time in calling someone up who'd done her wrong to give them a loud and colorful piece of her mind. But what was the point this time around? The only person she really needed to have it out with was Alan, and he'd find her sooner rather than later.

A shiver wracked through her again. She hadn't asked for this, didn't want it, and yet, it was the biggest constant in her life.

The fear, the running, the anger.

How badly she wanted to put all of them behind now that she had begun to rebuild her life. When faced with the very real possibility of losing everything she'd come to care about, she realized just how much she did care—and in a way, that terrified her, too.

Loving people meant giving them power over you. Alan was proof enough of that. Still, even if Virginia, Nolan, Jolene, Abigail, or Pastor Adam never intended to hurt her, they could easily do so by accident just as she could hurt them—just as she had by putting them all in danger now.

It wasn't long until Virginia showed up. She reached the house just as the police were packing up to say goodbye after their short visit.

"We'll keep you informed," the nice officer said with a sympathetic nod.

"Oh, dear!" Virginia cried the very moment the pair of policemen secured the front door behind them. "You must have been terrified. I'm sorry I wasn't here. I mean, I had no idea until Pastor Adam called me."

Harmony felt terrible all over again. Guilt, just like fear, proved to be an emotion in abundant supply. "Ginny," she said. "I'm so sorry I put you in harm's way. I had hoped he wouldn't come looking for me, but I should've known better."

"Hush, say nothing of it. It's not your fault, you poor, poor thing."

Nolan stood and made eyes toward the kitchen. "Mrs. Clementine, may I please have a word with you in private?"

The old woman looked disoriented for a second before nodding and following him out of the room, leaving Harmony alone with her Chihuahua.

"You wouldn't have let anything happen to me. Right, Muffin?" she whispered, stroking the dog's short fur. Her best defenses now would be quick thinking and this five pound warrior pup, Heaven help her.

But she just couldn't continue to put the people she cared about in harm's way. Maybe it would be better if did leave town, after all. This time, though, she wouldn't be running away from a life that had never fit her. She'd be preserving one she'd come to love deeply.

Virginia came back into the living room and sat beside Harmony on the sofa. "Well, then. Shall we work on our knitting projects for a while?"

The front door opened and shut, drawing Harmony's eyes toward the window where she caught a peek of Nolan's head bobbing across the front yard. It was the same window through which she'd spotted Alan earlier that day.

"Don't you worry," Virginia said, patting her on the knee. "He'll be back just as soon as he collects his things." Yes, the same could be said of Alan, too.

Harmony looked at her landlady askance.

Virginia got up to retrieve their yarn and needles, explaining as she went, "I offered him one of the spare bedrooms upstairs, but he says he'd feel much better sleeping on the couch beside Pancake."

So Nolan would be... moving in with them? Mrs. Clementine seemed pleased with this idea, and Harmony didn't want to disappoint her since she'd been the one to lead them all into trouble with her foolish secrecy.

"Thank you for being such a good friend to me," she said solemnly as the older woman handed Harmony her work in progress. She already knew there'd be no point in arguing Nolan's decision. Besides, she really would feel safer having him nearby.

Virginia sat back down, but kept her eyes fixed on her lap as she spoke. "I know you don't think it, because of this whole situation with your ex-boyfriend, but you've been a very good friend to me, too." She paused for a moment before adding, "Almost like the daughter I never had."

Harmony felt tears begin to prick in the corners of her eyes again. Kinder words had never been spoken to her, nor had they ever meant more. All her life she'd longed for a family, and now somehow she'd managed to find one when she wasn't even looking.

It wasn't pretend or imaginary like her relationship had been with Pastor Adam growing up. This sweet and giving woman sitting beside her now truly cared for her.

Her! The girl no one had ever wanted growing up, the damaged soul who had brought danger lurking into their lives.

Virginia Clementine had opened up her home and her heart when Harmony had so little to offer in return. It was she who had set down the roots that bound Harmony to this place, and it was because of her that Harmony couldn't run away scared now.

Not when she finally had something worth fighting for.

In that moment, despite the terrifying visit from Alan and despite the inevitable confrontation brewing, Harmony realized she'd later look back on this as one of the very best days of her life.

Chapter 33

HARMONY

The next day Nolan escorted Harmony to work at the diner while Pastor Adam showed up at the house to take care of some church business with Mrs. Clementine. Both dogs, of course, kept a watchful eye over everyone.

Alan didn't come back around that day, which felt like a relief and a disappointment wrapped into one. They both knew he'd be back. What she didn't know was why he'd chosen to wait or where he'd taken up residence while he bided his time.

"Stop thinking about it," Nolan said rather abruptly on their drive home after work. "I can see your thoughts keep going back to him, and you need to cut it out."

Harmony let out a sarcastic laugh. "Easy for you to say. You're not the one he's after, and besides, you're so big, you could probably just step on the guy and squash him like a bug."

Nolan snorted. "If only."

Pastor Adam was still at the house when the two of them returned from their shift at O'Brien's and a bit of "getting her mind off things" around the city. Abigail, Gavin, and little Owen had also joined them, and everyone appeared to be in good spirits.

MELISSA STORM

"Um, guys," Harmony said gently. "This seems like a really bizarre reason to throw a party."

Abigail laughed and shook her head. "You're right about that. We're just here to pick up Dad and then we'll be on our way. Otherwise, he'd never leave just so long as Mrs. Clementine keeps feeding him her delicious cooking."

The pastor put both hands on his belly and puffed out his cheeks. "My daughter knows me so well."

"I'll send some with you to go," Virginia promised from her spot at the stove. It wasn't even four o'clock yet, but apparently she'd started—and nearly finished—prepping dinner all the same.

Meanwhile, Abigail stepped closer to Harmony with a drawn expression on her face. "How are you holding up?"

"I'm fine. It's everyone else I worry about." Harmony attempted a smile, but it refused to come.

"You don't always have to be strong. Sometimes it's okay to let others take care of you, too. Believe me, I learned that the hard way." She gave Harmony a hug that was cut short by commotion near the door.

They both turned to see Abigail's little boy crawling fast toward the doorway, making a beeline for all the interesting shoes piled there.

"I don't think so, little one!" she scolded, luckily saving her son before he could put one of Harmony's work shoes into his waiting mouth.

"Give 'em here," Nolan said, holding his arms out to accept the toddler. "I've got a knack for them when they're this age."

"Enjoy!" Abigail said, plopping her son into Nolan's outstretched arms.

Something very strange happened in Harmony's chest as she watched her friend lift the baby up high into the air and make zooming airplane noises as they dipped from side to side.

Owen giggled nonstop, encouraging all the adults to stop and watch the happy little boy who was completely oblivious to the scary situation that had put the rest of them on edge.

"Dinner's ready!" Virginia announced a short time later. The clock had only just struck four.

"And that's our cue to get out of here," Abigail said, accepting her son back from Nolan. "Thanks for watching him. I can tell you're one of his favorite people now."

"Aww, and he's one of mine," Nolan said, rubbing the wild tuft of bright orange hair on top of the adorable kiddo's head.

"Wait," Pastor Adam urged. "Mrs. Clementine hasn't packed our to-go box yet."

"We're not taking a to-go box," Abigail said, drawing one hand to her hip and staring her old man down.

"Then we can stay?" the pastor asked hopefully.

"Not when we have a nice salad waiting for us at your house," Gavin interjected, sending a knowing look to his future father-in-law.

"But who wants salad when you can have this fine sugared ham instead?"

"Your heart, for one," Abigail said. "Your poor overstretched pants for another."

"Do you hear how she talks to me?" Pastor Adam asked Harmony with a dejected look upon his face.

"She does have a point," Virginia said. "Your waistline has seen better days."

"*Et tu,* Mrs. Clementine?" he asked in mock hurt.

"And it's about time, too," Abigail said triumphantly, nudging her father, fiancé, and son toward the door. "Welcome to Team Healthy Dad, Mrs. Clementine. Goodnight, Harmony and Nolan."

Nolan and Harmony joined Virginia at the table and began to dish up. Yes, it was far too early for dinner, but Ginny had worked hard on this meal and now needed someone to enjoy it with her, seeing as the original intended had been forced away before he could take even a single bite.

Their hostess sat quietly contemplating the ham and au gratin potatoes before her. "Do you think it's my fault that the pastor has become a bit hefty these days? He looks just fine to me, but if his heart is in trouble...

I'd hate to be the one to push him toward the grave. He's such a good, kind man. The congregation needs him for as long as they can keep him."

Nolan shook his head vigorously and waved his fork in protest. "What? No way. As a fellow cook, I can tell you that it's our job to make the food as delicious as possible. It's his job to control how much of it he eats."

"Actually, that seems more like it's Abigail's job," Harmony pointed out.

Virginia didn't join in the laughter that followed. She seemed genuinely distraught and surprised by the fact that Pastor Adam could stand to lose a few—*okay, more than a few*—pounds. "Well, I'd hate for the poor man to be deprived. Maybe I can work out some lighter versions of some of his favorite dishes. Do you think that would help?"

Harmony studied her friend. Clearly, this matter was of the utmost importance to her and needed to be figured out right then and there. "I think he'd love that," she said, wondering if Mrs. Clementine didn't also sometimes imagine roles for Pastor Adam that he didn't actually serve. It was really too bad Virginia was already married, because she and the pastor made quite a happy and well-matched pair.

Virginia nodded and speared a piece of meat with her fork. "Well, then, that's decided. We're all going on a diet... Um, starting tomorrow."

"*Nooooooo,*" Nolan playfully shouted, but then winked at her and took a giant bite of his potatoes. "Seeing as I'm staying here for the indeterminate future, I'd love to help in any way I can," he offered once he'd swallowed down his food.

Harmony sat silent and watched the two of them carry on. It felt just like a real family with everyone helping everyone, all while gently and lovingly teasing each other.

How had she managed to live so long without this?

And now that she knew how this felt...

How could she ever bear to be without it again?

Chapter 34

HARMONY

That evening the hours stretched on endlessly before them. Following their early dinner, Mrs. Clementine set to work scouring her recipe cards for substitutions she could make to create modified healthy versions of the meals Pastor Adam liked best.

This left Harmony with Nolan, Muffin, and Pancake, and several hours before any reasonable person would turn in for the night. Harmony also felt as if it were her job to occupy their house guest, since he was, after all, there as a favor to her.

"Want to walk the dogs?" Nolan suggested when neither could find any shows they wanted to watch on TV. She'd have to talk to Virginia about the wonders of Netflix and Hulu someday soon, although she doubted very much the old woman would appreciate a reason to be more sedentary—especially now that she'd jumped feet first into this new health kick.

Harmony glanced at Muffin who popped up and wagged his tail like a tiny rudder. He seemed to get all the exercise he needed without even needing to leave the house, but the larger Irish Wolfhound who currently resided here, too, would definitely need the chance to stretch his legs. As much as Harmony would rather stay put knowing that Alan was somewhere nearby and waiting to strike, it seemed a good idea to get out of the house a bit.

Fresh air being good for you and all that.

Besides, Nolan and the dogs would protect her, if it came right down to it. She knew that now.

"Sure. Let's go," she said, heading to the coat closet to fish out her sneakers.

Once they were outside, each holding onto a leash for one of their comically mismatched dogs, Harmony closed her eyes and sucked in a deep, cool breath of early spring air.

"Pancake likes to run, but I'll try to keep him at a decent pace," Nolan explained, already straining against the behemoth dog who wanted to give chase to a squirrel he'd spied near the edge of the yard.

"Actually, let's go fast," she said, surprising herself. It would feel nice to run off some of her anxiety, even though she'd never been much a fan of exercise before.

They all picked up the pace, but after a block, it was clear that Muffin's short legs stood no chance of keeping up with the lanky Wolfhound.

"Well, we can speed walk a little at least," she offered with an apologetic shrug. Moving fast also meant that they didn't have to talk quite as much. Even though Harmony felt safe with her friend, she was afraid of the feelings she'd begun to glimpse just beneath the surface of that friendship.

When they'd first met, Nolan had made his interest in her clear, and it seemed his attraction to her was still there. But how did Harmony feel? After making such a horrible mistake in choosing her last boyfriend, she was afraid to trust herself again. Nolan had become such a good friend. Did she really want to risk losing him for the chance that they could build something more?

Knowing herself, she'd probably freak out and ruin things right away, losing both the deep friendship and the possibility of an even deeper love.

"You seem lost in thought," Nolan pointed out, his breathing hardly labored at all despite the brisk exercise.

Lost.

That was a good way to describe it, for she didn't have any answers no matter how hard she tried to find them. She didn't know when Alan would be back or what he'd do once the two of them came face to face. She didn't know whether she could trust herself to love Nolan, no matter how good he'd been to her. And she didn't know how she could carry forward in both situations without horribly messing something up, something important. Like the lives of people she cared about.

"What are you thinking about?" Nolan asked with a tilt of his jaw.

"Alan," she answered simply. It was partially true and seemed like the easiest way out of a conversation she wasn't quite ready to have yet. Or ever.

"But you're smiling." He nudged her slightly, forcing her to look up at him.

"I am?"

Nolan nodded. "Here and there, mixed in with your usual frowns."

"Hmm," she responded simply.

"Now you have to tell me," he insisted with a piercing gaze that made her cheeks burn hot.

"I have to?" she asked sarcastically. If only he knew, he'd likely change his mind. If ever the time existed for the two of them to have the relationship talk, this was not it. Too many other things were currently unresolved. They needed to focus on dealing with Alan first, and then Harmony could decide whether she felt courageous enough to admit her new feelings.

"Yes, enlighten me. Tell me about those thoughts that are running through your busy, busy mind." He smiled, but she couldn't return the gesture. Why did everything have to be so confusing? Why was the only thing she could count on right now the fact that Alan would find her?

Should she tell Nolan how much his protection meant to her? That it made her realize things she wasn't ready to admit aloud?

Maybe she could get by with a partial truth. "I'm just thinking that other than this Alan situation—which, yes, is a hugely negative thing—I'm actually really happy."

He scrunched up his face and regarded her like she'd lost her mind. Maybe she had. "That's kind of weird," Nolan said with a quizzical glance.

"It is, isn't it?" She shrugged. "I don't know. I guess I just like my life these days. And the people in it."

"Well, we like you right back," he said, erasing the doubt from his face and flashing her an enormous grin. "Is that all you were thinking about?"

"What do you mean is that all?" Harmony hissed at him. "It's plenty!"

He shrugged. "Just seems like you're holding something back."

"How do you know me so well already?" She couldn't help but laugh despite her worry.

"It's a gift." He picked up the pace, forcing Harmony to do the same.

Once she'd caught up, she shot him a scalding glance. "Really. I'm serious. I want to know. Tell me how you do that."

"I just pay attention. I see you and your strawberry, marshmallow, gingersnap goodness, and you just make sense to me in a way little else has before."

Harmony giggled, then gasped for breath. "We should really make s'mores again sometime soon. I'm afraid you've got me hooked."

"See, I knew there was a reasonable person in there somewhere."

Good, he'd picked up on the change of topic. This man really did love him some s'mores, and it seemed he had started to love Harmony, too. Even though he no longer pressured her for dates and she needed more time to sort out her past before she could focus on even the chance of a future...

She realized then that, when the timing was finally right, she wanted to be with Nolan now and forever.

Chapter 35

PASTOR ADAM

Abigail and Gavin were dead serious about that salad, and regrettably had a second to go with it the next day. Even given all of eternity, I'll never quite understand the appeal of vegetables served without salt and butter. Now that Mrs. Clementine had turned on me, too, it looked like I'd really, truly be losing some weight and in the very near future.

Lord, give me strength. I can do all things through You. Yes, even this... Right?

As I was pouring myself a cup of coffee and adding organic soy milk to the mix—yes, organic soy milk, a double sin against my poor, sweet morning cuppa—my phone buzzed with a call from Mrs. Clementine.

"I'm not happy with you," I said, admittedly pouting.

"Oh, stop," she cajoled. "You act like losing weight is the worst thing that's ever happened to you."

She and I knew that, as unbearable as this diet was already proving to be, I'd suffered much worse during my days on this earth. The first awful thing was losing Abigail's mother—not to the Maker, but to her own wanderlust. We're still married to this day, though I haven't seen her in more than twenty years. The second horrible thing occurred when we lost Abigail's husband, Owen, during his service to our country.

Considering these events, I supposed I could get through a bit of bland eating. Didn't mean I needed to be happy about it, though.

"If it makes you feel any better," she continued, "I'm already adapting some new, healthy versions of all your favorites. Nolan has offered to help, too."

As a matter of fact, this news did make me feel better. For even if I had a worryingly low amount of butter and salt in my diet for the next few weeks, at least I had love and support by the heaping spoonful.

"That Nolan is a nice boy," I told Mrs. Clementine while rummaging in the cabinets for some powdered creamer or other hidden beverage fixings.

"So nice," my friend agreed. "And so good for our Harmony."

I bobbed my head. "Those two already love each other like crazy. Have you noticed?"

Mrs. Clementine sounded offended by the question. "Of course I have," she scolded. "Everyone in the tri-county area has probably noticed by now."

"You mean except for Harmony herself," I corrected with a chuckle.

She sighed. "Funny, isn't it? She has the perfect partner right in front of her nose and she can't be bothered to see it."

"I'd say she's probably keeping her eyes closed on purpose. Sometimes good things can be just as scary as the bad."

"Mmm," she responded, and we both reflected on this thought for a moment. I jotted down a reminder for myself to explore this as a possible topic for a future sermon.

"How's Muffin?" I asked, not ready to say goodbye just yet because it would leave me alone with subpar coffee and my worried diet obsession.

"Such a sweet little house guest," Mrs. Clementine cooed. "But he is just a guest. Isn't he? When do you suppose his work with Harmony will be done?"

I thought about this for a second to make sure I was content with my answer. "It'll be done when it's done."

"How very philosophical of you." I could just picture my friend rolling her eyes at me from halfway across the city. "And how will we know when that time comes?"

"The Lord will tell us when it's time, and I reckon Muffin will as well."

Chapter 36

HARMONY

Harmony chatted with Jolene as they prepared to open O'Brien's for breakfast that morning. She found the familiarity of their routine comforting as she filled the condiment caddies and Jolene put the coffee on. Today was Saturday, their busiest day of the week, and Harmony looked forward to losing herself in the hustle and bustle of the busy restaurant.

"Carolina called me up last night and said she's been offered a paid internship at her college. Can you believe it? My baby, an intern!" Jolene spoke of her daughter so often that Harmony felt as if they were already dear friends despite not having had the chance to meet her just yet.

"Congrats. That's wonderful. Carolina must be as smart as they come." She went to write out the day's specials on the chalkboard by the door while Jolene continued to work with the coffee.

"She sure is. No idea where she gets it from, but she is certainly making the most of it since heading off to school." Jolene paused and chewed on her lower lip. It was clear how much she missed her little girl despite wanting to be supportive of her big city dreams.

"Well, she's lucky to have a mom like you," Harmony offered with a reassuring smile. She'd had dreams like that once, that a simple change of location could give her a whole new life. Good on Carolina for actually making it happen.

"Oh, look at the time!" the other waitress cried. "I got so busy boasting that we forgot to open up the restaurant on time."

Harmony glanced up at the clock above the kitchen and—sure enough—they'd missed opening time by five whole minutes. When she went to answer the door, she found a few expectant diners waiting to be given reprieve from the chilly morning air.

"Good morning," she told them each as they shrugged out of their jackets and hung them on the old-fashioned coat rack by the door. "Take a seat where ever you'd like, and we'll come 'round with the coffee in a moment."

Jolene was already on it, wielding a pot in each hand. They'd already set out mugs and creamers on each table, which made getting started with their first batch of customers quick and efficient. It was part of the reason folks liked O'Brien's so much. They never had to wait to get fresh coffee and great eats.

Nolan's face popped into view through the kitchen window. "Can I get something started?"

"Hold your horses!" Jolene called from across the way, and Harmony chuckled at their easy banter. That's how life felt here, she realized, *easy*. Well, except for all the unwanted drama she'd brought with her from Alabama.

The front door swung open again and another group of diners entered.

"Good morning and welcome!" Harmony and Jolene both called in unison.

The group smiled and nodded, then took a booth near the large window that overlooked the street. A lone customer also entered behind them, keeping his head tucked down as he proceeded to the far corner of the dining room. Even without getting a clear view of his face, Harmony knew exactly who'd just arrived at O'Brien's—and that he wasn't here for breakfast.

This ends now, she told herself, striding forward with far more confidence than she felt. Hopefully no one else would be able to see the way her breaths came out as short, desperate puffs or that her chest had tightened so severely it felt as if her heart would burst.

"I heard you were looking for me," she told Alan with a biting stare as she slapped down a menu in front of him. "What do you want?"

He kept his eyes glued to the table and muttered, "The same thing I've always wanted—*us.*"

This man right here was the one she'd once loved, although that now felt like a lifetime ago. How could she have been so blind? Was she really so desperate for someone to belong to that she was willing to settle for someone who had never been right for her—and who clearly also wasn't quite right in the head, either?

"You and I? We're no longer an us," she told him in a low growl, feeling the fear ebb out of her the longer and more insistently she confronted him. Emboldened enough to go forward, she preferred not to draw the attention of the other diners or to worry Jolene and Nolan if she could handle the situation herself.

"I'm sorry I hurt you," he said, finally looking up at her with the pleading blue eyes she had once found so alluring. Now they seemed icy and threatening rather than beautiful. "That wasn't supposed to happen."

She crossed her arms to form a shield over her heart and show him she wouldn't be backing down. Not this time. "Yeah, well, it did happen, and it's not just something I can forget about."

"But you *can* forgive me. Please, it's all I ever wanted—for us to be together." Despite the emotion in his words, Alan didn't cry, didn't even frown. He merely voiced his thoughts plainly all while keeping a watch for her reaction. In a way, this version of Alan was even more intimidating than the loud, violent beast she knew he could become when pushed hard enough. But this wasn't about what he claimed to want, it was about Harmony and what she needed—and that was to be free of him once and for all.

"No, Alan," she said, casting a pity frown his way. "My life is here now."

"This isn't a life, Harmony," he hissed as he spread his palms out flat on the table before him then took a deep, measured breath. "It's just a vacation. Your real life is back with me in Mobile. We can still be happy. Give us another chance."

His rage began to bubble beneath the surface, and soon it would be boiling over. They were in a public place, though. He couldn't hurt her here.

She pressed forward with her arguments, willing him to understand and give up of his own volition before things escalated further. "I'm not entirely sure we were ever happy to begin with. I've made up my mind and I'd thank you to stop pestering me. I'm not going back, and I don't want to be with you."

He shook his head and looked down at his hands, still splayed on top of the table as if he were bracing himself for something. "You're so different now. This isn't my Harmony."

"Correct, I'm not your anything. I'm my own person and I get to make my own choices. I'm choosing not to be with you. I don't want to be your wife, your girlfriend, your anything. In fact, I never want to see you again."

And suddenly, he became kind and placating again. "C'mon, don't be like that. I've given you time to come to your senses, and now it's time to come home." He reached up and tried to take her hand, but she yanked it away before he could make contact.

"I'm not going anywhere with you," she said, loud enough that some of the other customers had started to sneak glances their way. She caught Jolene's eye, and she nodded and walked calmly to the back of the house.

"I've come all this way to get you back. Not just today, but I've been trying on every day I've had off from work. Do you know how much driving that is just to be turned down?" His hands began to shake. His skin became ruddy.

"I'm sorry you wasted your time, but we're over. You made sure of that the last time I saw you." She shuddered at the memory of his crazed declaration that she was already his wife, that they should...

Never again. She'd ignored too many warning signs, been such a fool.

"I said I was sorry," Alan told her, his brows knitting together in frustration. And then he began to rise to his feet.

"And she said you need to leave. Now I'm saying it, too. Get yourself out of here, or I'll do it for you." Nolan appeared at her side, a towering presence that comforted her but should have terrified Alan.

If Alan was afraid, though, he didn't show it. Instead, he pulled himself the rest of the way to his feet and stared Nolan down. "You think I don't know who you are? You think you can just swoop in and steal my girl right out from under me?"

That was when the first punch connected straight with Nolan's nose. A terrifying thwack reverberated throughout the restaurant.

Jolene grabbed Harmony by the waist and pushed with all her might until they were both safely hidden in the kitchen...

Leaving Nolan to take care of Alan on his own.

Chapter 37

HARMONY

Harmony struggled against Jolene's determined grip. The larger woman clutched her tightly from behind, refusing to let Harmony leave the kitchen.

"But it's *my* fight," she argued. "I have to make sure Nolan's okay!"

Jolene talked calmly despite Harmony's struggle. "Fighting ain't always the right thing. Let Nolan handle it until the cops show up."

"The police?" Did that mean it would all be over within minutes? Could they make Alan leave her alone for good? Harmony went lax in her friend's arms.

"Yes, I called them and they're already on their way. It's almost over, baby." Jolene's hold relaxed enough for Harmony to break free.

"I'm sorry. I have to be there!" she called back, knowing the other waitress had only been doing what she could to keep her safe. But it wouldn't be fair for Nolan to bear the brunt of Alan's anger. He'd never done a single thing wrong and didn't deserve this.

Passing back into the dining room, her eyes zoomed straight to the back corner where one of the customers now held Alan back so he couldn't hit Nolan again. From the looks of the smug smirk on Alan's face, he was the only one who had managed to throw any punches in the brief time Harmony had been kept away.

"Stop!" she shouted, forcing herself between them.

It was clear the customer wouldn't be able to keep Alan back much longer. Determination gleamed in his cold eyes.

"Stay back." Nolan pushed her behind him so that he was the one facing Alan's fury head on.

"This is the guy you want over me?" her ex challenged.

"It's not like that," she whimpered, terrified of what he might do next.

"Oh, please," he growled. "I followed you enough to figure things out. You spend every waking hour with this guy. Looks like he's been sleeping over, too. Funny, cuz that whole time we were together you claimed to be saving yourself. But now you seem just fine jumping into bed with the first loser who came along."

"Alan," she sobbed. "Please stop. Please go away."

"I believe the lady made herself clear," Nolan said through gritted teeth, though he kept both hands extended downward in a gesture of peace. "If you leave now, you won't have to explain yourself to the police."

Nobody said anything for a moment.

"Okay?" Nolan urged.

Alan still didn't respond, but stopped struggling to break free.

Nolan nodded, and the customer released Alan from his hold.

He immediately took another swing at Nolan, connecting with his jaw and forcing him to hunch over in pain.

The customer tried to grab Alan again, but he fought him off and continued to advance toward Nolan, punching, kicking, spitting, doing whatever he could to hurt the other man.

Nolan pulled himself back up to his full height but didn't return his opponent's advances. He just took one hit after the next while Harmony screamed and cried.

Jolene advanced from the safety of the kitchen and helped the customer regain hold of Alan. They each managed to hold him by an arm while the other diners watched wordlessly as this horror unfolded before them.

Harmony continued to try to appeal to Alan's better judgment. He had once been kind, once been someone she loved. It didn't have to be like this, but he was the only one who could stop it. "Alan, you can't force me to be with you, and even if you could, this is not the way to do it. Please, please just go away and stay away."

He laughed and attempted to jerk his arm away from Jolene, but she held on tight, her freshly manicured nails digging into his bare arm so hard they left little pinpoints in his skin. "How can I leave with your friends keeping me in this sucker hold?"

She looked to Nolan who collapsed onto the nearest bench seat, clutching at his jaw which had already bloomed with ugly purples and blues. A trickle of blood dripped from his nose and ran down his chin.

Meanwhile, Alan appeared completely unscathed, save for the indents from Jolene's fingernails.

"Are you okay?" Harmony asked, taking a step closer to her boss, her friend, her Nolan, and feeling so terrible that he'd taken such a beating at her expense.

Why hadn't he fought back? He had every right given the scene Alan had caused in the restaurant, given that Alan had thrown the first punch, given that Alan was clearly out of his mind.

"Why didn't you defend yourself?" she demanded, almost as angry with Nolan now as she was with Alan. It was so hard seeing his handsome face marred by the gruesome evidence of the other wild man's anger.

"I didn't want you to think I'm like him," Nolan mumbled. Though his voice came out weak and breathless, she understood every single word. He wanted her to know that he would never hurt her, that his love was just that—*love,* pure and simple.

Alan swore up a blue streak, but she no longer cared. The police would be here soon enough to take care of him. It was up to her now to take care of Nolan. That's what people did when they cared for each other.

Nolan had taken the full force of the other man's range so that Harmony wouldn't have to.

Despite all her fears, doubts, and reservations, she saw it now. God's true presence lived in Nolan Murphy. When faced with an evil before him, he'd actually turned the other cheek!

The door swung open again, and this time two uniformed police officers charged into the restaurant. She didn't know how much Jolene had told them during their brief phone call, but it wasn't difficult to figure out what had happened here. They marched straight up to Alan and read him his rights.

It was over.

Finally over.

Chapter 38

HARMONY

armony sat in the booth beside Nolan as the officer took statements from the customers. The other cop had already left with Alan in the backseat of their squad car.

Jolene flipped the sign to read *closed* and brought everyone sequestered inside the restaurant another round of coffee.

"Does it hurt real bad?" Harmony asked Nolan, wincing as she watched him wipe away the last drops of blood from his nose.

He sucked in air through his teeth and tried to smile, but his face was too swollen to complete the gesture. "Nah, I've been in way worse scrapes than this."

Somehow Harmony doubted that, but she didn't argue the point. This wonderful man had taken quite the beating on her behalf and now minimized his pain to help assuage her guilt.

The female police officer came to speak with them then, and Harmony scooted over to give her space to sit in the booth beside her.

"What a start to the morning," she said with a fleeting grin, then cleared her throat and narrowed her eyes at Harmony. "Can you identify the man who caused the altercation here today?"

"Yes, he's my ex-boyfriend, Alan White. He lives in Mobile, Alabama, but he came here today looking for me."

They exchanged particulars about her history with Alan, what they'd been to each other, what had caused her to run away.

"Were you aware that this same Alan White was arrested in multiple states for prior incidents of domestic abuse and one previous case of assault?"

A sinking feeling swirled in Harmony's gut, but she forced herself to keep her voice steady. "I had no idea, but it makes sense."

So she hadn't been the only one. How many other poor women had been scared and manipulated by Alan? Who were they, and how were they faring now? Had they managed to escape or...? No, she refused to think the worst.

The officer nodded. "Seems his record goes back clear to his eighteenth birthday. They're sealed before that, but it's possible he had some juvenile infarctions as well."

Harmony head spun as she tried to make sense of it all. Yes, Alan had been cruel to her when they were younger, but he'd been so charming and kind when they'd found each other again as adults. He hadn't grown kinder—just became better at hiding the darkness.

"How did he get by so long with hurting so many people?" she asked, needing to know, needing to understand how this could have gone on for so long.

The officer shook her head slightly, but kept her voice professional. "It seemed he'd stay focused on one victim for a couple years before moving on to the next. He'd get brought in, but no one ever pressed formal charges. A lot of folks are afraid to go through with it, but after he paid a visit to your house, we did some digging and saw a clear pattern of behavior there. Tell me this, how long were the two of you together?"

"About a year." Would Alan really have continued to stalk and plead with her for another year or more before giving up? She hated that her freedom would have meant another woman was cast into the same nightmare she'd just narrowly escaped that day.

Harmony looked to Nolan for encouragement, then said, "And I'd like to press charges."

"I figured you might. I still have more to get through here, but one of us will call you down to the station later today so we can talk in more detail." She nodded at Harmony, then switched her focus to Nolan.

"I'd like to press charges, too. Whatever helps keep him far away from Harmony as long as possible." He didn't have much to add after making this declaration since he only knew about his side of the fight and whatever little Harmony had told him before that day.

It wasn't long before the officer thanked him and headed over to the next table.

"I'm glad you're not backing down," Nolan said, reaching for her hands across the table. "That guy deserves to rot in jail."

She sighed and leaned back in the booth, still clinging to Nolan's hands which, unlike his face, were perfectly untouched. That's what happened when a fight ended up so one-sided. "I'm no expert on the law, but something tells me that even with us pressing charges, there will be no rotting away for Alan. Either he'll move on or he'll be back."

Nolan grimaced at this news, but didn't seem to have any information to add to Harmony's understanding of what was ahead. "Just to be safe, you should get a restraining order."

"Oh, I will," she promised. "But I'm not letting him run me out of my home. I belong here with all of you. It's where I've always belonged."

He squeezed her hands, and she felt the rapid beat of his pulse against her skin. "I'm glad you're staying. Charleston just wouldn't be the same without you."

She forced a laugh. "Oh, please, I'm just one out of more than a hundred thousand people in this city."

Nolan's eyes seemed to dance as he held her in his gaze. "No *just* about it. You're not just one. You're *the one.*"

Her heart leaped in her chest. Earlier she'd been so afraid to have this conversation with him, but now she was glad it had arrived. Watching Nolan defend her from Alan's advances without so much as raising a fist when he could have so easily overpowered the slighter man had cleared any last vestiges of doubt from her mind.

Nolan had never been *just* a friend.

"What are you saying?" she asked him, still afraid but also willing to face that fear. For him.

He lifted the napkin from his face that had been used to staunch the flow of blood and patted to make sure the wound had really finished bleeding out. When his tissue came away clean, he attempted a smile again.

"Isn't it obvious?" he asked. "Ever since that first day in the restaurant when you chewed me out for talking too much... That's how long I've loved you. When that creep was pummeling me with his fists but I knew you were safe, it was okay because I loved you. Right now, I love you. And I want to keep loving you forever, as long as you'll let me. *If* you'll let me."

"There's no ifs here. I love you right on back, Nolan," she told him shyly.

Nolan smiled so big at this news that the contraction of his facial muscles caused him a fresh flash of pain. "Worth it," he said, smiling again just to prove his point.

She chuckled and shook her head. After all this time, after so much worrying, sharing the nature of her feelings with Nolan had been as easy as taking down a breakfast order. It was comforting, familiar, delicious, and exactly what she needed to start the rest of her day—her life—off right.

"You know," she said thoughtfully as Nolan watched her with a smaller, albeit just as goofy grin. "I'd kiss you now if I wasn't worried about causing you more pain."

He leaned in closer to her on the bench seat and whispered, "But it will hurt even more if you don't kiss me. *Right here,* and as we both know, that's the very worst place to hurt."

He took her hand and placed it gently over his chest. His heart beat wildly, and it was all for her. It had always been for her.

Without thinking twice, she leaned forward and pressed a very light kiss against his swollen lips. It wasn't the kind of kiss you got in fairytales, but it was real and perfect and just for them.

Chapter 39

HARMONY

Three weeks later

Harmony could hardly believe how quickly her life changed after that fateful day in O'Brien's. Since then, Alan had been arraigned on charges of criminal stalking, domestic abuse, and aggravated assault. The kindly officer from the restaurant had informed her that he'd been unable to make bail and was awaiting his trial date behind bars.

With the immediate threat gone, Nolan and Pancake moved back home, leaving Virginia and Harmony to spend more time developing their close friendship as well. It had been Ginny's idea to start a ladies craft circle through the church, and Harmony had eagerly agreed to co-lead the group even though she was still very much a newbie herself.

She and Nolan saw each other every day at work and a few nights each week for dates or joint ventures to the dog park. Tonight's visit was bittersweet, because it would be their last time bringing Muffin. With his work done, it was time for the special little Chihuahua to return home to his brothers, sister, and mother.

Although Harmony would miss her Muffin dearly, she'd already submitted an application to the local rescue expressing her interest in a wiry little terrier mix that had lived more of its life at the shelter than in anybody's home. She instantly connected with the trembling gray mess of fur that reminded her of a mini Pancake.

But before she could move forward with her adoption of the dog she planned to name "S'moresy," she needed to give sweet little Muffin the perfect send-off. She and Virginia had worked overtime to knit his siblings matching sweaters and hats so that they could also stay warm and stylish, no matter what the weather. Somehow the tiny dog had doubled his belongings in the short time with Harmony, and she wanted to make sure he had every last bit of it when he returned to Pastor Adam's house that evening. That's why she and Nolan had needed to drive separately tonight. Both trunks were needed!

"Are you going to be okay?" Nolan asked, pressing a kiss to her temple as the two of them watched Pancake and Muffin chase each other through the park.

She nodded and put on as brave a face as she could muster. "It's not like it's goodbye. I've volunteered to help Abigail with the dogs when I can. Kind of my way of paying it forward."

It wouldn't be the same, they both knew that, but Harmony had always known the arrangement with her church dog would be temporary. And to think she hadn't even wanted him in the beginning.

"Muffin, c'mere, baby!" she called, which brought the little dog racing over. She hoisted him into her arms and showered him with kisses on his tiny apple-shaped head. "It's amazing how much love fits into this tiny, little package."

"Just imagine how much fits inside a giant one like Pancake," Nolan teased, scratching his Irish Wolfhound behind the ears.

Harmony set Muffin back down so he could go play, and her boyfriend pulled her into his chest.

"It's a good thing you're doing. You know that, right? Muffin loves you, but he has a great home to return to. That little shelter dog you've had your eye on, though, he needs you. He's never had anyone before, and now that lucky little guy will get to go home with the very best person I know."

"Thanks," she sniffed, refusing to cry. Muffin needed her to be strong.

"It doesn't just have to be that one dog," Nolan continued on. "Maybe one day when we're old and married... You know, like a few months from now, we can rescue one dog for each month I've known and loved you."

"So six?" she asked with a laugh. "Seriously, Nolan. Sometimes you're just ridiculous."

"There's that smile," he said, pulling her into a dancer's pose so they could look into each other's eyes. "I love that smile, but you know, you kind of missed the important part of that last bit I said."

"You mean about the six dogs?"

"That, and..." he nudged.

Harmony twisted up her face as if thinking hard, then sighed. "I have absolutely no idea/ I guess you're going to have to spell it out for me."

"Oh, you are incorrigible," he teased, swaying back and forth with her, neither caring that they were in the middle of a very public place and waiting for Abigail and Pastor Adam to join them.

"What I was saying is that I want to marry you, Miss Harmony King, and soon."

"Are you sure?" she asked. "I mean, I can be a lot to handle. Do you really think you're cut out for the job?"

"So sassy with me now! Can't a man declare his intentions without getting the third degree?"

"Are you sure you really want to marry me?" she asked again. As much as she loved Nolan and knew he loved her, she'd spent her whole life as the girl no one had wanted, the girl without a family. It was still hard to believe this sudden, tremendous change in fortune.

"People don't usually ask so soon, you know," she pointed out, mentally kicking herself for killing this otherwise romantic moment.

He laughed and took a deep breath. "Who says I'm asking? I'm simply letting you know that I plan to ask someday soon. I know how you need a bit of time to get used to some ideas."

She stood on tiptoe to kiss him. "Thanks for letting me know. I will definitely think about saying yes when the time comes."

But Harmony already knew what her answer would be. There was nothing left to think about. Nolan was the only man she'd ever wanted and the family she'd been waiting her entire life to find.

She'd once believed that people couldn't change, but she now knew better. With a little love, anything was possible.

Chapter 40

PASTOR ADAM

Abigail and I both went to the dog park to welcome Muffin back to our fold. When we arrived, we found Harmony and Nolan slow dancing right there in the middle of the park as if no one was watching. It warmed my heart to witness just how far that young woman had come since first returning to our city earlier that year.

"She looks so sad," Abigail said walking beside me. "But so happy, too."

I couldn't help but agree. "That, my dear, is the complex nature of life. Loving means losing, but not loving also means not living."

"That's a good one," my daughter told me, nudging my arm. "You should write that one down to use in a sermon sometime."

I drew out my phone and told that sweet Siri woman what I needed to remember so she could take a note. I still preferred Mrs. Clementine as my secretary, but Abigail had been working hard to get me to use the technology in my life somewhat more effectively.

"Over here!" Harmony called, waving us on over.

"I can't believe today is our last day," she told Abigail, wiping at an invisible tear in the corner of her eye. "You promise I'll be the first you call whenever you need help?"

"Promise," Abigail assured her.

Muffin came running over with his Irish Wolfhound friend. He'd grown a little chunkier since he'd last lived with Abigail and me but, boy, did that dog have hearts in his eyes whenever he looked at Harmony.

Harmony scooped the dog up and buried her face in his short fur.

"It was good for him, too," I told her. "You gave Muffin a purpose and the chance to be his own dog outside of the pack. I can see he loves you dearly."

Harmony sniffed and wiped at another tear. This one was big and fat and raced quickly across the slope of her cheek.

"And I love him dearly. It's funny..." She laughed here as if to prove her point. "At first I thought you two were crazy, throwing a dog at me the moment I hit town, but now I can see why you did. Loving this little guy opened my heart in a way I hadn't been able to open it before."

"And now you're surrounded by all kinds of love," I said, slapping Nolan on the shoulder. He and I both knew that it wouldn't be long until he managed a proposal. Those two had loved each other first as friends, which made their bond that much stronger. They'd soon be ready to join their lives together under the Lord's watchful protection.

She nodded. "I really am, and I have you to thank for setting it all into motion."

I smiled a big ol' grin. "Not me. The Lord working through me and Abigail and these wonderful, little dogs. And you, too."

"It's funny—once I turned eighteen I thought I'd never step foot in Charleston again, but even after all these years away, it's never stopped being my home. It's like my heart always knew where it belonged even when I didn't."

"God brought you back," I told her. "He never gave up on you. He never gives up on any of us."

"And neither does my dad," Abigail added, offering me a quick peck on the cheek.

Harmony hugged us both, then reluctantly placed Muffin into my

310

waiting arms. "I'm going to miss you, little guy," she cooed. "But I know you're ready to help somebody else now."

And I knew it, too...

I couldn't wait to see how the Lord would work His wonders through our beloved church dogs next.

**Are you ready to find out who the Church Dogs help next?
Carolina Brown had her whole life figured out, but then everything changed in an instant...**

CLICK HERE to get your copy of *A Surprise Visit*, so that you can keep reading this series today!

🐾

And make sure you're on Melissa's list so that you hear about all her new releases, special giveaways, and other sweet bonuses.

You can do that here: MelStorm.com/gift

Acknowledgments

This time around the bend, thanks goes out to all the usual suspects and a few new members of my support system as well. My biggest helpers when it comes to bringing the church dogs to life are first and foremost my two Chihuahua babies, Sky Princess and Mama Mila.

They are the ones who made me fall in love with this tiny dog breed and serve as the basis for the personality and actions of all the doggie goodness this series has to offer. They also stay glued to my side while I write each day, laying cozily in cat baskets on top of my desk or even inside my shirt (which happens to be Sky's favorite place to snuggle). If you've never had a Chihuahua lick the inside of your ear, you are missing one of the most special blessings this life has to offer!

My husband serves as the inspiration for many of my characters and for all of the romance. Yes, even though I'm the romance author, he's the one with the big, loving heart! He's been through some very tough times in his life, but he's emerged on the other side as a strong, faithful man and one heck of a daddy to our little girl. He is also one of the earliest readers of my books, dutifully giving me his feedback even though my stories have a way of making him feel sadness deep-down. I promise to give him a big thank you hug on your behalf, if you find that his sacrifice has been worthwhile.

My other early reader and my Southern inspiration is Angi Hegner, the world's best assistant and friend! Aren't I blessed to have so many world's bests in my life? She reads my chapters as I write them, devours those messy first drafts without so much as batting an eye at the horrible, glaring typos. She gets excited and holds me accountable, too. Without Angi, the books definitely would not get written in a timely manner. That's for sure.

My editor, Megan, is another God-send. She polishes my words and somehow makes my crazy schedule work for the both of us. Mallory Rock brings my stories to life with her art, and the church dog covers are my favorites yet! My proofreaders, Jasmine Jordan and Alice Shepard, are also fantastic at what they do and such a joy to work with.

My brother, Ron, has recently moved in with our family and has helped tremendously by cooking our meals and keeping the house clean, so I can write, write, write. I love you, little bwuzzuh!

And to you, my reader, thank you for enabling me to keep doing what I love each and every day. Thank you for opening your heart to my characters and their stories, and thank you for being wonderful you!

A Surprise Visit

CHARLESTON HEARTS #3

To Sky Princess and Mila:
My own personal Chihuahua darlings

About this Book

Carolina Brown couldn't be more different than her mama if she tried—and truthfully most of us believe she worked hard at precisely that. She worked hard at everything else, too, and set off to college to accomplish big things in the wide world. Unfortunately, God called her right back to Charleston when her mama suffered a near fatal accident that left her requiring round the clock care.

Now that poor young woman reckons her ambitions have reached a dead end. I say it's just a sudden turn toward a new destination she can't quite see yet. If Carolina is ever going to believe in herself enough to reach for happiness a second time, she's going to need some outside encouragement.

It's been a long time since she's come round to the church, but that's not going to stop me from coming round to her. Sometimes you've gotta meet people part-way, and sometimes you've gotta entrust them with one miracle so they can find the next for themselves.

I do believe Cupcake is the perfect Church Dog for the job. Now I'm sure you're wondering, can one little Chihuahua fix two broken lives? Stick around and see for yourself.

A SURPRISE VISIT is a touching and poignant story from a New York Times bestselling author that will warm your heart, bless your soul, and leave you smiling.

Prologue

PASTOR ADAM

S ome say that whenever it snows in Charleston, God is giving a miracle to His most favorite of places. I tried to remember that as the cold reaching fingers of the wind poked and prodded my cheeks, nose, and everything else not already covered up by my scratchy winter getup.

But the more I tried to be optimistic about the shocking turn in the weather forecast, the harder that miraculous snow swirled. Soon it had bleached out the entire sky so that it was hard to tell where earth ended and the heavens began. We had a veritable snowstorm on our hands just in time for the celebration of His birth.

I mumbled a quick prayer that those traveling tonight would remain safe and hugged my threadbare coat tighter around my shoulders. Head down, I fought against the wind, marching ever closer toward my destination.

Leave it to me to get so caught up in my Christmas Eve sermon that I'd forget my cell phone right there on the pulpit! Lucky thing I did, though, because as I finally reached the front doors of the sanctuary, I discovered a most disturbing sight.

Our locally famous nativity scene had been on the fritz all week, but

now the angels' glowing halos had plum run out of power, casting the entire display into darkness. And on Christmas Eve, no less.

Ignoring the cold, which had found its way straight up underneath my clothes, I stepped closer to investigate the source of our power outage. Last summer old Mrs. Clementine had taken it upon herself to plant a little garden right outside the church. How could I say no to her request when she said all the food from our newly christened vegetable patch would be donated to feed the hungry?

And so, with more than a little trepidation, I said *yes*, and unfortunately so did every little critter within a twenty-mile radius. Even with the crops resting for the winter, I had no doubt that one of Mrs. Clementine's rabbit friends had tried to make a home of Christ's manger—and a snack of His power cords.

Upon closer inspection, I found that—yes, just as I'd suspected—a tiny ball of brown fluff had nestled into the nativity right there between Mary, Joseph, and the kindly shepherds who'd come to pay their respects.

Darn varmints!

Well, that's what I wanted to think, but then I stopped myself. These poor creatures hadn't expected the sudden snowfall either. They just wanted to get warm, and maybe God had sent me back to offer assistance on His behalf.

My toes began to go numb, but I tried to ignore that tingly sharpness as I stepped in for a closer look at the trembling animal.

Imagine my surprise when I found not just one creature, but five!

Right there next to the little Lord Jesus lay a mother dog and her four newborn pups. How they'd managed to survive this long was truly by the grace of God.

I didn't want to leave them, but I couldn't carry them all at once either. At least not on my own. After retrieving the box that our latest batch of hymnals had arrived packed inside, I stripped off my scarf and made a little nest. Then one by one, I lifted the mama and her puppies into the cardboard carrier and brought them into our church to get warm.

My lungs could scarcely take in a single breath of air until I made sure

that each pup was alive and well. Only by the glory of God each of these tiny newborns moved just enough to show me they were okay. You must understand these dogs were hardly bigger than my own thumb. They could have easily been mistaken for rat pups if not for that brave mama dog.

A quick search on my newly retrieved phone confirmed that these were not just any dogs. They were the most diminutive of all dog breeds.

I didn't even stop to question why the Almighty had sent me five Chihuahuas in need as an early gift for His birthday. I didn't have to, because right then I knew beyond the shadow of any doubt these dogs were meant to find us. Surviving that cold Christmas Eve outdoors was only the first of many miracles that mama dog and her pups would bring to our congregation...

Chapter 1

CAROLINA

Sixteen months later

Carolina Brown approached the crowded bus stop with a happy skip to her step. Out of all the political science majors at her college, she'd been one of the few to land this prestigious internship right in the nation's capital. It even paid!

For a first-year undergrad to receive this honor was practically unheard of, but her mama had always promised she was destined for great things. Ever since Carolina was a little girl in pigtails, her mother would sit her on her knee and say, "Sugar, there are two kinds of people in this world. The first is like me. We're happy just getting by. It's the simple life for us. But the other type? The type like you? Well, you're made to change the whole world."

And so, change the world Carolina would.

She'd settled on politics as her career path back when most kids still wanted to be ballerinas or firemen. Her perfect grades in school and stellar test scores landed her a full-ride scholarship to the college that she'd labeled as the second choice on her very lengthy list of possibilities, which was just perfect considering her mother's waitress earnings didn't leave any wiggle room for a spendy tuition bill.

She missed her mama back in Charleston, but the two still found time to speak on the phone several times a week and were just as close as ever. After all, it had always been just the two of them against the world. According to Mama, her dad's brains made her smart, but it was she who'd taught Carolina to have a strong work ethic and a kind heart. Brains were all well and good, but it was the other two traits to which she most owed her beginnings of success.

The city bus arrived with a booming hiss as it slowed to a stop, and Carolina made sure she was the very first to board. Although the raw mileage didn't amount to much, it would be a long commute due to the constant heavy traffic flow running in, out, and through the Capital. She kept her eyes glued out the window, not wanting to miss a single second. Perhaps on future journeys she'd bring a book to keep her company, but today she was far too excited to even try focusing on anything else.

After today, she'd be a right, proper politician. Just an intern for now, but everyone had to start somewhere. And this was the beginning for her.

When the bus entered the outer limits of D.C., Carolina almost died right there from true bliss. It wouldn't be long before she moved to the city herself. She'd save every penny from this internship, earn another scholarship for law school, and then she'd become a permanent resident of the greatest city within the greatest country in the whole wide world.

She didn't deny that America had its problems, but you didn't stop loving something just because it wasn't perfect. In fact, you loved it that much harder to help it fix those problems and discover new levels of greatness. That was precisely Carolina's plan. She didn't exactly know how she'd leave her mark on history, only that she would find out when the time was right.

She'd serve her country and her fellow citizens by using the talents God and her mama gave her. It all started today.

The lighted signs that hung near the bus's ceiling flashed the name of her stop, and Carolina rose to exit with a dozen or so fellow commuters. A moment later, she was there right on the sidewalk that led straight up to Congress. She considered pinching herself to make sure it was all real, but no. This wasn't the kind of dream come true that just randomly plopped into one's lap. She'd worked hard for this. Even though she was young, she'd given everything she had and then some to making this day a reality.

The skip returned to her step as she approached that beautiful domed building. A hand rose to heart reflexively out of respect for the power, history, and symbol of freedom that stood before her. She'd been here on school trips before, but this was different. Now she wasn't just a tourist. She belonged here. She'd always belonged here.

Gosh, it was just like coming home, only better.

Her phone jangled in her satchel, playing her silly "Yankee Doodle" ringtone for all within passing distance to hear.

Oops, better silence it now. That would have been so embarrassing if it had gone off in a meeting! She was already the youngest intern of the bunch, which meant she'd have to work that much harder to prove she wasn't just some kid. And "Yankee Doodle" certainly didn't help.

While flicking her volume switch to the off position, she glanced quickly at the screen. The missed call sported a Charleston area code, but it wasn't a number she recognized. *Hmm.*

A new notification popped up to inform her that she had a voicemail. She pressed to accept it and lifted the phone to her ear as she continued the blessedly short walk to her destination.

"Hi, Carolina. This is Officer Franklin with the Charleston Police Department..."

Carolina stopped so fast the person behind her ran clear into her back. "Sorry," she mumbled, giving all her attention and energy to the message that continued to play out in her ear.

"There's been an accident, a pretty bad one. Your mother is on her way to the Medical University of South Carolina now. We saw that you were the last person she called so figured you'd be the one to notify. Um, it's probably best you come immediately. We aren't—"

Carolina ended the call abruptly and then turned around and ran back toward the bus stop as fast as her feet could carry her.

Yes, today was the first day of the rest of her life. Hopefully it would be one she'd want to keep living.

Chapter 2

CAROLINA

Carolina drove straight home to Charleston without taking any breaks. Regardless of her determination to get there as quickly as possible, it still took more than eight hours to reach her mother's bedside. The whole way she'd murmured one quiet prayer after the next.

"Dear God, please let her be okay. Please help my mama," she'd chanted almost as the chorus to a song she couldn't quite get out of her head.

As her desperation grew, however, her prayers took on a rougher edge.

"Don't take her away from me. I'll do anything. I'll never leave her again, if only she'll be okay," she begged the God she'd always trusted and respected, although she had major questions about that commitment now.

After all, what good would it do changing a world that didn't include its very best person? Why would the Lord allow her to work so hard and tirelessly for something, only to grab it away at the last possible second? And why would He allow her beautiful mother to suffer like this?

The sun hung high in what would have been a beautiful day if not for the dark worries and fears pouring forth from Carolina's heart. Not even a single cloud crowded the sky, but her eyes filled with the precipitation of tears.

Today, she was the storm.

And she blew into the hospital, a cyclone of demanding anxiety.

"Where is she?" she cried to the crowd of nurses standing near their desk. "Where's my mama, Jolene Brown?" Her fingers gripped the edge of the counter so tightly, her knuckles turned white. Still, she felt nothing but the fear surging through her.

The oldest nurse licked her lips and took a step forward. Her bright blue scrubs pinched at the armpits, suggesting she'd recently put on a good deal of weight. The heavy bags under her eyes hinted at a lack of sleep. Was this really the person best qualified to care for her mother now?

"Come with me," the nurse instructed.

And then Carolina was following her wordlessly down the hallways of the intensive care unit. There were so many things she wanted to ask, but first, she had to see her mama. That would tell her everything she needed to know, or at least answer the most important question: *Is she okay?*

The nurse paused outside an open doorway and offered a sad smile. "She's right in there. Go on, and I'll call for the doctor so he can update you directly."

Carolina thanked the woman, swallowed hard, and then ducked her head while entering the sterile room. It was the exact opposite of how her mama preferred to keep things at home. There, everything was alive with color—bold prints and proclamations and an explosion of well-kept clutter that showed the world she was too busy enjoying her life to worry about the housekeeping. She even had a replica of that sexy leg lamp from "A Christmas Story" amidst her collection of odd, chuckle-inducing decor.

In this place, though, everything was devoid of color, clean, tidy...lifeless.

When her eyes locked onto her mother lying unmoving on the bed, she let out a gasp that properly combined her panic at seeing her mother unconscious but her relief at noting the steady rise and fall of her chest.

Carolina didn't even remember rushing to her mother's side, but suddenly she was there. "Mama?" she asked, moving the blankets aside to find and squeeze her hand. "I'm sorry it took me so long, but I'm here now."

Her mother made no indication she'd heard Carolina's words or even that she knew her daughter had come all this way to be at her side. Her eyes didn't open. Her fingers didn't squeeze Carolina's back. But the heart rate monitor continued to beep steadily along, promising there was still life in there somewhere.

"Mama?" she asked again, her voice breaking on the simple two-syllable word.

Soft footsteps approached from behind, and Carolina waited, unwilling to look away from her mother for even a second. Even as she cried, she resisted the urge to pinch her eyes closed tightly to relieve the wellspring of tears that had badly blurred her vision. Still, she could see clearly enough to make out Mama's form, to make sure she was still there with her.

"She's in a medically induced coma," the patient voice that hovered just above her head explained, its speaker coming around the bed to face her.

Carolina trembled as she forced herself to ask the impossible question. "Is she going to wake up?"

The doctor nodded. He was wrinkled and grandfatherly. He looked like someone you could trust, and she now needed him to say that everything would be fine in the end. "We think so, but we can't be sure," he said gently, waiting for a moment to make sure Carolina understood.

As the full impact of these words hit her right in the heart, Carolina gasped and bit down on her knuckle.

The doctor waited for a few seconds before explaining further. "There was a lot of swelling in her brain. The coma is a precautionary measure to help bring that swelling down."

"Her brain?" Carolina mumbled without removing her hand from her mouth. She needed the sweaty, earthy smell of her skin to keep her grounded. "Does that mean...?" She couldn't even bring herself to finish that horrible sentence.

"We don't know. It's too soon to tell," he answered quickly. "But we're going to do everything we can to bring her back to us."

The doctor placed a hand on her shoulder and offering a consoling smile. "I can tell your mother meant a lot to a good many people. Half of Charleston has gathered in the waiting room to await an update on her condition. Perhaps you'd like to go say hello?" He smiled again, cleared his throat, then left the room just as quickly as he'd entered.

Now it was just Carolina and Mama again, same as it had always been.

What would she do if she lost the one person who'd always given everything for her?

Chapter 3

CAROLINA

arolina finally left her mother's bedside when she could no longer delay her need to use the bathroom or to get a drink of water to wet her very dry throat. Just as the doctor had mentioned, an overwhelming number of their neighbors, friends, and her mother's coworkers filled the waiting room.

Nolan Murphy, the owner of the diner where her mama worked, was the first to rise and wrap his arms around Carolina. Hardly a moment later, the others came forward and everyone huddled piled on to form a giant group hug. Some of the folks who'd come out Carolina had known her whole life, while others she scarcely recognized. Yet still they were all here for her and because they loved her mama every bit as much as she did.

"It's a terrible thing, what happened," the freckle-faced Nolan said before returning his mouth to a firm line. It looked as though he were trying not to burst into a fresh round of tears himself.

She found it unnerving to see a man as tall and generally happy as Nolan Murphy break down in agony. If someone as big and smiley as him couldn't hold it together, then what chance did regular, little Carolina have?

And he was just one of many huddled together in misery.

The pastor of the church they'd attended off and on through Carolina's childhood had also come to lend his support. "Your mama's smile could brighten up even the dreariest of days. She always had a friendly greeting and a full pot of coffee for anyone who stopped in at the diner. Which I was happy to do all too often," he added, placing a hand on his sizable midsection and offering a far-off smile.

The pastor's daughter spoke next. "I'm not sure you remember, but I used to babysit you when you were small. My name's Abigail."

Carolina noticed that now she had a baby of her own straddled on her hip, a gorgeous red-headed boy in denim striped overalls. Carolina smiled at the baby and reached for one of his pudgy hands to give it a squeeze hello. There was something about this innocent, young life she found calming while her old, familiar world continued to crumble at an alarming pace.

"We're all here for you and for your mother now," Abigail said. "Is there anything you need us to bring you to make waiting more comfortable? I know how close the two of you are, so I'm guessing you won't be willing to set up shifts to give you some time off to rest at home."

Carolina shook her head sadly. "No. As long as she's here, I will be, too."

"The whole city is praying for your mama now, and we believe He will make her better," the pastor added, clasping his hands reverently before him as he glanced toward the ceiling and murmured a quick prayer.

"I know that sometimes it's easier not to talk when things get tough. That's what I went through when I lost my first husband, Owen." Abigail paused." To help you now, we brought someone to help keep you company and lend support without asking for a single word in return... Gavin?"

Abigail stepped back, and a handsome man walked forward with a stout, little fawn and white Chihuahua in his arms. "This is Mama Mary," he said.

Carolina took in the bright vest the tiny creature wore proclaiming it as a therapy dog. It sat silent and contented in Gavin's arms as Abigail continued the introductions.

"She's one of our famous church dogs and our very best therapy dog of the bunch. That's why we brought her here to wait with us and lend comfort where it's needed."

The dog watched Abigail lovingly, wagging its tail gently the entire time she spoke. When Abigail finished speaking, Mama Mary at last turned to Carolina with a questioning glance.

"Would you like to hold her?" Gavin asked kindly.

Yes. Carolina realized then how much it would help to have something soft to hug in her arms while she waited for only God knows how long to get an update on her mother. She nodded and opened her arms to the shivering creature.

Gavin passed the little dog to her and it immediately began to sniff and lick Carolina's hands.

"Thank you," she said. "Thank you for everything."

Carolina clung tight to that little ball of fur for the next several hours. A couple of times Abigail borrowed Mama Mary to take her outside for a bathroom break or a drink, but she always returned the Chihuahua to Carolina the moment she came back.

Slowly, the other visitors began to trickle away. Each left his or her cell number asking to be informed the minute there was any news on Mama's condition. Abigail, however, told Carolina not to worry about it. She or her father would make sure everyone knew, in due time, said that Carolina didn't need another thing to worry about just then.

By the time night fell, only Abigail remained at her side.

"You don't have to stay," Carolina said with a weary smile. She truly appreciated all the support, but everyone else had lives and families of their own to get back to. This must be especially true of a young mom like Abigail.

"I want to," the other woman said, placing an arm around Carolina. "My dad and husband can handle little Owen on their own tonight. This is where I need to be right now."

Carolina murmured her thanks and laid her head on Abigail's shoulder. At some point she fell asleep, and the slumber that followed was blessedly sound. This was the first time in all her life Carolina had been content to rest without dreams. If her mama didn't make it through this, soon she might also be living without dreams or aspirations, too.

One thing was for certain—Mama was the very heart of who Carolina had become. And without her heart, well...

Life just wouldn't be worth living anymore.

Chapter 4

CAROLINA

A few days later, the doctors finally woke Carolina's mother from her drug-induced coma. They kept Carolina out of the room until after they'd run a battery of tests and secured whatever urgent knowledge they needed to help them determine what would come next with her care.

By the time Carolina was finally ushered into the tiny hospital room, she found her mother resting on a slight incline and still connected to a crazy amount of tubes, wires, and monitors. She had to fight hard to prevent herself from running over and clutching her poor mama to her chest as she cried giant tears of joy at seeing her awake at last. Instead, she approached slowly, as if the slightest bit of commotion could upset the delicate new balance the medical staff had worked so hard to achieve.

Her mother spoke first. "My darling girl," she croaked, her voice unnaturally hoarse, her eyes unnaturally vacant.

"Mama," Carolina cried as she wiped at the fresh rivers of tears that ran down her cheeks. Her words, too, surged out in a rapid deluge. "I came as fast as I could. I've been waiting here all this time. I'm so glad you're going to be okay."

"Did they tell you?" her mother asked without blinking, smiling, or adding any type of inflection at all.

"Tell me what?" Carolina asked with a giant smile, hoping it would help to ease her mama into one as well. The doctors had said many things, but she hadn't heard much after finally learning that her mother was awake and that the damage to her brain had been minimal. She still had her mama, after all. That was the thing that mattered most—in fact, it was the only thing that mattered at all.

"I can't walk," her mother informed her. Her mouth remained open slightly after delivering these words and she sucked in deep, rasping breaths across her chapped and flaking lips.

Carolina shook her head and continued to grin wide. If Mama needed her to be the optimist now, then that's exactly what she would be. "You're just weak from all that extra rest they gave you," she cooed. "You'll be back on your feet in no time."

"*No.*" Her mother let out a beleaguered sigh and widened her eyes as if begging Carolina to understand. "No, I can't walk." Each word came out slowly, definitively, one weighty proclamation after the next.

"Ever again?" Carolina asked, following a ragged intake of breath.

Her mother closed her eyes and nodded subtly.

It took Carolina a few moments to gather her thoughts and force the bright outlook this situation so desperately needed. "Oh, don't say that, silly Mama. Medicine has come a long way these days. I'm sure with lots of patience and the right physical therapy, you'll be walking again before you know it."

"No," her mother answered firmly, staring straight into her daughter's eyes with a pitiful expression. "And please don't make me say it again. It's already hard enough without having to keep explaining."

Carolina bit her lip to keep from saying anything more. She was so happy to see her mama awake again, but it didn't seem like that enthusiasm was returned. In fact, it felt as if she'd somehow managed to make everything worse.

Mama took a long pause to catch her breath before continuing, "The accident damaged my spinal cord. I can't walk, and I'll never be able to again. Do you understand?"

Carolina nodded and begged her tears not to fall. Her mother needed her to be strong right now, not to make things harder than they already were. "You're still with me," she said at last. "That's the only thing that matters now."

She moved a chair to her mother's bedside and sat holding her hand, feeling so relieved and grateful each time she felt her mother's pulse beat in time with her own. After several minutes of companionable silence, she whispered, "How did you get in that terrible car wreck to begin with?"

Mama hesitated, her hand tensed and she gently moved it out of Carolina's grasp. "I don't want to talk about that."

Post-traumatic stress—that had to be it, and Carolina should have known better than to press her for details she wasn't yet ready to offer. Had less than one year of college really changed things between them so much?

The woman lying in the bed beside her looked so familiar yet felt somehow also like a stranger. To change the world, would Carolina have to let go of the parts that mattered most to her?

That was when she remembered the bargain she'd made with God. Those desperate murmured prayers echoed back to her now: *Don't take her away from me. I'll do anything. I'll never leave her again, if only she'll be okay.*

God had kept up His end of the deal, and now it was time for Carolina to keep up hers.

"Mama," she said, waiting for her mother to shift her gaze back toward her. "Don't you worry about anything. We'll get you the fanciest wheelchair money can buy and then we'll bedazzle it to make it just as special as you are. And I'm coming home. I'll be there for you every step of the way."

Her mother squeezed her hand but gave no other indication she'd heard Carolina's emphatic promise. Well, that was fine. Knowing Mama, once she'd rested up and regained some of her strength, she'd be trying to push her daughter out the door again.

"Don't worry about me," she'd insist. "You have such important things to do."

Carolina had no doubt her internship had already been offered to another candidate. She could try again in the fall semester. Perhaps they'd take pity on her, give her a second chance considering the circumstances.

But would that allow enough time to help Mama through this drastic life change? And would she ever feel safe again knowing her mother was so far away? What if something else happened and she wasn't there?

All these questions swirled together in Carolina's mind, but she couldn't find a clear answer to any of them.

Just take things one day at a time. Everything in due time.

All her life she'd been in a hurry to move on to the next thing. Now, for Mama's sake, she'd need to take her time. All her plans hadn't necessarily been discarded, just postponed. Then again, maybe it had been a mistake to leave Charleston at all.

Oh, she wished she knew. Then maybe she'd stop blaming herself for this horrible tragedy that had befallen her dear, sweet mama.

Maybe I don't deserve to be happy, she thought before heading out to the hall so she could finally let her tears fall unencumbered once more.

Chapter 5

PASTOR ADAM

The call came in late Thursday afternoon.

"Abigail," I yelled for my daughter, thankful that she spent the better part of her days working from my home even though she and her new family had officially moved into a place of their own.

Abigail peeked out from the kitchen where she was fixing a healthy snack for the both of us. "Oh, my phone," she exclaimed, abandoning the apple she'd been slicing and making a dive for her cell phone.

"It's Carolina," she told me before clicking over to answer the call. She nodded and said "mm-hmm" and "oh" a bunch before concluding with, "We'll be there just as soon as we can" and ending the call.

"Jolene's up," she informed me, even though I'd already figured out this particular bit of good news for myself.

"How is she?" I asked hesitantly. The way my daughter now worried her lip hinted that it wasn't all good news.

"Paralyzed," Abigail said with a frown.

"Oh," I said softly. Poor Jolene. She loved flitting about the diner like a butterfly surrounded by blossoms. Being forced to stay still would be utter torture for her.

"That's what I said, too." Abigail looked lost for a moment before bending down to pick up Mama Mary and giving her a good, long cuddle. "Carolina said she's not quite ready to talk about it yet."

"I'd imagine it's very hard news to digest," I said, keeping my rear glued to my favorite reclining chair. I was eager to be at the Brown ladies' sides, but first my own daughter needed some talking through things.

"We'll take up a collection this Sunday," I said, watching for Abigail's reaction. "And I'm sure Gavin and his friends would be more than happy to build some ramps at her home. Right?"

Abigail nodded. "Her whole life is going to be different now."

"Yes, but Jolene is a fighter, and she has a lot of people on her side." I knew the Lord would provide a way, that He never gave us anything we couldn't quite handle, but this was a much bigger thing than most of us had ever needed to handle. Besides that, Jolene—bless her heart—was one of my Easter and Christmas churchgoers rather than a regular. Even the most devout Christian would have a hard time wading through something like this. Was Jolene's faith ready to withstand it? Was Carolina's?

"Carolina," she murmured as if reading my thoughts. Abigail met my eyes as she took in a shaky breath. "Jolene will rise above. I know she will. But I don't know how Carolina is going to be about accepting help. She's put everything she worked for her entire life on hold to be with her mother now, and..."

Her voice cracked and fell away. My poor Abigail had been raised without her mother and then lost her first husband during his military service. Although she had a very fulfilling and happy life now, she had an uncanny ability for finding and diagnosing people's pain.

I could also tell she had the sparks of a plan that excited her. "What do you suggest?" I asked casually.

"You saw how much she liked having Mama Mary with her during all that waiting. Do you think one of the puppies could help her—help them both—at home?" The term *puppies*, of course, was a misnomer. The Chihuahuas were all grown now, although four of them had just been little things when I first found them in our church nativity scene.

"Well, if Jolene truly is paralyzed, she'd be a prime candidate for a service dog. While we get her on the waiting list, perhaps one of our tiny therapy dogs can help in the interim. But that's only if they want it. They both have to face a lot of changes now and the hard work that comes with them."

"Yes," Abigail agreed. "But sometimes it's helpful to not have to think or speak or do anything but pet a sweet, little dog. Besides, weren't you the one who forced Muffin on our friend Harmony practically the very moment she came to town?"

I chuckled. "That I did."

"And didn't Muffin help her out of a tough spot?"

"That he did. Are you thinking we need to send Muffin out on a long-term assignment again?" I brought the dogs to church with me for my counseling sessions each week, but sometimes our congregants benefited from a longer time with one of our dogs. If my daughter was right, then Carolina and Jolene might also fall into that category.

"Not Muffin," Abigail answered with a quick shake of her head. "Somebody new this time."

"Cupcake, do you think?" I asked, eyeing the scrappy little guy who was picking on one of his siblings across the room. "He's the best fighter we've got. Perhaps he'll inspire them."

"Yes," Abigail said, racing over to offer me a tight teddy bear hug. "Cupcake will be absolutely perfect."

Now we just had to find out whether the Brown ladies would agree.

Chapter 6

CAROLINA

Carolina and her mother had a steady stream of visitors straight through the night. Even after Mama had drifted off for some much-needed rest they continued to filter through the room, pausing to chat with Carolina, offering help should she need it, and sharing their favorite memories of the chatty waitress the entire city so adored.

She was surprised that the pastor and his daughter were among the last of the visitors to arrive, having fully expected them to turn up first. Abigail entered with a tiny white dog following closely at her heels. He, too, wore a miniature service dog vest, which explained how she'd managed to trot him right into the intensive care ward.

"Is she sleeping?" Abigail asked, hardly above a whisper when Carolina rose to offer her a hug hello.

The women parted, and Carolina glanced back at her mother's still form. "Yes, for now."

"Would you mind leaving me to pray with her alone for a little bit?" the pastor asked, resting his hands above his portly midsection.

"Sure," Carolina conceded. Some fresh air might do her good. At least now she knew what they would be up against and that her mama would live to see another day. Many more, at that.

Abigail looped the leash over Carolina's hand and smiled. "This is Mama Mary's son Cupcake."

The little dog wagged its tail so vigorously at this greeting that his entire back half shook. He looked exactly like a thinner, more energetic version of his mother. People often said the same thing about Carolina and her mama, too, seeing as they both shared blonde hair, fair skin, and those same chubby cheeks everyone seemed to find so angelic.

Carolina couldn't help but smile as the three fell into step on their way down the hall. "A boy named Cupcake," she said with a chuckle. "Well, I never."

"The Sunday school kids named all the puppies, and it seemed they had baked goods at the top of their minds at the time." Abigail laughed, too. The three of them clopped through the ward together. Although normally lighter of step, Carolina's feet fell heavily now, such was her immense fatigue.

"Thanks for bringing him by," she told Abigail as she kept her eyes glued to the merry little canine trotting alongside them. "Mom will be happy to see him when she wakes up. She's only been awake for a few hours and already she's complaining about how bored she is."

Abigail snorted and shook her head. "That's our Jolene, all right."

She paused to wait for Carolina at the exit. "Actually, we brought Cupcake for you," she revealed.

Carolina took a moment to digest this revelation as she passed through the sliding glass doors and into the open air outdoors. She'd enjoyed waiting with Mama Mary before, and the only way she was helping Mama now was by offering her company, so why not add the furry companion to the mix? It did seem odd that Abigail had chosen to bring a different dog this time, but perhaps the mother Chihuahua was needed elsewhere.

"Well, thank you," she said at last. "He seems just as sweet as his mama."

"Cupcake is sweet, but he's also a little bit spicy. He's actually our alpha pup. He'll listen to Mary, but he's forever telling his brothers and sister what's what."

"Sounds a bit like my mom," Carolina remarked, glancing up toward the darkening sky.

Abigail wrapped her arms around herself even though it wasn't the slightest bit cold. "My father and I put out some feelers about a service dog for your mom," she said as she watched Carolina watch the sky. "It will take some time, but we think a well-trained Golden Retriever or German Shepherd could make both of your lives much easier as you adjust to the new way you'll need to do things from now on."

A service dog? Carolina had begged for a dog growing up, but Mama had always said it would be unfair since they didn't have enough time to look after it and the poor thing would be lonely whenever Carolina was at school and Jolene was at work. Instead, they'd adopted a string of well-intentioned but mostly standoffish cats to round out their little family.

Maybe the dog would be a blessing to the both of them, especially if it was trained to help her mama get around.

"That's a great idea. Thank you," she mumbled.

Abigail smiled and shifted her attention toward Cupcake as the little dog sniffed around the grass. "My husband and some of the other men from church are going to install ramps and get your mother's bedroom moved downstairs. You'll just have to let us know a good time to come by, and they'll take care of everything to welcome your mama back home."

Carolina reached up to swipe at a fresh well of tears. "That's very kind of y'all. Thank you for taking such good care of us."

"There's one more thing," Abigail said with an added surge of warmth in her voice. She waited for Carolina to glance over at her before continuing. "We want you to look after Cupcake for a while, too."

As much as she liked the little dogs and Abigail, too, why hadn't she chosen someone else to ask this favor of? Surely, she must understand how much extra was already on Carolina's plate these days—and she'd hate to do an improper job taking care of the sweet, little Chihuahua who was now growling at a bird that had winged over to a nearby tree branch. Besides, wouldn't they soon have a service dog to take care of as well?

She shook her head quickly. "What? Why? Is there not space at your house? If that's the case, then I suppose—"

"No." Abigail laughed and waved her hands. "It's not like that. We don't need you to, but we think it might do you some good to have someone other than your mama to keep you company as the two of you adjust."

"I don't know..."

"We won't force this on you, but please think about it. Getting used to her new limitations is going to be very frustrating for you both. There will be anger, tears, saying things neither of you mean. I think it may help to have an impartial friend who will always be happy to see you and can offer you a pair of big, nonjudgmental ears when you need them."

"Okay, I'll think about it," Carolina promised, even though she already knew the answer would be no. Who in their right mind would add something more to her plate when it was already so full she could barely keep it from clattering to the ground?

Cupcake turned back to her excitedly and let out a tiny, high-pitched bark.

He sure was cute, but cute didn't fix any of their problems now.

Carolina would have to lean on God and the community for that.

Chapter 7

CAROLINA

When Carolina returned to her mother's room, she found a young man waiting outside the door. His dark, curly hair appeared unkempt and his clothing suggested he may have come straight from the gym. It hardly seemed appropriate attire for a hospital visit.

"Can I help you?" she asked, finding him familiar, though not someone she could readily identify. Maybe he just had one of those faces.

The strange visitor straightened and cleared his throat. "Oh, um, I came to see Mama Jolene, but someone's already in there praying with her and it felt rude to interrupt."

"I'll just go check on Dad," Abigail said, handing Cupcake to Carolina before she let herself into the room and clicked the door shut behind her.

"Who are you, and why are you calling my mama *Mama?*" Carolina demanded, holding tight to the dog in her arms.

Cupcake seemed to sense her upset because a low growl sounded in his throat.

"I'm Levi, and your mama is a friend of mine. Whenever I drop by the diner, she always has a fresh dish of water for my dogs." He offered his hand to Cupcake, who gave it a vigorous sniff and then relaxed into Levi's palm.

Carolina had spent many weekends helping out at the diner during her high school years, yet she had never seen Levi and his dogs—at least not there. He was handsome in a way she didn't quite trust. What did this young charmer want with her middle-aged mother? How was their relationship close enough to warrant a visit the very same day she woke from her coma? And if he were actually important to her mama, wouldn't she have mentioned him on one of their many nightly phone calls?

She met his dark eyes. They were too dark, too easy to hide secrets within. "Why do you bring your dogs by the diner?" she demanded. "Can't you give them water at home?"

Levi chuckled. "Well, I suppose I could do that, but they aren't *my* dogs. I walk them for their owners and O'Brien's is right on our route."

"Oh." Carolina shifted her weight uncomfortably. Levi still seemed familiar to her, but it had nothing to do with the diner or walking dogs. "Do we know each other from somewhere?" she asked.

"I sat behind you in eighth grade math," Levi said with a shrug and an apologetic smile. He looked every bit her opposite then. Where she was unwelcoming, he proved friendly. She was fair and dainty, but he was tall, strong, and dark. Yet if he was to be believed, they both cared deeply for her mama.

"Feels like a lifetime ago, doesn't it?" he said as he placed his hands in his front pockets and began to rock back and forth on his heels.

She continued to study him, unsure of what to say. "Did we have any classes together in high school?" she asked, unable to recall a single one on her own.

"No, my family moved that summer. I went to high school in Virginia."

"But you're back now," she said flatly. If they'd attended middle school together, then that meant he was a recent graduate, too. Why had he come back to Charleston, and why was he walking dogs past her mother's diner every day?

"I like it here, and I want to go to school at the community college, too."

She raised an eyebrow in question. "Want to?"

"I'm putting in a year at work first to help save up and to meet the residency requirement for lower tuition," Levi explained, unmoved by her rudeness.

"How very pragmatic," she said as she ran her fingers along Cupcake's soft fur.

They both looked to the door, but it was still shut firmly with Pastor Adam and Abigail inside.

"And you went off to D.C.," Levi spouted off. "Where you landed a prestigious paid internship, working on Capitol Hill."

"How did you...?"

"Your mama's very proud of you," he said with a laugh. "She tells everyone everything about you, whether they want to hear it or not. I also know your first crush was on Freddy Franklin back in second grade."

Heat rose to Carolina's cheeks. She hadn't thought about that before, but if Levi was truly a friend of her mother's, then that meant he knew all the sundry details of her life—including her goals, ambitions, likes, dislikes, first word as a baby... you name it. And yet she knew absolutely nothing about him.

"I never minded," Levi said with a shrug. "In fact, I like hearing how the other half lives from time to time."

She laughed sarcastically at this. "Other half? *Hardly.* In case you forgot, my mother is a waitress and I don't have a father."

He shrugged again. "That's where you come from," he pointed out. "Not who you are. And going by everything I've heard from your mama, you are definitely one of a kind, Carolina Brown."

They fell silent until at last the door opened again and the pastor and Abigail emerged with hellos for them both.

"She's up now," the pastor said, "and asking for you."

"I'll tell my mama you stopped by," Carolina told Levi before disappearing back into the room. She shut the door behind her and took a deep breath in.

The other half? Her!

She'd need to have a talk with Mama about her boasting when the time was right. At least she probably wouldn't need to see the over-informed dog walker again any time soon.

Mama had lots of friends, and already it was proving a challenge to keep up with them all. Surely everyone knew how crowded her hospital visiting schedule had already become. As for Levi, he'd gotten his requisite visit in, paid his well wishes, and now he could go back to whatever it was he liked to do with his evenings.

Carolina was done, and maybe now that her mother wouldn't be able to work at the diner any longer, she'd be done, too.

Chapter 8

CAROLINA

"W ho were you talking to out there?" Mama asked. Her voice had begun to sound a bit more like its usual self, but there was still a dry rasp every time she spoke.

"Someone named Levi," Carolina answered flippantly, joining her mother at the bedside.

"Oh, Levi!" Mama appeared authentically happy at the mere thought of him. "How is he?"

"Pushy," Carolina grumbled as she tucked her light blonde hair behind both ears. "And apparently somehow he already knows me like kin. How did that happen, Mama?"

Her mother attempted a laugh, but it broke apart into a scratchy cough. "Can't I be proud of my daughter?" she wanted to know.

Carolina forced a smile. She still felt uncomfortable with a near stranger knowing so many intimate details of her life and history, but this wasn't the time to get into any fights with Mama. "Maybe with fewer personal details next time?" she suggested with a soft hum.

Her mama sighed and clasped her hands on her lap. "Oh, baby girl. I don't think there's gonna be a next time."

"Hush. Don't you talk like that." One thing everyone loved so much about Mama was that she was perpetually kind, positive, and friendly. Was this a minor setback, or would the accident forever change her to the very core?

"Well, you know I can't return to work like this," she pointed out with a sigh as she glanced pointedly at her immobile lower half. "It may have just been a waitressing job, but already I feel lost without it. How will I pass my days? How will I keep up with the town gossip? How will I do anything at all?"

"We'll figure it out," Carolina promised. "We just need a little time, is all."

"We have plenty of that at least," Mama said, cracking a small smile that dissipated all the tension that had begun to build between them.

A soft knock sounded on the door.

"Come in," Carolina called, lifting her head to see what new visitor would enter next.

Levi popped his curly head through the doorway with a big hammy grin. "I just couldn't leave without first offering my wishes directly."

Cupcake perked up with a happy little whine. For the first time, Carolina realized that Abigail had left without taking him with her. Did this mean that she'd inadvertently agreed to that ridiculous plan to add the tiny therapy dog to their household? If she had, then it was all Levi's fault for distracting her in the first place.

Carolina frowned, refusing to welcome someone she'd already very clearly dismissed. Couldn't she and Mama have any time to themselves?

Mama, on the other hand, smiled and said, "That's very nice. Thank you."

Levi crossed the room and bent down to give Mama a kiss on her cheek. "I think I'm going to have to find a new walking route. It's only been a few days, but already O'Brien's just isn't the same without you there."

Carolina cleared her throat, ready to lay into him. Mama had only just begun to feel better after sharing her worries of how she'd fill her days going forward. Now Levi wanted to rub that in her face?

"I think you better do just that," Mama said, surprising Carolina with the mirth that lighted in her voice. How come it was okay when Levi said things like that? What made him so special to her mama?

Carolina rose and motioned toward the door. "Well, now that you've seen her, we should get back to—"

"Oh, you hush up," Mama said, looking suddenly cross. "Levi can stay as long as he'd like."

"Then I guess I'll give you two some privacy," she mumbled. It was one thing to step aside so the pastor could pray over Mama privately, but quite another to abandon her post to some young kid who hardly knew her mother at all.

"If that's what you want," Mama said. "Even though you know you're welcome to stay."

But Carolina wanted to go. For some reason, Levi had gotten under her skin and she didn't want to stick around to figure out why, especially since Mama seemed to be enjoying his visit so much.

She set Cupcake on the ground and let him lead her out of the room. She hoped that by the time she returned, Levi would be gone.

Chapter 9

CAROLINA

The next several days passed in a busy blur. Carolina stood watch as her mama began a rigorous schedule of both occupational and physical therapy appointments. The hospital loaned her a starter wheelchair until her specially fitted and customized one could arrive.

Carolina herself only left to oversee construction at the house. As Abigail had promised, a number of men from the church banded together to install ramps, move her mother's bedroom to the main floor, and install other accessibility updates to the house. Pastor Adam even helped to sell Carolina's sedan and use the insurance payout on Mama's totaled car so that they could upgrade to a minivan with a handy ramp already installed.

Before anyone could take a moment to catch their breath, a full week had passed since Mama had woken up and the doctors said she was ready to head home. Carolina had a good many people to thank, but mostly Pastor Adam and Abigail who had rallied the community to make their transition home easier—and also Nolan Murphy, her mother's employer who had chosen to offer his employees a top-notch health insurance plan that made all these additions and changes financially feasible. It even gave them a bit of nest egg to live from until either Carolina or Mama found a way to return to work.

Work would come in due time. Today they'd finally be leaving the hospital and returning home.

"Are you ready to head home, Jolene?" the nurse asked, squatting down so that she was the same height as Mama in her loaner wheelchair.

"Only one way to find out," Mama said, accepting the proffered clipboard to sign her long-awaited discharge forms.

"We'll miss you around here but are so happy you're doing well enough to leave us." The nurse rose and turned her overly enthusiastic face toward Carolina. "Why don't you go pull your vehicle around and your mother and I will meet you outside after we discuss a few quick things?"

Carolina looked to Mama, who simply nodded and motioned for her to go ahead. What did they have to discuss that Carolina couldn't hear?

She was puzzling over just this thing when Abigail called to her from the waiting room, then jogged to catch up. "Hey, there!" the pastor's daughter called. "Heading home?"

"I'm starting to think you know what's going to happen before even I do," Carolina answered with a chuckle, her mood instantly lightening. Abigail had truly been a lifesaver this past week and a half. She'd be forever indebted to the other woman's kind help.

"I was hoping to catch up with you before you left," Abigail said between slightly labored breath. "Figured I might be able to help with a few things."

"Oh? Like what?" They continued walking side by side toward the exit, something they had done together many times during the past ten days.

"Well, Cupcake has missed you something terrible these last couple days. Maybe after you get yourself and your mama settled at home, I could bring him by?"

"Maybe," Carolina said dismissively. She'd asked Abigail to take the Chihuahua back to her house when she'd been so busy with all her mother's appointments that she'd not been able to take him out in a timely manner—and he had piddled all over the hospital floor. Yet another bit of evidence that she didn't have the time for a dog right now. Maybe the whole service dog notion was a bad idea, too.

"I'm not going to force you," Abigail continued in a hurry. "But I just want you to know that the option is still open. Also, my dad and Nolan have decided to throw you and your mama a welcome home surprise party, and I wanted to warn you. You're going to get ambushed by about fifty of your mother's closest friends the very second you return home."

Carolina groaned. "I get that everyone loves Mama, but do we really need all these visits? I don't know about her, but I could really use a break." She felt ungrateful given all the community had done to help, but she was too exhausted to worry about appearing rude.

Abigail nodded enthusiastically. "I hear you on that one. That's why I wanted to give you a heads up. Gives you time to come up with an excuse or at least brace yourself for impact."

"Thank you." Carolina stopped walking and hugged this friend who was roughly ten years her senior, who'd even babysat her back in the day apparently. It felt as if she'd seamlessly picked up that role again, too, during this long time at the hospital. "Thank you for everything. Somehow, you've known exactly what we've needed these past couple weeks, and it's meant a lot to the both of us."

Abigail squeezed her back. "That's what I'm here for."

They reached the parking lot, and Abigail waved goodbye. "I need to go check in on things at the surprise party—but I'll see you real soon. Okay?"

"Okay, bye!" Carolina took a deep breath as she slid behind the wheel of her new minivan. The middle row of seats had been removed and outfitted with a place to secure her mother's wheelchair in place. This made it so Carolina wouldn't have to somehow summon the strength to lift her mother up and into the vehicle, and they wouldn't have to call someone bigger and stronger every time Mama wanted to go out.

For her part, Carolina still had no idea how Pastor Adam had managed to find an appropriate vehicle so quickly. Sure, it was secondhand and smelled strongly of disinfectant, but it was also perfect for what they needed. How their two old beat-up sedans had secured a high enough price to afford such a specialized van, she still didn't quite understand.

But she was grateful.

And also very tired.

She still didn't know what the future held, but at least now they were finally on their way to finding out...

Chapter 10

PASTOR ADAM

I could hardly contain my excitement as I waited for the Brown ladies to pull up in their new handicap-accessible minivan. We'd found quite the deal on that fancy state-of-the-art vehicle, and our congregation had shown their generous spirit by rallying to raise the needed funds to purchase it when the Browns' older vehicles didn't fetch quite enough to cover the full cost of their new van.

While I hated to see anyone faced with struggles, it always made my heart swell to see how readily the church was willing to help in times of need.

Today's surprise party was just the first two of welcome back festivities being thrown in Jolene's honor. So many more folks wanted to attend than would fit in her small yard, that we had to promise a second party following next Sunday's church service. We kept everything outside today, of course, so that neither Carolina nor Jolene would have to worry about tidying the mess and could simply focus on enjoying themselves. Besides, I had more than enough volunteers to wrap up the post-celebratory cleanup as soon as we all decided to call it a night.

My daughter pulled up to the house first. She'd been our look-out at the hospital, which meant the guests of honor would arrive any moment.

Cupcake hopped out of her car and trotted up to me, a miniscule ball of waggly energy. Abigail followed behind at a more leisurely pace.

"Hey, Dad. Had to stop home and get him on my way over," she explained.

"Does that mean Carolina agreed?" I grunted from exertion as I stooped down to bring the Chihuahua into my arms. I'd miss the little fellow while he was away, but I was also so happy that one of our church dogs had been called to perform a new miracle in someone special's life.

"Not yet," Abigail said without breaking her smile. "But I have a sneaking suspicion she will soon enough."

Harmony King came over to join us and immediately took Cupcake from my arms. "Hello, darling Cupcake!" she cooed. "Tell your brother Muffin I miss him!"

Harmony had been the very first to care for one of our church dogs for an extended time, and she was now a frequent visitor both to our house and the church for visits with both the dogs and myself.

"Nolan's ready with the buffet," she informed us. "I hope everyone brought their appetites."

I rubbed my over-sized belly. "I sure did," I pretended not to notice as my daughter shot me an exasperated expression. Yes, I was supposed to be on a diet these days, but special celebrations, such as today's, were obviously exempt.

Good food was like good company—always meant to be enjoyed one hundred percent.

"Wait..." Harmony glanced between my daughter and me, then clasped a hand over her mouth and giggled. "You're planning to give him to Jolene. Aren't you?"

I chuckled as a way of offering my confirmation. Were my intentions really so obvious? Well, I guess that's what happened when you followed the Lord's plan.

"Carolina, actually," Abigail corrected. "Do you think it's a bad idea?"

Oh, my dear daughter. Even after rediscovering her faith, she still had far less conviction than one needs around these parts.

Harmony shook her head. "It's a great idea. I don't really know Carolina personally— just what Jolene would tell me over shared shifts at the diner—but I imagine this has got to be hard on her. Perhaps even more than her mama."

"She's still a bit unsure," I said with a not-so-subtle wink.

"I'll talk to her," Harmony immediately volunteered. "Tell her how much Muffin helped me during my lost days."

"That's a fabulous idea," Mrs. Clementine, my church secretary and one of my dearest friends, said. She'd just finished circulating through the crowd and now returned to us with a bottle of raspberry Snapple in hand.

Harmony handed Cupcake back to me, then hugged the woman who had become like a mother to her during their brief time living together. I delighted in the fact that our little community constantly found new ways to become more like family than neighbors.

"Look!" Abigail cried and pointed toward the four-way stop a couple blocks down. "That's them!"

Somebody placed a cardboard party hat on my head and pushed me to the front of the crowd. Cheers of *surprise* and *welcome home* rose into the air like paper lanterns, each carrying a special prayer of recovery and solace for our guests of honor.

Carolina pulled right up into the driveway amidst all the cheers, then raced around the vehicle to open the door for her mama.

I craned my neck, eager to catch a glimpse of Miss Jolene.

And wouldn't you know it? The woman who always had a smile for everyone now had huge, fat tears streaming down her face.

Chapter 11

CAROLINA

Carolina stopped struggling to unclasp her mother's chair when she noticed the big, heavy tears rushing over her cheeks. "Mama, are you okay?"

"More than okay," she answered, giving her daughter a pat on the shoulder. "I just can't believe they're all here for me."

"A lot of people love you," Carolina pointed out. "They all want to make sure you're okay and to make sure you know you can turn to them for help if you need it." She bent forward to work on releasing the chair once more and was met with another pair of deft hands that effortlessly performed the right maneuver to free her mother from the van.

"Thank you," she said appreciatively as she brushed aside the hair that had fallen in front of her face like a curtain. Once her vision was no longer blocked, she saw that it was her mother's young friend Levi who had come to their aid.

"Nice to see you again, Carolina Brown," he said with a lingering smile that made her face burn with heat.

They stared at each other a moment until Pastor Adam joined them at the van, helping to guide Mama and her chair down the ramp.

Levi stayed close by Carolina's side as they all followed Pastor Adam and Mama into the yard. The throng of partygoers parted like the Red Sea as their small party approached the buffet where Harmony and Nolan stood with their arms linked.

"Well, look at that. I couldn't come to the diner, so you brought it here to my front yard," Mama said with a chuckle, accepting hugs from them both. Soon she was absorbed into a lively conversation as everyone filled their plates to bursting.

Levi leaned into her shoulder and whispered, "I'm sorry if we got off to the wrong start the other day."

Carolina shivered from his sudden nearness and the enchanting feel of his warm breath in her ear. "It's fine," she said, all the while hating how her body reacted to his proximity.

He straightened back to his full height, which was a good deal taller than Carolina stood. His dark, curly hair looked just as messy at it had during their first meeting, suggesting that maybe it was just his look. Instead of workout clothes like before, he wore a nice button-down shirt with dark wash jeans today.

Everyone had dressed up a little for the party—everyone except Carolina and Mama, who hadn't received enough advance warning to do so. She glanced down at her comfy sweatpants and old T-shirt and suddenly felt terribly underdressed.

Levi shook his head, bringing her attention back to his words rather than his appearance. "It's not fine. I shouldn't have assumed that we'd be friends just because Mama Jolene and I are."

Carolina sucked in air through her teeth before she could stop herself. She hated that he called her mother *Mama*. That name had always been reserved just for her use.

Levi slapped his forehead. "You don't like it when I call her Mama Jolene, do you? I keep making one mistake after the next."

She offered him a gentle smile. "It's just been a rough couple of weeks."

"Can we start over? I'd really like to start over."

Her smile widened as she asked, "Does that mean you'll forget all the sordid details Mama's already revealed about my life?"

"Sordid?" He laughed. "Hardly. Everything she's said has only made me want to get to know you even more. Maybe that's why I messed up so badly when we first met."

"It wasn't that bad," Carolina said with a shrug, feeling guilty from her overreaction. He loved her mother and only wanted to help, just like everyone else here. So why had she only taken out her frustrations on Levi? "I'm sorry I was rude before," she said.

"Like you said, it's been a rough couple weeks." He smiled at her again, and she felt the last of her resistance melt away. Maybe they could find a way to be friends after all.

"I still don't understand how you and my mama know each other so well, though."

They walked up to the buffet table now that the line had dwindled and began stacking waffles, sausage, bacon, and eggs on their plates. After all, O'Brien's was famous for its world-class breakfast and served little else. Not that anyone ever ventured far from Nolan's delicious morning dishes. Carolina's mouth watered as she took in the generous spread.

Levi scooped two giant servings of cheesy grits onto his plate. "Like I said, she always makes sure my dogs have water when I stop in."

"And that's enough to justify a hospital visit?"

He tilted his head to the side as he balanced three giant biscuits onto his rapidly growing tower of food. "It's not just that. We'd talk, too. I don't know what else to say. I knew right away that she's a very special person. It's kind of like she's the sun, sucking us all into her gravitational pull." He searched the crowd until he found Mama and smiled at her for a moment before turning his eyes back to Carolina.

"If I didn't know better, I'd say you have a crush on my mama," she pointed out with a laugh as she debated adding a second helping of bacon to her plate.

Levi stopped smiling suddenly and took a step back from the table. "It's not like that," he mumbled, unwilling to look at her. "Not at all."

Carolina laughed nervously but didn't risk saying anything more. Why was it so impossible for the two of them to get along for more than a few minutes at a time?

Chapter 12

CAROLINA

evi drifted away after they'd finished filling their plates, leaving Carolina to work on the dreaded task of mingling. And mingling while attempting to eat was pretty much the worst thing ever.

Luckily, Abigail found her a few minutes into the awkward ordeal. "You looked like you might need saving," she said with a wink. "Go ahead and eat, and I'll run interference."

"Bless you," Carolina said, digging into the feast.

Cupcake barked excitedly from the ground, which startled a piece of bacon clear out of her fingers.

"Hey, what's he doing here?" she asked with a suspicious glance toward Abigail as the Chihuahua wolfed down his ill-gotten treat.

Abigail's smile didn't waver. "Just checking things out, catching up, saying hello."

"You're not planning on leaving him here, are you?" Carolina managed between bites. "Because I don't think I can take any more surprises today."

"Nope." Abigail bent down to scoop up the tiny critter, who immediately began to frantically and loudly sniff the air around Carolina's plate as if hoping that more of the tasty morsels might find their way into his belly. "He'll be ready when you ask for him, though."

Carolina stuffed a large bite of waffle into her mouth to stop herself from saying anything more on that. Other than the pushy thing with the dog, Abigail had been her best support and closest companion these last couple of weeks, and the last thing she wanted was to appear ungrateful.

It still felt strange that her hometown had changed so drastically in the less than a year since she'd gone off to college. All her high school friends had also scattered away from the city to attend their own dream colleges. Those from her graduating class who'd remained in town weren't ones she'd taken the time to get to know well. As soon as she was able, she'd filled her entire class schedule with Advanced Placement classes, which meant she'd rarely seen the students who weren't racing down the gifted track alongside her. So, if she needed company now that she'd expectantly returned, all that was really left for her were Mama's friends.

The possibility of forming any new relationships terrified her poor introverted self. Sure, she was able to come out of her shell when debating politics in class or talking about one of her many academic passions—but most people didn't want to do or hear about these things. They wanted to discuss their jobs, kids, favorite TV shows, and the like. Carolina had never been great at talking about any of those things, and she always worried she was boring anyone when she started in on the things *she* liked to discuss.

Mama, on the other hand, could make friends with just about anyone and talk about pretty much anything. Levi was proof enough of that. Sometimes Carolina regretted not getting her mother's extroversion gene, but then again, she found all the peopling her mother did utterly exhausting.

Perhaps that was why she liked Abigail so much. Abigail was content to remain silent just as much as Carolina was. She really had understood what Carolina needed instantly. Was that because she'd babysat her back in the day, or was Abigail the same way herself?

Her mother's boss, Nolan, came over to join them, and Abigail immediately ran interference as promised. "Great turnout," Abigail said, clasping a hand on his arm. "And even better food."

"Thanks," he said with a charming smile. "Jolene's worth it."

"How are you holding up?" he asked, turning toward Carolina just as she'd popped another bite of breakfast sausage in her mouth.

"Um..." she mumbled.

"She's really tired," Abigail answered helpfully.

"I bet you are," Nolan said. "A lot of folks love Jolene and want her to know they're for her during this time. I don't imagine the visits will dry up for a very long time."

Carolina swallowed. "I'm starting to think you're right."

"That's what I came over here to tell you," he continued. "If you ever need to escape for a while or want a few extra dollars to treat yourself and your mama to a nice day out, you're always welcome at O'Brien's. We're still trying to find a way to welcome your mama back to work, but I'm afraid we're not quite as handicap-accessible as we probably should have been all this time. We're working on righting that now, though."

She nodded and smiled. "Thank you, Nolan. That's very kind of you."

"No pressure, though. Okay? Harmony says she can handle the extra tables as long as she needs to."

She gave him a thumbs up, almost losing hold of her half-emptied plate in the progress. "Got it."

"Well, I'll let you two ladies get back to it." He offered them a quick wave before disappearing back into the crowd.

As she watched him go, she caught sight of Levi across the yard and shot a smile his way. He not only didn't return her smile, he also spun around so that his back was to her.

Had her harmless joke really upset him that much? If so, how could she make things right? She'd hate to hurt this strange—but important—friendship for her Mama.

She considered marching right up to him and demanding they talk this thing out, but then her nerves got the better of her and she returned to standing in silence next to Abigail as the rest of the crowd buzzed merrily around them.

Chapter 13

CAROLINA

Carolina worked up the nerve to approach Levi later that evening, but he immediately shrugged her off. By the time the party wrapped up, she was even more frustrated than she'd been following their first meeting at the hospital.

When the last of the cleaning crew dispersed, Carolina pushed her mother's chair up the brand-new ramp and in through the kitchen door.

"I'll let you help me through the threshold this one time," Mama said with a warning glance. "But after this, I power my own chair. Got it?"

"Good," Carolina answered as she made a silly face. "Because even on wheels, you're kind of heavy."

The two laughed together, finally allowing themselves to relax after all they'd been through the past couple weeks—both good and bad. It felt so good to be home. Here they could start to work toward normal again.

There was still one thing Carolina needed to understand before she could allow herself to relax for the evening, though. "Mama?" she asked, plopping down onto the living room couch and placing an arm over her head.

"Hmm?" Her mother wheeled back and forth as she tried to find the best place to angle her chair in front of the TV.

"What's the deal with that Levi guy?" she asked, pulling herself back into a sitting position with a giant sigh.

"He's a good guy," Mama answered distractedly.

"Well, I was talking with him today and he suddenly shut me out."

"Did you say something you shouldn't?" she asked, giving up on her task and turning her chair to face her daughter.

The house felt cold after having spent so many long days in the over-heated hospital. Carolina grabbed the afghan that hung over the back of the couch and tossed it over her legs, but it did little to warm her. "I don't think so. I mean, I was just teasing him."

Mama shook her head in dismay. "You know you and humor don't always get along. What did you say?"

"I just asked if he had a crush on you."

"Carolina!" Mama gasped. "I'm old enough to be that boy's mother."

She shrugged, trying even now to play the slight off. "I know but..."

"But nothing," Mama said with a stern look. "You owe him an apology next time he stops by."

Carolina hated knowing that her mother was right just as much as she hated having inadvertently hurt Levi's feelings. "Why is it so crazy to think he could have feelings for you?" she insisted. "You're still a good-looking woman, Mama."

Mama took in a deep breath. "I'm guessing you don't know why he and I have become such good friends lately?"

She waited a moment, knowing her mama would break down and share with her if she asked in the right way. "No, neither of you would explain it to me."

Mama took a few deep breaths before finally explaining herself. "His mama died last year, and my baby moved far away. We both lost someone important, so we took comfort in each other."

A niggling worm of guilt burrowed deep down into Carolina's chest. "I still called you all the time," she argued. "You're the one who encouraged me to go to the best school to help me achieve my dreams. I don't under—"

"I'm not blaming you. I'm incredibly proud of you, and I love you so much, but it didn't mean that I wasn't lonely. In fact, that's what..." Mama's voice trailed off and she set her mouth in a firm line.

"What?" Carolina urged. "What were you going to say?"

Mama bit her lip. "Never mind. I shouldn't have said anything."

"Tell me," Carolina begged. Mama had never been able to keep a secret for long. Whatever it was now, she'd get it out of her eventually, but she'd feel so much better if she knew now.

The older woman continued to hesitate, unwilling to even look at her daughter as she mumbled, "I'm worried you're going to take it wrong."

"Please just tell me."

"I was on my way to surprise you," she murmured, hardly above a whisper. She didn't have to say anything more than that, though, because Carolina understood instantly. The accident that had almost claimed her mama's life had actually been all her fault.

If she'd been less ambitious...

If she'd chosen a closer college...

If she'd come home to visit more often...

If, if, if.

"I'm sorry, Mama," she said, swallowing back her tears while trying to keep her voice strong. "I'm so sorry."

Her mother wheeled her chair forward so she was touching the edge of the couch. "Hey, stop," she said. "What happened is in no way your fault. If anything, it's mine. I'm the one who should've been driving safer. I'm the one who chose to swerve on the expressway to avoid hitting a pesky squirrel. Actually, now that I think about it, I'm pretty sure we should blame him more than anyone else. Stupid squirrel. I bet he's holed up in some huge tree having a great laugh about all the trouble he's caused."

Carolina sniffed and attempted a smile.

"I mean it," Mama said, knitting her brow. "Tell me you understand that it's not your fault."

"I do," Carolina said to appease her mother. But no matter what

Mama said, Carolina knew she was the one who deserved the blame for this horrible tragedy—not Mama, and certainly not some silly squirrel.

It was Carolina who had ruined everything. And it was Carolina who didn't deserve a second chance at her dreams, not when she'd already stolen all that was left from the one person who had always given her everything.

Chapter 14

CAROLINA

Carolina sat up late in her room, hugging her knees to her chest as she tried to keep her crying quiet to avoid disturbing Mama.

She'd always wanted to change the world.

Well, finally she had, but it was nothing like she'd imagined.

Instead, she'd received her penance for trying to be more than she was. She only wished Mama hadn't been the one to pay the price for her pride. Now Carolina had an even harder time even looking at her in that chair, knowing that she'd been the one to put her there.

It was terribly selfish—she knew that—but she needed time to work out her feelings before she and Mama could go back to being one big, happy family. They'd almost fallen into their old, familiar pattern, but then Mama's revelation had slapped Carolina cold in the face.

She knew her mother didn't blame her, but that didn't stop Carolina from blaming herself. And she'd spend the rest of her life, doing her best to make things up to her.

The next morning, she rose early following a brief, fitful sleep. After listening quietly at the door and making sure Mama wasn't up yet, she quietly got dressed and snuck out of the house. Nolan had kindly offered her a shift at the diner whenever she needed it, and today she needed it. Sure, the time away from Mama and the way of keeping her brain busy was more important than the money, but she could use her tips to buy Mama something nice on the way home.

If Nolan was surprised to see her show up at O'Brien's, he didn't show it.

"Good morning, you," he said simply with his signature welcoming grin. "Aprons are under the counter. Can you start by putting coffee on?"

Carolina was grateful for his quiet acceptance and quickly got to work. As always, the diner was packed from the very moment it opened. How Harmony expected to manage the daily rush on her own, Carolina had no idea. Maybe she should plan on coming each day to help out, encourage Mama to sleep in until she could make it home from the breakfast shift.

Around ten, the crowd of early-morning diners began to disperse, finally giving Carolina a chance to relax a little. She poured a cup of coffee for herself and checked her text messages. Sure enough, there was one from Mama.

I'm sorry if I hurt your feelings last night. I love you and will see you when you get home.

Of course, that text only made her feel more guilty, seeing as Mama was blaming herself for Carolina's issues. At least she'd found the note Carolina had written and taped to the TV, not knowing where else to leave it.

Went to grab a shift at O'Brien's, she typed back, her thumbs flying furiously across the tiny screen. *Be home in a couple hours. Love you.*

"Everything okay?" Nolan asked from behind the kitchen window.

"Totally fine," she said, offering a quick smile. "Just catching my breath. It sure was busy today."

"Business has been good." He grabbed a soapy rag and began to polish the stainless steel warmer.

"Are you sure Harmony can handle all this on her own each day?" she asked with an equal measure of hope and dread. Her inner critic had been blessedly quiet while she focused on taking and delivering orders that morning. On the other hand, if she took over her mother's job full-time, it would officially put an end to her dreams to do something else with her life. Was she ready for that step?

Nolan glanced curiously at her as he continued to wipe down the counter. "Are you asking for a job?"

She swallowed and nodded. "I could use a way to keep myself busy, and it looks like you could use another waitress."

"Fine," Nolan said with a frown which surprised her. "You're hired on a provisional basis."

"What does that mean?" Carolina was familiar with the term when it came to provisional governments, but she'd never heard of a provisional waitress before.

"It means that you can help out for a while, but you're not allowed to stay long-term. In fact, the moment I see you're settling in here will be the very same moment I fire you for good."

"What? Why? Am I not a good waitress?" Even worse than settling was being deemed not good enough for her last resort plan. She thought she'd done a good job today, but maybe she had moved a bit too slow or not smiled enough at the customers.

Nolan studied her for a moment before coming around from the kitchen to stand beside her. "This isn't what your mama wants for you. It's not what you want for yourself, either."

She folded her arms over her chest. "Yeah, but it's where I am now."

"It doesn't have to be," he said gently.

She sighed. "Well, it looks like Harmony can manage from here. I'll see you tomorrow at six."

"Carolina, wait." Nolan followed her as she untied her apron and put it in the linen hamper. "I'm not trying to upset you or make you feel unwelcome. I just don't like to see you hurting."

"It's okay, Nolan. I understand. I do. I just have a lot of things to work out right now, and I guess I'm not doing a very good job at it."

"Big changes take time," he said with a nod. "I'll see you tomorrow."

Carolina said a quick goodbye to Harmony, then pushed through the door and out onto the street. These past few days had been so confusing, but finally she had clarity about one thing, and that was a start.

She drew out her phone and dialed Abigail's number. It looked like she and Mama would be welcoming Cupcake into their home after all.

Chapter 15

PATOR ADAM

I was idling over a long, lazy breakfast when my daughter charged into the dining room waving her phone triumphantly. "Told you!" she shouted.

I pushed my meal aside. Hopefully she didn't notice the bacon residue on my otherwise mostly polished plate. "What has you so happy this early in the morning?"

"Early? It's already past ten o'clock." Abigail pulled out the chair beside me and took a seat. "Usually you're up and active long before now."

"I guess all that partying yesterday took it out of me." No escaping the fact I was getting older by the day. "Now, what did you tell me?"

"Carolina texted me on her way home from work. She asked if it would still be all right if she took Cupcake in for a few days."

I cleared my throat and tilted my head before asking, "Just days?"

Abigail seemed unfazed. "I'm sure it will turn out longer than that."

"Did she say what made her change her mind?"

"No, and I didn't force it. Carolina's much more reserved than her mama. If she wants us to know, then she'll tell us herself."

I nodded. "True enough."

"Will you help me gather his things?" Abigail asked, popping back up to her feet in the effortless way of youth.

I grunted as I slowly pulled myself to a standing position. My knees made a cracking noise, but otherwise felt fine.

My daughter frowned at me. "When's the last time you checked in with the doctor?" she demanded.

I waved away her concern. "I'm fine. Just old and fat."

Now her hands were on each hip the way her mother used to do whenever she got frustrated with me, too. "Dad, you know I don't like it when you talk like that."

"Sorry, dear. I'll try to be better," I said as I shuffled away.

Over the next half hour or so, I packed a few large boxes with toys, bedding, food, bowls, leashes, and more while Abigail updated and printed off a fresh copy of her church dog care manual.

"Are we going now?" I asked after loading the last of the boxes into her trunk.

"I am," she said pertly. "But you're not."

I stared at her, awaiting an explanation. We'd done this together the last time, so why not now?

"Mrs. Clementine is coming by to take you on a walk. Make sure you take Mama Mary, too. She needs exercise just as bad as you do."

I sighed. Apparently, my diet wasn't enough. Now I'd be exercising, too.

"It's because we love you and want to keep you around as long as possible," my daughter explained, offering me a conciliatory kiss on the cheek.

"Yeah, yeah, I know," I grumbled playfully. A walk in this beautiful weather sounded like it might be nice. Ever since Harmony had come to town, Mrs. Clementine and I had become even closer friends, and I enjoyed her company better than almost anyone else's. She needed the companionship, too, since her husband's most recent promotion kept him away from home nine days out of ten.

379

"Give Carolina and Jolene my best," I said to my distracted daughter. "And make sure they come to church this Sunday for the surprise party."

"Will do," she said before returning her focus to the computer. I guess that meant I was dismissed. As much as I enjoyed being involved in the church dogs' comings and goings, I loved seeing my daughter take ownership of the program. She'd really come a long way since moving back home.

And I couldn't be prouder.

Chapter 16

CAROLINA

Carolina fired off a quick text to Abigail the moment she left O'Brien's. Now that she'd thought about it some more, both her and her mother could use a cuddly distraction. Besides, Abigail had been right about everything else lately, so why not this?

She tucked the phone back into her purse and quickened her pace down the block. She'd nearly reached her parking spot when a cluster of six or seven dogs rounded the corner followed by one very familiar dogwalker.

"Levi!" she called as she jogged over to him. "I'm sorry about the other day. I didn't mean to overstep," she said once she caught up.

"Hey, Carolina. Take this guy. It'll make it easier for me to talk." He handed her the leash to the biggest dog in his sidewalk pack, and they fell into step together.

"My mama told me about your mama," she said gently. "I'm sorry. I didn't know."

He sighed and looked toward the sky before returning his gaze ahead. "As much as I wish she wouldn't have said anything, I guess I can't really complain."

"If it's any consolation, she held back on your Social Security number, blood type, and favorite sports' teams." Carolina bumped into his shoulder playfully. Since he was so much taller, though, it was really a nudge to his arm.

"Oh, good," he answered with a chuckle. "Then all my darkest secrets are safe for now, it seems."

"I thought about it some more, and I don't mind if you call her Mama Jolene," Carolina offered. "It's weird to hear anyone except me say it, but I can tell she likes it."

"It's just... well, it feels weird to call her only by her first name, but it's also not quite right to call her Mrs. Brown or Ma'am." Levi scrunched his features together in thought, a gesture which she found absolutely adorable.

She nodded and offered a shy smile. "I understand."

His eyes found and held hers. "Me too," he answered with a giant sigh. "And a good thing, too, because I was really getting sick of avoiding each other. I'd much rather have the chance to get to know each other and to know it's okay when I want to come by for a visit with... uh, your mom."

"Mama Jolene?" she offered.

"Fine, have it your way," he said with a laugh.

"I'm headed home now if you'd like to tag along."

"I'd love to, but I kind of have six dogs and their owners depending on me right now. Besides, I'm sure both you and Mama Jolene could use a bit of a rest after the huge surprise party last night."

"You're probably right about that." Carolina practically tripped over her feet when the big dog in her grip lunged for a squirrel further down the block.

"Easy, Killer!" Levi cried, transferring all of his leashes to one hand and giving a firm yank to the taut leash Carolina just barely managed to keep hold of.

The dog instantly shifted his focus back to the walk and gave the leash a bit of blessed slack.

She was just about to ask if *Killer* was a name or a description when Levi picked up their conversation from before.

"What about tomorrow?" he asked, surprising her. "I'll be done walking the dogs at around eleven and have the afternoon off before I pick up my shift at the barbecue shack."

This surprised her, too. "Another job?"

"One of many," he said with a mischievous smile that felt a bit out of place given the context. "Remember, I'm saving up for school next year."

School—that was something she could talk endlessly about, if given the chance. "What are you going to major in?" she asked him.

"Don't know yet." How could he not know? Levi was obviously an inquisitive guy, and he was working so hard. How could he not even know what he hoped to accomplish next?

She motioned toward the dogs with her chin. "Then why all the hustle?"

He shrugged. "I'm working to set up a life I'll love."

"But you don't know what that life will entail."

"Nope. At least not yet. I'm only nineteen. I have tons of time to figure out what comes next."

Carolina thought about this. They were the same age, yet she'd known exactly what she wanted from life until about two weeks ago. "How do you plan to figure it out?"

He laughed. "You're asking if I have a plan for making a plan? I don't. I'm just going to put myself out there, keep my mind open, and see what happens."

"But aren't you scared?"

"Honestly, no. I guess I have faith that everything will work out okay in the end."

"And until then you're going to walk dogs and serve barbecue," she mumbled.

He laughed again. "Yeah, why not?"

Carolina looked back over her shoulder and realized they'd wound up a long way from her car. "I should get home before Mama starts to worry."

Levi eased the dogs to a stop. "Wait. Give me your number before you go."

"But you already have Mama's," she pointed out as shyness suddenly overtook her.

He rolled his eyes at her. "Which is great for when I want to talk to her. But when I want to talk to you, I'll need your number for that."

Her cheeks flooded with a fresh rush of heat. "Oh, right." They exchanged phones and punched in their numbers for one another, then Carolina gave Killer's leash back to Levi and tucked her hair behind her ears.

"Tell Mama Jolene I said hi." He tightened the leashes in his hands and offered Carolina one last smile before continuing on his way.

"See you tomorrow!" he shouted as they walked away from each other. "I'm looking forward to it!"

"Me too!" she called back, smiling to herself.

Tomorrow.

Chapter 17

CAROLINA

Carolina stopped by the store to grab a bouquet of wildflowers for her mama before coming back home. When she arrived, she found her mother sitting in the kitchen waiting. It didn't escape Carolina's notice that she'd taken extra efforts with her hair and makeup that day and even put on her nicest earring and necklace set.

"Are those for me?" her mother asked, clasping her hands before her face in delight.

"Of course, they are." Carolina gave her mama a quick kiss and handed her the bouquet while she set to work finding a vase.

"I owe you an apology," she mumbled as she moved toward the sink. "I'm sorry I just rushed out of here this morning. I'm obviously not handling things as well as I should be."

"Nuh-uh," Mama said with an exaggerating shushing sound that followed. "Shoulds are not allowed in this house, and you know it. Everyone handles challenges at her own pace. It's okay if you need extra time. And by the way, I'm sorry, too. I knew better than to say anything about the reason I'd been on the road that morning, but sometimes my big mouth runs off without me noticing."

Carolina shook her head. It was nice that Mama didn't blame her, but that didn't change the fact she still felt terribly guilty, would probably always feel guilty. She chose to switch to a more pleasant topic rather than upset them both any further. "I decided to accept Abigail's offer. I hope that's okay. I just figured we could both use the extra little bit of joy these days."

"I was hoping you would," Mama said with a conspiratorial smile. "What with all those years growing up that you begged for a dog, I'm surprised you didn't jump at the first chance to say yes to Cupcake."

Carolina shrugged as she poured the plant food into the vase and stirred. "I guess it just seemed like one more thing to take care of when my focus should really be on you."

Mama pushed her chair over toward her daughter and offered her both the flowers and a stern look. "Let me focus on me. I'm a big girl, and I can take care of myself with or without the use of my legs, mind you."

Carolina didn't know how to respond to that. Luckily, Mama only paused for a short while before carrying right on with what she planned to say. "I sure am happy to have you home, but you should also be preparing to return to school just as soon as you can."

Carolina's face burned under the heat of her mama's gaze. This was another topic she wasn't quite ready to talk about yet. "I already took the rest of the spring semester off," she murmured. "Maybe I'll go back in the fall."

"What? No *maybe*, young lady. I did not raise you to give me maybes."

"You look pretty today," Carolina said, praying Mama would glom on to yet another subject change and stick with it this time.

Mama fluffed her hair and batted her eyelashes. "Well, I had some extra time on my hands, and I didn't quite know what to do with myself, so I did this."

"I may need you to give me a makeover before too long." Carolina frowned at herself in the reflective door of the microwave that hung over the oven. She hadn't gotten a single haircut since going away for college last fall, and she no longer wore makeup, preferring to spend the few minutes she saved by skipping these beauty rituals to catch up on either her sleep or her studies.

"I can do you one better," her mother said. "How about we head to the salon tomorrow for a girls day of pampering?"

"Actually, I invited Levi over for tomorrow," she said, hoping her mother didn't notice her blush. "Maybe the day after?"

A self-satisfied smirk spread across Mama's face. "I thought you two weren't on speaking terms."

"We ran into each other on my way home from the diner and cleared the air."

"Good," Mama said, running a finger idly on the arm of her chair while Carolina worked on arranging the flowers inside the vase. "I have a feeling you two will become fast friends. You're a lot alike, you know?"

Carolina took the spring bouquet out to the living room and placed it on the coffee table. "Why would you say that? We seem like perfect opposites, if you ask me."

Mama followed. "You know better than to jump to conclusions, darling. Sometimes things aren't the way they seem, and sometimes they're exactly what they seem," she countered. "But you know what? Figuring out what's what is pretty much the best part of life. Wouldn't you agree?"

"Sure," Carolina answered with a smile. At least Mama was back to her usual ways. Maybe Carolina would be able to rediscover some of herself soon, too.

Chapter 18

CAROLINA

Hardly an hour passed before Abigail showed up with Cupcake for his big move-in day.

"Hey, sweetie," Mama cooed in a cutesy voice. "It's good to see you again, little one."

In response to this warm welcome, Cupcake hopped right up into Mama's chair, which delighted her to no end.

Abigail placed a hand on Carolina's elbow to draw her attention. "While those two are getting reacquainted, why don't I show you what you need to know about taking care of the little guy?"

Carolina nodded and followed her out to the car to unpack the Chihuahua's things. "Thanks again for dealing with my wishy-washiness over this. I think Mama and I will both enjoy having Cupcake around for a time. Although I do worry we'll both get too attached for our own good and have a hard time giving him back when the time comes."

Abigail placed a giant bag of food in Carolina's outstretched arms. "Never mind about saying goodbye when you've only just said hello. Life's too short to focus on goodbyes."

"Okay, then what should we be focusing on?" She shifted the bag in her arms and considered the other woman's wise words. Lately life had given her all kinds of hellos and goodbyes. Was she looking at them the wrong way?

Abigail grabbed the last box from the car, and together they headed back inside. "I wrote up an instruction manual for you, and of course you can call me any time with questions. Chihuahuas are part of the AKC Toy Group, which means they were bred to be companion dogs. Cupcake will probably stay glued to one of your laps pretty much nonstop. He's a lot of personality in one very tiny package. Actually, after Mama Mary, he's pretty much the dog in charge. He's always had this way of bossing the others around until he gets his way. That includes humans, too, by the way. He'll have you both wrapped around his little paw in no time at all, I'd wager."

Carolina laughed at the prospect of being pushed around by such a tiny, shivering creature. "I think we can handle that," she said. "Mama will love having him on her lap. I guess that's a very big plus to spending all day in a chair. You never really have to shoo your dog off."

Abigail nodded. "Make sure you get some time with him, too. He's a trained therapy dog, so he's good at handling unfamiliar situations. But more than that, he's great at reading people's emotions and offering cuddles just when they need them."

"Which, from what you just told me, is pretty much all the time?" Carolina, for her part, could definitely use a good cuddle or two these days. But would it be enough to move on past the overwhelming guilt that plagued her day in and day out?

Abigail winked. "You betcha." Which question had she answered? Or had it, perhaps, been all of them—even the ones Carolina hadn't been brave enough to voice aloud?

She pushed her emotional baggage back to the dark corners of her mind and decided to focus on the business part of their arrangement. "And you have info about feeding him and taking him to the bathroom in that packet you brought?"

"I do."

"How long do you reckon he'll stay with us?"

Abigail shrugged. "Don't know, but we'll both know when the time is right for him to come back to Dad and me."

Carolina wanted to argue, to press for an exact date so that she knew what she and Mama would be working with. She knew better than to accept a gift while also making demands, though. It still felt incredibly odd that both Abigail and Levi felt it was better to go forward without a set plan. Not knowing tended to drive her nuts, and somehow, she doubted this time would prove any different.

Abigail helped Carolina set up Cupcake's bed and bowls in the kitchen, then the two of them rejoined Mama in the living room.

"All good in here, Jolene?" Abigail asked, hovering near the entryway rather than fully joining them in the seating area.

Mama laughed as Cupcake stood on his hind legs to lick her neck. "All good," she said. "Although if we don't feed him soon, I'm worried he may just turn me into his next meal."

Abigail chuckled. "He doesn't eat until six, but it's all in the folder I gave your daughter. If there's nothing else, I'm going to head out. Text me tonight to let me know how things are going?"

"Absolutely," Carolina said. "But why are you leaving so soon? You only just got here."

"Yes," Mama said. "At least stay for a glass of sweet tea or some lunch."

"It will be better for Cupcake if I leave fast. Besides, y'all need some time to yourselves. You'll see me again soon." She hugged them both and gave Cupcake a scratch between the ears. "Make sure you come to church this Sunday, by the way. Dad has something for you."

"We'll be there," Mama promised. "Thank you again," she called, waving Cupcake's tiny paw after Abigail.

Okay, so now what?

Chapter 19

CAROLINA

"Let's go on a walk," Mama suggested a few minutes after Abigail left. "Show our new roomie the neighborhood."

Carolina agreed, knowing the fresh air would do Mama some good. She was also happy she wouldn't have to futz with the van again just yet. "Let me just go grab his leash."

Once outside, Mama set the pace and Carolina followed along with Cupcake trotting at her heels. "Everything looks different from a couple feet down," she mused, sweeping her gaze from side to side as they navigated the quiet little suburb.

"How'd you sleep last night?" Carolina asked. It was Mama's first night back in her own bed since the accident, after all. Another wave of guilt swept over her. She should have asked how her mother was feeling earlier rather than rushing out of the house first thing in the morning as a way of hiding from the situation.

"Okay, I guess," Mama said, slowing her pace slightly. "I woke up once and wanted to use the bathroom, but then I was afraid that if I struggled with that whole crazy setup in there, I'd be up for good. So, I held it and plan to stop drinking fluids by six at night. At least until I get used to things."

Carolina also had a hard time maneuvering around the extra handles installed at the edges of the toilet but didn't say a peep about that. Instead, she said, "The fresh air is nice."

"Yes, the change of scenery, too. To be honest, I'm already getting pretty bored being laid up in the house like I am." That was her mama, always moving a million miles a minute. This had to be torture on her.

"I'm sorry. Is there something I can do?" Carolina asked, keeping her eyes fixed on Cupcake as an excuse to not have to make eye contact.

Mama sighed. "I know you want to help, darling girl, but this is something I need to figure out for myself. Nolan says he's working on changing up the diner so I can come back and work, but honestly, he's already gone to more than enough trouble for me. I'm wondering if I shouldn't try finding another job to keep me busy. Maybe answering phones somewhere?"

"But you love waitressing," Carolina argued. Granted, most people worked as servers as an in-between job while they worked toward what they really wanted to do, but Mama had always loved feeding people while also getting the opportunity to visit with the whole town each day. Carolina honestly couldn't picture her doing anything else.

"But waitressing doesn't really work for me anymore," Mama reasoned. "That probably means it's time for a change of plans."

They walked another couple blocks in companionable silence.

Mama spoke next. "So, Levi's coming over tomorrow, huh?"

Carolina smiled as she remembered their brief encounter that morning. "Yup, I invited him."

"Good. Maybe he'll have some ideas on a new career for me. Do you know that boy works no less than four jobs?"

"He says he's saving up," she offered with a shrug.

"He is, but I also reckon he's trying on all kinds of lives to see which suits him best."

Carolina considered this. "That's a nice thought. I guess I've always used books for that."

"Yeah, and when has all your knowledge about being a nineteenth century Russian doctor come in handy?" Mama asked with a laugh.

Carolina chuckled, too. "Fair point. Right now, I'm trying on your life at the diner. Nolan gave me a job but says it can't be permanent."

"Good man," Mama said with a smile. "I'm glad he's protecting my interests while I'm not there to do so myself."

"Hey now, there's nothing wrong with being a waitress," she scolded. "Today actually went pretty well. I enjoyed it."

"No, you didn't," Mama said with a very sarcastic *pffffh*. "Perhaps you didn't hate it as much as you suspected, but I guarantee you didn't enjoy it."

Carolina shook her head. "There's no winning with you on this, is there?"

"Nope," Mama answered with a giant hammy grin. "And don't you forget it."

"How could I?" Carolina shot back, twisting Cupcake's leash around her hand tight.

"Carolina," Mama said gently. "You know I just want to see you reach your dream."

"I still have plenty of time to work my way up to Capitol Hill," she pointed out. Even though she knew she could go back, Carolina wasn't sure it would be the right decision.

"That's not what I meant," Mama said. "Your dream has always been to change the world, and there's more than one way to do that."

Carolina contemplated this for the rest of their walk. Had she been short-sighted by not considering any other options? Was she missing something important when it came to planning out her life, or like Abigail and Levi, would she be better off waiting to see what life had planned for her rather than the other way around?

Well, whatever the case, she still wasn't convinced that she deserved to find happiness for herself—at least not until she helped her mama regain all that she'd lost.

Chapter 20

PASTOR ADAM

My first day of this new-fangled exercise regimen was not going well.

Mrs. Clementine somehow got it in her mind that we would be doing a three-mile walk that day. Not even halfway through, I was already sorely regretting that decision.

"Here," she said, placing her water bottle in my sweaty hand. "You look like you could use this more than me. Drink up."

I took a long, appreciative chug, then ran the back of my hand across my lips. When I tried to hand it back, she waved me off.

"It's all yours," she said with a gracious smile. "But when we go walking tomorrow, make sure to bring one of your own."

"Tomorrow?" I asked in horror. I still wasn't sure I'd make it through today.

"Yes. We want to get healthy, don't we?"

"You're already fit as a fiddle, and I'm happy just as I am," came my feeble protest. I honestly can't say why I even try arguing with Mrs. Clementine when she never ever lets me win.

"You're stubborn is what you are," she said with a big old eye roll.

We both laughed. We often ribbed at each other, and that was precisely what made our friendship so strong.

"Where is Mr. Clementine stationed this week?" I asked as we rounded the corner to start a new loop. He'd received a promotion this past year and was on the road far more than he was ever at home. Although my friend rarely showed a crack in her happy façade, I worried that distance between those two was doing anything but making their hearts grown fonder.

She sighed. "Minnesota? Michigan? Honestly, it's hard to keep up anymore."

"You'd tell me if something wasn't okay, right?"

She blew a raspberry, completely undermining the seriousness of the moment. "Everything's fine. Never you worry."

Of course, I knew better to push it, especially since Harmony would be moving out of Mrs. Clementine's home and into a place of her own before too long. I was worried my friend had become far lonelier than she cared to admit. Hopefully she was at least laying her burdens at the Lord's feet, if not on my shoulders.

"So, Abigail said the Browns agreed to take Cupcake off your hands?" Mrs. Clementine said, flowing seamlessly into this new change of topic.

"That they did," I answered. "And not a moment too soon. I've done more than my fair share of worrying about them both as of late."

"Jolene will be just fine." She made a dismissive hand gesture before drawing her face in consternation. "It's the daughter I worry about."

"Same here," I confided. "Any ideas how else we can help?"

Mrs. Clementine placed a hand on my forearm as we continued ambling down the block. "You've already done more than enough. Charity is a wonderful thing, but not when it stops someone from experiencing life for themselves. I worry if we do too much, Carolina will stop fighting for what she wants and just go any old place we lead her."

"That's a fair point," I admitted, constantly impressed by my friend's wisdom when it came to these things. "You know you never have to worry about that with me, though. Right?"

"Oh, I know you'll fight your healthy living plan until the day you die," she shot back with a chuckle.

"It's much easier when I have you to help me get through it," I said truthfully.

"Well, that's what friends are for," Mrs. Clementine retorted with a sweet smile. "Now, do you think we can go a little faster on this next lap?"

"No way, you crazy woman," I argued, but then sped up my pace all the same.

Chapter 21

CAROLINA

Carolina woke up excited for her visit with Levi that afternoon. After breezing through her shift at the diner, she came home and attempted to take some time tending to her appearance, but it turned out comically bad. She eventually gave up and pulled her hair back into its signature high ponytail, then scrubbed all the overly bright makeup from her face. The last thing she needed was Levi thinking she was trying too hard to impress him.

Sure, she was intrigued by both the man himself and his unlikely friendship with her mama, but that didn't change the fact that they were hardly acquaintances right now. They needed much more time to get to know each other before deciding what turns their relationship might take in the future.

Still, no matter how friendly, handsome, and possibly inspiring she found him, a romantic entanglement between them could never work. For starters, they were both way too young for anything so serious. Who knew where life would take them by the time they both found careers and homes? It seemed Mama would push and push until Carolina rediscovered her dream, but right now Carolina just didn't know if she'd ever feel comfortable leaving her dear mother behind again.

Look what had happened the first time!

The more she thought about it, the more she landed on the conclusion that maybe she just wasn't meant to change the world. Maybe it would be enough to make just one person's life better while she could. And maybe that person had been Mama this whole time.

She felt a fierce sense of loyalty to the only family she had, but she knew that commitment ran both ways. She and Mama likely had many fights in their future as each tried to sacrifice her own needs to make sure the others were met.

Cupcake, who had been snoozing on the bath mat while Carolina attempted to get ready, suddenly woke up and began howling.

"Stop, you," Carolina scolded as the little dog whined and frantically scratched at the crack beneath the closed bathroom door. The very moment she opened the door, the Chihuahua was off like a shot.

"Whoa, hey there!" Levi said from the other side of the kitchen screen door.

Carolina quickened her pace and found the little dog whining and jumping, trying to burst through the door to greet their visitor. She scooped him up but had a hard time keeping hold of him as he wiggled and wriggled and tried to fly through the air toward Levi.

"Wow, boy. We hardly know each other." Levi laughed as he petted the whining dog on its head. "But I'm happy to see you, too."

"Mama's in the living room," Carolina said, setting Cupcake down again now that he'd calmed a bit.

Levi stayed rooted to the spot and lifted an eyebrow. "Will you be joining us this time?" he asked.

"I suppose I can do that," she said, even though that had been her plan all along. She still felt terribly embarrassed for how she'd behaved during his visit with Mama at the hospital, but they were well beyond that now.

He gestured for her to go ahead and then followed her into the living room.

Carolina seated herself on the loveseat, and Levi sank down beside her after giving her mother a quick peck on the cheek.

"You look lovely today, Mama Jolene," he said, then glanced at the floor before murmuring, "You too, Carolina."

Mama giggled. "Oh, you charmer. Isn't he a charmer, Carolina?"

"So charming." Carolina rolled her eyes but was glad to see her mother so happy.

Cupcake hopped up on Mama's lap in the chair and beat a rapid rhythm with his tail, which never seemed to stop wagging unless he fell asleep.

"So, catch me up," Mama said. "What have you been up to these last couple of weeks?"

Levi didn't miss a beat. "Mostly worrying about you. Walking the dogs. Serving barbecue. Cleaning hotel rooms. The usual."

"How's your father?"

"Also, the usual." Levi turned toward Carolina and explained, "He's had a hard time talking to me since my mom died. I guess I'm too painful a reminder of what he's lost, and he's just not ready to confront how deep his grief runs yet."

"That's terrible," Carolina said as she shook her head.

"We all handle pain in our own way," Mama interjected.

Levi tapped his fingers on his knees, looking as awkward as Carolina felt. It was hard to get to know him with Mama's over-the-top enthusiasm leading the conversation. Carolina had never been effusive like that. If anything, she'd become extra reserved as a way of counter-balancing her mother.

"The weather's getting really nice," Mama said. "Carolina and I took a good long walk yesterday, and it was just what I needed."

"We're starting to see the spring break crowd pass through now," Levi said with a drawn-out sigh. "It makes for extra work at the hotel."

"I can't believe it's that time already," Mama said, shaking her head. "Time sure does fly. What are you doing this weekend?"

Levi laughed. "Other than working, you mean?"

"Yes, other than that. If memory serves, ArtFest will be in Mount

Pleasant this week, and it's one of Carolina's favorite festivals of the year. You two should go together."

"Mama," Carolina warned, "he doesn't have to take me anywhere he doesn't want to. It sounds like he's plenty busy as it is."

Levi crossed his legs and turned toward her. "Actually, I'd love to go if you're up to joining me. It's been years since I saw the art fair, but I have good memories of it."

"Sure," Carolina said, feeling a bit trapped by her mother and Levi's twin grins.

Mama clapped her hands together in delight. "Well, that's decided then. Pick her up tomorrow at noon. I'll make sure she's ready."

As much as Carolina loved ArtFest and also wanted the chance to get to know Levi better, Mama's zeal at pushing them together made her extra uncomfortable. Why did a simple visit to a free community festival suddenly feel like the prom? And did Levi even want to go, or had he been backed into it every bit as much as her? Because Carolina had no doubt now Mama was trying very hard to play matchmaker between the two of them. Was this why she'd befriended Levi in the first place? Had this been her plan all along?

Well, it seemed they'd all find out soon enough.

Maybe even tomorrow.

Chapter 22

CAROLINA

T he next morning, Mama woke Carolina up by shaking her prone figure in bed. "Wake up, sunshine!"

Carolina pulled the covers over her head. "I don't have to be up for work yet," she grumbled.

"You don't have to be up for work at all," Mama corrected. "I called Nolan and told him you needed the day off."

"What? Mama, why?" Carolina kicked the covers off and pulled herself to a sitting position. "This better not be about the art fair thing with Levi."

"Of course, it's about the art fair thing with Levi." Mama rolled herself back to give her daughter space to get out of bed.

"It's no big deal," Carolina grumbled. "Just two new friends being forced to spend time together."

"He's picking you up at twelve, and we have a lot to do before then," Mama pressed. "Our appointment is at seven. Belle agreed to open early for us given our emergency. But before that, we need to stop by the hospital to get my new chair."

"Your new chair arrived?" she asked. "That's good, but what's this about an appointment at Belle's? I really hope you don't mean Beauty by Belle."

"Of course, I do. We have to get you gussied up for your big date this afternoon."

"Mama," Carolina yelled. "This is not the eighteen hundreds, and we are not the Bennett family."

"Of course not. We're the Browns," Mama said with pride.

Carolina would have rolled her eyes if she didn't have the dregs of sleep still stuck in the edges. "It's a Jane Austen reference... You know what? Never mind."

"Does that mean you're going to stop fighting it and just go with the flow?"

No wonder Levi and her mama were friends. Carolina, on the other hand, was getting very sick of this *go with the flow* business. "I'll agree to all your plans so long as you agree to stop calling it a date."

"It's just semantics," Mama shot back.

Carolina tapped her foot impatiently. "Do we have a deal or not?"

"Fine," Mama said with a huge, drawn out sigh. "Think you'll be ready to go in about an hour? I'm going to take Cupcake for a quick walk before we head over to the hospital."

Carolina bit her lower lip and nodded.

Mama wagged a finger sassily. "And before you make a peep, I know it won't be a *walk* for me. My arms need to get stronger, though, and I enjoy the fresh air and sunshine."

"You know," Carolina pointed out. "If you enjoy being outside so much, maybe you should come to the festival with us."

"But it's a—" Mama stopped abruptly when she caught herself. "I'm not ready to navigate those kinds of crowds just yet. Besides, you two will have a much better time without me slowing you down."

Carolina shook her head and frowned. "Yeah. Sure."

"Yup, uh-huh. See you in a bit. C'mon, Cupcake." Mama left just as quickly as she'd arrived, the little dog merrily trailing her out of the room.

Carolina gathered her outfit for the day before heading to the shower.

How could she just take life as it comes when she had a hard time taking a shower without first laying out her clothes? These days everything seemed to take on a constant edge of anxiety from not knowing what would come next. It was definitely not a way she wanted to live her entire life.

Thinking on this, she returned to her room to check in with things on her computer before getting ready for the day. She'd been horribly negligent of her email these past couple weeks, and the number of unread emails gave her a mini panic attack. She was still clearing out her email, making sure to unsubscribe the time wasters and properly file away the important messages, when Mama and Cupcake returned from their walk.

"Still not ready?" Mama asked with a shocked expression. "Well, c'mon. I'm sure Belle and her girls will wash your hair before getting started anyway. Actually, on second thought, let's skip the hospital. I'm sure Pastor Adam wouldn't mind taking me by while you're out with Levi. It's probably better that you're showered and clean before spending the full day outdoors. Enough with the computer, go wash up!"

"Yes, Mama," Carolina said, gently closing the lid of her laptop and heading to the bathroom to do as instructed.

She felt better, lighter now, that she had at least cleaned out her email inbox. What made her sad was how few emails she had from the university. It was as if she were out of sight, out of mind. The only messages she got were the safety news and other campus-wide updates. Her professors had already removed her from the online class portals, and none of her new study partners had written to check in.

It felt strange that she could so easily be removed from life there, when even after a year away from Charleston, she was still very much a part of the town life.

Maybe Charleston would always be home, no matter how much she tried to fit in elsewhere... or maybe she was just worrying about things needlessly.

Regardless, she had to get it together before her outing with Levi that afternoon. The last thing she wanted was to slip up and confide all her problems in him, knowing he'd just turn around and share them with the one person who couldn't know the truth about what was on Carolina's mind these days.

Mama had enough to worry about without adding Carolina's struggles with guilt over the past and confusion over the future to the top of the heap. She would just have to keep swallowing those terrible feelings down until she got used to the taste.

Chapter 23

CAROLINA

Carolina and her mama were the very first customers to arrive at Beauty by Belle that day. In fact, they arrived before any of the stylists did.

"Why do we need to be here so early?" she asked with a poorly hidden yawn.

"Because we're getting the works," Mama proclaimed enthusiastically.

"Uh oh. What does 'the works' entail?"

"It's a surprise, but you'll see soon enough," Mama said, making a lip-zipping gesture.

Oh, great. Carolina suddenly had the sneaking suspicion that she would be very embarrassed when she met up with Levi later.

An old car pulled into the empty parking lot and a red-haired woman popped out, then took quick, small strides toward the salon door. "Sorry I'm late!" she cried.

"It's okay," Mama said. "I think we might just be a bit early. Will Belle be coming in today, too? By the way, I'm Jolene and this is my daughter Carolina."

"I'm Avery," the woman said as she struggled to twist the key into the lock. "She'll be along in about an hour. I'll get you two set with your color first, then she'll come and help with the rest."

"Color?" Carolina demanded of her mama just as Avery finally popped the lock on the door and motioned for them both to follow her inside.

"Yes, color," Mama answered without the slightest hint of apology. "I need to cover these grays, and you need something fun. Look good, feel good. That's my mantra."

The stylist nodded approvingly. "Your light hair will hold pretty much any color you want," she said as she zipped back and forth opening the blinds along the storefront. "I, for one, think you'd look gorgeous with a cotton candy pink."

Mama clapped her hands together like a gleeful toddler. "Oh, yes, that would be perfect. Do that."

"Don't do that," Carolina shouted in a panic. She'd never been a pink girl growing up, and she wasn't a pink woman now.

"Why don't you grab one of those magazines and thumb through to see what you like?" Avery suggested. "We need to pick a haircut for you, too."

A cut, too? Well, at least that she needed. It seemed Mama wasn't skimping on their visit one bit, and Carolina was glad she'd already banked a couple shifts at the diner to help pay for it all. From the sound of things so far, she'd need to work at least another full week to cover the expense, but it was worth it to see Mama this happy.

Anything to keep her smiling, Carolina said to herself.

"Let's do the pink," she called aloud without so much as picking up the magazine. "You know more about this stuff than I do. If you think it will look good, I trust you."

Mama blew her a big, smacking kiss. "You know what, Avery?" she said, wheeling after the stylist. "I think I'll go pink, too. It sounds fun!"

"You've got it, boss," Avery said with a tired smile that made Carolina wonder if perhaps she hadn't slept well the night before. "How about your haircut?" she asked, glancing toward Carolina now.

"I don't know," she admitted. "It's been driving me nuts lately, constantly falling in my face and stuff. I guess just do whatever you think will look best."

"Are you okay with a big change?" Avery asked with a widening grin as she bent forward and ran her fingers through Carolina's still-wet hair. "Because that's kind of my specialty."

"I'm in your capable hands," Carolina said, hoping she wouldn't regret that later.

"Isn't this fun?" Mama clucked a short while later when they were both seated in the lounge with their heads full of foil. "We're like twins!"

"Well, it's definitely more fun than working a shift at the diner," Carolina mumbled with a wry smile.

"See!" Mama said. "I knew you didn't like it."

"I like helping out," Carolina corrected.

"Well then, darling, the best way to help me is just to be here with me like you are right now." Mama reached over and squeezed Carolina's knee affectionately. "Now let's catch up on gossip."

They spent the next half hour chuckling over photos and stories from the latest fashion magazines. It felt nice to have this no-pressure day with her mama. At least it was no pressure as long as they both kept mum on her upcoming afternoon with Levi.

The salon owner Belle joined them a little past eight, passing out cups of coffee all around. "Good morning," she trilled.

Carolina took a big, appreciative sip, but immediately regretted it. The coffee tasted like sweetened charcoal. *Blech.*

Luckily, Avery came to collect her while Mama went off with Belle. "Are you ready?" She asked, swishing her scissors demonstratively.

Carolina took a deep breath and closed her eyes. "Ready."

The first snip came uncomfortably close to her skull. And even though she'd vowed to keep her eyes squeezed shut the entire time, Carolina couldn't help but take a sneak peek.

Avery caught her eye in the mirror. "You said you were okay with a big change," she reminded her. "With a bone structure like yours, a pixie will look gorgeous on you. And then you won't have to worry about hair falling in your face for a good, long time."

Carolina was more startled by the pink color than the shortened length, but even she had to admit it looked perfect for her. Funny how just two weeks earlier she'd been wearing a department store pants suit with her hair swept back into a bun as she approached Capitol Hill for the first day of the internship that wasn't meant to be. Now she sat wearing jean overalls while her head increasingly came to resemble a child's lollipop.

Well, she could use a little sweetness in her life. If that meant looking like a confection, then so be it. Each time Avery snipped the scissors, Carolina felt half a dozen pounds lighter until finally it felt like she was floating.

Today would be a good day, after all.

And perhaps it could still be a good life, too.

Chapter 24
CAROLINA

J ust as Mama had predicted, they barely had enough time to finish all their pampering before noon. By the time they left the salon three and a half hours later, they'd both received haircuts and colors, deep-cleansing facials, massages, manicures, and pedicures. Talk about the works!

Carolina had to admit, she felt great—and she looked pretty dang good, too.

"A new look for a new life," Mama had remarked as Carolina drove them home.

When Levi came by to pick her up for the festival no more than fifteen minutes later, he had to do a double take. "Who are these gorgeous pink ladies?"

Mama giggled and blushed while Carolina hid her face.

"*Mmm,* pink ladies. That makes me crave apple pie," he added with a laugh.

"Oh, good idea!" Mama said. "I'll make some for us all later this week."

"I can't wait," Levi answered, holding the door open for Carolina so they could be on their way.

Before she could make a move, though, Cupcake shot past in a blur of fur and joyful barking.

"Come back, you!" Carolina cried, chasing helplessly after.

"We could take him with us," Levi offered.

"No, he's gotta keep Mama company while we're out."

"She could come with us, too," he said.

"Believe me, I know, and I've already tried to no avail." She caught up to the dog and guided him back inside, then pulled the door shut quickly before he could escape again.

"He causing trouble for you?" Levi asked as they both strolled toward his car still idling at the curb.

She blushed when he opened the passenger door and waited for her to climb in. The simple chivalrous motion brought their bodies close together for a split second, but that second was enough to set Carolina's nerves on edge all over again.

"Not really trouble, per se," she answered once Levi joined her in the car. "But we are still learning about each other bit by bit."

They both buckled their seatbelts, and Levi pulled the car forward. "You know, I do have quite a bit of experience with dogs. I'd be happy to give you some pointers."

She folded her hands in her lap and kept her eyes focused straight ahead. "Sure. What have you got?" she asked.

He shook his head and laughed. "No, not now. Let's just enjoy ourselves today. I can come by another day to help you train Cupcake. He is a therapy dog, so I'm guessing he's already pretty well trained. But I'd also guess he's probably using the new living situation to push boundaries and find out what he can get away with."

"Sounds like Mama," she said with a laugh of her own.

"Speaking of Mama Jolene..." Levi's breath hitched as he glanced nervously toward Carolina. "I have a bit of a confession to make."

"Uh oh," Carolina said. "Don't tell me she's tricked you into some kind of nefarious secret agenda for today."

"Well, actually, it was the other way around," he admitted before Carolina could ask what he meant. "I asked her to help set us up."

She hadn't expected that, especially given how he'd run from her at the party. "What? Why?"

He kept his eyes on the road ahead, and so did she. "Why not? I like you and want the chance to get to know you. When your mama is around, it's hard to talk much to you because you're so quiet and she's so..."

"Loud," Carolina finished for him.

"Hey, you said it, not me."

They both chuckled.

"Remember how I sat behind you in seventh grade math?"

She nodded.

"I had a huge crush on you back then, too," he confessed with a very noticeable blush across his handsome features.

Wait, did this mean he had a huge crush on her now as well? Carolina smiled and said, "Oh."

"Yeah."

They fell silent for a few moments.

"Since we're sharing secrets today," Carolina said, keeping her eyes trained straight ahead. "I've got a bit of a crush on you, too."

That was all the encouragement Levi needed to remove one hand from the steering wheel and hold it out to her palm up. Her breathing hitched as she placed her hand in his, and he gave it a tight squeeze. They held hands the rest of the drive to the festival, and Carolina's heart beat in her throat, keeping her from talking much.

Even though she didn't know him well yet, she liked Levi. It meant a lot that her mama liked him, too. But that still didn't mean she was ready for a relationship just yet. What if she opened her heart to Levi only for her entire world to collapse yet again?

She'd always lived life ruled by her head.

Now seemed like a terrible time to start listening to her heart.

Today. They could have today, but then she had some difficult decisions to make.

Chapter 25

PASTOR ADAM

I made it over to Jolene and Carolina Brown's house around lunch time.

Jolene greeted my arrival with a huge smile and a head full of newly pink hair. "What do you think?" she asked, running a hand with matching pink fingernails through her hair, then suddenly frowned. "Unless of course you don't like it. If you don't like it, keep quiet and don't ruin my fun."

"It suits you very well," I answered with a chuckle. "What prompted the change?"

She smiled sweetly again before declaring, "If people are going to stare, I'd much rather have them staring because I'm fabulous than because I'm in a chair."

That made good sense, I thought. "Speaking of chairs," I said. "Are you ready to trade this old model in for something new?"

"Oh, am I ever. This one has a particular smell I find rather unpleasant. Besides, it's so plain and boring. Doesn't go with my new hairstyle at all."

"Well, then let's get you into a new set of wheels, kiddo."

Jolene laughed. "Kiddo? I'm not even fifteen years younger than you."

I laughed again. Jolene always had everyone laughing. It was part of the gift of her joyous personality. "I stand by my choice, *kiddo.*"

"Oh, wait," she cried halfway out the door. "We should bring Cupcake, too. After all, he is a therapy dog. Could you just help me get that special vest on him?"

"But of course." I helped the Chihuahua into his service vest and Jolene into the van, then the three of us were on our way.

"Where's Carolina today?" I asked when we stopped at our first traffic light.

"A date," Jolene revealed with an energetic shift in her voice.

Well, this was a surprise. Carolina had only been back in town a short while and already she'd managed to land herself a boyfriend? I didn't know how she found the time, but a part of me was impressed by her ability to juggle work, home, and now romance, too.

"An old flame from her high school days?" I asked, locking eyes with Jolene in the rear-view mirror.

She shook her head but continued to smile like the cat that ate the canary. "Nope. My friend Levi."

I thought back to the party and remembered the well-mannered young man I'd spoken to briefly as part of my circulating. "I'm guessing you had something to do with this," I said with a chuckle.

"Well, of course I did," she said straightening in her chair. "They're both so shy, it makes me want to scream."

"How about you, Jolene?" I wondered aloud. "Anyone special in your life these days?"

"I should ask you the same question," she shot right back.

The light freed us from our wait, and I pulled through the intersection. "Fair point," I conceded.

At the hospital, I was not at all surprised to find that Jolene's new special-order wheelchair was decked out with purple trim. "If you'd have known about your new hair, you could have ordered your chair to match," I quipped.

She moved herself into the new chair, refusing any help from me or the nearby nurse. "Or maybe I'll change my hair to match before too long."

"How is it?" I asked as she twisted and turned to check out the various features of her new ride.

"Perfect," she said with a giant sigh of relief.

"How do you make it go?" I wondered, bending down to examine it myself.

"Uh, with my arms," she said sarcastically while making a silly face that showed me exactly what she thought of my well-meaning question.

"Don't you have a little joystick to steer yourself around? I always thought that looked fun."

"This is a manual power-assist chair," she said proudly. "The best of both worlds, but for now, I like powering my own chair. Have to get my exercise in somehow."

She patted her lap and waited for Cupcake to hop up. "See? Perfect."

"I can see that." I laughed again. Jolene had a way of bringing the happiness right out of people. It's why all of Charleston loved her so dearly.

Suddenly, a terrible thought surfaced in my mind. "Shoot. Speaking of exercise, Mrs. Clementine will have my hide if I'm late for our daily walka-bout. Do you think maybe you'd like to join us?"

"I can think of nothing I'd like better," Jolene answered. She placed a hand on each of the two big wheels that flanked the sides of her chair and moved herself rapidly toward the exit. "C'mon, slowpoke!"

Oh, yes, she and Mrs. Clementine would make a fine pair when it came to torturing me this afternoon.

Chapter 26

CAROLINA

"How do I look?" Carolina said, turning her head from side to side to show off her new face paint. They'd started their afternoon by grabbing a delicious lunch to eat as they walked up and down the festival. Carolina hadn't planned to spend any money, but once the face painting booth popped into view, she knew she had to treat herself to this small indulgence. After all, it was a tradition she'd kept since childhood.

"Like the most beautiful thing I've ever seen." Levi offered her a hand to help pull her up from the artist's chair.

"Thank you so much," she said to the kindly woman who had painted an intricate pattern of swirls and stars on each side of her face. "I love it."

"Does he want something, too?" the artist asked with a smirk as she cleaned off the brushes and sponges she'd used on Carolina.

"No, thank you," Levi said at the same time Carolina shouted, "Yes!"

All three of them laughed.

"How about a compromise and I just do half of his face?" the artist offered with an exaggerated wink.

"Pick something good for me?" Levi asked, settling into the chair now himself.

Carolina flipped through the album showing off all the beautiful possibilities, then held the book up so she could indicate her choice while keeping it hidden from Levi. "That one," she said, knowing instantly that it would suit her companion perfectly.

"Good choice," the artist said, squeezing greens and golds onto her palate.

"Don't I get to see?" Levi demanded.

"You will. After she's done," Carolina teased. "Until then, we'll keep you hot with anticipation," she added as a small hint to the design that was currently being brought to life on his face.

About five minutes later, he had a beautiful dragon tail that started at his hairline and wrapped around his chin, complete with glittering flecks of gold.

"Why a dragon?" Levi asked, admiring the artist's work in the little mirror she held before him.

"Clearly it's because you're her knight in shining armor," the woman answered for Carolina. "You two make a cute couple, by the way. Enjoy the fair."

"So, I'm your knight in shining armor, huh?" Levi teased when they'd left the painter's tent and were once again walking through the festival hand in hand.

Carolina shoved him playfully as she shook her head. "Those were her words, not mine."

"Okay, so what are your words then, Ms. Brown?" he asked, pulling her closer to his side.

"You're my dragon," she said with a goofy laugh. "You know, a powerful, mythical creature who hoards gold. Wait, that came out wrong. It's because of all your jobs and the fact you're saving up. I meant—"

He snapped his teeth close to her face. *"Raaaar!"*

He was so stinking adorable.

She couldn't help it. She leaned in and placed a sweet peck right on his non-dragoned cheek. "Thank you for today," she said. "I'm having a really nice time."

Levi lifted his hand to the place where her lips had just been. "I am having the very best day ever," he countered with a flirtatious grin. "We should hit all the festivals this summer. Imagine how fun that would be. It's like visiting a new world every single weekend."

Carolina let go of his hand and reached to tuck her hair behind her ear, only that familiar safety blanket wasn't there anymore. She'd shorn it all off earlier that day and dyed it pink to boot.

"What's wrong?" Levi asked, stopping mid-stride.

She picked up the pace, forcing him to follow after. "Nothing," she murmured, searching the aisles for a distraction. "Look, handmade jewelry. Let's go check it out."

"Please don't lie to me." Levi stopped again and held tight to her hand so that she couldn't make it very far herself. "I can tell something's wrong. Let me help."

"It's just I don't know if I'll be around this summer," she mumbled as she tried to yank him toward the jewelry exhibit.

He came with her this time. "Will you be heading back to D.C. so soon?"

"I don't know if I'll be going back at all." She picked up the first pendant she saw and held it up in the light. "Don't you think this would look lovely on Mama? It's got a purple stone which ordinarily is her favorite color."

Levi completely ignored her attempt to change the topic. "I thought you were one of those people who had your whole life mapped out," he insisted.

"I was, until..." She widened her eyes and made a flippant gesture with her hands to say what she didn't feel like putting into words just yet.

His face fell. "Oh."

Carolina slipped out of the booth and into the main walkway, pushing a hand into each pocket to discourage Levi from trying to hold onto her hand just then. She was already getting far too comfortable with him. It would only make leaving harder, if that time ever came. "Can't we just enjoy today and not worry about tomorrow?"

He looped an arm over her shoulders as they walked deeper into the crowd. "That's a bit nihilist of you, but if it's what you want, I guess I can respect that."

"It is," she insisted.

"Okay, then we're agreed. Hey, let's go dance to some music up by the main stage." Levi led her through the throngs of festival goers. When they reached the main stage, he took her hand from her pocket and spun her in a lively dance.

And while Carolina enjoyed herself well enough, the rest of the day was covered by a dark cloud. Why had she assumed she could last even a few days without a plan?

She felt so lost now.

Chapter 27

CAROLINA

When Carolina returned home, she found her mother waiting outside in a fancy new wheelchair.

"Hey, sugar darling!" Mama cried. "How was your da— I mean, your *not* date?"

"It was fine," Carolina answered, coming over to offer her mama a quick hug. "I see you went with purple."

"Nice, right?" Mama answered with a contented smile. "It moves like a dream, too. Want to go for a stroll? I'm eager to show this puppy off."

She shook her head with laughter. Oh, it felt good to be home with Mama. "A stroll?"

"Yes, a stroll," she insisted. "I took a walk with Pastor Adam and Mrs. Clementine earlier this afternoon, and the three of us came up with it. *Stroll.* It has *roll* right in the name. You walk. I roll. Stroll is the perfect word for what we do."

Carolina chuckled at her mother's never-ending enthusiasm. Why couldn't she have inherited her easygoing nature? "Sure, let's go for a stroll. Although, I've gotta say, *walk and stroll* is mighty cute, too."

"Ooh, you're right." Mama's eyes lighted mischievously. "And I thought of that just now all on my own, too."

"You sure did," Carolina said, happy to see her mother having such a good time determining new lingo to describe her activities. "I'll just go grab Cupcake from inside."

"No need," Mama said, hooking a thumb over her shoulder. "Look back there."

Carolina circled around the side of the chair and found the Chihuahua snoozing on a special shelf attached to the back of Mama's chair. It even had raised edges so that the tiny dog wouldn't accidentally roll off.

"Wow, that's cool!" Carolina cried. "I can't believe your wheelchair came with a custom dog bed."

Mama positively beamed. "It didn't. I made this myself."

Okay, now she was seriously impressed. "What? Haven't you only had this chair for a couple hours?"

"Yup, and it took far less than that to see the need to add a few of my own modifications. Cupcake had a hard time walking the whole way with Pastor Adam, Mrs. Clementine, and me earlier, but he wasn't secure on my lap and I needed my hands for powering myself along, so I came up with this beauty. Neat, right?"

"Neat? It's fantastic!"

Her mother waved off the compliment. "Oh, you flatterer, you."

"I'm serious. I saw lots of great art at the festival today, but you know what it was missing? Practical art. You know, art that also serves a purpose. I bet a lot of folks in wheelchairs would like having a mobile doggie shelf like you do."

"Oh, hush. It's not art, just a practicality."

Wasn't that what she'd just said? Sometimes Mama glommed right onto compliments, and other times she could be hard to convince. Apparently, she needed a bit more coaxing before she'd accept Carolina's praise today.

"But it's purple," she told Mama. "And, wait, is that embroidery along the edge?"

"Maybe." Mama tried but could no longer hide how happy the

compliments made her. "Hey, now that we're all here and caught up, let's get strolling along."

Carolina walked a couple paces behind her mother so she could see the doggie shelf in action. It held firm even when they turned sharply at the end of the driveway. "Have you thought of any other accessories you could make to go with it?"

"I only just got the chair this afternoon," Mama said.

"Yes, but you were in that other chair for over a week. Surely you must have had some ideas on how to improve it."

Mama stopped and waited for Carolina to fall into step beside her. "Why the sudden interest in my chair?"

"I just really like your new one. It's so stylish, and so you. That shelf is just the cherry on top of the fabulous sundae you have going on." This was all true, but also, she didn't want to talk about Levi or the awkward turn their date had taken that afternoon. She'd much rather stay focused on her mother than herself.

"Okay, now you're speaking my language," Mama admitted. "By the way, I like it, too. Not being able to walk isn't quite as bad with a luxury ride like this."

Carolina rolled her eyes at that comment as she searched for a way to keep the conversation going on this current track. "How is getting around the house in this new chair? Easier?"

"Much," Mama said with an animated nod. "I've even learned a couple new tricks."

"Tricks?" She could just imagine Mama out there on a skateboarder's halfpipe, flipping around in her chair like Tony Hawk. "You're being careful, right?"

Now Mama rolled *her* eyes. It seemed most days were measured in how many eyerolls they could shoot back and forth between them, and this day was no exception. It meant things were getting normal again.

"If I move my weight to the side before I transition to a new surface, it's easier to get the momentum to make the switch. Things like that. Also,

I have this nifty little button here." Mama pressed something on the side of her chair and suddenly she zoomed forward.

The unexpected acceleration woke up Cupcake who barked merrily and crawled from his shelf over Mama's shoulder and into her lap.

"Wait for me, Speed Racer!" Carolina cried as she jogged after them, doing her best to stifle the laughter bubbling within. She loved seeing her mama exuberant like this. She'd returned to the same woman Carolina had known her entire life. Somehow, she'd managed to turn her accident and the confinement in the chair into a new adventure rather than an obstacle.

There was a lot she could learn from her mama, but first, she'd enjoy the rest of their day together.

Chapter 28

CAROLINA

When they returned from their stroll around the neighborhood, Mama and Carolina found Levi waiting for them on the front porch. Cupcake, of course, immediately hopped down from Mama's chair and raced over to greet their guest.

"Levi," Carolina said simply, not sure what else she could say.

"I'll just give you two some time to yourselves," Mama said, heading for the ramp as she called for Cupcake to follow her inside.

"I was almost home from dropping you off when I realized I couldn't leave things the way we had," Levi explained. He steepled his fingers before himself, which made her nervous that a serious discussion was on its way. Hadn't he agreed to leave well enough alone that afternoon?

Carolina came down to sit beside him on the steps. "What way? We had a nice day."

He shook his head and sighed. "Something happened after we got our faces painted. You pulled back and weren't the same after that."

Carolina dropped her voice low just in case Mama was eavesdropping from somewhere nearby. "I already told you why."

And I don't want to talk about this with you—or with anybody—right now, she silently added.

"Yeah, and I thought about that, too," he explained. "You said it's because you don't have a plan and that scares you, but honestly, Carolina, we're nineteen. Most people our age don't have a plan yet, and that's okay."

She raked a hand through her new short hair and fixed her eyes on the ground. "I'm not most people. I'm me, and I need to know where I'm going before I get there."

"But why? What are you so afraid of?"

Why was he pushing her like this? She'd already told him this topic was off limits. Did he think that no longer applied now that they weren't at the festival?

Carolina wanted so badly to answer—if only to get him to leave faster—but in truth, she didn't know why she'd lived her whole life afraid of being taken for a surprise. Maybe it was just an innate part of her personality, or maybe somehow a part of her had anticipated what would happen to Mama.

Whatever the case, she felt the way she did, and there was no sense in anyone telling her she should feel differently. She couldn't just magically snap her fingers and stop worrying.

"I can't answer that," she said at last, turning hesitantly to face him.

"Can't or won't?" Levi demanded. His voice held undertones of frustration, which only served to stoke the rage within her. She was angry about so much these days—what had happened to Mama, what she'd left behind in D.C., the lot of it. Yes, she'd gone on one sort of date with Levi, but that didn't give him the right to dictate her life. If she wasn't ready to make a decision yet, he couldn't force her. The fact he was even trying showed he wasn't the man she or Mama had assumed him to be.

"You know what?" she said as she jumped to her feet. "I've had quite enough. You barely know me and yet you think you can just show up and make all these judgments about me? That won't win you many friends in life, Levi."

"Yeah, well, maybe I'm not trying to make friends," he shot back.

"Maybe I'm trying to help you. I care about you. I care about your mama. And I want you both to stop hurting already."

"Shows what you know," she sputtered, practically shaking with rage. "Mama is happy as a cat in pajamas these days."

Levi's features pinched together. "Is she, though?"

Wow, he'd said the one thing that was even worse than the words he already uttered. It was one thing to boss Carolina around, but to speak unkindly of Mama? She was done.

"That's between me and Mama," she said through clenched teeth. "I think you need to go."

"But, Carolina, I'm only—"

"Go!" she shouted. "Go away and leave us alone. We'll be just fine without you and your know-it-all attitude."

"I just want to help," Levi said softly as he pulled himself to his feet. "But I can see you're not ready to be helped. As much as you complain about it, you like living in fear. I bet you like feeling guilty, too. You're using your guilt as an excuse to not be brave. You think you're punishing yourself, but you're not. You're punishing those who love you instead."

"So now I'm selfish, too?" she shouted with a frustrated groan as she threw her hands up in the air. "If you won't leave, then I will. Have a good life, Levi. I'm done."

Chapter 29

CAROLINA

"What happened out there?" Mama asked when Carolina came tearing back through the house following her confrontation with Levi.

"I don't want to talk about it," she mumbled before locking herself in her room.

Why couldn't Levi leave well enough alone? She had enough on her mind these days without having to worry that he'd randomly show up and push the boundaries of her comfort zone. He may have heard all about Carolina from her mama, but she still barely knew anything about him. How did her agreeing to go on one lousy date with him give him permission to judge her? To think he knew how to live her life better than she did?

At the end of the day, it didn't. Nothing gave him permission to have a say in her life. The audacity, that's what made her so furious.

A soft knock sounded at the door. "Carolina? Baby?"

She used her palms to wipe away the fresh tears that had soaked her cheeks before answering, "Yes, Mama?"

"Can I come in?"

Carolina got up to unlock her door and opened it to find her mother staring up at her. It felt so odd, towering above her mother like that, but she'd get used to it soon enough. She had so many things to get used to—to accept—these days. What was the point in fighting any of them anymore?

"Did Levi say something to upset you?" Mama asked with a wilting look. "I'm sorry. I should have never pushed you to—"

"No, it's not your fault," Carolina said, crossing the room back to her bed. "It's not even his fault, really. I'm just not ready for what he's after."

"And what is he after?"

"Honestly? I don't know."

"Okay, then what are you after?" Mama amended.

Carolina shrugged, feeling so stupid and childish in that moment. "I don't know that, either."

Mama chuckled sadly. "That's the problem with life, isn't it? So much of the time we don't know what we want, but that doesn't stop us from striving for it all the same."

Carolina's tears had silently begun to fall again—or perhaps they'd never stopped falling in the first place. "How do you figure it out?"

Mama rolled forward and lifted a hand to her daughter's cheek. "Eventually we just do. Maybe it's our hearts, our conscience, or God. I'm not really sure. All I know is that the answers will come if you're patient."

Carolina sniffed and shook her head. "That's easier said than done."

"Oh, I know, my darling girl." Mama searched the room until she found a box of tissues, which she retrieved for her daughter. "That's part of being nineteen and wanting to change the world. Sometimes we have to change ourselves first. Help ourselves before we can help others."

"Aren't I helping you?" Carolina asked as she pulled a tissue from the box and wiped at her runny nose. "I'm trying so hard."

"I know you are, and yes. I had a perfectly lovely day today. It stinks that I can't walk, but that's not going to change. The only thing I can change is my attitude, and that's what I'm working on." Mama opened her arms wide and Carolina leaned into them.

"You're always so upbeat and happy," she murmured into her mother's pink hair that matched her own. "It's why everyone loves you."

"They all love you, too. Your strength, intelligence, ambition. From the very first moment I held you in my arms, I knew you were special." Mama stroked Carolina's hair until Carolina pulled away from her embrace.

She didn't feel like she deserved to be comforted right now, especially by the one person she'd hurt most, both with her ambition and her indecision. She just couldn't accept Mama's kindness some days.

"But how?" Carolina asked with another sob. "I haven't even done anything yet."

Mama placed a hand on Carolina's chest. "It's your heart. It's always been your heart. It seems like maybe you've stopped listening to it lately, and I blame myself. I've been dragging you all over the place because I so love spending time together. But what you need right now is some time to yourself so that you can figure things out."

"I don't know how," Carolina admitted. "I want to, but I can't."

Mama grabbed her daughter's hand and pressed her lips to it gently. "Yes, you can. Just listen to that little voice. It'll steer your ship home."

With that, she left the room and pulled the door shut behind her.

But poor Carolina was more troubled and more confused than ever.

Chapter 30

PASTOR ADAM

Sometimes the Lord is subtle. This afternoon, however, He was anything but.

"Pray!" He shouted straight into my heart like it was a megaphone.

At the time, of course, I was out grocery shopping, but I heard the call, stashed my buggy with a kindly cashier, and headed straight to the parking lot as instructed. I knew better than to ignore a direct call from the Lord, no matter how inconvenient it might seem at the time. Once in the privacy of my car, I folded my hands over the steering wheel and closed my eyes.

"Dearest Father," I started, then paused to listen to my heart for direction. Immediately, a picture formed in my mind's eye, and I knew exactly who I was meant to be praying for so urgently that day.

"Dearest Father," I began again. "Your child, Carolina, is hurting. She's lost and afraid. Show her your mercy and the power of Your love. Place a guiding hand on her life. Help her to know that You have a plan for her life. Open her eyes to see."

I recited *Psalm 23*, envisioning our dear, sweet Carolina as that lost little lamb. Whether or not she liked it, she'd returned to our flock here in Charleston, but still, she wasn't comforted. She was afraid, unsure, and even angry with God. This was the perfect combination for Satan to work his dark magic.

No wonder the Lord had called on me so urgently to lift that child in prayer.

I spent a good while in my car talking with God before I returned to collect my buggy and finish my shopping. I continued to think about Carolina and her mama Jolene for the rest of that day.

Despite my worry, I knew the Lord would provide a way for the both of them. I also certainly felt better knowing they had a church dog in their midst.

Tomorrow was a church day. Perhaps it wasn't too late to change my sermon to speak directly to both of them...

"God, give me the words to reach their hearts," I murmured before I locked myself away in the study. It was going to be a long night.

Chapter 31

CAROLINA

Carolina really did not want to go to church that Sunday. It wasn't like she and Mama had ever really been regulars, but Pastor Adam and Abigail had insisted they make an appearance —and they'd done so several times over the past week. Perhaps regular attendance was part of their church dog program, or maybe they believed that the Browns needed an extra helping of God following Mama's accident.

Whatever the case, Mama was up early and dressed in her Sunday best, which meant they'd definitely be attending service despite Carolina's unvoiced objections.

"Oh, Cupcake," she murmured to the little dog nestled in the crook of her arm. "I'm too tired for this today."

She'd stayed awake long and late, trying to listen to that still small voice in her heart as Mama had suggested. She'd hoped a clear and obvious answer would come to her, but that morning, she felt just as confused as ever. If she didn't make a decision about where to go or who to be next, then life would decide for her—and she probably wouldn't much care for the answer it came up with.

"Are you getting ready yet?" Mama called from the living room.

Cupcake immediately hopped off the bed when he heard Mama's voice, then booked it straight to the bedroom door where he began to whine and scratch in earnest.

"Yeah," she answered, pulling herself to her feet sluggishly.

Once again Carolina looked so plain next to Mama, even with her stylish new hairdo, but at least the short hair made getting ready much faster in the morning.

Less than half an hour later, they were seated in the front row of Eternal Grace Church, waiting for the service to begin.

The regular churchgoers flocked to both Carolina and Mama to offer their greetings, blessings, and hugs. Everyone sang some praise and worship songs, and then Pastor Adam took the pulpit.

He took a quick drink from his water bottle, then stepped up to the microphone attached to his podium. "Dearly beloved," he began, then broke out in a huge grin, making eye contact with both Carolina and her mama.

"Funny how we tend to only start wedding ceremonies that way, isn't it?" he quipped. "Dearly beloved. Dearly beloved. Well, that's all of us, all the time. At least to God."

He paused to let this sink in as he continued to make eye contact with the various congregants seated in the audience before him.

"Yes, we are dearly beloved by our heavenly Father all the time. Do you understand just how amazing that is? He loves us dearly *all the time.* Not just when we're at our best. Not just when we're following His plan for our lives, but all the time. Every single second of every single day."

Mama reached out to grasp Carolina's hand while Pastor Adam paused again. He had a definitive preaching style that didn't exactly match his normal way of speaking, but Carolina found that she liked it all the same. It was simple and easy to understand. And with how sleep-deprived and utterly confused she'd been of late, the easy to understand part was pretty important these days.

"When you're at your worst, when you're sinning up a storm, when you can't even find a reason to love yourself, you are still His dearly beloved. When you're at your worst, that's when He's got you the most. He's willing to leave ninety-nine other sheep behind to go find you, His beloved and lost little lamb. It is not an aggravation. It is not an inconvenience. God will go out of His way to meet you right where you are, because *that's what a good father does.*"

He hit the pulpit with the open palm of his hand on each of those last six words to drive the point home.

"Don't be like Adam and Eve in the Garden. Don't hide because you're naked. Lay it all bare to the Lord. After all, He made you. He already knows what you look like."

Laughter sprung up throughout the audience, and Carolina found herself chuckling, too.

Pastor Adam wagged a finger at the crowd as he, too, struggled to stop laughing. "Of course, I'm not talking about being without clothes. I'm talking about being afraid, angry, sad, confused, unsure, *guilty.*"

Carolina gulped hard. Okay, now it felt like the pastor was speaking directly to her. How did he know she'd been feeling exactly as he said?

"God knows your heart and it's impossible to hide from Him," he continued. "So why try? You can't run. You can't hide. So why not go directly to the Father? Lay your burdens at His feet. Stop trying to do it all yourself. He's ready and waiting. He wants to help, so go ahead and let Him. Let us pray."

Carolina bowed her head with the rest of the congregation and placed a hand on her heart. She'd come so close to giving up on herself, giving up on her dreams, but God hadn't left her for a second.

She smiled as Pastor Adam's timely words sunk deeper and deeper into her heart.

God wants to help. I just need to let Him.

Chapter 32

CAROLINA

O nce Pastor Adam finished his full sermon and closing prayer, he surprised Carolina by calling her and Mama to the front of the church. When they joined him there, a cheer erupted through the crowd. Some of the congregants even lifted hand-painted signs that read *We love you, Jolene* and *A foundation built on faith never crumbles.*

"My goodness," Mama said, wiping the fresh tears that had begun to form at the corners of her eyes. "What's all this about?"

"Your brothers and sisters in the Lord wanted to celebrate with you, but not everyone could attend our first surprise party, so..." Pastor Adam turned toward the crowd and gestured for them to lift their voices.

"Surprise again!" everyone cried.

Several men entered from outside the sanctuary carrying long folding tables, which they placed at the front of the church. Next came Abigail, Mrs. Clementine, Harmony, and Nolan, each carrying a giant platter of finger foods which they laid on the tables before coming over to hug Carolina and her mama.

Mama kept crying the whole time everyone came up to say hello, to pray over her, or just to chat. After the first dozen or so folks had come forward, someone achingly familiar approached.

Levi.

First, he hugged Mama and gave her a swift kiss on the cheek, then he turned to Carolina. "I'm sorry about the other day. I was too harsh."

"Yes, you were," Carolina whispered as she searched the crowd to make sure no one was watching their awkward exchange.

Levi's eyes grew wide. She felt the sincerity in his words, but that didn't change all the horrible things he'd said before. "Can we start over? Please?"

"We can't just keep starting over," Carolina mumbled with a sigh. "That's no way to build a relationship. Or a life."

He shook his head. "You're right. Of course, you're right. Just know that I'm sorry. I was too hard on you and way too soon. You need time to deal with everything that's happened, and you need to do that on your timetable. Not mine."

"Thank you for understanding," she said, forcing a smile. She wished she was ready to fully forgive him, but she needed to work out her own issues before attempting to repair their fledgling relationship. "I do need to work through things on my own time. And alone. At least for now."

"So, you're saying you need some space?" he asked, placing a hand on her shoulder and giving it a squeeze before letting it fall away.

She nodded hesitantly.

"Please don't make it forever. I'll do whatever it takes to help make things right." He leaned forward to brush a kiss against her cheek, then disappeared back into the crowd.

Maybe he left the church after that, because Carolina certainly didn't see him again.

Abigail kept her company for the rest of the party, though, seeing as there were long lines to speak with both her mama and Pastor Adam.

"How's Cupcake?" Abigail asked over shared croissants.

"He's been wonderful for Mama. He really gets her out and about, and she even invented this special wheelchair attachment to keep him near where ever she goes," Carolina explained. She was so proud of her mama's creative invention that she told everyone who would listen.

Abigail laughed. "That's great! I'm definitely not surprised your mother's making lemonade out of all these lemons, and I'm glad Cupcake is there to help. How have *you* been?"

Carolina sighed and threw the rest of her croissant in the trash. "I've been. That's about the best answer I can give."

"I understand that. I wallowed a lot longer after my first husband, Owen, died. It just felt like nothing was as it should be in the world. I didn't know how I could possibly go on when everything that mattered had been stolen from me."

"What turned things around?" Carolina asked, wrapping her arms around herself.

"I was pregnant with Owen's baby when he died. That alone kept me going even though I felt no joy about expecting my first child. Not the way everyone says you're supposed to feel. Instead I felt helpless, guilty, pathetic."

Carolina noticed that Abigail hadn't answered the question. "Do you still feel that way?" she prodded gently.

"Sometimes," Abigail confessed. "But most of the time, no. I couldn't see it at the time, but God had so much more waiting for me—falling in love with Gavin and getting married again, getting to keep a part of the love I lost through my amazing little boy, reconnecting with the church and community, and the church dogs, too."

This surprised Carolina. She didn't know the full origin of the church dogs, only that they'd been discovered in the nativity scene one cold and snowy Christmas Eve. Pastor Adam said the dogs worked miracles. Was his daughter the first to benefit from them?

"They helped you?" she asked.

"More than I can possibly put into words. That's why it was so important for me to entrust one of them to you. My dad says they're miracle workers, but I think they're just a constant reminder that God is there and that he loves us."

Carolina let out a long breath. Everything was clicking right into place now that she was willing to search for the pieces. "Just like his sermon today," she said.

"Just like his sermon today," Abigail repeated with a nod.

Carolina thought about her conversation with Abigail for a good, long time. While Cupcake was a constant reminder that God was there, her mother's wheelchair served as an equally constant reminder of all that had gone wrong in their lives. Could one ever cancel the other out? Could she learn to be strong and find new happiness the way Abigail had?

One thing was for certain: she wanted to try.

Chapter 33
CAROLINA

s the days continued to pass, Carolina began letting go of her
guilt bit by bit. She still didn't know what would come next,
but she was more open to the possibilities. Sometimes life went
exactly according to plan, but sometimes flexibility was needed in order to
make it through.

Carolina reminded herself of that constantly. Every time she looked at
Cupcake, she remembered the Pastor's sermon and Abigail's experience of
finding life and love again after her own tragic loss.

They'd all made it through, and now she could, too. After all, God was
on her side—just as he'd always been. Knowing that made it easier to take
any new struggles that popped up in stride.

Most days she worked breakfast at the diner, but every single day she
and Mama would go for a stroll with Cupcake. Sometimes twice per day, if
Mama was lucky.

"Why do you like it so much?" she asked on their constitutional
that day.

Mama shrugged. "I just do. It makes me feel normal, like I'm still part
of the bigger world. Every day I get stronger and can make it longer or
complete the same distance in less time. I like that, too."

Cupcake joined them every single time, of course. He'd start off by trotting merrily at their side, but as the distance stretched on, he'd grow tired and have to be placed on his specialized shelf. Even from that vantage point, he loved all the fresh air and interesting sights just as much as Mama did.

"For all the strolling you do, you should start a club," Carolina quipped as they rounded the corner to start their third loop of the neighborhood.

"Ha, maybe I should!" Mama took this as encouragement to increase their pace so that even her daughter had a hard time keeping up with her.

They moved on to discuss other things, but Carolina couldn't get the idea of a club out of her mind. Mama had always loved bringing people together. Usually she'd done that with a hot breakfast and a fresh pot of coffee, but much as Nolan was trying to find a way to make things work back at the diner, they'd both be better off by moving forward rather than slipping back.

The truth was things had changed, and maybe that was okay.

Hardships didn't have to be the end. Instead, they could provide a chance to prove how much you wanted something.

What Mama wanted was to be a part of the community, to bring people joy and to gossip about all the latest town news while doing it. A strolling club could help her do that. And at the same time, she could help others meet their own goals for companionship, health, or any number of other things.

Yes, this had to happen, and Carolina was pretty sure she knew how to get started.

"C'mere, Cupcake," she called, then patted her lap so he would jump up. She stroked the Chihuahua as she spoke to him. "You've inspired Mama, and that's inspired me. Can you do me a favor and help me plan a special surprise for her?"

Cupcake barked and wagged his tail with a boisterous series of thump-thump-thumps.

"*Shhh,* we don't want Mama to hear us before it's ready." Carolina

439

petted the dog until he calmed a bit, then spoke again. "We need to plan a secret visit to Abigail. Do you want to go see Abigail?"

Cupcake barked again and ran impatiently toward the door. Okay, she'd probably asked for that.

She fired a quick text to Abigail to ask if they could drop by, then waited until Mama was distracted over fixing dinner to sneak away with Cupcake in tow.

When she met up with Abigail, Carolina explained her idea about the club, which had now evolved into a much more detailed and complex plan to surprise Mama.

Her friend's eyes flashed with mirth. "I love it," she said, rubbing her hands together. "Now, tell me how I can help."

"You do the church's bulletins and slides, right?" Carolina asked, referring to the gorgeous new designs that Eternal Grace featured each and every week.

"I do. It's kind of a way of honoring my past life as a graphic designer. These days I spend more time tending to the church dog program and other church activities, but I still find time to design those for my dad every week."

"They're beautiful," Carolina said enthusiastically. "And I was hoping you could help me design a few things for Mama. I have a little saved up from working at the diner. If it's not enough, though, I'll make more soon enough."

Abigail sucked air in through her teeth and raised a hand to her chest as if utterly scandalized. "Carolina, you wound me. Of course, I'll do it for free. The Lord has blessed my family with more than enough money from Gavin's job as an endodontist. Let me do this as a gift for your mama, and so that when this whole thing becomes a nationwide sensation, I can let everyone know that I was there right from the start."

On the drive home, Carolina had to work hard to calm her racing heart. Now Abigail saw the strength of her idea, too. It wasn't just a pipedream. This could really happen—and soon.

Oh, Mama would be so pleased.

Chapter 34

CAROLINA

The next day, Carolina awoke to an excited string of texts from Abigail.

Inspiration struck last night her first message said. What followed was a series of digital mock-ups, each more perfect than the last.

"Thank you so much!" Carolina texted back. "These are even better than what I was hoping for."

Awesome. I'll email over the high res images in a few!

Carolina still had several more people she'd need to ask for help with what was turning out to be a very big idea, and the next person she needed to reach out to was Levi, which meant it was time to clear the air between them at last. She took a deep breath before giving him a call.

"Hello? Carolina?" he answered after the first ring.

"Hi, Levi," she said softly.

"How are you?" he sputtered. She imagined him stumbling around his apartment to find the best signal. Even though she'd never seen the place, she could imagine perfectly what Levi's home might look like. She bet it was full of needful clutter just like the one she shared with Mama.

"Is everything okay?" he pressed.

"Everything's great," she answered, a smile creeping across her face.

She hoped he'd hear it in her voice. She was finally done being angry and ready for what came next.

"I've missed you," Levi said. "Are you ready to see me again?"

She nodded, even though he couldn't see the gesture from the other end of the line. "Yes. I missed you, too, but I was also hoping I could get your help with a surprise for Mama."

They made plans to meet up that afternoon and, true to his word, Levi both appeared on time and in secret. He texted her from the curb in front of their house so that she could come outside and talk with him in his car.

Boy, was it hard to plan anything without Mama knowing, but she at least had to try.

When Cupcake followed her through the door, she decided to let the little dog come with her. After all, he'd been a huge part of what had set this all in motion, and she knew he could feel the shift in Carolina's emotions as a newfound excitement replaced her long-standing anxiety.

Once she was seated in the car with Cupcake in her lap, Levi turned to her with huge, shining eyes. During their week apart, she'd almost forgotten how handsome he was, how much kindness he always wore splashed right across his face for all to see. It reminded her of Mama's special way with people, and suddenly she understood what had drawn them to each other. Not just the need to fill gaps in each of their lives, but also a shared spirit and enthusiasm for life.

"Thanks for coming," she mumbled, feeling shy now that they were together. She raked a hand through her short, pink hair as she searched for the right words to start this conversation. She needed to put that aside and be her former courageous self. Growing up, she'd never been afraid to fight for her own dreams. Now she needed to stand up and fight for Mama's.

"You look good," Levi said with a slow, shaky breath out. "Lighter somehow."

She raised an eyebrow and chanced a smile. "Are you telling me I've lost weight?"

He fell over his words as they all tried to push their way out of his mouth at once. "No. I mean, maybe. You did—"

Carolina burst out laughing. "Relax, I'm just teasing you. I do feel good. Happier now that I have something to work toward."

"You finally figured out what you want," he said, watching her for confirmation of his assessment.

"Sort of," she admitted. "Right now, I want to do something special for Mama. And that's enough for the time being."

"I like it," he said, reaching for her hand but pulling back before he made contact. "Tell me how I can help."

"Well..." She grabbed his hand and held it tight as she explained about the club and everything else she had planned for Mama's big surprise. When she finally finished, they both wore the widest smiles that could fit on each of their faces.

"She's going to love that," Levi said. "It's absolutely perfect."

"I hope so. She deserves to be happy more than anything."

Levi squeezed her hand. "And so do you, Carolina. So do you."

Chapter 35

PASTOR ADAM

I wasn't expecting anyone that day, but I still kept my open office hours at the church, just as I did every Tuesday. Not long into their start, Carolina Brown strode through my door with our blessed church dog, Cupcake, trotting happily behind her.

I'd taken Brownie with me to the office that day, and she immediately perked up at receiving this surprise visit from her brother. The two immediately fell into play stance, and it wasn't long before full-blown zoomies were taking place right there in my church office.

Carolina took a seat on the couch and crossed her legs at the ankle. Of course, we both watched the reunited siblings play for a spell before talking much with each other.

Finally, I cleared my throat and asked, "What brings you by today, Ms. Brown?"

"I have a proposal for you," she answered before rooting around in her bag and pulling out a packet of papers, which she promptly handed to me. "I'm starting a club, and I'd like the church to sponsor it."

"A club, huh?" I said, studying the cover page on the folder she'd handed me. Instantly, I recognized my daughter's brilliant work. "Walk and Stroll," I read aloud, running my fingers across the decorative words and the silhouette of a man, woman, child, baby stroller, dog, and even a person in a wheelchair that ran along the text.

"It's for Mama," she explained with a smile so confident I almost had to question if this was the same girl I'd seen during last week's service.

I laughed. "Yes, I remember our stroll together with Mrs. Clementine. We came up with that term together, you know."

Carolina nodded. "I do know, and I love it, by the way."

I flipped through the papers she'd handed me, liking what I saw more and more with the turn of each page. Looking back up at her, I asked, "So why the club now?"

And, bless her, she didn't miss a beat. "Every single day Mama drags me and Cupcake out for a stroll. Sometimes twice. It's become her favorite thing, and I just find it so inspiring that she's committed to physical fitness given her change in circumstances. Don't you?"

I sucked in my overstuffed midsection and nodded. "Why, sure, I do. Is that why she does all that strolling? To stay fit?"

"It's just one of many reasons," Carolina explained. "I think more than anything she wants a hobby to fill her days. When she worked at the diner, she loved visiting with all the customers each and every day. The Walk and Stroll club will allow her to help and inspire others while still providing her a way to socialize and—I'll be honest here—gossip every single day of the week, excluding Sundays, of course."

I nodded along. Everything she was saying sounded good, but more than that it was *how* she said it. Judging by her extreme enthusiasm in sharing this idea with me, I could tell it would be a huge hit with the community.

"And what does your mama think of all this?" I asked carefully.

"She doesn't know," Carolina explained before rushing to clarify. "*Yet.* She doesn't know yet. I want it to be a surprise and, given the recent rash of surprises led by yours truly, I figured you'd like this one, too."

I nodded enthusiastically, finally letting my belly go back to its full size which was at least somewhat smaller than it had been before starting my new forced healthy living plan. "I do. Very much. Now how can the church help?"

"We don't need much," she said. "Just a place for walkers to meet and park their cars, an announcement in the Sunday bulletin and maybe on the church website, too. That's it for now, but as the club grows, we may need help organizing charity walks and other types of community events."

"You haven't even officially started yet and already you're planning for such big things down the road," I said thoughtfully.

Carolina was unapologetic. "I am. With Mama at the wheel, this club is going to go on to accomplish great things. Even if it's just making people a little less lonely. But like the church dogs, I think Walk and Stroll also has the possibility to change lives and deliver miracles."

I chuckled despite myself. "You were always such an ambitious young lady, and you had me convinced from the very start of the conversation," I confessed. "Now, tell me how I can help get this wonderful idea started."

Chapter 36

CAROLINA

The next day, Carolina stuck around the diner after her shift to help Nolan and Harmony tidy up and close down for the day. When everything was done, she asked Nolan if he could spare a few minutes to chat over coffee.

He'd happily agreed, and now they sat together in the corner booth, each with a copy of her proposal before them.

"Walk and Stroll?" Nolan asked with a chuckle. "Well, this has your mama written all over it."

Carolina laughed, too. "This is for Mama, but you're actually going to want to turn to page seven for the part I want to discuss with you."

"Mama Jolene's Dog-Walking Company," Nolan read aloud. "Well, I'll be."

"Levi helped me come up with the idea, and he even helped me invent an add-on for her chair to help hold the leashes for bigger dogs. Mama designed her own special shelf for the little ones to rest on when they get tired. Of course, she'll only be able to walk a couple at a time, but it's a good way for her to earn income and have fun doing it. We're even working on a design for an emergency brake with the high school robotics team to make sure she's kept safe should any of the dogs ever get out of hand."

Nolan thumbed through the pages, his smile growing with each new insight into the project. "You've really thought of everything," he said, looking up at last. "I'm impressed."

She nodded. "I've tried my best to be thorough."

They each took a sip from their coffee cups before Carolina continued.

"I know you've been looking for ways to bring Mama back to O'Brien's, but I think it's time for her to start something new. We appreciate all you've done for her, both before and after the accident, and I will stay on as a waitress however long you need to find a full-time replacement. Mama loved working here each day, and I know she'll miss it, but I really hope she'll love this new venture, too."

"She will," Nolan said with a huge grin. "Oh, Carolina, you have really done your mama proud. All that bragging she's always done about you is well founded. I couldn't have come up with something more perfect for her if I'd tried. And actually, I did try! I tried really hard, but I like your idea so much better and I know she will, too."

Carolina would normally have blushed at such a kind compliment, but today she stayed strong and focused. She'd worked hard on this plan for Mama, and she was excited to see it come to fruition.

"There's more to the proposal, too," she pointed out. "Take a look at it when you have some time to really sit with it and review all the parts. There's one more thing, too."

"Yes?" Nolan wrapped both hands around his coffee cup as he hung on her every word.

"I'd also like you to consider investing. We need a little money to start things up, but I'm not asking for a loan. I'm asking for you to take part ownership and to help guide us along. You've done great things with your business, and I believe with your guidance, Mama will become quite the entrepreneur herself."

"You just keep impressing me more and more," Nolan said, shaking his head in apparent disbelief. "How much do you need to get started?"

She tapped her index finger on the proposal once more. "Not much, but it's all in there. Pay particularly close attention to pages seven through twenty-three as you read." Carolina stood and gathered her purse and empty coffee mug.

Nolan stood, too, and extended his hand forward, which Carolina shook without a moment's hesitation. "I'll read over this tonight and come back to you tomorrow with any questions, notes, or ideas. From just the little you've shared with me today, though, I know I want in. This shake is my promise that we'll be doing business together soon."

"And my promise that I'll give this everything I've got." Carolina squeezed his hand tight to solidify their promise to each other, their promise to Mama.

"There was never a doubt in my mind," Nolan answered.

After they said goodbye, Carolina pulled out the notebook she now kept with her all the time and checked off the item that read, "Talk to Nolan about investing."

She scanned the list for what was left. Now far more items had been crossed out than still remained for completion. Bringing her eyes back up to the very top of the list, she mumbled the words aloud, "Make things right with Levi."

Yes, it was time.

She brought out her phone and fired off a quick text: *May I take you out for a second try on our first date?*

Chapter 37

CAROLINA

Later that afternoon, Carolina and her customized white minivan pulled up right in front of the barbecue shack where Levi worked part-time. She didn't have to wait long for him to come outside and gawk at the dainty, tiny form behind the driver's wheel of the large vehicle.

He shook his head and motioned for her to roll down the window, which she did. "What are you doing here?" he asked. An expression of amused disbelief overtook his features.

She turned and put both of her arms up on the window frame so that she was facing Levi head-on. "Picking you up for our date, of course."

"I could have picked you up!" he argued with a good-natured laugh.

She shrugged. "Yeah, but it's more fun this way. Besides, I know exactly where we're going already, so hop in."

Levi raced around the van and climbed into the passenger seat. "You know this isn't what I'd have chosen to wear for our date, right?"

She glanced over at his black shirt emblazoned with a giant red pig and the words, "So good, you'll pig out!" It was paired with black jeans and black sneakers to match.

"Well, I think you look great," she said with a smile before bursting out in huge peals of laughter.

Levi didn't laugh along with her, but he didn't look upset, either. "You know, when I said yes to this date, I thought we'd agree on a time together before making it happen. I didn't realize you'd surprise me at the end of the lunch shift."

She beat a peppy rhythm on the steering wheel before transitioning to drive. "Surprises are better, though. Don't you think? I mean, I hope you think so, because I have another planned, and it's just about fifteen minutes away."

"No, no surprises! Tell me now," Levi insisted.

"Not on your life," she shot back. She reached forward and turned on the radio. "I don't think I ever found out what kind of music you like," she said with a frown.

He laughed at her long face. "But I know yours, courtesy of the Mama Jolene Information Network."

"That should be a real thing," Carolina said. "I mean it already is, but I'm glad there's a name for it now. Are you going to tell me what you want to listen to or not?"

"Same as you—*92.5 for Kickin' Country*—but I prefer the sound of your voice to anything else."

She wondered if he'd have reached out to hold her hand then, had she not been the one driving. As it was, she definitely needed both hands on the steering wheel to safely drive this giant vehicle around the city.

"Mama was right about that, too," she quipped. "You are such a charmer. Sometimes a bit too charming for your own good."

"I don't know whether that's an insult or a compliment, but either way, I'll take it." When Carolina peeked over at Levi, he wore a giant, relaxed smile.

They continued to chat amicably as Carolina navigated the roads that would deliver them to their surprise destination. It was funny how much easier things were now that she'd finally allowed herself to relax and enjoy getting to know Levi rather than worrying about whether this was the right time or if he was the right guy. They'd figure both those things out eventually, but first, she had to give them a chance to build a relationship at a natural pace.

And in Charleston, that natural pace was often slow and languid.

She pulled into a massive parking lot and took a space near the very back. Unbuckling her seatbelt, she said, "Since Mama is about to be the Charleston Walk and Stroll Queen, I figure I shouldn't embarrass her by parking upfront when I have two perfectly good legs to get me where I'm going."

Levi got out of the van and strode around to join her. "And where is that?"

She'd expected him to know by now. "Don't you recognize it? I mean, there was a giant sign when we drove in."

"I was too busy looking at you," he answered with a dreamy—albeit cheesy—smile. "You know, I really love that new hairstyle on you."

She giggled and raised a hand to her collarbone demurely. "Stop flirting for one second and take a look around. I know you'll recognize it if you try."

Levi squinted at the building at the other end of the lot, recognition at last dawning on his face. "Are we at the community college?"

She nodded proudly and pulled a stack of papers from her bag. "Yes, we are. We're here to hand in my application for next year."

He studied her for a second. His expression didn't give anything away. "Doesn't everyone do that electronically now?" he asked after a moment.

She rolled her eyes at him. "Usually, but this is symbolic," she said, each word slowly to really drive the point home.

Levi nodded, but still had a goofy look on his face. He raised an eyebrow and asked, "Hey, are you going to make a speech now?"

"Yes, I am. Now stop teasing me and listen, because I worked hard on this."

Levi drew quiet and motioned for her to proceed.

"We're here today to turn in my application. After lots of thinking and even more listening to my heart, I realized the Capitol can wait. I still want to go back someday, and I still fully intend to change the world, but right now I want to do that a little closer to home. I want to spend time with Mama and help her get her new enterprise off the ground, and I want to spend some time getting to know you, too, Levi. After all, we're only nineteen. We have our whole lives ahead of us. Rather than rushing, I'd like to take some time to make sure I get things right."

Levi swallowed hard but didn't say anything.

"Would that be okay with you?" she asked. Silence was not the response she'd expected to receive after making this huge, life-changing proclamation, especially since she suspected it was what Levi had wanted for her—wanted for them—all along.

He simply nodded, still unable—or choosing not—to speak. That meant it was up to her to decide what came next.

"Well, then..." She closed the distance between them and leaned in to place a kiss right on his cheek.

But Levi had other plans. He grabbed her from beneath and picked her up in his arms, then gave her the kiss to end all kisses. It made Carolina so deliriously happy, she almost forgot what they were here to do.

But then Levi began to march forward, still carrying her in his arms.

"What are you doing?" she asked.

"Carrying you over the threshold to our new college," he answered without missing a beat. "It's symbolic."

Chapter 38

CAROLINA

The following few weeks passed in a blur.

A very complicated blur.

Carolina worked hard to get all the pieces in place for Mama's new club and business, even taking it upon herself to learn some web design from Abigail so she could get everything set up before she did the big reveal at the surprise party she had planned for Mama.

It didn't take long for Mama to become suspicious, however.

"Where are you always sneaking off to without me?" she demanded on more than one occasion, then threw a right fit when Carolina simply answered, "You'll see" with a mischievous smile.

Finally, the day of the party arrived and Levi had come to pick Carolina up so that they could put the last-minute preparations in place.

Mama was onto her, though.

"Just where do you think you're going, young lady?" she asked, blocking the door with her chair as she petted Cupcake on her lap.

Carolina hedged. She hated lying, but they were so close to the big reveal that she couldn't possibly spoil it. "Out with my boyfriend," she said glibly.

"You're very lucky I approve," Mama grumbled. "But when I helped set you up, I didn't realize you'd spend every waking moment with him instead of me."

"Oh, Mama," she whined, losing a bit more of her resolve each time Mama questioned her these days. "You know it's not like that. I'm also working at the diner, and..." She stopped herself just in the nick of time, but Mama noticed this hesitation and called her on it.

"And? See, that's the part I want to know about—that mysterious *and* of yours." She crossed her arms over her chest and stared her daughter down.

"Mama," Carolina warned. "Just let me go."

"I want to come, too," she insisted. "Quit leaving me out of things. I'm getting mighty bored strolling around here all by myself."

"It won't be for much longer," Carolina promised, bending down to give her mother a kiss on the cheek. "Tell you what. I'll come back in about an hour and take you someplace fabulous to make it up to you. How does that sound?"

"Well, I don't want to twist your arm or anything," Mama complained with a sigh.

"You're not," Carolina insisted. "I want to spend the afternoon with you. I'll be back soon. Two hours tops, I promise."

Finally, Mama relented and removed herself from the entryway.

Carolina, of course, raced out before she could change her mind.

"That was not easy," she said once she'd seated herself in Levi's car. "Mama is definitely suspicious."

"Then it's a good thing she'll finally learn what we've been up to at last. I'm pretty sure I would have cracked under her next interrogation, anyway."

Carolina laughed. "I almost cracked today. Man, she is a tough cookie."

"Then it seems she'll be a great businesswoman, just as you suspected." He nudged her with his elbow and smiled.

"You said it," Carolina agreed as Levi drove them to the Eternal Grace Church.

Pastor Adam, Abigail, Nolan, Harmony, and a few other helpers were already there. Abigail had taken it upon herself to decorate with giant printed mockups of each logo. She'd even projected the new website right onto the twin screens that hung at the front of the church. Everything looked absolutely perfect, and the food smelled great, too.

"What's this?" Carolina cried when she spotted a table overflowing with brightly wrapped gifts.

"That was my idea," Nolan's girlfriend Harmony said. "Jolene's starting a new life, and that definitely calls for presents."

"But so many?" Carolina couldn't stop smiling, even as she was scolding the other woman. "What all is in there?"

"You'll just have to wait and find out. After all, there may be a surprise or two in there for you, too," Harmony said before drifting off to help Nolan with the food.

Wow. Well, now she understood how Mama must have felt being subjected to this surprise in progress for weeks. She was dying to know what Harmony had planned and if any other surprises had worked their way into the big reveal.

Focused on getting to Mama as soon as possible, Carolina checked over the venue, then dropped the last of the supplies off in Pastor Adam's private office round back.

"That should be everything," she said, returning to the group that had assembled in the sanctuary. "Now I just need to go and get the guest of honor."

Chapter 39

CAROLINA

When Carolina came back home to pick up Mama, she said, "I'm taking you somewhere for a surprise. Please don't make me spoil it before we get there."

Mama's face instantly fell. "But—"

"*La la la,* I can't hear you," Carolina sang, pushing a finger into each of her ears. "We'll also be listening to music on the drive over, and loudly at that. Now c'mon!"

She saw Mama move her mouth in protest, but the words came out blessedly muffled. Once in the car, she cranked up the radio and resisted looking at her mama in the rearview mirror, enabling her to deliver them both to Eternal Grace safely and without the secret getting spoiled.

Levi stood waiting in the parking lot and was quick to help Mama from the back of the van while Carolina dislodged the earplugs and took a deep breath to steady herself. This was it. The moment they'd all worked so hard for.

"What are we doing at the church?" Mama wanted to know.

"Just wait two minutes and you'll see," Levi shot back with a smile.

"It doesn't even need to be that long!" Mama called as she raced ahead of them both and burst into the sanctuary.

Once folks got over the shock of her sudden appearance, they all shouted, "Surprise!"

She brought both hands to her mouth and gasped, then turned to Carolina who'd just caught up and whispered, "Did you forget your mama's birthday? Because I hate to break it to you, but it's not today, and you've already thrown me two welcome home parties. So, what else could this possibly be?"

Carolina laughed and rolled her eyes.

Levi did, too.

Stepping in to serve as the voice of reason, Abigail approached them and said, "Let me give you a tour."

Normally, Mama didn't like anyone pushing her chair when she was fully capable of moving it around herself, but on this day, she relaxed and let Abigail guide her around the sanctuary.

"What is all this, my darling girl?" she asked her daughter when Abigail stopped them both in front of the Walk and Stroll display.

"This is your new strolling club, Mama. The church has agreed to sponsor it to give everyone a place to meet. Now folks can come join you for your daily strolls—parents, kids, dogs, babies, and even other people in wheelchairs."

Levi picked up one of the custom water bottles they'd had printed with the Walk and Stroll logo and handed it to Mama. "You inspire a lot of people already, and now you can reach even more."

"My dad has already signed up to be your first member," Abigail revealed. That really said something since all of Charleston knew just how much Pastor Adam hated to move if he had a choice to sit still.

Mama had genuine tears in her eyes now. "I love it so much. Thank you."

"Well, we're not done yet," Nolan said, appearing then to navigate Mama toward the next display.

"It is my great pleasure to introduce you to Mama Jolene's Dog-Walking Company!" he shouted, getting Mama and the rest of the crowd hyped up.

Carolina took one of the brochures Abigail had printed up and handed it to Mama. "As we've already established, you love strolling. And you love dogs, too, now, thanks to our Cupcake. So why not combine the two and make a little money while you're at it?"

Levi spoke next. "I already talked things over with my dog-walking customers and informed them I'll be stepping down in order to free up my schedule some so that I can spend more time with my lovely girlfriend."

He squeezed Carolina's hand before announcing, "They've all said they'd love to transfer their business to you once you're up and running. And with all the hard work Carolina's already put in, that can be as soon as tomorrow if you want it to be."

"I've bought us some advertising in the *Post and Courier* that starts running next week. That should bring loads more business our way," Nolan added.

"Us? Our?" Mama asked as she unfurled the brochure and studied it with a big old smile on her face.

"Nolan's agreed to invest and guide you as you get started with both new businesses," Carolina told her, giving it a moment for everything to sink in. She knew she was bombarding Mama with a lot all at once, but she also knew her strong, brave, inspiring mama could handle it just fine.

"Both?" Mama asked, her mouth hanging open in shock after the single word eked out.

Carolina grabbed hold of Mama's chair with a big flourish and pushed her toward their final display.

"Wheelie Crafts," Mama read aloud. "Practical Art for Practical People."

Carolina strode around the chair and crouched before Mama. "Remember when I said a lot of folks would be interested in your custom doggie shelf?"

Mama nodded as tears continued to fall down her cheeks and straight into her open-mouthed smile.

Carolina couldn't hide her absolute bliss as she straightened to her full height once again. "Well, I hate to say I told you so, but I put up your new

459

Etsy site last night, and you already have five orders," she said, pointing toward the new website displayed on the twin projectors." More than fifty people also favorited your store so that they can see what other products you add next!"

"Oh, my word!" Mama cried as her hands trembled from the weight of this final surprise. "No wonder you've been so busy these past few weeks. I can't believe you did all this for me."

"Well, believe it," Levi said as he placed an arm around Carolina's shoulder and hugged her into his side. "Your daughter loves you more than anything in this whole world, and she wants you to be happy. We all do."

"But what about your dreams, darling?" Mama asked, bewildered.

"Well for starters," Carolina answered, bending down to hug her mama tight. "Seeing you happy is one of them. I'm going to take a year or two to help you get started with your businesses and club while taking classes at the community college. After that, I'll take another run at D.C. I've got plenty of time. Did you know I'm only nineteen? I can't even run for president for another sixteen years!"

Laughter erupted throughout the crowd, and Carolina's was the loudest of all.

"So, it seems you have it all figured out," Mama said, clutching a hand to her chest.

"Well, not everything," Carolina said. "But that's part of the fun."

Chapter 40

PASTOR ADAM

As I watched Jolene and Carolina Brown embrace, cry, and embrace again, I couldn't help but be reminded of my own daughter and me. Sure, we're different, but that's part of what made us fit together so well.

Carolina had gone above and beyond to make sure her mama would keep being happy, even after a life-changing accident took away so much of the happy world Jolene had already established. And our church dog, Cupcake, had helped to inspire what would come next for them, so that those two very special ladies could continue to inspire first the city, and then the rest of our great country.

Who knew? Maybe Carolina would see her biggest dream come true one day. She definitely had my vote when that time came, and thanks to my daughter, Mrs. Clementine, and the new Walk and Stroll club, I had a sneaking suspicion I'd be around for many more years to come.

Abigail and Harmony both stood beside me as Jolene dug into her giant stack of gifts. Folks had brought her all kinds of things, but mostly crafting supplies and books on business. Jolene squealed with delight as she opened each one.

"So, another church dog has worked his miracle," Harmony, who had been blessed with a miracle from our Muffin, said.

"Seems that way," my daughter answered, holding Cupcake in her arms as we all watched the festivities unfold. "Does that mean you're ready to come home?" she asked the little dog after laying a smooch right on the top of his head.

"That was record fast," Harmony mentioned. "It took Muffin months to work his magic on me."

"Well..." I said as I watched the pink-haired ladies with the last name of Brown continue to celebrate at the front of the crowd. "Jolene has the biggest heart of anyone I know, and her daughter has the smartest head. I'd expect nothing less from either of them."

"Too right," Abigail said while Harmony nodded at our side.

"Oh, look!" my daughter cried a few moments later. "Carolina's found her surprise."

We remained perfectly silent with our eyes glued on the younger Brown as she opened the gift box and brought out a...

"Turn around?" she read from the lone notecard that she'd found tucked into the box. Behind her, Levi stood holding a shivering little Chihuahua who was missing both its front legs.

"Oh my gosh, what did you do?" Carolina cried.

"We rescued this little guy from a kill shelter," Abigail stepped forward to explain. "Nobody wanted him because... Well, because he's a little different. But we just knew you and your mama would be able to get him strolling in no time."

Carolina took the dog from her boyfriend's arms and cried big, fat tears into its short fur. "Hi, darling," she cooed. "What's your name?"

"This is Rex," Levi said. "And he's all yours."

Carolina took the little ball of love over to her mama and set him on her lap.

"My, oh my!" Mama proclaimed. "We're the perfect matched pair. I can't use my legs, and you can't use your arms. But don't worry, little Rex. We've got huge adventures ahead of us."

I had no doubt about that.

"There's one last thing," Carolina said, as if suddenly remembering. She raced back to my office and returned with a thin stack of papers.

"Just sign here and here and here," she said, flipping through the pages. "And you'll be an official small business owner."

"Carolina Brown," her mama said. "You've really outdone yourself this time."

"And so have you," I whispered to the sweet church dog in my daughter's arms. "Well done, Cupcake. Well done."

Ready for more heartfelt and heartwarming stories? Then make sure you're on Melissa's list so that you hear about all her new releases, special giveaways, and other sweet bonuses.

You can do that here: MelStorm.com/gift

What to Read Next!

More Church Dogs of Charleston will be coming soon. While you wait, why not try this other great faith-based romance featuring a tiny church in Sweet Grove, Texas?

Ben Davis has lived in the shadow of his family's mistakes for years. Forced to give up all his dreams, he wonders if death by his own hand might be the only way out. A desperate plea sent to the God he isn't even sure he believes in is soon answered by a series of miracles that bring Summer and Ben crashing into each other.

Summer loves the busy life of the city, but agrees to spend the season in Sweet Grove, running her aunt's flower shop while figuring out what to do with her life after. One thing's for sure, she's a terrible florist. Luckily, her latest mishap leads her to a man with pleading, soulful eyes she's all too happy to get lost in.

Ben tells Summer she's his miracle, but Summer's not so sure she sees it that way. Can he convince her to share the rest of her life with him before the seasons change? And might the tiny town have a place for Summer to finally, truly call home?

If you love tales of faith, hope, and finding home, then don't miss your chance to fall in love with Ben, Summer, and the entire town of Sweet Grove, Texas, in this heartwarming romance.

A Summer in Sweet Grove is now available.

CLICK HERE to get your copy so that you can keep reading this series today!

Sneak Peek of A Summer In Sweet Grove

Ben Davis had once believed in God. He had once believed in miracles, fate, divine intervention, and all the similar lies people tell themselves to get through the day. Perhaps if he still believed, he wouldn't find himself so tempted to never get out of bed—not even to eat—and to eventually die a slow, private death in the only place that still offered him any comfort at all.

On this day, a Thursday, he spent longer than usual blinking up at the ceiling and wondering if he should just end it all with a swift bullet to the brain. After all, that's what his older brother, Stephen, had done seven years ago. He'd wandered into the town square and shot himself clean in the face for all of Sweet Grove to see. People still talked about it to this day, and those who didn't speak of it definitely thought of it.

Like his mother, Susan. She waded through the memories, attempting to silence them with the bottle. But even though the liquor often ran out, her grief remained endless, unquenchable.

Ben wasn't saddened by the loss of his brother. Even though he sometimes felt as if he should be. No, he was angry—rage was another unquenchable commodity in the Davis household. Stephen had selfishly chosen to end it all. He'd hurled his issues straight at Ben, who, ever since that day, had been tasked with paying the mortgage, tending to their mother who had spiraled down the dark path of addiction, and without an outlet to enjoy any of the things he had spent years working toward and hoping for.

He'd turned down his full-ride scholarship to college, because he needed to take care of things in Sweet Grove—things that only got worse the more his mother was left to grapple with her grief. Recovery remained a summit she just couldn't reach, no matter how hard she climbed. So he'd turned the university down year after year, and eventually the admissions board had stopped asking.

Which left him here today, staring up at the popcorn ceiling above his twin-size bed, no longer bothering to wonder if life could ever be any different. At 6:12, he placed one foot after another onto the shaggy carpet and went to clean up for work. At 6:25, he was out the door with a piece of half-toasted bread in one hand and a banana in the other. He had five minutes to make the short walk from the quaint—and "quaint" was putting it kindly—home he shared with his mother to the local market where he worked as a bagger and delivery boy. Yes, even his job title suggested a temporary arrangement, a job better suited to a boy than the twenty-four year old man he had become.

"Good morning!" sang his boss, Maisie Bryant, as he tromped through the sliding glass doors. Each morning she arranged a fresh display of local produce and other seasonal specialties right at the front of the shop. As always, she took great pride in her work.

Ben hated that his boss was only a couple of years older than him. Maisie had managed to escape town long enough to earn a degree before returning to run her family's grocery store. While he didn't know the exact numbers, he could bet that the youngest Bryant child made at least triple what he did for the same day's work. But that was life for you—or at least for Ben. Never fair, not in the least.

"Don't I get a hello?" Maisie teased him as always. Some days he liked her chipper demeanor. This was not one of those days."

"Hi," he mumbled. "I'm going to go check the stock. See you in a bit."

"Wait," she called before he could manage to make his escape. "I'll handle the stock. The staff over at Maple's called, and they need a delivery first thing. Think you can handle that? The purchase order is on the clock desk."

"Yeah, I got it."

Ben hurried to put the order together and load up the designated Sweet Grove Market truck. A smiling red apple beamed from the side of the cargo box. He hated that thing, but he did like having the opportunity to drive around a little, let the wind wash over him as he rolled about town. It sure beat walking everywhere, and since it offered his only opportunity to get behind the wheel, he relished every chance he got. Occasionally, Maisie would let him borrow the truck to head into the next town over and lose himself in the sea of unfamiliar faces.

He'd once loved living in the type of place where everyone knew everyone, and everyone looked out for everyone, but he hated how people who had once been his friends had begun to pity him. Ever since Stephen's death, they couldn't even look at him without betraying that sadness. Ben had become a reminder of how fragile life could be, of how everything could go to hell in the briefest of moments. And though their words were kind and their smiles were omnipresent, Ben knew better. He knew that he'd become a burden to them all, that his presence brought them sorrow.

At first he'd tried to redirect them, to speak of something—anything —else, but after a while he just grew tired. It was easier to avoid them than to constantly have to apologize for the blight his terrible, selfish brother had brought onto their town. He'd have left if he could. By vehicle or bullet, it didn't matter.

But his mother needed him. And as small and insignificant as it seemed, so did Maisie.

So he remained, day after day.

And so began another dark morning for Ben Davis.

Summer Smith arrived in Sweet Grove right around that awkward time of day when the sun was starting to set and ended up in her eyes no matter how hard she tried to look away. She loved sunshine, which is why she'd jumped at the chance to attend college in Southern California, but now those four years had reached their conclusion and had left Summer more confused than ever about her future.

Thank goodness her Aunt Iris needed her to run the Morning Glory flower shop for the season. Aunt Iris was going off on some fancy cruise she'd been saving up for half her adult life. True, that didn't speak well of the money to be earned being a small-town florist, but, then again, Summer had never been much taken with flowers anyhow.

The problem remained that she'd never really been much taken with anything. And now that she'd reached that pivotal stage of needing to pick a career and finally set down roots, she was hopelessly lost. Two months, one week, and three days—that's how much time she had to figure it out. At that point, Aunt Iris would return from her sail around the world and be ready to take back her shop and home. So for the next two months and some-odd days, Summer would be living a borrowed life. Luckily, she'd always liked her Aunt Iris.

Her aunt greeted her at the door wearing a brightly colored blouse with leaf fronds printed along the neckline, and with freshly dyed hair that still smelled of chemicals. "Oh, there's my Sunny Summer!" she cooed.

Summer laughed as her aunt hopped up and down, holding her tight. The hug probably could have lasted for days if a loud screeching hadn't erupted from deep within the small ranch house. Iris let go of her niece and breezed through the doorway, dragging the smaller of Summer's suitcases behind her.

"Oh, enough, Sunny Sunshine!" she called in the direction of the screeching, leaving Summer to wonder if her aunt affixed *Sunny* to the start of everyone's name these days.

The shrieking continued, growing louder as they made their way back toward the living room. There, in the far corner beside the small stone fireplace, sat a large iron cage with a colorful blur of feathers which screamed its lungs out.

Iris rushed over and unlatched the cage, then drew out the little yellow and orange bird on a delicately poised finger. "Now that's not how you make a good first impression. Is it, Sunny?"

The bird ruffled its feathers like a marigold flower, then shook itself out.

Iris laughed. "Much better. Now meet Summer." She puckered her lips and blew a stream of air at the little bird, who made a happy bubble-like noise. Iris then offered the parrot to Summer who took a step back.

"I-I just . . . You didn't say anything about a bird!"

"Oh, Sunny won't be any bother. Besides, you'll be grateful for the company once you're settled in and looking for a bit of fun."

"I tend to prefer the company of humans."

"Sunny is the human-est bird you will ever meet. Aren't you, my baby?" She placed the little sun conure on her shoulder, and he immediately burrowed below the neckline of her blouse and stuck his head back up through the hole, making Iris look like a strange two-headed monster. Summer had to admit that Sunny *was* cute. Maybe she and the bird could come to some kind of agreement during their months together.

Iris—bird in tow—showed Summer around the house, pointing out which plants needed to be watered when and taking extra care when it came to describing the needs of her little feathered friend.

"Is that it?" Summer asked when the two had settled onto the loveseat following the grand tour.

"Pretty much. What else do you need to know?"

"How to run the shop, for one. Also, what am I going to do with myself to keep busy during the nights?"

"I've written everything down in a big binder and left it for you near the cash register. Everything in the shop is clearly marked as well. You'll use the key with the daisy head to open up. Hours are eight to three. And as for how you'll keep busy . . ." Her eyes flashed as she bit back a Cheshire cat-size smile. "Life in a small town is never boring. You'll see."

"But, Aunt Iris, aren't you worried I'll mess things up?"

Iris waved a hand dismissively. "You'll figure things out. Besides Julie will be there for the first couple of days to give you on the job training."

Summer wasn't sure whether her aunt was talking about running the shop or about life in general. Either way, Summer sure hoped she was right.

What happens next?
Don't wait to find out...

Head to my website to purchase your copy so that you can keep reading this sweet, heartwarming series today!

Acknowledgments

Thank you to my family, friends, and readers—many of whom fall into more than one of those groups. You are my constant source of inspiration, but even more than that, determination!

My books simply would not get written were it not for a number of people in my life who support my dreams, crazy schedule, and the need for an occasional shoulder to cry on. There are so many people who fall in this category, that it's impossible to list and thank them all. Some of my most consistent helpers are Falcon Storm, Ron Rayner, Angi Hegner, Becky Muth, Mallory Crowe, Evelyn Adams, and so, so many more.

I also have a number of people to thank for helping me work out story details, polish my prose, and giving a happy, shining face to my stories. These folks include many of those listed above, plus Megan Harris, Mallory Rock, Alice Shepherd, Jasmine Jordan, and my own personal Super Reader team!

I must also mention my darling daughter, Phoenix, and my crew of fur babies, especially those of the Chihuahua variety. My tiny tri-color girl, Sky Princess, in particular, is with me for every single word and basically every single moment of my life. She cuddles inside my shirt when it's cold, wags her butt at me when I need a smile, and even gently nudges me awake when I'm having a bad dream at night. She also makes sure that the inside of my ears are always perfectly clean and ready to pass even the most vigorous of inspections.

Sometimes the perfect animals land in your life. Treasure every single moment with them, because life is too short to do anything but.

Also by Melissa Storm

ALASKAN HEARTS

Get ready to fall in love with a special pack of working and retired sled dogs, each of whom change their new owners' lives for the better, and a sprawling ranch located just outside Anchorage helps its patients regain their lives, love, and futures.

The Loneliest Cottage

The Brightest Light

The Truest Home

The Darkest Hour

The Sweetest Memory

The Strongest Love

The Happiest Place

TEXAS HEARTS

Sweet and wholesome small town love stories with the community church at their center make for the perfect feel-good reads!

A Summer in Sweet Grove

A Supper in Sweet Grove

A Sunday in Sweet Grove

A Wedding in Sweet Grove

Someone in Sweet Grove

❦

CHARLESTON HEARTS

A very special litter of Chihuahua puppies born on Christmas day is adopted by the local church and immediately set to work as tiny therapy dogs.

A New Life

A Fresh Start

A Surprise Visit

❦

THE SUNDAY POTLUCK CLUB

This group of friends met in the cancer ward of the local hospital. They've been there for each other through the hard times. Now it's time to heal...

Home Sweet Home

The Sunday Potluck Club

Wednesday Walks and Wags

Manic Monday, Inc.

❦

THE ALASKA SUNRISE ROMANCES

Brothers, sisters, cousins, and friends—are all about to learn that love has a way of finding you when you least expect it.

In Love with the Veterinarian

In Love with the Ski Instructor

In Love with the Slacker

In Love with the Nerd

In Love with the Doctor

In Love with the Football Player

In Love with the Rodeo Rider

In Love with the Pastor

In Love with the Paramedic

SWEET STAND-ALONES

Whether climbing ladders in the corporate world or taking care of things at home, every woman has a story to tell.

Saving Sarah

A Colorful Life

A Mother's Love

A Girl's Best Friend

Love & War

About the Author

Melissa Storm loves a good cry. She believes, that whether happy or sad, tears have a way of cleansing the soul. Perhaps that's why her books have been known to make readers grab the nearest box of tissues and clutch it tight while visiting her fictional worlds. Hey, happily ever afters mean that much more when they're hard won, right?

As a *New York Times* and multiple *USA Today* bestselling author, Melissa is always juggling at least half a dozen new story ideas at any given time. She is married to fellow author Falcon Storm, mom to a precocious human princess, and keeper to an entire domestic zoo full of very spoiled cats and canines. Melissa is the owner of Novel Publicity and also writes under the name of Molly Fitz.

Find Melissa on Facebook @MeetTheStorms or sign up for her newsletter and receive an exclusive free story, *Angels in Our Lives*, along with new release alerts, themed giveaways, and uplifting messages from Melissa at **melstorm.com/gift**

Printed in Poland
by Amazon Fulfillment
Poland Sp. z o.o., Wrocław
26 June 2022